"Reading Jeremy Robinson is dangerous for your sleep pattern. He spins monster yarns so well that you cannot stop turning pages. Giant monsters, creepy islands and writing that is both smart and furious in intensity and pace."

— Famous Monsters of Filmland

"Project Nemesis turned out to be the first book in years where I read it from cover to cover in just under a day. I kept my eyes peeled on those 250 or so pages as if it was crack! It was that good! Nemesis is a true American Kaiju by every definition. This is a definite must for any fan of the Kaiju genre. It gets a full fledged 5/5 rating."

— Kaiju Planet

"A brisk thriller with neatly timed action sequences, snappy dialogue and the ultimate sympathetic figure in a badly burned little girl with a fighting spirit... The Nazis are determined to have the last gruesome laugh in this efficient doomsday thriller."

— Kirkus Reviews

"Relentless pacing and numerous plot twists drive this compelling stand-alone [SecondWorld] from Robinson... Thriller fans and apocalyptic fiction aficionados alike will find this audaciously plotted novel enormously satisfying."

— Publisher's Weekly

"Robinson blends myth, science and terminal velocity action like no one else."

— Scott Sigler, NY Times Bestselling author of NOCTURNAL

"Just when you think that 21st-century authors have come up with every possible way of destroying the world, along comes Jeremy Robinson."

— New Hampshire Magazine

ALSO BY JEREMY ROBINSON

Kaiju Novels
Island 731
Project Nemesis
Project Maigo
Project 731

SecondWorld Novels
SecondWorld
Nazi Hunter: Atlantis
(aka: *I Am Cowboy*)

Standalone Novels
The Didymus Contingency
Raising The Past
Beneath
Antarktos Rising
Kronos
Uprising (aka: *Xom-B*)
Flood Rising
MirrorWorld (2015)

The Jack Sigler Thrillers
Prime
Pulse
Instinct
Threshold
Ragnarok
Omega
Savage
Cannibal (2015)

The Continuum Series
Guardian

The Chesspocalypse Novellas
Callsign: King
Callsign: Queen
Callsign: Rook
Callsign: King – Underworld
Callsign: Bishop
Callsign: Knight
Callsign: Deep Blue
Callsign: King – Blackout

The Antarktos Saga
The Last Hunter – Descent
The Last Hunter – Pursuit
The Last Hunter – Ascent
The Last Hunter – Lament
The Last Hunter – Onslaught
The Last Hunter – Collected Edition

Writing as Jeremy Bishop
Torment
The Sentinel
The Raven
Refuge:
    Night of the Blood Sky
    Darkness Falls
    Lost in the Echo
    Ashes and Dust
    Bonfires Burning Bright
    Refuge Omnibus

PROJECT
731

JEREMY ROBINSON

BREAKNECK MEDIA

Cover design copyright ©2014 by Jeremy Robinson
Cover art by Cheung Chung Tat. Used by permission.

Printed in the United States of America

Visit Jeremy Robinson on the World Wide Web at:
www.jeremyrobinsononline.com

For TOHO,
whose productions inspired me as a child,
and still do to this day.

PROJECT
731

PROLOGUE

"Looks like a ghost ship."

Sean Johnson's hands squeaked over the Zodiac's rubber skin, holding his body steady, but not his nerves. As the newest addition to the five-member black ops team, he wanted to prove that he was the right man for the job. He'd been recruited straight out of the U.S. Military Academy, just days after graduation, and here—not five days later—he was on a mission, slipping through the glassy sea, concealed by the night's darkness.

He never thought of himself as an exceptional student. He was mediocre, at best, in all things. So it came as a surprise when he was interviewed and recruited by a secret division within DARPA, the Defense Advanced Research Projects Agency. DARPA was the brains behind the U.S. military, and despite the word 'Defense' being in their name, he knew that much of what they developed was actually used for offense. Drones, weapons systems, advanced armor and the stuff of science fiction movies.

Johnson's night vision goggles were one of those advances not yet released to the public, or even to the standard military. Though it was dark, in the middle of the ocean, with no light sources other than the stars and a faint crescent moon, he could see, as clear as day, in full color. Accessing countless online photos, videos and satellite images, full color was rendered and projected on top of the standard green night vision, which could still be used in situations where no reference was available. So as he looked at the backside of the approaching derelict research vessel, he could clearly read the name printed on the aft: *Darwin*.

All he knew about the ship was that it had been searching for the *Magellan*, its sister research vessel, which had been lost at sea. Contact with the *Darwin* had been lost years ago, the ship presumed sunk in a storm. But the *Darwin* hadn't sunk. Instead, it had made slow revolutions around the Pacific, following the North Pacific Gyre, circling the massive garbage patch it had been tasked with studying alongside *Magellan*. After years at sea, the currents had set the ship free, sending it toward the U.S. West Coast, where it had been spotted by fishermen.

"It looks like a ghost ship because it *is* one, you dumb shit." The reply came from the man behind him. Shadow. Johnson didn't know his real name, but like all the men in the BlackGuard, his codename reflected the clandestine nature of their black ops team.

Johnson wasn't recruited for his brains. He knew that. They wanted him for two things: his skills as a soldier and his 'unwavering loyalty.' Their words. While he wasn't sure about his skills on the battlefield, they were right about his loyalty. With no brothers or sisters and both his parents deceased, the military was the only family he had left. He would follow every order to the letter.

So when they asked him to join this night mission off the coast of Oregon, to inspect a derelict ship, he hadn't questioned why DARPA was interested, what they were after or whether it was dangerous. He'd simply said, "Yes, sir," to the man he knew as Silhouette, leader of the BlackGuard. Silhouette sat at the Zodiac's aft, operating the engine, which was impossibly silent—more DARPA tech.

Johnson thought better of replying to Shadow. Instead, he looked to the others, hoping to find a pair of sympathetic eyes. He found none. The other men on board the Zodiac, known only as Obsidian and Specter, kept their goggled eyes straight ahead, on target, which was exactly where Johnson realized he should have been looking.

The *Darwin* was just fifty feet ahead, sitting still in the nearly placid sea, eerily peaceful. The research vessel, its faded blue metal hull showing patches of rust, was larger than Johnson had expected, despite knowing there had once been fifty people on board.

Fifty people...damn. What happened to them?

"Eclipse," Silhouette said. "Prep for landing."

Johnson looked up at the vessel now looming above them. At two-hundred-seventy-feet long and three thousand tons in weight, it was the largest ship he'd seen up close. Most of the hull rose up, thirty feet above them, but the dive deck on the back was accessible by boat. He remained locked in place, watching the deck get closer.

"Eclipse!" Silhouette hissed, making Johnson flinch. He was still getting used to his new callsign. "Tie us off."

When the Zodiac bumped against the dive deck, Johnson stood on shaky legs and straddled the distance to the deck. The up and down motion of the Zodiac was much faster than the big ship's, and it threw him off balance. He stumbled forward and caught himself on the ship's aft ladder, but not without cramming his face against the cold hull.

"Amateur," Shadow grumbled from the Zodiac.

Ignoring the comment, which Johnson knew was what his drill sergeant had called 'fuckup bait,' he tied the Zodiac to the dive deck without a word, moving quickly, fighting his shaking fingers. "Good to go," he said, praying he'd tied the knots right.

Moving silently, the five-man team scaled the ladder up onto the *Darwin*'s aft deck. The deck was clear, swept clean by winds and rough seas over the past years. If anything had been left on the main deck, it was gone now. A crane for moving small boats, ROVs or supplies sat alone and bent on the deck, coated in rust, a solitary chain swaying in the breeze.

"Two teams," Silhouette said, his voice a whisper, but clear through the earpieces the BlackGuard wore. "Shadow, Obsidian: sweep below decks. Take Eclipse with you. Specter and I will clear the labs and bridge before rendezvousing with you."

Without verbal confirmation, Shadow and Obsidian, looking their part in all-black tactical gear from head to toe, moved toward a nearby hatch. Johnson followed, not giving voice to his questions. *What are we looking for? Why are we whispering? If the ship is abandoned, why are we all carrying KRISS Vector submachine guns?* The future weapon fired heavy hitting .45 caliber rounds at high speed, without recoil or muzzle climb. It made them exceedingly deadly and accurate. A little overkill for an empty research vessel. But his job was to obey, not question, and that's exactly what he did.

The interior of the *Darwin* flickered to night-vision green for a moment before flickering back into full color. The ship's interior, along with just about every piece of equipment and object inside, was identified by some distant computer, labeled, colorized and illuminated.

The floor was empty except for a pile of clutter at the end, too distant for his eyes or the computer to distinguish. The walls were white and clean. Spartan.

Shadow opened a hatch to the left and swept the room on the other side, left to right. "Clear."

Obsidian continued forward, stopping to open the next hatch. While he swept the room, Johnson took his cue from the others and continued to the next hatch, which was already open.

"Clear," Obsidian said, behind him, his voice gruff and baritone. He was a massive man, but he moved with the swift agility of the rest.

Johnson, on the other hand, had to lean against the doorframe when a wave canted the ship to the side, nearly throwing him inside the room he was supposed to be checking. Holding on to the hatch with one hand, he scanned the room from left to right, remembering to keep his weapon raised halfway through the sweep. As he lifted the submachine gun, his vision flickered in and out of night vision, muddling the image. Squinting like it would help, Johnson took a step inside the room. "Something is—"

The image resolved, exploding into full color.

Johnson stumbled back with a shout, pulling the trigger on his weapon. He toppled back into Obsidian's large arms without firing a shot; the safety was still engaged, blocking the trigger from depressing fully.

Shadow walked past him, entering the room while shaking his head in disgust. Obsidian propped him up and grumbled, "Pull your shit together, kid. You haven't seen scary yet."

Yet, Johnson thought, standing up. He imagined the two corpses inside the room. Could there be anything more horrible? He knew the answer. More horrible things existed. Three-hundred-foot-tall horrible things. City destroyers. But they had come and gone. Even Nemesis, the three-hundred-fifty-foot tall Kaiju with ominous glowing membranes, plated armor that modern weapons couldn't get through and the ability to harness the sun itself as a weapon, who had left her mark on Boston and Washington D.C., was dead. And he had never seen those giant monsters up close.

His thoughts returned to the bodies. Sealed away from the humid ocean air outside, they hadn't rotted normally and hadn't been consumed by insects. He re-entered the room and stood next to Shadow, while he inspected the dead. Obsidian stayed in the hallway, watching the ship's interior, gun raised. The bodies were petrified. Husks of what they once were. Dried leather stretched over bones. Frozen in death, sprawled beside what looked like an operating table, the corpses told a violent story, torn open as they were, from the inside out. Gnawed on. Surrounded by dark stains. This is what happened to the crew of the *Darwin.*

This is why we're carrying the KRISS submachine guns. But... "The *Darwin* went missing two years ago. Whatever did this is gone or dead now."

Shadow looked at Johnson, but said nothing. Instead, he toggled his invisible throat mic. "Silhouette, evidence of Dark Matter confirmed. We have corpses. Over."

Dark Matter. To most, it was the theoretical stuff that held the universe together, but to the BlackGuard, it was the code name for whatever target they'd been assigned on a given mission. Johnson hadn't been told about the Dark Matter, but apparently, they were after whatever had done this to these people.

Johnson fought the chill threatening to shake through his body.

Silhouette's confident voice came through all the headsets. "Copy that. It's the same up here. Ten total. Continue forward. Will join shortly. Over."

"Copy that." Shadow stood. "Out." He turned to Johnson. "Good news. You're on point."

Everything in Johnson's being, from his cells to his soul, shouted at him to run, to admit he wasn't cut out for this, that they'd put their faith in the wrong man. But he ignored the urge, refusing to abandon his family. *Be strong*, he told himself. *Be smart. Show these assholes you can be one of them.*

With a nod, Johnson stepped back into the hall and led the way, sweeping two more empty rooms before reaching the end, and the piled debris. Another body, torn apart, inside out. He knew the dead held no real interest, so he continued past without pointing it out.

As they moved to the second deck, he picked up the pace, growing more confident with each room swept. After finding ten more bodies, he became numb to the mounting number of dead, seeing them as objects, not victims. *I can do this*, he thought, opening another door, seeing a corpse, and then moving on. *I can do it.*

But Johnson's subconscious was a whirlwind of observations and unanswered questions. Each person had been killed violently as something had emerged from within them. Not something... some*things*. Each body had three holes, sometimes merged into one gaping wound, but never more than three. Had they been infected with a flesh eating disease? Parasites? How was the entire crew affected before they could call out a mayday and report their position?

It wasn't his job to know or discover the answers to these questions, so when they reached the far end of the second deck hallway, he continued down the metal stairs to the third deck. The label on the closed hatch read, *Living Quarters, Mess, Galley.*

"Silhouette," Shadow said, his voice just a whisper through the earbuds. "We are on deck three. ETA? Over."

"On your six," Silhouette replied. "Thirty seconds."

Johnson looked back, curious if they should wait, but Shadow urged him forward with a two finger point.

Knowing that Silhouette would soon join them and see him in action, Johnson threw himself into the task of clearing rooms. He moved quickly, efficiently, sweeping the many bunkrooms, sometimes finding bodies, sometimes not, but never looking back to see if Silhouette had joined them.

The room at the end of the hall was labeled *Messdeck*, but Johnson barely registered the sign, or that the space beyond would be different from all the rest—until he opened the door and looked inside.

Everything was black.

Green night vision returned, revealing a white-green floor covered with dark stains. But the rest of the large space was impenetrable darkness. "What the—I think my goggles are broken."

Then the darkness moved, spreading out along the floor. A sound like static filled the air: hundreds of hard, sharp points striking the floor.

"It's alive," he said, stepping back, thumbing off the safety on his weapon.

"Hold him," Silhouette said.

Johnson tried to turn around, but he was stopped by three sets of hands that felt robotic. Impossibly strong. He fought, a scream building in his throat, but Silhouette's next words shocked his system silent.

"Nighthawk, this is BlackGuard. Come in. Over."

"We read you BlackGuard. What's your status? Over."

Silhouette looked up as Johnson craned his neck back. "Sorry, son, but you were the crappiest soldier we could find that wouldn't be missed."

The sentence struck Johnson in the gut, and it was quickly followed by a constricting tightness that had nothing to do with his emotional state. He was locked in a coiled grip that tightened over his midsection. Then, stabbing pain.

Once, twice, three times.

"Dark Matter acquired," Shadow said.

Gunfire, painfully close, filled the metal hallway with ear-splitting noise, flashing light and the stench of gunpowder. With a shriek, the coiled tightness fell away. But twisting pain blossomed anew, roiling in Johnson's gut.

"It's happening fast," Specter said.

The hallway shook as Obsidian slammed the hatch closed and said, "The lock is broken."

Specter, the smallest and fastest member of the team, took the door. "I'll give you a head start and catch up."

Johnson was propped up. Silhouette pulled a plastic cap off a syringe with his teeth, and jabbed the needle into Johnson's belly. Johnson's vision blurred as the pain in his gut intensified. Tightness wrapped him again, but this time it was cold. Freezing. He was turned around and around, wrapped tightly in a translucent blue plastic, each revolution adding to the chill.

They're freezing me.

"Nighthawk, evac on the aft deck in two mikes. Exfil will be hot. Repeat, exfil will be hot. Over."

"Copy that," Nighthawk—whoever that was—replied. "We'll be waiting. Out."

Johnson felt himself lifted up. When he saw the hall again, it was from Shadow's shoulder.

"Let's move," Silhouette said. And they did. The journey on Shadow's shoulder was rough, made worse by the pain in Johnson's gut, which had slowed some, but nausea was sweeping through him. He left a trail of puke behind them. He watched the puke as the goggles tried to colorize it, and he noticed blinking lights along the walls. Bricks of C4 had been planted on the walls, their detonators blinking readiness.

"On my way," Specter said through the comm. Ten seconds later, gunfire. Fast and continuous.

Then they were outside. The ship's exterior was no longer silent and still. The violent chop of rotor blades filled the air with thunder and kicked up mist from the ocean below. Spotlights lit up the deck.

Gunfire grew loud behind them, spilling from the still-open deck hatch. "Almost there," Specter said. "Very hot."

Johnson felt himself tossed into the helicopter, his body temperature dropping by the second, robbing consciousness. The pain in his gut was almost gone, along with the rest of his feeling. He watched as the BlackGuard opened fire from inside the chopper, shooting at some unseen enemy. Then, Specter dove inside, held fast by Obsidian. The helicopter rose up and peeled away, giving Johnson a momentary view of the *Darwin*, its upper decks alive with hundreds of moving, unidentifiable black spots.

And then, with a bright flash, the *Darwin* exploded, erased forever. As the roar and pressure wave shook the helicopter, Johnson rolled onto his back and looked up at his teammates. Only Shadow looked back, his squinted eyes revealing a smile. *"Now* you've seen scary."

NEMESIS

1

"Stop moving," she says.

"I'm itchy," I tell her.

"You didn't roll through poison ivy again?"

"Four leaves, shiny green. No way."

"Poison ivy has three leaves."

"Shit."

A faint scratch, barely a whisper, silences us. Collins, whose fiery hair and personality are hidden by full-body camouflage, lowers her goggle-covered face to the ground, blending in with the leaf litter that surrounds and covers us. I lower my head, too, knowing that concealment is the only course of action. If our enemy is within a hundred yards, something as small as passed gas would give our position away.

So we wait in silence. I can hear Collins breathing through the earbuds that let us communicate over distances without having to shout. While the scent of damp earth and decaying leaves seeps through my facemask, I picture our future together. It's totally inappropriate, both because I'm kind of in the middle of something and because my face is in the dirt, but I find it hard not to think about. I picture her in a wedding dress, red hair in curls, orange-brown eyes blazing. My mind's eye travels south to her... *No*, I think.

The wedding dress I've conjured is far too revealing, so I mentally censor the image to something more conservative. These camo fatigues are a little tight, and I don't want to relive the last day I ever wore sweat pants in high school.

"Pervert," Collins whispers.

"What?" I say, too loud. "How did— Get out of my head, woman."

"You're adjusting," she says.

I freeze. Without realizing, I've reached down and shifted my boxer briefs. I generally prefer straight boxers, but that's not always comfortable when in the field. A good sprint can leave a guy feeling like Sugar Ray Leonard discovered a new punching bag.

"What was I wearing this time?" she asks. "Bikini? Lingerie?"

I turn toward her, seeing only the side of her facedown head. "First, kudos on the confidence. How do you know I wasn't thinking about a Kardashian?"

"You sound too nervous for that."

"Too nervous? I'm not nervous at all." *Shit, shit, shitty-shit, shit.*

I can't tell her the truth. We've been together for two years now. She knows how I feel, but she was married once before. The man abused her. Hardened her. I need to make sure that the idea of marriage hasn't been ruined for her. Ted Watson and Anne Cooper, our co-workers at the Department of Homeland Security's Fusion Center – Paranormal division, FC-P for short, were married six months ago, before the birth of their son. Collins was a bridesmaid, but I couldn't read how she felt about the situation. I might need to come right out and ask her, but that will kind of ruin the surprise...which I haven't planned yet. To lead her away from the truth, I need to give her something embarrassing, something to justify the nerves she's detecting.

I sit up, revealing myself to the enemy. "Uhura."

Collins sits up beside me. "What?"

"Uhura. I was picturing you as Uhura."

Collins lifts her facemask so I can see her squinting eyes.

I take her silence for not understanding, despite the fact that I know her fantasies probably involve Jean-Luc Picard. "Star Trek...

Communications officer. Tight red uniform. Short skirt. Speaks Klingon."

"Heghlu'meH QaQ jajvam."

I have no idea what she said, but Collins's Klingon sounds flawless.

I lift my mask away, smiling wide. "Oh my god. Where were you during my teenage years?"

A thud reveals the arrival of our enemy. I turn to the new arrival and casually say, "Oh, hey Lilly," before giving Collins my full attention again. "Seriously, you know Klingon?"

Collins acknowledges Lilly with a wave, but otherwise ignores the girl, which is impressive, since the now six-foot-tall cat-woman with bright yellow eyes, black fur-covered body and long twitching tail is still amazing to witness—even after we've known her for a year.

"I had Watson teach me a few phrases. Thought you'd like it."

"Thought right," I say. "Bonus points for Collins." I pantomime a scrolling scoreboard, complete with ticking sound effects.

The ridiculous conversation has the desired effect.

"You guys will never beat me if you don't take this seriously," Lilly says.

"We're playing capture the flag," I say. "It's hard to take seriously. Not all of us are kids."

Lilly's pupils narrow and lock on me. Predatory. Intimidating.

I smile.

She stomps her foot. "I am *not* a kid."

"You're what, six years old?"

"I age differently than...humans...than regular people."

I'm pushing the conversation into dangerous territory here. Lilly's teenage self-esteem issues, unlike most, are rooted firmly in reality. While other teenagers feel like freaks, Lilly pretty much is one—at least to the outside world. To us, she's family, and a part of the team.

"That doesn't mean you mature any faster," I say.

Lilly pulls back. Sucks in a breath. "I know what you're trying to do."

I grin. "You do?"

"I know that Dad is hiding beside you." I turn to the long lump next to me, the camouflage fabric of Mark Hawkins's fatigues hidden beneath the leaves. Lilly reaches out and taps my head, and then Collins's. We're officially captured.

"Okay, Dad," she says to the stationary lump. "You can come out."

I still get all choked up when this girl, who looks every bit the killer, speaks in such kindhearted tones, and gives those she loves honorary familial titles. We're all uncles and aunts these days.

Hawkins doesn't budge. Lilly nudges his still form with her sleek, black-furred foot, the retractable claws currently hidden. The leaves fall away, revealing an empty boot and pant leg.

"Oh my god," I say in my very best sarcastic tone. "What did you do? You vaporized him!"

Lilly is too smart to fall for the continued distraction. She knows she's been had, and like a true competitor, she's once again on the hunt. Finding Hawkins proves easy. Even I can hear him running through the woods, which means one thing.

"He's got the flag," Collins says, sounding a little stunned. Despite her surprise, Hawkins was the logical choice for flag retrieval. He's a first class tracker, trained by Howie Goodtracks, his unofficial adoptive father, who also happens to be a Ute Indian. After learning the trade from Goodtracks, Hawkins became a Yellowstone Park Ranger, specializing in finding lost, and sometimes dead, hikers, climbers and vacationers. An encounter with a grizzly bear ended that career, along with the bear's life.

We've run through this simple exercise twenty times. At first, we were cocky. How could Lilly stop the whole group of us, in the woods, by herself? But she has—every single time. We've never even spotted her flag. Whether she catches us all, or simply steals our flag out from under our noses, we've never stood a chance. But this time...

I stand up, cup my hands to my mouth and shout, "Run, Mark! She's coming!"

Lilly hisses at me and then she's off and running, a black blur between the trees, and then in them, leaping from trunk to trunk, branch to branch.

Collins stands up and brushes herself off. "You know he's screwed, right?"

"Nah," I say, feeling less hopeful than I sound. "Hawkins is like a jackrabbit, and he's got a head start." I catch a glimpse of Lilly soaring between two-hundred-foot pine trees in the distance. "Yeah, he's screwed. Let's go watch."

We run down the wooded hill toward the field at the bottom. Mark is making the same run, maybe a quarter mile to the west. If we hurry, we might reach the field in time to see him get tackled. Moving in a straight line, we reach the field and stop, watching the tree line to our right for any sign of Hawkins or Lilly. *Did she catch him already?*

A line of flags running through the middle of the field delineates the two sides. If Mark crosses the line, we win, and we seriously need to, otherwise all the sage wisdom and experience we have to offer Lilly will fall on deaf ears. She needs to know she's not invincible. So far, all we've managed to accomplish is the opposite.

I walk out into the field, watching the line of tall pines for any sign of movement. All I see are puffs of yellow pollen being swept into the air on the breeze. Normally, in an open space like this, I'd be worried about someone spotting Lilly. In public, she wears a pretty badass looking suit—think Snake Eyes but with a woman's figure, and no swords—she doesn't need them. But the federal government, at the President's insistence, was inclined to give the FC-P one hundred acres of land in Willowdale, Maine, where Collins served as Sheriff for a time, and where Nemesis was created in a secret lab disguised as an abandoned Nike missile site. The lab, leveled after Nemesis's escape, is now hidden at the core of a massive, fenced-in preserve. We have fresh *No Trespassing* signs threatening prosecution, and the latest in high tech monitoring, which Watson can watch from the Crow's Nest (the FC-P's headquarters) back in Beverly, Massachusetts.

"See anything?" I ask.

Collins starts to reply in the negative, but she stops short and points. "There."

Hawkins is distant. Small. His head barely visible above the tall, yellow grass, despite his height. He's wearing just a T-shirt and shorts, which is supposed to be my uniform, and he's running in a sprint, like Tom Cruise in...well, in every Tom Cruise movie ever made. His arms, rising and falling, are a blur.

As Collins and I jog toward the action, I let myself think, *he's going to make it*, but I quickly follow that thought with, "Holy fuuuu." I never finish the expletive. I'm too stunned.

Lilly explodes from a tree in a cloud of yellow pollen. She's at least seventy-five feet up, and arcing downward toward Hawkins, who is oblivious to her aerial approach. I nearly shout a warning, but I realize Lilly would disqualify the win, *if* we won.

"Just a little closer," Collins says, and I smile. She hated this at first, but once Lilly started getting cocky, she's been on board.

For a moment, I think Lilly is going to land on top of him, but she lands right in front of him in a crouch, her back turned. Hawkins doesn't miss a beat, diving over Lilly and rolling back to his feet. He doesn't bother running now. It would be a wasted effort. He'll be tagged in less than a second.

Lilly strikes, reaching out for Mark's back.

But he manages one last move before Lilly tags him. He throws the flag, which is wrapped around its metal post. It tumbles through the air, landing just short of the dividing line.

Lilly thrusts her hands in the air. "Yes!"

Collins and I stop nearby, close enough to watch what happens next.

After a few seconds of victory dance, Lilly notices her three silent observers, stops and misreads the situation. Again. "Sorry," she says. "That was over the top."

"Bonus points for apologizing, but..." I point to the flag.

Lilly's head snaps around, just as a blond head of hair, perfectly hidden in the yellow grass, rises up to reveal the lithe Dr. Avril Joliet. As a biologist and oceanographer, she lends her scientific prowess to the team. But to Lilly, she's 'Mom.' Like Lilly, she's prone to impulsivity and is widely considered the reason we lost the first five capture-the-flag matches, but over time, Joliet learned how to operate on a team. And as she casually bends over from her position behind the dividing line to pick up the flag, she delivers us our first win.

We don't gloat. We don't need to. Lilly is upset enough as it is, kicking grass and grumbling. She turns on Hawkins. "How did you get past the girls?"

The 'girls' are Lilly's immaculately conceived brood of three black cats, which lack her human traits, yet are unlike any other big cat species on the planet. They are jet black, like pumas, the size and build of Siberian tigers, and they're incredibly intelligent. While they can't speak, it's clear they understand most of what we say, and they don't view us, or people, as prey. That's not to say they're not dangerous, but they are absolutely devoted to Lilly, who gave birth to them by laying eggs... True story. I wasn't there, but Hawkins swears by it. And that's just the tail end of the weirdness he endured along with Joliet and Lilly on an island in the Pacific.

"Bacon," Hawkins says with a shrug.

"Wha—" Lilly's head lolls back, her mouth open in a silent groan. "Bacon? For real?"

"Good game," I say to Lilly, willing to leave it at that, and I raise my hand.

To my surprise and delight, she gives me a high five, and says, "Next time, I'll feed the girls first."

While the others hang back and talk and joke about the match, I stroll away and pull out my cell phone, tapping on a contact's name and placing the phone to my ear. It rings six times and goes to voicemail. Although we're in East Nowheresville, there's always cell service on the preserve. I made sure of it.

She should be answering. She always answers. On my way back to the others, my heart starting to beat faster, I try again with the same result.

Collins must see the look of concern on my face, because she asks, "What is it?"

I lower the phone. "Something's wrong. Maigo's not answering."

2

The black Suburban sits alone on what remains of the paved road leading to the ruined laboratory. Not far from here is a large cabin that belongs to the FC-P. Hawkins, Joliet and Lilly spend most of their time here, training in the woods and hiding from the public—Lilly for obvious reasons, Hawkins and Joliet because they're convinced they're being hunted by someone within the government, specifically within DARPA. While Joliet is now part of the team, her involvement is off the books, and Hawkins works under a fake name, Dustin Dreyling, though we just call him 'Ranger' when on mission.

I'm out of breath when I reach the Suburban, having run the distance. The others aren't far behind. Lilly, as usual, is several steps ahead. Unable to see through the tinted glass, I reach for the SUV's door.

"She's not in there," Lilly says. "I already checked."

I believe her, but I open the door anyway, looking for clues. Maigo's cell phone is in the back seat, where she'd been sitting. No signs of a struggle.

Maigo is kind of a solitary soul, except when it comes to me. We've maintained the bond developed while she was inside Nemesis—while she *was* Nemesis. It really is impossible for anyone to fully understand what she's going through. Lilly gets what it's like to not be fully human, and the two girls have made a connection. And I have a vague understanding of what it's like to share a head with a three-hundred-foot-tall *Kaiju*. I got a taste of Maigo's world, too, when I slipped my consciousness inside the Kaiju, Scylla. But Maigo...

She was once a normal little girl. She lived and went to school in Boston. Her mother was Japanese, and her father was a wealthy, white business man—and a murderer. He killed Maigo's mother, and then, when the then ten-year-old girl walked in on the scene, he killed her as well. Maigo's recollection of her previous self begins and ends with her own murder, the memory hazy but real, passed on through her cells.

Using Maigo's harvested organs, General Lance Gordon—who is now dead, thank God—fused her DNA with that of an ancient, long dead Kaiju, who we now call Nemesis Prime, and whose origins are still a mystery. If mythology is to be believed, she was the ancient Greek goddess of vengeance, a role she filled again when the Maigo clone grew and changed, into a colossal monster. Nemesis reborn. She carved a path of destruction from this very spot in Maine, all the way to Boston, eating people—which Maigo remembers—whales and anything else she came across on her route. The smorgasbord fueled Nemesis's rapid growth. The creature found Maigo's father in Boston, turning him to dust, along with half the city. Then there was that whole mess in D.C., where instead of eating people, Nemesis was protecting them, though she was really just there to protect me. The monster Nemesis gave her life to save us, and somehow left Maigo, who was arguably the monster's soul and conscience, behind in a giant chrysalis. Maigo was reborn again, this time as a teenage girl. She has no real age, but our best guess is sixteen, a few years younger than Lilly appears...though she's also technically much younger.

The point is, Hawkins and I are now the father figures for the two most screwed up teenage girls that have ever lived. How the hell that happened, I'll never understand, but here we are, doing our best to protect and raise two girls who shouldn't exist, but do.

And right now, I feel like a pretty big failure.

Or maybe I'm just being overprotective. We're in the deep woods of Maine, at a fenced-in preserve with a halo of motion-sensitive security cameras. If Maigo had approached the fence, Watson would have called. And I've got two of the world's best trackers with me.

I turn to Lilly, whose acute senses can track most anything. "Find her."

She bounds off the Suburban's roof and darts into the woods. It won't take her long to search the entire preserve if she needs to. I hope it doesn't come to that.

Hawkins arrives, quickly assesses the situation and without saying a word, he goes on the hunt for a trail. While Lilly can instinctually track, Hawkins is a pro, teasing out details from the environment that even the cat-woman can miss.

Collins and Joliet arrive last, looking a little too casual for my taste. "You could help," I tell them, still scanning the vehicle for any hint of foul play. While no one, and I mean *no one*, knows about Maigo's, Mark's or Joliet's true identities, not to mention Lilly's existence, the very public nature of the FC-P's past exploits has made some of us celebrities. We're targets for conspiracy theorists, secret hungry corporations, rival governments and worst of all, fanboys.

If someone took her... The thought stops me short. I glance back at Collins and Joliet, who are basically the yin and yang of feminine body types—Collins the Amazon, Joliet the almost boyishly figured sprite. I'm about to complain again, but I stop myself and turn to them. "What do you know?"

Collins grins. "She's a teenage girl who actually has good reasons to feel boatloads of angst."

"So...she's what? Off brooding somewhere? She was alone here. She could have brooded in solitude without leaving."

Joliet actually laughs and sighs, but she might as well have offered a condescending, "Men." She tries to hide the humor when she sees my annoyance, and slugs my shoulder. "C'mon, lighten up. Odds are she's fine, and I'm willing to bet you can find her first. No one knows her or understands her better than you. Just take a minute to step out of your panic and think. Where would she go?"

I sigh. I hate it when Joliet is right, mostly because she usually is. Collins, too. I'm surrounded by women who are better than me at everything, except, as Joliet has pointed out, understanding Maigo...and just about everything weird, whether it be Kaiju, Bigfoot, chupacabra or anything else supernatural. What started off as a dead-end job for a slacker agent has really become my life's calling. "Fine," I say, and I wander away from the Suburban.

I don't pick my direction for any other reason than it takes me away from the others. *Think like Maigo,* I tell myself. But how can anyone think like Maigo? Not only is she fairly silent most of the time, she also doesn't share a whole lot. After me, she speaks to Watson the most, primarily because they like the same cartoons. But that's all surface level. And...

I stop.

I'm standing in front of the burned out concrete rubble. It's all that's left of the lab where Nemesis, and Maigo, were born. I've looked at this mass of debris several times, remembering my visit here with Collins, when a young Nemesis nearly made a snack of us, and we faced off against Katsu Endo, aka, a pain in my ass who has gone missing.

I'm about to turn away when I notice a gaping hole where there used to be none. Someone moved a large chunk of rebar-infused concrete to the side. "What the..."

Ever prepared, I pull a small flashlight from my cargo fatigues and turn it on. There is a tunnel beyond the hole, large enough to crawl through, leading down. *To the basement*, I think, and then I remember what I found there two years ago—what I thought had been destroyed along with everything else.

I know where she is.

The tunnel's rough surface assaults my hands, knees and back as I push through the tight downward grade, flashlight gripped in my teeth. *Top secret father of the year award, here I come.* The tunnel is fifty feet long, descending at least three stories. The deeper I go, the more it becomes clear that this straight shot down was not formed naturally. Someone made this tunnel.

Maigo.

She's been holding out on me.

While the rest of us have been training in the woods, assuming she was back here, nose in a book, she's been excavating a tunnel back to the scene of her first...what? Murder? Meal? She was still part human at that point. Thinking about what I'll find and how it will affect her, I move faster, skinning my knees and embedding a few pebbles in my palms.

The tunnel ends at a four foot drop, where part of a hallway remains intact. The walls are scorched and cracked, but the fire was smothered before the whole place could be consumed. Flashlight aimed forward, I creep down the hallway feeling a little spooked. If Maigo, who is half Japanese with straight, long hair that often hangs in front of her face, steps out looking like Samara from *The Ring*, I'm probably going to scream. Accepting the potential for future embarrassment, I push on, finding a ragged hole to the left, where there was once a door labeled *Morgue*.

My mind flashes back to the first time I entered this room. Well, 'entered' is a gentle way of saying, 'ran for my freaking life into this room.' I was with Collins, though not yet really *with* her. We hid in separate coolers meant for corpses. How many dead were left down here? *At least one*, I think, and I step around the corner. I sweep the flashlight through the liquid black, death-scented space, its ceiling ragged and sagging. And then all at once, I'm sent sprawling back into the hallway, gagging for a moment before finally screaming.

3

"Well..." I cough and push myself up against the far hallway wall. "That was way worse than I expected. Seriously, were you *trying* to scare me?"

Maigo steps into the ruined doorway, lit by the diffuse light from my flashlight, which now lies on the floor, pointed at a wall. Even though I know it's her, and that I'm in no danger, I can't stop the chills that shake through my body. Not only is her hair hanging in front of her face, but she's also covered in dust and debris, her pretty self hidden behind layers of gunk. Worst of all are her eyes, the pupils fully dilated and black in the near absolute darkness.

Speaking of which... I glance around Maigo, back into the morgue. She had no light.

Definitely holding back. But why?

"I killed them," she says.

"Not helping."

"I'm being serious."

Her eyes shift slightly, sparkling with the first signs of tears. The girl who was once a three-hundred-fifty-foot-tall destroyer of worlds needs a hug. I climb to my feet and reach my arms out. She falls into them, crushing herself into my embrace. While this is all new and strange to me, the connection she felt to me, as Nemesis, has not dulled. I have seen into her mind, and she has seen mine. We know each other in a way most parents can never really know their children. And as we stand here, underground, in the dark, away from the outside world, that connection takes root in my psyche. Without realizing it, I've started crying, too. The pain this kid is dealing with...it's just not right.

"I killed them," she says again.

"Is the woman still there?"

I feel her nod against my chest. "The word, too. *Nemesis*." She pronounces the word with a Greek tang, the way people might have said it in ancient Greece, but without the "oh my God it's going to step on me" terror.

"I remember," I tell her, "but that wasn't you."

"Part of it was," she says. "But it's not just the woman in the next room." She releases me and takes a step back. "It's everyone."

Ouch. Nemesis killed upwards of ten thousand people between here and Boston, many of which she ate. If Maigo really can remember each individual death... No wonder she's so quiet. Well, that and being squirted out of a Kaiju like a chick in an egg. That can't be too good for the psyche either.

"Look," I say, "I know you remember doing everything that Nemesis did. They're your memories. You feel like you made those choices. But it wasn't just you in there. The space was shared."

"Still is," she says, and it takes a colossal effort to hide how this makes me feel—heartbroken and terrified.

"What do you mean?" I say, the words coming out slowly. "Some part of Nemesis's consciousness is still—"

She shakes her head. "Just memories."

"But Nemesis started... She was created..." There's no easy way to say this. "You both began life together, right? You both have the same memor—" The answer pops into my mind. "Oh. Oooh. Really?"

She nods and turns away, looking back into the dark morgue like she can see just fine. "Nemesis Prime. Her memories started as dreams, but are coming back faster. I can't remember the end of her life, but I *can* remember the beginning." She looks back at me. "So can you."

I would like to forget it, but she's right. During one of our surreal connections inside the head of Nemesis, we relived the monster's beginning. The ancient Nemesis Prime had endured tortures beyond description and had been infused with the ability to detect injustice and the desire to seek vengeance, no matter the cost.

"She wasn't born a monster," she says. "They made her one."

Dammit, just once I would like the rabbit hole to not go down so deep. "They?"

"I don't know what they're called. Or where they're from...other than..."

I raise my eyebrows. "Other than..."

She looks up.

Aliens.

Double dammit.

If I've got the story right, Nemesis Prime, captured by an alien race, was turned into an injustice-seeking vengeance-delivering machine, and sent to Earth to...what? Judge us? Keep us in line? Destroy us? Or maybe she was just entertaining these aliens, the destruction of ancient cities broadcast throughout the galaxy. But it's not their motivation that really bothers me. It's their existence. An alien race capable of containing something like Nemesis Prime would be a problem far greater than any one Kaiju. Or even a dozen. The FC-P would need some kind of miraculous extraordinary help to keep them from making short work of the human race.

"If it makes you feel better," she says, "it was like ten thousand years ago."

It doesn't. "Ten thousand years? But that predates the Greeks by...a lot."

"She was around for a long time, sometimes hibernating long enough for people to think she had died, but when she wasn't sleeping..."

"I get it," I say, putting a hand on her shoulder. "You're bearing a weight I don't think anyone else but you could handle. If you've still got a little bit of the Kaiju muscle in you, that's probably a good thing."

Her eyes go wide. "You sure about that?"

"As sure as I am that you've been hiding it from me."

Caught, she turns away again, this time entering the morgue. I recover the flashlight and follow. We stop in front of a pile of bones. Above her, scrawled in now dark blood by Maigo's then clawed hands, is the single word:

Νέμεσις

Greek for Nemesis.

"When were you going to tell me?" I ask, before Maigo can distract me with ancient tales of woe.

"I didn't..." Her head sags.

"You thought you would change again?"

"I don't want to be *her* again. I don't want to kill any more people. I don't want to *eat* anyone!"

I rub my hand over Maigo's back the way my mother used to do mine. "You're not changing."

"I'm getting taller! And heavier!"

"You're sixteen...we think. You're still growing. Give it another year and you'll be done." This seems to resonate. As she calms, I mentally pat myself on the back. This parenting stuff isn't too bad. Of course, we haven't yet addressed the non-standard stuff. "So...what can you do? Besides eat people."

Maigo flinches away, but she's smiling. She gets my sense of humor, which can sometimes be morbid and is almost always inappropriate. She swats my shoulder, and for the first time, I can see just how much she's holding back. "Dad!"

Whoa...

Dad.

This is new.

While Lilly jumped right into dubbing everyone uncle, aunt and in Maigo's case, sister, Maigo has never once called me anything other than 'Jon.' She's almost formal with people, her emotional boundaries strict and rigid.

I play it cool. "So let me guess. You can see in the dark. Any other sensory stuff?"

"Mostly just the eyes. I can see really far, too. And I can feel this... I don't know what it is. But I remember what it felt like to be me. To be *just* human. And the me now, in my head, is different. I feel something like static, but faint. Sometimes I feel it pulse, but most of the time it's just a steady pull. I've gotten good at ignoring it."

"Huh." I have no idea what this could be, and I'm certainly not the person to figure it out. That's more up Joliet's alley. "And you're strong, right? Dug a hole all the way down here."

"Yeah," she says, smiling this time. "I'm strong."

"*How* strong?"

"Stronger than you." She laughs, and I feel a weight fall away. She's returning to herself. Quiet. Reserved. And sometimes funny, but usually only when it's just the two of us.

"Stronger than Lilly?"

Her grin widens.

"Really?" I'm genuinely surprised.

"Don't tell her," she says. "I don't think she'd like that."

"Lilly doesn't like a lot of things, but she gets used to it. Speaking of which, we beat her today."

"Then definitely don't tell her about this."

"We'll keep this between you and me until you're ready," I say, "But if you're worried about changing, Joliet can probably run some tests...or wait...did Ash have the feminine talk with you yet?" I make air quotes with my fingers when I say 'feminine.'

"And now things just got weird." She steps around me and heads for the door.

"Really? We can talk about eating people, ancient goddesses and what it feels like to be a Kaiju, but we can't have the feminine talk?"

"If you say 'feminine talk' one more time, I'm running away." She heads into the hallway and walks out of view. She's seriously embarrassed and fleeing, which is a good thing. Once again, the day is saved by Jon Hudson's wry wit. Emotional bomb defused.

As I follow her back up the tunnel, my mental defenses fade. The seriousness of what we've just discussed seeps into my gut, twisting it. We've got some hard times ahead of us. She really has endured an inhuman amount of torture, from the returning memories of Nemesis Prime, to her time as a Kaiju and now, trying to figure herself out as a human being, while somewhere in a Boston graveyard, the original Maigo lies dead. Could there be a more screwed up situation?

After we reach daylight again, I help Maigo dust off. I'm expecting cheers and a "How did you find her," from Lilly. Instead, I hear my name shouted by Collins. "Jon!"

"Here!" I step out from around the rubble, Maigo beside me, once again folded into herself.

Collins stands beside the Suburban with Joliet and Hawkins. She's on the phone. Lilly is perched on top of the vehicle. None of them were looking for us. Either they had complete faith in my ability or whoever Collins is talking to has bad news.

My phone chimes. I glance at the screen. Cooper and Watson both called me. I must have lost my signal while underground. "What's happening?"

Before Collins can answer, Hawkins speaks up. "It's them. It's DARPA."

This puts me on guard. I spin around, looking for danger. "They know you're here?"

"Tillamook State Forest," Collins says in her best 'chill out' voice.

"In Oregon," Joliet says, doubling the effect of Collins's statement. "It has nothing to do with us."

"You heard the report," Hawkins says. "A turtle with eight legs and a tail."

The description is instantly familiar. Hawkins's BFSs. The Big Fucking Spiders. We have a detailed account of what happened to him and Joliet during their stay at what they call 'Island 731,' where a surviving group of World War II Japanese scientists called Unit 731—responsible for some of the worst atrocities and human experimentation ever performed— continued their research under the supervision of a clandestine group within DARPA. Lilly, and her monstrous mother, who was actually named 'Kaiju,' were a direct result of that genetic research, which also created a variety of monstrous chimera, the worst of which were the BFSs. Part spider, part turtle, part who-knows-what, the creatures had eight legs, were protected by a turtle's shell and had prehensile tails with scorpion- like stingers at the end. They were able to reproduce rapidly, by injecting their spawn into the guts of their victims. The young would tear free, fully grown and able to breed, within a minute. They were a nightmare scenario, as deadly as a Kaiju, but spread out. Impossible to stop.

"And it has everything to do with us," Hawkins continues. "They're not going to find us here, but we can find them there." He turns to me, eyes blazing.

These are the people who committed some of the worst crimes against humanity, and they weren't World War II scientists. They were modern-day, American scientists working for the government. In the past year, while subtly seeking them out, we've found nothing. They're buried deeper than I can look without being noticed. But now...

"I made you a promise," I tell Hawkins. "Looks like it's time to deliver."

4

"Tell me, how do you feel?"

Sean Johnson's eyes fluttered open. Hazy white filled his view. "What? W—where am I?"

"You're safe. How do you feel?"

"Cold."

"Understandable." To Johnson, who felt like he might fall back asleep, the man's voice sounded colder than the chill wracking his entire body. He had never felt such pervasive coldness, down to the marrow.

"I can't feel my body," Johnson said. "Did something happen?"

"Something? Yes. But your back is fine, if that's what you were thinking."

A ghost-like apparition slid across Johnson's view, white on white. Just a subtle shift in the light ahead. "I'm having trouble seeing."

"It's from the cold. Nothing to worry about."

"Why am I cold?"

"You're safe," the man said. "Are you experiencing any pain? Anything at all?"

"I t-told you," Johnson said, teeth chattering, "I can't feel anything."

"Good. That's good."

Johnson's exasperation grew. He couldn't feel. Couldn't move. Couldn't really see. "W-why is it good?"

"Still nothing?" the man asked again. "Nothing at all?"

"No, I—" But then he could feel something. It wasn't pain. It was...like lifted weight. He felt lighter...and a steadily increasing sense of tiredness. "Is something happening?"

A sigh. "Mr. Johnson, I'm normally remiss to discuss the particulars of what I do with my...patients. But given your situation, I feel that full disclosure poses no risk. Do you understand?"

"No. No I d-don't. What's happening? Where am I?"

"You're back at DARPA," the man said.

"In Virginia?"

"Oh, no. Not remotely. We are still on the West Coast. But that's hardly the most interesting line of questioning. You're no doubt feeling something *now?*"

Johnson tried to look down, but found himself unable. "I can't move my head."

"You're restrained."

"Why?"

"It's better for you."

"Why? What's happening to me!" Johnson's voice cracked with desperation, his heart beating faster, adrenaline surging and returning some small sense of feeling to his brain. And in that fraction of a second, his body sent a faint signal, detected by a few sentinel neurons, which received and repeated the message—*I am dying.* "Oh God. You're killing me!"

"Me? No. But yes, you *are* dying." A blurred-out form slipped into view. A man. Dressed in white. But concealed, like he stood behind a wall of frosted glass. "Do you really want to know how?"

"Tell me," Johnson said. If he was going to die, he wanted to know why.

"You don't remember?"

Johnson searched his memory. He was on a mission with the BlackGuard. His first mission. To the *Darwin*. They searched the ship. There were bodies. So many bodies. With holes from where something had come out. But then...what happened? "There was a room. It was dark. And—and the dark, it moved. It was *alive*. It was—"

All at once, he remembered. "It attacked me. Put something inside me! The Dark Matter. And the others...oh my God, I was *never* on the team. I was just—"

"A vessel," the man said. "Not as dumb as everyone thought. But dumb enough."

Johnson's vision began to fade. A strange taste filled his mouth.

"Take comfort in the fact that you have done this organization, and perhaps your country, a great service. It is a more honorable death than you would have managed on your own. Now then, would you like to see your gift to us?"

The man didn't wait for Johnson to respond, perhaps because he could see Johnson's fading lucidity. He rubbed his arm against a hard, clear surface, scratching away a thin layer of frost and revealing his face, which wasn't a face at all, but the reflective mask of a biohazard suit.

The man rapped his gloved knuckles on the glass, creating a hollow gong that echoed in the tight space. He spoke with a sing-song voice, like there was a dog nearby. "Here. Over here. Come say hello."

The sharp *tick tack* of small, hard limbs striking the floor filled the air. With a shriek, a black blur launched at the cleared glass. Claws scrabbled for purchase, while a dagger-sized stinger at the end of a long, wiry tail struck the glass three times.

The man on the other side showed no reaction. No fear. No surprise. Johnson couldn't see his face—couldn't see much of anything as his vision narrowed—but he detected a hint of pride from the masked stranger.

"Goodbye, Mr. Johnson. I believe it is time for you to fulfill your secondary role."

Johnson was too weak to ask what that meant, but he had his suspicions confirmed when he faintly felt a series of pin pricks travel up his body. The black shape crawled over his face, eight legs twitching with energy. As the monster's mandibles turned toward his wide eyes, Johnson used the last of his life to scream.

No one heard him.

No one missed him.

And within the hour, when the feast came to an end, there was nothing left of him.

Dr. Alicio Brice turned away from the containment unit, which was a five-inch-thick glass dome, fifteen feet across and ten feet tall at the apex. Like many of the other units on this level, it held a biological threat. Not a virus or bacteria or anything else belonging to the realm of the micro. Those kinds of things were kept in the basement. Brice dealt exclusively with the macro, the killers that existed outside the human body, but would be happy to consume it just the same. Some came from nature—various big cats, snakes, spiders and crocodilians, all the most efficient killers mother nature had conjured up.

But there were the others, the best and worst creations of man. Some came from the island before it was destroyed, like these newest additions, which he called Tsuchigumo, or Tsuchi for short. In Japanese mythology, the Tsuchigumo were a race of spider-like phantoms. The *Yōkai*. Like the chimera now consuming Johnson's body, they could take on many forms, spiders and turtles most common among them. They were deadly and crafty. The name fit.

"You did well, Silhouette," Brice said, as he turned around and removed his mask. Though it wasn't necessary, he always wore a mask when dealing with uncomfortable situations. He'd never been good with people and was even worse with people about to die. The mask helped. Hid his emotions. He'd always wished he could be unattached, like a sociopath or a Vulcan, but he felt emotion like anyone else. He had experienced sorrow for Johnson since the moment he had chosen the unexceptional, very alone boy to transport the Tsuchi. But any misgivings he felt were dwarfed by his ambition, his desire to change the world—or perhaps even remake it. In his line of work, where emotions could be a liability, masks helped.

It was why he could speak to the man known only as Silhouette, whose eyes were always hidden behind those reflective sunglasses that made him look more like a State Trooper than the leader of the BlackGuard. He and his men—Shadow, Obsidian and Specter—were the best at what they did, which was to serve none other than GOD—the Genetic Offense Directive. In extreme situations, they could mobilize military assets if 'national security' was at risk, as they had done to ensure the island's destruction. Most of the time, the BlackGuard did GOD's dirty, wet and covert work.

GOD was an arm of DARPA, and their research was defined by two words: weaponized biology. Few in DARPA knew of GOD's existence, and none of those few saw a need for oversight. Plausible deniability was essential for this kind of work. Killer robots remained acceptable, while anything organic was seen as abominable, despite being cheaper and deadlier. Aside from the island's loss two years previous, they were making progress far faster than labs who had to abide by federal regulations. While the island had been GOD's first outpost, their headquarters was now located on the mainland, hiding in plain sight. And thanks to their many patents and shell corporations, not to mention a sizable black budget that increased by five percent every year since 1959, they had more resources and a larger GDP than many small nations.

Silhouette gave a curt nod, but said nothing. His penchant for silence unless asked a question was another one of his redeeming qualities.

"No witnesses, I presume?" Brice asked, using the reflection in Silhouette's glasses to fix his blond hair, sweeping it over the top of his head to cover the growing bald spot. He'd considered following Silhouette's example and shaving his head clean, but he hadn't found the time. He waved his hand, brushing away his words. "I know there weren't. Silly question. And the ship? Sunk?"

"To the bottom," Silhouette said.

"Were there many Tsuchi?"

"More than a hundred. In the mess hall."

"And they're all dead?"

"They can't swim."

"Would you say there is a margin of error?" Brice sat behind his gleaming white desk, which held only a laptop. He bounced twice in the swivel chair and then spun in a slow circle, marveling at the scope of his work. The three-hundred-foot-long lab was one of fifteen he oversaw, three per floor, housed in the building's top five floors, which he had deemed *Incubators*. A row of glass domes, each containing various species or mixes of species, stretched from one end to the other. On the far side of the space was an empty walkway, at the center of which sat his solitary desk. No windows. No co-workers. Just Brice and his creations. But this incubator wasn't a functional lab. It was simply his office, where the best, and most dangerous creations were kept under his watchful and admiring eye. The real work happened in the other nineteen incubators, which held as much lab equipment as glass domes, and in the more recently constructed five-hundred-foot-long hangar next door, which was less of an incubator and more of a morgue. "If there were one hundred fifty Tsuchi on board the *Darwin*, would you say there might have been a .75 percent margin of error?"

"Do you have a point?" Silhouette didn't like games. Didn't like much of anything.

"No fun," Brice said, and swiveled his laptop monitor around. "This was taken from a dash cam and uploaded to Flickr an hour ago. Note the red circle with the words, 'What the hell is this?' above it. Can *you* tell me what this is?"

Silhouette showed no reaction beyond a tightening of his lips.

"What do you think the odds are, that amid the chaos, a Tsuchi survived and found itself afloat on a piece of debris that later washed up on shore? Certainly higher than .75, yes?" Brice turned the monitor back around and looked at the grainy image. No one outside GOD could identify the creature in the image. Most people would believe it to be yet another cryptid hoax. They would give it a name. Something catchy. And make documentaries about it.

The trouble was, if they actually went out looking for it, and found it, it wouldn't be long before the whole world knew about the Tsuchi. And that could lead to trouble worse than exposure. If a Tsuchi reached the general population before controls had been implemented, life on Earth would be fundamentally changed forever. North and Central America would fall first. South America, too, if they didn't think to destroy the Panama Canal's three bridges. Then, when winter arrived and the arctic ice reached out across the top of the world, Greenland would fall. Then Russia, Asia, Africa and most of Europe. Only the island nations would survive. All because Silhouette had allowed the .75 percent margin of error to exist. It didn't matter how it had happened, it only mattered that he corrected the error before it was too late.

The stoic BlackGuard leader knew this as well as Brice did, so he simply turned around and headed for the door at the end of the lab. "We'll find it."

"Be sure that you do. And if you encounter anyone who has seen or come into contact with the Tsuchi..."

"Scorched earth," Silhouette said. "We'll leave nothing behind, living or dead."

5

"Are you serious?" I ask Hawkins.

He's bent over a dirt trail leading into the Tillamook State Forest, which is 364,000 acres of temperate rainforest sitting atop the Pacific Coast mountain range, defined by the Jon Hudson dictionary as: a crap-ton of trees on top of really tall peaks that are separated by lots of streams and rivers. But that's the good news. If Collins were here, that would sound like a good time. Instead, I'm with Hawkins, in search of a single creature the size of a basset hound...with eight legs, a shell back and an egg-laying stinger.

Hawkins shuffles back without standing, pointing to the sand around the trail head. "Look closely. Two lines of staggered impressions."

We left the FC-P preserve in Maine just twelve hours ago. Woodstock, our surly helicopter pilot had picked us up so we could get a head start, while Collins and Joliet got Maigo and Lilly settled. All four women had protested for different reasons: Joliet because she had more experience than me, Collins because she was more badass than me, Lilly, because she was more badass than me *and* had more experience, and Maigo...because she was secretly more badass than me and she doesn't like to be geographically distant from me. At least one of them isn't as badass, though Joliet can certainly handle herself.

But this was Hawkins's show. The BFSs were his personal nemeses. He knew what they could do and how to kill them. And he wanted me, and only me, on the advance search. He claimed it was because a smaller team would move faster and quieter, but I'm not sure anyone believed him. At first I thought I detected a little bit of sexism. He is kind of a macho, rugged wilderness guy. But then, during the six-hour flight from Boston to Portland, I realized the truth. Mine is the only life he felt comfortable risking. It's a horrible kind of compliment.

I bend down, my legs protesting after being crammed in an airplane seat for six hours and then a compact rental for another hour and a half. The only time not spent sitting in the past eight hours was the walk from the plane to the rental agency, who had mistakenly given away our much roomier rental. Despite my tired legs and bleary eyes, I see what he's pointing at. Two sets of tracks, which look too small to be anything large, head up the path toward the forest. I look back. The coastline is a sliver of blue, just two miles away. Hawkins says we're lucky it hadn't attacked anyone on its way to the woods, which was most likely because it wasn't comfortable, being so far out of its habitat without its brood. Apparently, the BFSs are social creatures. But now it's in the woods, where lots of living things will make for convenient, rapid fire incubators.

"I see them," I say, following the tracks to the edge of the woods, where they disappear. "But they stop here. Did it turn around?"

Hawkins stands up, hands on his hips. He's dressed in black fatigues, like me, to better hide in the shadows of the dense forest. While I've got my balding head concealed by a black beanie cap—I prefer red—he has his full head of hair held down by a black bandana, tied back. I'd like to think we look super cool and dangerous, but I'm pretty sure we look more like weekend warriors trying to relive our childhoods. Of course, the weapons we carry shatter that image.

We've both got .45 SIG Sauer P220 handguns, which pack a serious punch. I'm also carrying an MP5 submachine gun, and Hawkins has an insane looking AA-12 automatic shotgun that can shoot twelve rapid-fire shells with minimal kick. All this for one BFS, which if Hawkins is right, could become many BFSs if we don't kill it before it finds victims. I'd brought up the possibility of bringing in extra fire power. The FC-P has the option now. But he's seen these things use military forces as breeding grounds. We could throw a hundred men at them and end up having three hundred more BFSs as a result. At least with Hawkins and me, there would just be six more.

Until they reach Portland, population: 600,000, which isn't including all the suburbs.

"Look again," Hawkins says, and he waits until I find the trail, fifteen feet up, etched into the bark of a Douglas-fir.

"Got it." The fresh scratches and punctures lead around the fourteen-foot-diameter tree, rising steadily before disappearing again. I point to the next tree, where the trail continues, rounding a second, three-hundred-foot-tall Douglas-fir. If the BFS climbs too high, we'll never find it. But this one appears to prefer being near the ground. The trail continues deeper, and I notice it's following the human-made walking trail. It's just 6:30 in the morning, so we're the first ones here, but that doesn't mean there isn't anyone camping.

Hawkins stops me with a hand on my shoulder. Points to my MP5. "Safety off."

"Not exactly protocol," I say.

"There's a good chance you won't have time to switch the safety off later," he says.

"If we find it."

"When it finds us."

I thumb the safety off. "You know, when Collins and I do these things, I usually get laid."

He cracks a smile. Hawkins has a sense of humor, but he doesn't crack many jokes. He's a serious guy most of the time, which isn't surprising given the number of scars he has—the worst of them from that grizzly bear he killed. Claw marks right over his chest. "I'm afraid that the only eggs getting fertilized will be the ones injected into your gut. Good news is, you'll get to see the live birth before you die."

His smile widens. An uncommon joke. He must be nervous, which makes me nervous.

I pat the puncture-resistant armor we're both wearing. It covers most of my soft spots, and it's strong enough to stop a razor-sharp KA-BAR knife thrust by Chuck Norris. "I'm wearing protection."

"We'll see," he says, the smile fading as he steps into the shaded rainforest.

"I'd rather not."

"Then keep your gun up, and stay quiet. Try not to speak unless you're being attacked."

"Copy that," I say, getting serious. The time for jokes is over. The time for screaming and shooting and potential worst-death-ever-at-the-hands-of-a-genetic-freak has now begun.

We walk for an hour in complete silence, listening to the sounds of the forest. Birds, insects and water—lots of water. Aside from a foot-long banana slug, which looks like a cross between a banana and a living turd with tentacles, we haven't spotted any large game. This could be a good or bad thing depending on what kind of glass-half-full, glass-half-empty kind of person you are. I'd like to think I'm a glass-half-full kind of guy, but then I see the BFS's trail returns to the ground, where it disappears again.

The path has turned to brown stone. The roar of a waterfall drowns out the forest. It's just ahead, hidden by fifty feet of looming trees.

Hawkins waits for me to catch up. He leans back to whisper in my ear. "Stay sharp. This is an ideal hunting ground."

I nod, having spent enough time in the woods in search of Wendigos, Jersey Devils and hairy drunk men pretending to be them, to know that the water draws prey animals to drink, and the noise helps drown out the approach of the predators that hunt them.

MP5 braced against my shoulder, I follow Hawkins around the massive tree trunks separating us from the river. Sounds easy, but I'm walking backwards. Any predator worth its claws will attack from behind, so I don't give it a chance. Part of me says that I need to show my back, so the BFS will attack, but if Hawkins is right, it won't matter. The B in BFS could also stand for *brazen*.

We exit the rainforest onto a slab of stone overlooking the river, which descends down the gently sloping mountainside over a series of five-to-ten-foot-tall waterfalls. The rush of water is deafening. If Hawkins and I were talking, we'd have to shout.

After scanning the area, I give Hawkins a 'what now?' shrug. He points two fingers at his eyes and at the surrounding rainforest. The trail. Right. If the BFS simply passed through, the trail would pick back up on the other side, assuming it didn't travel up or down the river first. He must be thinking the same thing, because he points at himself and then points upriver, and then he points at me and downriver.

I nod and head downriver, hopping over layers of stone, polished by years of rising and subsiding waters. I pause at the edge of a ten-foot drop. White water falls beside me, plunging into a black pool carved into the stone below. I can't jump down, so I sling the MP5 over my back and slide over the side. The rock's edge is craggy. Plenty of hand and footholds. Just a few feet down and a short jump.

But I don't make it all the way.

I stop, clinging to the stone like a gecko trying to blend in. Something has set off my oh-fuck-o-meter.

It's behind me, I think, but I can't see it. So I jump, spinning around in the air and reaching for the MP5. While wrestling with the weapon, I realize I should have drawn the handgun. Would have been much faster.

But it doesn't matter, because when I take aim at the river behind me, nothing is there. Just rocks, water and a killer view. But nothing deadly. So why the hell did my instincts go haywire? I've stood before a high rise-sized Kaiju without pissing myself. I don't scare that easily. Not without a reason. So I look for one.

The woods are dark. A perfect hiding place. But the trees show no signs of passage. The stone riverbanks are obviously empty. The rushing waters are no place to hide. That leaves the pool of water. Hawkins said the BFSs avoided water. That they couldn't swim. But the best predators sometimes make exceptions. I turn toward the pool of water, depth and rotting leaf litter turning it black, like a BFS.

I aim the MP5 at the turbulent, dark water, but hold my fire. The rounds will lose their lethal force shortly after striking the water. I'm going to have to wait for it to—

I almost miss the burst of black emerging from inside the waterfall. The sneaky bastard must have been hiding in a pocket, clinging to the wall, waiting for some idiot—me—to focus his attention on the murky pool. The MP5 comes up and spews a string of rounds into the air, but all miss the mark. The BFS, which really does look like a big fucking spider's turtle love-child, is too fast.

It strikes my chest. Its ugly face, with its five buggy eyes and twitching mandibles just inches from my nose, elicits a scream. The impact knocks me back onto unforgiving stone, my head splashing into the river, where it is dowsed by the waterfall.

As water crushes out my scream and tries to force itself down my esophagus, something constricts around my waist. And then, as the corset from hell is fully tightened, I feel Hawkins's worst nightmare become reality, as something impacts my gut three times in rapid succession.

The spawn are implanted.

Already gnawing at my organs.

At least the river will drown me before they tear me apart from the inside out.

6

Aww, c'mon, I think as I'm dragged out of the water. The asshole mutant spider won't even give me a merciful death. Some part of my brain wonders if the host has to be alive for the young to grow, but the rest of me vacillates between coughing up water and shouting.

When my head clears the water, I see Hawkins standing above me, holding the BFS by its thrashing legs, its prehensile tail still wrapped around me, still punching holes in my gut. But why? I thought these things implanted three young, and then it's wham-bam-thank-you-ma'am, you're dead. I feel the impacts, over and over, but not the sharp sting of a puncture wound. *The armor is doing its job.*

The knowledge frees my mind and body from the terror of being eaten from the inside out. I draw the knife sheathed on my belt and swipe the blade over my stomach. I feel a moment's resistance and then the blade—and me—are free.

The BFS shrieks as red gore and some kind of viscous white nastiness oozes from its severed tail. Its thrashing is so violent that Hawkins loses his grip and resorts to tossing the thing away. Neither of us has our heavy hitting weapons ready, so we both draw our hand guns and make like we're skeet shooting. The problem is, the eight-legged skeet is fast and not moving in a straight line. We each fire four shots, only one of mine striking it and taking off a leg. But the missing limb doesn't even slow it down as it lunges into the forest—on the far side of the river.

Hawkins offers his hand and pulls me up to my feet.

"You okay?" he asks, holstering his sidearm and readying the shotgun.

I look down at the puncture-resistant armor. It's full of holes—and wriggling things. *What the hell...* I lean down for a better look. They look like larva, white and plump, their tails spinning frantic circles. When one of them slips further into the armor, I realize they're working their way through it.

Spinning in a circle, muttering a string of curses, I remove the armor and throw it to the stone riverbank. After lifting my black neoprene shirt and confirming none made it through, I calm down and focus on the situation. We still have one BFS on the loose, but with its tail severed, it won't be multiplying. It's also left us a nice bloody trail to follow. We'll find it and kill it. There's no doubt about that now. It might even bleed out by the time we find it. But these little squirmy bastards present a problem. Collect and study, or exterminate?

Hawkins makes the call before I can, stomping on the armor until each and every larva is a white smear. When he's done, he looks up at me, back at the mess he's made and then back to me. "You okay with this?"

"I'm just upset you beat me to it," I say. "Now let's go take care of mom."

After finding a wide, shallow stretch of river, we cross into the woods on the far side and quickly pick up the trail. We don't even see it at first. The trail of gore smells ungodly, like Satan himself left a skid mark through the forest. The bloody smears move from tree to tree, but slowly shift lower until reaching the ground.

"Why did it move to the forest floor?" I ask.

"Blood loss," Hawkins says. "Doesn't have the energy for leaping between trees. It won't be much further."

Open space and bright light ahead reveals a break in the forest. While the BFS is missing its tail, it could still be deadly. If there is any kind of civilization ahead, people could be in trouble. I double-time my pace and reach the clearing ten seconds before, and more out of breath than, Hawkins. "Dammit," I mutter between heaves.

Hawkins steps up beside me and repeats my curse when he sees what I'm looking at. A large swath of the forest has been cleared. All that remains are severed trunks and layers of old, dry, branches, many of them blackened by rot. It's the perfect place for a BFS to hide.

I'm about to say this could take a while when I spot the blood trail. "There." I follow the trail with my finger until I'm pointing into the distance, where an aberration mars the bleak landscape.

"What is that?" I ask myself, pulling out a pair of binoculars. I put the lenses to my eyes, find the object and focus. An RV. The FC-P is generally quiet work. Nearly all the reports of strange animals we get turn out to be real and friendly or just plain bogus. But when things go wrong, they go colossally wrong. If anyone is inside that trailer, they're in trouble.

I lower my binoculars just as Hawkins lowers his own pair. "Let's go in quiet," I say. "Weapons hot. But we can't go John Rambo now. Not until we know that RV is empty."

He gives a silent nod and we strike out, side by side. Moving through the debris of a hacked-down forest turns out to be a slow and noisy affair. Although we're back in silent communication mode, there's not a single place to step where there isn't a branch to break or a pinecone to crunch. If the injured BFS is still alive, it knows we're coming.

When we're within twenty feet of the RV, which looks one part rock star tour bus and one part retiree home, I motion to Hawkins and point to the far side. He nods, and we separate, each rounding the large vehicle. I scan the sides of the thirty foot long RV, but spot nothing unusual. The door is closed. The window shades are drawn, and the front windshield is covered by a reflective visor.

When we reconnect on the far side, Hawkins breaks his silence. "Abandoned?"

I shake my head. "No way. These things cost a fortune, and this one doesn't look that old. Maybe they're still inside."

"Maybe."

"I'm guessing college age. Sex. Drugs. Alcohol. In the woods."

"Sounds familiar," Hawkins says. A slight grin.

"I have no idea what you're talking about," I say, and I head for the door. I'm about to knock, when a *tap, tap, tap* stops me in my tracks. I find the source of the sound just above and to the side of the door. A mix of white and red, like milk and strawberry syrup, drips from the RV's roof, onto a branch. I motion for Hawkins to watch the roof, and he aims the shotgun up over my head.

I raise my fist next to the door. "Ready?"

"Just duck if you hear me shoot."

"Right," I say, and I give the door three hard pounds. "DHS! Anyone inside?"

Silence is the only reply.

I knock again. "DHS! If anyone is inside, respond now or we will enter."

I wait for a moment, fist raised and ready to give a final warning before flinging the door open. Before I can knock, Hawkins gives my shoulder a quick tap. When I look back, he points to his ear. *Listen.*

I hold my breath and turn my full attention to what may or may not be beyond this door. Then I hear it. The *thunk* of something moving. A shuffle. A bottle falls over, rolls, stops. Someone is inside.

I step back from the door, waiting for it to open. But it doesn't. Whoever is inside must be in a stupor. "Told you. Drugs and alcohol." But as the sound grows louder and more distinct, I'm less sure of my assessment. My instincts decide I'm wrong long before my intellect. I step back away from the RV as the sound—like a hundred nails being whacked into the RV's interior walls—grows thunderous.

"I think I woke something up," I say.

"Some*things*," Hawkins says. Our eyes meet. "It's already bred. The one we found might not have even been the one in the photo. We can't win this fight."

"How many could be in there?" I ask.

He shakes his head as we continue backing away. "One or two, we could handle. Four...maybe. More than that..."

He's painted a clear enough picture. I get it. The noise coming from inside the now-shaking RV indicates a much larger number. "We need help."

"We don't have that long."

Our conversation is cut short when the RV door flings open and slaps against the vehicle's exterior wall. A cloud of black flies buzz out, concealing the view. When the insects dissipate into the air like smoke, a single, tailless BFS fills the doorway, very much alive, and if I'm not mistaken, pissed off. Its shaking limbs reveal barely contained rage. The inside of the RV behind the creature is slathered in blood and body parts, painted with the insides of people and various woodland creatures.

"Just keep walking," Hawkins whispers. "Running now will just trigger their pursuit. Let's get as far away as we can first. Wait for them to make the first move."

Walking backwards, through the uneven stretch of crisscrossing branches and stumps without making any sudden moves is tough to do. But we keep moving, slow and steady...for all of five seconds. Then we're frozen by what happens next. Living black flows from the top of the RV. Like sludgy water from a broken water main, the BFSs rise from below, congregating on the roof in a writhing pile of twitchy hairy limbs and wriggling tails.

My armor is gone, I think, and I fight to maintain my slow and steady pace. How many of them are there? Twenty? Thirty? More flow out of the doorway, their sharp talons piercing the RV's metal hull. The massive vehicle is transformed into a living ball of BFSs, the way daddy longlegs pile together against the cold. But these things aren't cold. They're hunting.

Us.

But what are they waiting for?

I step back. The branch beneath my feet rolls and sends me toppling backwards. Hawkins is quick to catch me, but the damage is done. By the time I'm upright again, the BFSs have launched themselves toward us.

We don't bother firing into the mass of shell-protected monsters. From this range we wouldn't do much good, and neither of us want to get any closer. The only thing keeping us alive right now is distance, so we do our best to maintain it, bunny hopping through the field of fallen trees.

Our pace quickens when we enter the forest, which is mostly clear, thanks to the thick pine canopy blocking out the sun. But that also means the BFSs will move faster, too, and that's a problem, because like most creatures with more than two legs, they can outpace a human being with little effort.

The sound of a hundred little daggers puncturing tree bark fills the forest. They're gaining on us, taking the high ground, probably flanking us. They might not be intelligent, but most predators are born with instinctual strategies for hunting, and who knows what was programmed into the DNA of these things.

Through the chaos of the monsters pursuing us, the sound of my feet pounding the ground, my equipment rattling and my heavy breathing, I hear something new. Voices. Commanding and authoritative. *Military*, I think, but my half full glass is now totally empty. *How did they get here so fast? We didn't tell anyone. And—*

I tackle Hawkins, and we fall into a field of tall ferns. Before he can complain, I put my hand over his lips and mouth the word, "Listen."

The voices grow louder as the unknown group of men rounds a large Douglas-fir.

"I've got movement on the Flir," a man says, referring to a thermal imaging device. "Up ahead. Half a click and closing fast. Looks like a lot of them."

"Get ready," a second man says. "We're not here for Dark Matter. This is a straight forward slash-and-burn op. When we're done with the Tsuchi—"

Sushi? They named the BFSs Sushi? Because they eat people raw? That'd make us the sushi... In the fraction of a second it takes me to wonder all this, I replay the word in my head, hearing the subtleties of its pronunciation. I've been immersed in Japanese culture, trying to keep that part of Maigo's heritage intact. Granted, it mostly involves us watching anime—*Ghost in the Shell*, *Akira* and her favorite, *Gaiking*, which are beautiful and horrifyingly violent at the same time, but I've heard enough of the Japanese language to speak a few phrases and recognize the nearly silent T at the word's start.

Tsuchi...

"—we need to track down and eliminate anyone that has come into contact with, or is in a position to reveal, them. Understood?"

What I understand is that these men not only know about the BFSs, but like us, they are here to eliminate them, and anyone else who has evidence that the...Tsuchi, are real.

The number of vehement instances of "Yes, sir," that reply is disconcerting. We have unknowingly led one army toward another, and we're currently caught in the crossfire.

Hawkins catches my eye. We're both laying face down, sniffing the wet earth beneath the curling fronds of a fern ceiling, cloaked in shadow, thanks to our garb. While the unknown force of men and the frenzied horde of genetic monstrosities close in from either side, he points in the direction of the voices, then stabs his finger into the soil between our heads. He etches a series of lines in the dirt, but I can't see it. Then he slowly pulls his hand away, revealing a single word:

DARPA.

7

"Auto-turrets, here and here," the man in charge says. I can't see him yet, but the way he gives orders and the way the others follow them reveal his role. I can't see anyone else, either, but now that they're almost standing on top of us, their individual movements are clear. I count four, which is far fewer than I previously thought, and not nearly enough to face what's coming, though the words, 'auto' and 'turrets' are promising. Granted, these guys might be part of Hawkins's rogue DARPA group, but four guys with guns is preferable to an army of BFSs.

I breathe slowly, MP5 gripped tight, waiting for someone to trip over me. I keep my eyes locked in the direction of the men's voices, assuming that Hawkins is doing the same.

"ETA?" the man in charge asks.

"Contact in thirty seconds."

Hard metal presses against the side of my head. I glance toward it without moving and see the barrel of a gun. I look beyond it, toward Hawkins, and see nothing. Sneaky bastard.

"That's just enough time for you to tell us who the hell you are and why you're here." The voice has a trace of a southern accent, but mostly it's just intensely grouchy.

I take my hands off the MP5 and raise them above the ferns. No sense in lying, as anything short of the truth will likely result in a bullet punching a hole in my head. "Jon Hudson. DHS."

"Get him up," the man in charge says.

I'm lifted by the back of my shirt. Free of the ferns, I see the four-man team, all cloaked in black, head to toe, including armor like mine, but more futuristic looking and not partially missing. Their faces are covered with round, reflective goggles that I suspect are more than stylish.

The man in charge stands beside one of two devices that look like a Porsche had babies with a mini-gun. The barrel of the weapon sweeps back and forth, no doubt guided by an array of motion and heat detecting sensors. I can hear the second one behind me.

"Who are you?" I ask.

"You can call me Silhouette," he says. "Why is the FC-P here?"

He knows who I am. It shouldn't surprise me. A lot of people know who I am, but I'm sporting the beginning of a beard now and my face is covered in dirt. That means he knows my name, which still isn't impossible. But he quickly identified my name with the FC-P. *We're on these guys' radar.* Hawkins is right to be afraid of them.

"Reports of spider-turtles is kind of our thing," I say, "though if I'm honest, I'm pretty far out of my element right now." I motion at the sophisticated weapons and take the opportunity to glance at the other men. Other than size differences, there's no telling them apart. "I'm sure as hell happy to see you guys. And I'll be happy to lend my gun to the fight, which, by the way, will start in three...two..."

Silhouette nods at the man holding me, and I half expect to get a bullet in the head, but I'm freed instead.

An auto-turret kicks off a round, the sound muffled by a sound suppressor. I glance at the weapons held by the four men. I'm not really a gun guy, but it goes with the job. I recognize the weapons as KRISS Vectors, which are technically future weapons not yet available to the military. Definitely DARPA. The weapons, unlike the turrets, are not sound suppressed, and not raised. Clearly, they think the two turrets will win this fight for them.

Rounds start flying, the turrets snapping back and forth. I turn uphill, back the way I came, and I see a wall of living black flowing toward us, on the ground and in the trees. Rounds chew up the forest, killing more trees than BFSs, but getting the job done...slowly. The weapons are targeting the nearest BFSs first, taking down one after another, but the mass, as a whole, is getting closer.

When the first unsuppressed weapon barks to life, I jump, not just from the sound, but because the round fired punches a hole in a BFS dropping down from above—toward my head. There's a loud crack as the shell is punctured. The round hits the far side of the shell and doesn't exit. Instead, all that energy snaps the creature to the side. It lands in the ferns next to me, and I waste no time unloading ten rounds into it, only stopping when the writhing tail falls limp.

I turn to the shortest of the four men, who shot the BFS, and nod my thanks. In response, he points up. I follow his finger and see more BFSs overhead, leaping through the trees, out of the auto-turrets' range. I aim up and fire, the rest of the mysterious four-man team joining me. While the MP5 rattles in my grip, I can't help but wonder where Hawkins went.

"Too many," the biggest of the four men declares without much emotion, before taking a precise shot that drops a moving BFS two hundred feet up.

Geez, these guys are good.

"Give me thirty," Silhouette says, tapping his ear and turning away.

The other three continue shooting, and so do I, but it's a losing battle. The BFSs are still closing in, from above, and now from the sides. They're avoiding the auto-turrets. Smart little assholes.

Through the gunfire, I catch two words spoken by Silhouette. "Scorched earth." I don't know who he's talking to, but as someone who has dealt with a three-hundred-foot-tall monster capable of creating its own scorched earth, I understand the concept. They're going to torch the forest, which means they also know what kind of danger these things present. And since there's nothing I, nor the vanished Mark Hawkins, can do about this many BFSs, it's the right call. In fact, so far, I'm glad these guys are here. Without them, Hawkins and I would have already given birth to our own small broods.

More words filter through. "One mile radius," and "Three mikes." His voice is suddenly clear when he turns around, once again addressing the group. "EVAC in two mikes, boys, payday in three." As he says the words, he points his handgun at my chest. "Sorry, Jon, scorched earth includes you, too."

"Ahem," a familiar voice says. I turn to find Hawkins standing behind the short man who saved me, knife blade against the man's throat. Hawkins's face is now slathered in mud, no doubt to protect his identity.

None of the four men seem ruffled by this turn of events, including the man with a knife to his throat.

Silhouette looks at his watch and lowers his weapons. "We don't have time for games, Specter."

The small man gives a faint nod. "Shadow, Obsidian, you're with me." The trio heads downhill, leaving the expensive, and still-firing auto-turrets behind. All around, the BFSs close in, focusing on the three people present rather than on the three leaving. "Specter, catch up when you're done."

I look at Hawkins, his confused expression no doubt matching my own.

"Buddy," I say to Specter, "Your pals just sold you out, so if you know a way to—"

Before I can finish speaking, the man's foot comes flying up, slips past his own head and connects with Hawkins, who spills backwards. The blade pulls across the man's throat, but doesn't cut through his suit's fabric.

The *tick-tack* of sharp feet punching through bark grows louder all around. I ignore it and fire at the man, nearly point blank. Each shot is a hit, straight to the chest, but the rounds don't even faze him. With normal body armor, the rounds are absorbed, but the impacts are still powerful enough to crack ribs and bruise skin. Whatever this guy is wearing diffuses that energy, allowing him to do what happens next.

The short version is that he kicks my ass.

The long version is that he kicks the weapon from my hand, follows that up with a spinning kick to the side of my head and then a second spinning kick, in the opposite direction, to my legs. The effect is that I'm spun through the air, onto my back, dazed and breathless, all in about the same time it took me to fire three useless shots.

Hawkins fares no better. In fact, he's still recovering from that single kick to the forehead. We're at this guy's mercy, and as his handgun comes around and draws level with my forehead, I'm pretty sure there isn't much mercy to go around.

But then he pulls the trigger and proves me wrong. The bullet punches into the dirt beside my head. He's either a horrible shot, or he meant to miss. When he fires again, without adjusting his aim. I know it's the latter. But why?

Before I can ask, he pistol whips his own face, twice, drawing blood and shattering the goggles over his head.

What the hell?

Without a word, he turns around and pulls the goggles off his head, tossing them over his shoulder. When the goggles land beside me, he takes off running, like a little lightning bolt. He's out of sight in seconds.

"Hawkins," I say, scrabbling to my feet. The static click of an approaching tree-scaling army grows louder. They're just seconds way. "Run!" I snag the goggles, then grab the man and hoist him up.

With a shake of his head, Hawkins's wits return, and he shoves me ahead. "Go!"

I start running without any real sense of where I'm going. What I do know is that this whole place, for a mile all around, is going to be scorched earth in less than three minutes, and there is no way we are getting outside the target area in time. "Which way is the river?"

A springing BFS, eight arms outstretched, stinging tail reaching toward my gut, is cut down by a spray from my MP5. It writhes on the ground as I run past, and it nearly strikes me. "What?" I shout back to Hawkins, whose reply was drowned out by the gunfire.

He points past my head and to the right. "That way!"

We turn together, running downhill now, picking up speed. But we're not alone. BFSs give chase on all sides, including in front of us. Five of them come at us, too many for the MP5 to handle on its own. "Hawkins!" I shout and move to the side. Taking the lead, Hawkins unleashes seven rapid-fire shots from his AA-12 shotgun. The incredibly loud weapon sounds like thunder for a moment, and sets my ears to ringing, but the effects are undeniable. The five BFSs have been reduced to sludge. We run through them, the river now audible, the air growing moist.

Over the sound of the nearby river and the ringing in my ears, I hear something new. A distant, but growing roar.

A jet, unlike anything I've seen before.

It streaks overhead just as I'm about to shout my warning. Something small falls from its gullet, dropping toward us. Eyes flicking between the small object and the path ahead, we explode out of the woods and into the clear, stone river bed.

"Find a sinkhole!" I shout, searching the area, but finding only shallow pools and the waterfalls that feed them.

Above, the single projectile coughs and shatters, turning into multiple bombs, spreading out over a large area. Just then, a second bomb falls from the jet. And a third. This whole area is about to get wiped clean.

"Here!" Hawkins shouts, and yanks my arm. Before I can see what he's found, he throws us both over the side of a waterfall. All I can see below is frothing white. If we hit stone, at least we'll probably be dead or unconscious when the bombs hit. But we don't hit stone. Instead, we plunge into a ten-foot-deep pool, barely big enough for two, and we're held there by the force of the water dropping down above us.

That's when the very earth around us shakes, and a wave of pressure crushes the air from my lungs. I fight the urge to surface and breathe, not because I don't need to, but because the surface of the water now glows bright yellow.

The world above us is burning.

8

"You!" Alicio Brice said, snapping his fingers at a man whose name he couldn't recall and perhaps never knew. "What's happening?"

The man was a member of the science staff. The white coat and ID badge told Brice that much. The man, a heavyset fellow with a bushy beard and thin spectacles, leaned over the glass dome containing the Tsuchi.

"They look dead," the man said.

"What's your name?" Brice asked.

"Wood," the man says. "D-David."

"Well, Wood D-David," Brice said, his temper flaring. "What, in your personal opinion, could be the cause?"

"I...I don't know. I'm a geneticist."

"As am I." Brice crossed his arms. "I'm also your employer. So do yourself a favor and postulate."

The big man leaned in close, breath fogging the glass. "Ahh. Well...I'm assuming all the environmental systems are functioning?"

Brice nodded.

"Then, ahh...what are they? I've never seen these specimens before."

"They're new," Brice said.

"Chimeras of some sort," Wood said. "Spider. Turtle. A few other traits thrown into the mix. The genetic integration is amazing. Are these from the island?"

"Fewer questions, more ideas."

"Uh, well, when was the last time you fed them?"

It had been nearly twenty four hours since the Tsuchi had devoured Johnson. Could their metabolisms be that fast? Would they need to eat again already? There had certainly been enough waste material, long since swept away by the automated cleaning system.

To test the theory, Brice tapped out a few keys on his laptop and watched as a fresh piece of raw beef rose into the containment unit. The three Tsuchi, all laying on their backs, motionless legs clutched inward, remained still. The scent of raw meat failed to lure them from sleep. Could they really be dead? He didn't think they could have starved. The Tsuchi on the *Darwin* had lasted years at sea, most likely in some kind of hibernation state. Was that what they were doing now?

Only one way to find out.

"I need you to inspect one for me," Brice said.

"M-me? I'm hardly qualified to—"

"You're here," Brice said. He knew he could call in help, that there were other people just minutes away, who were more qualified. But time was of the essence, and he hadn't known this man's name. That meant, should the worst occur, the man was expendable. "That makes you qualified. You do like your job, don't you?"

The big man actually appeared to be debating his answer, but eventually acquiesced with a sigh. "Just...tell me what to do."

"Very good." Brice set his fingers to work on the keyboard. Inside the Tsuchi unit, the floor came to life. Two small circles opened in the floor. The robotic limbs slipped into the space and twisted toward the nearest Tsuchi. The three stubby digits at the ends of the arms opened and gently gripped one of the creature's rigid limbs. It didn't flinch.

If the Tsuchi were dead, it would be a significant loss, but not catastrophic. They could harvest the creatures' DNA and start anew. There was also a chance that they could collect and implant the Tsuchis' eggs and artificially implant them into hosts. If that worked, they would have new, adult specimens in minutes. How the Tsuchi grew so quickly was one of the secrets he needed to unlock. If only the island had been more closely monitored, they wouldn't be in this predicament, but reverse engineering was always easier than trial and error. And while Brice was a brilliant man, the mind behind the Tsuchi had been...insane, at best. Probably worse.

The Tsuchi body was pulled toward a clear plastic tray, collected and pulled down through the floor. "Over here," Brice said, snapping his fingers, while walking to a biological safety cabinet on the far side of the massive incubator space. They arrived at the same time as the Tsuchi, the tray rising up behind the protective glass wall where two thick gloves hung limp. The Tsuchi was still rigid, seemingly clutched by death.

Biting his nails, Brice stood beside the unit and waggled his free hand at it. "Go ahead."

After a moment's apprehension, Wood put his hands into the glass-mounted gloves, reaching inside the container without exposing himself to what was inside. "That stinger looks pretty nasty. Should I—"

Brice waved his fears away. "The gloves are made from nanocrystalline cellulose, the same material our bullet-proof, puncture-proof and shock-proof armor is made from. Your hands are perfectly protected. Now, if you wouldn't mind...pull off a leg."

"W-what? Why?"

"If it's dead, what does it matter?"

"What if it's alive?" Wood asked.

Brice shrugged. "Then we'll know it's not dead."

Lips pursed, brow damp with sweat, Wood turned to the task at hand, reaching out with the thick gloves. At first, he touched the body gingerly, ready to pull back. But after a few moments of prodding, he became more comfortable, lifting the Tsuchi up and turning it around. "It's lighter than I thought it would be."

"Most of the weight comes from the shell," Brice said, "but on the inside, even that is mostly porous, like a gel-filled honey comb."

"You've dissected one before?"

"Heavens, no. I have merely studied reports from those who have."

Wood stopped still and turned to Brice. "But you would, right? If given the chance."

"Yes, yes," Brice lied. "Of course. Now please, concentrate. All this talking will give me a migraine."

Wood tried to hide the shake of his head and the roll of his eyes, but he failed. Brice decided he'd fire the man regardless of his participation. But not until they were done. Not until he knew what step to take next.

The Tsuchi, laying on its shelled back, spun around under Wood's guidance. He stopped it, took hold of a limb, and pulled. The leg didn't move.

"Pretend it's a wishbone," Brice said. "You look like you've had a go at your fair share of turkeys."

With a sigh, Wood leaned forward, face near the glass, and put his weight into the leg, holding the body still with one hand and pulling with the other. The limb slowly relented. And then, as though connected, all eight limbs snapped open. Wood let go of the leg, but still held the body in place. "What was that?"

"Reflex," Brice guessed. "The last of its neurons firing in response to your pull."

"It felt like it was resisting," Wood said, looking back.

Brice's reply was cut short, replaced by wide eyes and gaping mouth. Wood saw the reaction and turned toward the containment unit. The Tsuchi's legs were all still splayed wide, but the long tail and its needle-tipped stinger hovered in the air like a coiled snake.

Wood withdrew the hand that had been holding the leg, but when he pulled back the other, the Tsuchi's eight limbs snapped closed like a bear trap, not puncturing the gloves, but applying pressure. "It has me!" He tugged his arm hard, gripping the top of the unit, his face inches from the glass.

A sharp crack, like a suppressed gunshot, silenced Wood's panic.

"What happened?" Brice asked, trying to look around his counterpart's now still body. He gripped Wood's meaty shoulder and turned him around. The first thing he saw was the glass, a spider-web crack emanating from a small hole. The second thing was a hole in Wood's temple, a single drop of blood leaking out.

Wood looked stunned, like he wanted to say something but now lacked the mental capacity to do so. Instead, his face twisted, as though in slow motion, into a mask of pain, followed by the most ear splitting howl Brice had ever heard. He understood what was happening, even if Wood did not.

"Sneaky devil," Brice said to the Tsuchi, still clinging to Wood's arm. The creatures weren't dead. They'd set a trap. He glanced at the Tsuchi dome and confirmed it. The other two were up and about, hopping around, trying to find a way out, perhaps sensing a shift in the action outside the glass dome.

Cracking glass brought his attention back to the contained Tsuchi. It was stabbing at the glass, shattering it. It would eventually be able to break free.

"Not quite sneaky enough," Brice said, lifting a plastic cover on the side of the containment unit. His finger hovered over the now visible red button. He turned to Wood, appeared serious for a moment, but then laughed. "Sorry. Sorry. I'm sorry. It's just that I was about to tell you that you were fired, and now I have to do this. Would have been like an 80s' action movie."

Wood's only reply was more screaming.

"Levity is lost on the dying, I suppose." Brice pushed the button.

The inside of the containment unit filled with white hot flames.

Wood's scream rose several octaves and was joined by a shrieking, melting Tsuchi. The glass shattered and the flaming creature dove out, but fell still upon hitting the floor.

The large scientist, on the other hand, ran. The flesh of his left arm had melted away, leaving his radius and ulna bones protruding from charred skin, the bones of his arm dangling limply on slowly stretching connective tissue.

"Stop!" Brice shouted, but the man's mind was lost.

Wood ran the hundred fifty feet toward the exit, gripping his head. Brice followed as best he could, but the last time he'd run anywhere was as a child, some forty years ago. He shoved through the double doors a few seconds behind Wood. When he entered the hallway, he found the other, much heavier man, running for the far end and the elevators. If Wood escaped, the results could be catastrophic. Brice couldn't catch the man, but he could head him off at the pass, digitally. He pulled his cell phone from his pocket, accessing the building's digital security measures. He quickly tapped in a code, locking down the elevators. Next, he locked all the stairwell doors. Last, he alerted security to a containment breach. Within thirty seconds, there would be an army of heavily armed men capable of dealing with the situation. And if Brice was right, that's about the same time Wood's body would...give birth.

Brice began backing away, intending to lock himself inside the incubator, leaving security to handle the messier, and more dangerous, work. But he stopped short when the lumbering, screaming scientist barreled straight past the elevators and the stairwell door.

What is he...oh no!

Brice saw what was about to happen, and tried shouting out, but nothing could stop the big man's charge. Weighing more than three hundred pounds, the prodigious Wood struck the window at the far end, moving at an impressive clip for his size. Momentum carried all of his girth into the pane, which didn't shatter. Instead, the whole window popped free and fell away.

Brice ran to the end of the hall, listening to Wood's scream fade with distance, and then, all at once, it was cut silent with a loud smack. Moving fast, Brice nearly fell out of the window himself, but he caught the frame and clung to it, looking down. Wood's body, fifteen stories below, appeared wider than before, a pool of dark red slowly seeping out. But the gore wasn't what held his attention, it was the man's bulging head. With a crack audible from fifteen floors up, Wood's head split open and burst. But it wasn't a brain that emerged. It was a scrabbling, still growing Tsuchi. The creature, smaller than the one that birthed it, perhaps because it had been implanted in the man's head, rather than his soft gut, stumbled to the side, found its footing and then scrambled inside the open cargo door that led inside Building-K, the 200,000-square-foot morgue.

Working the phone, Brice quickly triggered the bay door to close, and then he locked down the rest of the massive building. Next he redirected security, and unlocked his own floor. The Tsuchi had to be caught or destroyed at all costs. He took consolation in the fact that the BlackGuard were scheduled to return soon, and that the Tsuchi required living hosts to multiply. Looking down at the massive morgue, Brice shook his head and thought, *thank God for that.*

9

Hawkins and I survived the blast beneath the water, but nearly drowned as a result. It took some last-second teamwork to escape the torrent of water pouring over us—water that had gotten hot enough to burn—but we survived. And from what I saw, we were the only survivors inside a square mile. The mysterious DARPA hit squad had done their job. But did they do it well enough?

So far, it seems that way. Hawkins found no traces of the things, and there hadn't been any more reported sightings. We almost got cooked, but we also got lucky.

Not that you'd be able to tell by talking to Hawkins. While I'm feeling happy to be alive and not the proud father of three baby-killing machines, he's upset that the DARPA guys got away. Stopping the BFSs, or Tsuchis, was our primary goal, but Hawkins wanted more. He wanted a lead. But it seems that our only lead is cracked, waterlogged and lacking in clues.

"So you're telling me they're useless?" Hawkins says, pacing in front of the long window back at the Crow's Nest. The view looks out on Beverly-Salem Harbor, which is now under repair. Two years ago, Nemesis, on her way to Boston, made a pit stop in the harbor, decimating the area with a fiery detonation matching the power of the cluster bombs dropped on the Tillamook State Forest. A year later, Nemesis returned, this time with Maigo's consciousness at the forefront, battling a smaller Kaiju named Scrion, and protecting me. The view outside the window now is blessedly clear and calm.

Can't say the same for the view on the inside. Hawkins's pacing is making everyone nervous. The office space is clean, each of our desks separated and the neatness contained, evidence of Cooper's continued influence. The walls are covered in maps, with pins showing the locations of active FC-P cases, closed cases and general reports of weirdness. There is a global map specifically for Kaiju threats. It hasn't been used in a year. There are pins showing the locations of Nemesis sightings, as well as the five Kaiju born from Nemesis Prime, all now dead, along with Nemesis. The last pin was placed in Washington D.C. A large red question mark was drawn next to it, by Maigo. She, like me, would like to know where Nemesis's body was taken.

Two days after the battle that leveled much of the capital, also under reconstruction, Nemesis's body simply vanished in the night. I haven't been able to find out who took it, how they managed to move her, and where she was taken. Monster or not, Maigo came from the creature, and she did save Washington, probably the world and on a more personal note—me.

"I can't turn them on, but I've never seen anything like this," Watson says. His chubby face is flushed. He's been intimidated by Hawkins since they first met. Hawkins is a big guy with a deep voice. Where I'm casual and chummy, he's rugged and serious. But this is the first time Watson has seen him angry. He turns his attention away from

Hawkins and back to the futuristic goggles left behind by the man known as Specter, who for some reason spared our lives. "*Nobody* has seen anything like this. Best guess, they're some kind of vision-enhancing goggles. Like night vision, but something else. There's all sorts of sensors in here, but I can't tell what they're for. Batteries. A transmitter."

That perks up my ears. I take my crossed legs down from my desktop and sit up. "Transmitter?"

"Yeah," Watson says, happy to have me in the conversation. He's got the goggles opened up on his desk, its insides laid bare.

"Not GPS, I hope?" I'd have to adopt a self-flagellation policy if I led them straight to us.

"No, nothing like that, though we might be able to trace the signal back to its source."

Hawkins stops his pacing. "You said it wasn't working."

"Because it's not *on*," Watson says, losing his patience. "The insides are still soaking wet." To my surprise, he stands up, facing Hawkins down. "Do you want me to turn the power on now? Fry everything inside? You might be a magician in the woods, but we're not fly fishing or tracking down a deer, here. Just—just, leave. Go find a tree to climb."

Watson sits down, picks up a hair dryer and resumes the task of drying the goggles' insides. I meet Hawkins's eyes, offer him a consolatory smile and the motion for him to leave with my head. He's not exactly pleased, but he follows my lead.

To his credit, Hawkins stops next to Watson and taps him on the shoulder.

The hair dryer cuts off. "What?"

"Sorry," Hawkins says. "I just get nervous...about Lilly."

Watson moves his head in a weird way that I can't discern as a nod or a head shake. It might be both, some inner battle between competing emotions. Then he waves his hand behind his head. "I get it. Just give me some space."

"You got it," Hawkins says and leaves, heading downstairs to where everyone else is currently congregated, having dinner. The

FC-P headquarters is in what once was a large brick mansion set atop the highest point of Powder Hill in Beverly, Massachusetts. The insides feel old and regal, with thick wood floors that creak when you walk on them, wide staircases with polished banisters and large brick fireplaces on each floor. It feels like a museum, but with bedrooms, computers and kick-ass WiFi. The kitchen, where Collins, Cooper and Joliet are waiting for us, is large enough for a gourmet chef to have a field day. I mostly use the microwave. The building is old, but it has stood the test of time, an assault courtesy of the deceased General Gordon and the ghost of old Mrs. Rosen, who most of us believe still roams the house, spying on the weirdness that is our day to day.

When Hawkins is gone, I push myself toward Watson. The chair rolls over the wooden floor and doesn't stop until it bumps into Watson's desk. I lean my head back. "So..."

That's all it takes. He's already smiling.

"Piss or shit?" I ask.

"What?"

"Which one was it?" I say. "You're only this grumpy on days when you've been pissed on or shat at. So which was it."

He glances at me without moving his head. "Both."

"Gross."

He lifts his right hand up. Wiggles his fingers. "There was a hole in the wipe. Fingers right through it. Have you ever had bright yellow crap under your fingernails?"

I've endured a lot of horrible things in the last few years, but nothing as horrible sounding as that. I wince and lean away from his hand. "Nasty."

"Our talks are always so helpful," he jokes.

"It's what I'm here for." I spin around and face the desk, looking at the open goggles. The insides are a mess of wires and small microchips. They're kind of like Google Glass on steroids. Beyond that, I'm clueless, and so is Watson, so I stick to the personal stuff. "Getting much sleep?"

"A little."

"How about Coop?"

"Less."

"Listen..." My hesitation draws his eyes. "I want you guys to take a break soon. I know you believe in what we do here. We all do now. But you guys are wearing yourselves out."

He opens his mouth to argue, but I cut him off. "I know, I know. We need you guys, and it's true, but we need you at a hundred percent, not half-asleep and covered in poo. Just...when you're done with the goggles, take a few weeks. If I need you, I can reach you at home. You don't need to be here."

"Cooper's not going to like it," he says.

"She'll get over it."

"Just...try not to ruin the place while we're gone. And don't let Paul Bunyan use my computer. Or Lilly. Or you." He smiles. "Maigo can use it, though. Kid's got a mind for this stuff, you know. She's a pretty good hacker already. Showed her a few tricks, but she's moved pretty far on her own."

"I didn't know," I say.

"She must be holding out on you," he says, smiling.

"You have no idea." I stand and pat his shoulder. "I'll leave you to it, then. Just let me know the moment you figure something out. Then you and the missus are out of here, okay?"

He just nods as I show myself out.

An hour later, after a long meal, while being regaled by Woodstock's stories, some of which are either exaggerated or totally fabricated—much to Lilly's delight—I find myself on the second floor balcony, beneath the Crow's Nest, with Collins and Maigo. Hands on the brick wall, I look out toward the darkening ocean. It's eight o'clock, but the summer sun is still setting behind us, casting the long shadows and orange light out toward the water. The still-charred land provides a dark, but stunning contrast to the color.

"It's beautiful," Collins says, standing next to me, two of her fingers atop mine, our affection now reaching a more comfortable level. After returning from Oregon, bruised, singed and alive, she crushed me with a hug that might have caused more pain than nearly being fire-bombed did, but we're pretty casual with our affection now, trying to stay professional. While the FC-P is now made up of three couples, two teenage girls and a foul-mouthed pilot, we still try to keep the mushy stuff for after hours.

When I don't reply, Collins taps my head. "Where are you?"

Before I can answer, Maigo does. "He's thinking about how to propose."

My eyes widen so far it feels like they might peel off the whole top of my head. I turn around slowly, away from Collins, and glare at Maigo, whose hood of long black hair covers her face and conceals the smartphone she's staring at. But I'm not just upset at her for revealing this private detail, I'm also wondering how the hell she knows what I was thinking.

Maigo reaches around and pulls the shade of hair away from her face to reveal apologetic eyes. "Sorry. I shouldn't have—"

"How did you know?" I ask.

"Wait, what?" Collins says, and I suddenly realize I've just confirmed what Maigo said. "She was right?"

"Nevermind that," I say, keeping my eyes well clear of Collins's gaze. I sit down at the outdoor table, across from Maigo. "You're *still* holding out on me."

She looks up at me, but says nothing.

Collins sits down beside me. I can feel her staring at the side of my head, but I don't look. To acknowledge her means to answer her question, and I'm not ready for that. It's why I was *thinking* about it.

"Spill it," I say to Maigo.

"Jon..." Collins says.

"Hey!" a voice shouts, making all of us flinch. It's Watson, from the window above. "I did it! They're working. I know where they are!"

I stare at Maigo for another moment, and then stand. "Saved by the chubby man with the future goggles."

"That makes two of you," Collins says, standing.

I acknowledge her for the first time, unable to stop my smile. "Yes. Yes it does."

10

Watson is generally uncomfortable being the center of attention. He'd normally balk at having this many people standing around him, watching him, but he barely notices that the gang is all here. Me, Collins, Cooper, Woodstock, Hawkins, Joliet, Lilly and Maigo. We're more like a weird dysfunctional family than a government agency, but my superiors don't need to know that. With Joliet, Lilly and Maigo being off the books, and my relationship with Collins not public knowledge, only Cooper and Watson are under the DHS's ever-bureaucratic microscope that says office relationships are a faux pas. Not that any of us have to worry. Since saving Washington D.C., and securing the current President's unshakable trust, we're becoming fairly autonomous.

"Once the circuitry dried out, it was pretty user friendly. You said a soldier was wearing it, so that's probably why."

"You sayin' soldiers ain't smart?" Woodstock, a long since retired Marine, says, stroking his white mustache. I told him mustaches were creepy without an accompanying beard, but he waved me off and said all the hipsters were doing it and that he was finally back in style.

"I'm saying they made the glasses easy to operate while in the field," Watson says, with that 'I had crap under my nails last night' snip creeping back into his voice. "Which is probably important for when you're getting shot at."

"S'pose," Woodstock says, which was as close to an apology as he'll ever get.

"What do they do?" I ask.

Watson hands the goggles to me. They're still open, with wires trailing down to his computer. "Put them on."

I slide the goggles over my eyes. I see nothing unusual, just the people around me. "Am I supposed to be seeing something?"

"Button on the right," Watson says.

I feel the right side of the goggles and find the small, flush button. I press it once. Words spring into my vision, quickly identifying Cooper and Collins, listing their full names and affiliations with the DHS. I turn to Woodstock and the words 'Chief Warrant Officer 5, Richard Woodall, U.S. Marine Corps, Retired,' slip into view beside his face, followed by his FC-P employment status. When I look at Hawkins, the name displayed is Dustin Dreyling. Wherever this information is coming from, it's a government source, picking information from official records before delving into the DMV. But then new information appears, correctly identifying Dustin Dreyling as an alias for Mark Hawkins.

That's not good...

Around the room, various objects are identified. Weapons. Maps. Computers. Even the view through the window is correctly identified as Beverly-Salem Harbor. But when I turn toward Lilly and Maigo, the names disappear, replaced by blinking dots. The words 'identity unknown' appear over Maigo, which is to be expected, but a more disturbing message is displayed over Lilly, 'Dark Matter identified.'

Dark Matter?

Before I can ask what it might mean, Watson presses the button again, erasing the words. "Watch what happens now," he says, and he claps his hands twice. The lights go out.

"Seriously?" I say. "Who installed a clapper?"

"I put it in when I was pregnant," Cooper says. "When walking wasn't fun."

A hundred different jokes flit through my mind, but they're all silenced by what happens next. For a moment, the room is displayed in standard shades of green night vision. But then I can see. Perfectly. Well, almost. Colors flicker to life as I look around, slowly at first, and then as fast as I can move, including clothing and faces. "Are the lights on?"

"You can see fine, right?" Watson says.

"Perfectly."

"The goggles send information to a server and then receive color information. It all happens in real time. Whatever computer is on the other end must be amazing, like quantum amazing, storing data on everything—people, places, everyday objects, exotic objects, and then using that information to colorize the wearer's night vision."

"Or identify targets."

"Right," Watson says, "And I was able to trace the signal back to its source. Back to the super-computer's location. They're in Lompoc, California, north of Los Angeles."

"Uh," Cooper says in her tone that says she's about to point out something obvious that the rest of us missed, but shouldn't have. I turn to her colorized face, her hair tied back tight, her eyes looking at me over the thick, black-rimmed glasses. "If the goggles are communicating with a computer operated by the people who designed these things, and who nearly killed Hawkins and Hudson in Oregon, isn't it likely that we're not only receiving data, but sending it?"

Watson's response is quick. He yanks the wires attached to the goggles, tearing them out. Then he stands, pulls the goggles from my face and slams them down on the hardwood floor.

"I'm sorry," he says. "Damn. I'm sorry."

"GPS could still be active," Maigo points out, and I wonder how she knows about such things, despite Watson's revelation that he's been teaching her.

Watson shoves his way past the group and tosses the goggles into the fireplace and douses them with the lighter fluid Woodstock likes to use when setting a fire. The ambiance is nice, especially during the winter, but I think Woodstock just likes setting fires, which is once again proved when he quickly strikes a match and tosses it into the fireplace. The goggles catch, slowly melting into acrid smelling slag. Happily, the flue is open and most of the foul chemical smoke rises up and out the brick chimney.

"Who did you look at?" Collins asks me, but the real question, barely disguised, is who did they see.

"Everyone," I say. "Except for me, which is good."

"How is that good?" Hawkins asks.

"Because I'm supposed to be dead," I say. "Probably better if they continue believing that."

"But you looked at me," he says.

"You were covered in mud in Oregon. They won't make the match."

"But they know we have the goggles," Cooper says. I have a love/hate relationship with how often she's right.

"You could have recovered them while looking for us," I say. "And that Specter guy spared us and gave us the goggles for a reason."

"Maybe to track us down," Hawkins says.

"The FC-P's location isn't exactly a secret from other government agencies," I say. "They wouldn't need—"

"Not you," Hawkins says, glancing toward Lilly.

Shit.

Collins places her hand on my arm. "Did it identify either of the girls?"

"Not Maigo," I say.

"They know who I am?" Lilly asks, sounding surprised and nervous.

I shake my head. "You were identified as 'Dark Matter.'" I turn to Hawkins. "Any idea what that means?"

"It means," says a new voice, feminine and vaguely familiar. I spin around, reaching for my sidearm, and I see a face I haven't seen in a year, not since Washington D.C.—Maggie Alessi. "That none of you are safe here."

Alessi was Katsu Endo's right-hand lady at Zoomb, the technology giant behind the rebirth of Nemesis, whose interference has had long and destructive consequences without much in the way of repercussions, mostly because of its massive ties to Washington and lucrative government contracts. While Hawkins's thorn has been DARPA, ours has always been Zoomb. It shouldn't surprise me that they are, once again, involved in shady dealings, but it does. Endo and Alessi were instrumental in stopping Gordon and a handful of Kaiju from turning the world into a human-life-free zone. While I still hold a grudge against Endo, it's mostly for kicking my ass on a few occasions. He's still a fugitive, and it's still my job to bring him in, but I had no plans on tracking the man down. He's earned that much.

I have a lot of questions for Alessi, specifically about Zoomb's potential involvement with Nemesis's disappearance, but the problem she's just posed dwarfs them all.

"Who will come?" I ask, drawing my weapon, but not aiming it at her. She's unarmed and dressed like a civilian. She's not here to hurt us. If she's telling the truth, her goal is quite the opposite.

"The BlackGuard," she says.

"Who?" Hawkins asks.

"The men responsible for destroying the Tsuchi in Oregon."

I don't miss the fact that she used the same name for the BFSs as the BlackGuard she's talking about.

"The DARPA special ops team," Hawkins says. He's fishing, but he doesn't let on.

Alessi's momentary surprise is confirmation enough, but she says, "How much do you know about them?"

"Enough to know they're bad news," I say, "which brings us back to the problem at hand. When are they coming?"

"I don't know," she says, "but if they've seen Lilly, they'll come for her. Soon."

Alessi and Endo both know about Lilly. They've seen her in action. They don't know her origins, and they didn't ask, but they've obviously kept quiet about her. But now, it seems, we've put the crosshairs that Hawkins has always feared right on Lilly.

"You need to leave here," Alessi says. "All of you."

"I suppose you have someplace for us to go?" I ask. "I'm sure Zoomb would like to get a peek at Lilly."

"And at her," Alessi says, pointing at Maigo, "but they don't know about them. About *either* of them. And we're going to keep it that way."

"Why?" I ask, unable to restrain my skepticism. "Does Endo want to keep them for himself? Or is he simply waiting for the highest offer?"

"That's not fair," Alessi says. "He saved your life."

"He also serves himself."

Alessi is silent for a moment and finally says, "Endo's allegiance remains where it has always been."

After leaving the Japanese Defense Force, Endo served under General Gordon, and then in the private sector, working with Zoomb, but in each of those instances, he was involved in all things—

Maigo screams and falls to the floor, clutching her head.

The conversation with Alessi slips from my mind, all fears of exposure and impending BlackGuard doom forgotten. I hurry to her and fall to my knees. "Maigo what's—"

My voice is cut short when I reach out and take her hands. The physical contact acts like a conduit, slamming me into Maigo's mind for a moment. We stand across from each other, both ten years old again, on Christmas morning, dressed in footie pajamas and staring at each other. I reach out for her, opening my mouth, but then the world becomes a blur.

Heat surrounds me, pulsing in the darkness.

Maigo is here, too. I can feel her.

Where are we? I think.

Back. The mental voice belongs to Maigo.

Back where?

Stabbing pain fills my body, pulsing through me three times, growing in intensity like a migraine headache.

She's alive, Maigo thinks to me.

Who... And then I know. *Oh my God...*

My eyes snap open, and I sit up from the floor, where I must have collapsed. Maigo sits up next to me, pulled from the strange mental connection.

I grip her shoulder. "Was that?"

Maigo nods, looking relieved and afraid.

Collins crouches next to me. "What happened? Jon, what's—"

"It's Nemesis," I say, turning to Collins, feeling terrified, but unable to prevent a smile from forming. "She's alive."

11

"Alive?" Woodstock looks aghast. "Bullsheeit. We saw the ol' girl die."

"We never really confirmed it," I say, head spinning. While I have to admit that part of me is relieved, I'm also filled with dread. If Nemesis is alive, more people are going to die, and it's our job—my job—to stop her. The problem is that I don't know if I can, and not because of our previous bond, though that weighs heavily; it's because I'm pretty sure we're not capable. A nuke might do it, but we'd be killing a lot of people along with her, and there's no guarantee that even that would work. There's still so much we don't know about her. She's not of this Earth, after all. "We didn't even know how."

Collins crouches beside me. "Jon...I know you had a connection with Nemesis." She glances at Maigo. "You both did. But she was dead. Whatever you're feeling now is—"

"It's her," I say, a trace of annoyance in my voice. I'm not used to being doubted. Granted, up until this very moment, I would have balked at the idea of Nemesis's revival. But I know what I felt. "She was in pain."

"Fightin' with the Devil, most likely," Woodstock says.

Maigo shoots him a look so serious that he raises his hands and backs away. "Let's try not to forget we're talking about a monster who killed thousands of people and very nearly ate me an' Betty, on more than one occasion."

"We thought you'd taste bad," Maigo whispers, and given the lack of reaction, I think I'm the only one who heard. Nope. Not quite. Collins's eyes have opened a touch, but she's staring straight ahead, restraining her response. The three of us will talk about it later. Maybe.

"Is it possible you're feeling something else?" Cooper asks, ever the pragmatist. "Something new? Something created from Nemesis's remains, the way that Nemesis was created from the corpse of Nemesis Prime?"

It's a good thought, but the connection was too familiar. I shake my head slowly.

Watson pulls at his hair a bit. Nemesis's rebirth is triggering some anxiety I haven't seen in the man since he became a father. He calms when Cooper puts her hand on his shoulder, but he still voices his concerns. "There are contingencies to activate. Protocols. But we don't know where she is. Don't know where she's going. What should we do?"

"I think," I say, standing to my feet and pulling Maigo up, "we should ask the only person who doesn't seem surprised by the news." I turn to Alessi. "How long have you known?"

"Eight months."

"*Eight* months?" I so want to punch her, but she'd probably kick my ass, and that would get me nowhere but a hospital room...and chocolate pudding. Tempting.

"Penis envy doesn't suit you, Jon," she says.

I cough and sputter. Not only has she just said this in front of two teenage girls, it's the kind of accusation that, when defended adamantly, makes the accused look guilty.

She doesn't give me time to figure out a defense. "Just because we can do what you're not able, doesn't mean we're working against you."

"Who *are* you working for?" Collins asks, and I'm relieved the conversation is moving away from my manhood.

"I'm still employed by Zoomb, though I'm currently on leave. But Endo...that's complicated," she says.

"Like the ending of *Lost* complicated, or peace in the Middle East complicated?" I ask the question, but then realize the answer. "Whoever is paying the bills, he's not really working for them, is he? You mentioned Endo's allegiance earlier. It was never to Gordon or Zoomb. It was always to Nemesis."

She doesn't deny it, but refuses to reply.

"And you're okay with that?" I ask. "I know he's your half-brother, but is your allegiance to *him* so blind that you—"

"He doesn't know I'm here," she says. "I came to warn you off because...you're good people."

This confession takes me a little off guard and puts her ribbing in a new light. Maybe she's not trying to get under my skin? Maybe she's just palling around? "Would Endo have stopped you from warning us?" I still don't really know where he stands, and I have serious qualms about his moral compass.

Her frown tells the answer before she speaks. "I didn't want to give him the chance to make that call. It would have...strained our relationship. And I haven't heard from him in a week, which means he's pre-occupied."

"And you won't tell us where he is?" I ask.

She shakes her head. "He'll get in touch when its important."

"Well, thanks for the warning," I say, "but if Nemesis is alive, we can't—"

"They'll come for you." She looks at the girls. "For them."

"We'll take precautions," I say. "But this is what we're here for. This is what we do."

"They do it better," Alessi says.

"DARPA?" Hawkins asks. He's a bit red in the face, showing admirable restraint. Alessi has information he's wanted since escaping Island 731.

"GOD," she says, to eight confused listeners. "Genetic Offense Directive. They're a black operation under the umbrella of DARPA, but without really any oversight. The island she's from—" She nods at Lilly. "—was one of their projects."

"They're the ones in Lompoc," Hawkins says.

Alessi sags in defeat. "You're not going to listen to me, are you?"

I look at the resolute faces around me. The FC-P won't back down from a Kaiju. They're not about to back down from a shady government agency. But, these people are also my responsibility. Two of them aren't even adults. Sure, they might argue that point, and they might also point out that physically, they're more than ready, but they're still my responsibility.

"We're going to Lompoc," I say, "but not all of us."

"Cooper. Watson. Take mini-Cooper and go on a vacation. Pay in cash. Go dark. They might not be interested in you, but why take chances." Watson is about to complain, but I silence him by clamping my fingers and thumb together. "There isn't anything you can't do on the road from a laptop. Just a few days, until this clears up."

They both nod. Now comes the hard part. "Hawkins. Joliet. I need you both to take the girls and—"

"Not a chance," Hawkins says. "I'm coming with you."

"Not your call," I say, matching the serious tone of his voice. "I know what this means for you, but if these GOD assholes are coming for Lilly and Maigo, I'll feel better knowing you're with them."

"But," Lilly says, and I clamp my hand at her.

"I'm not about to deliver you to them," I say. "These guys are better than us." I look at Hawkins, waiting for a challenge. He doesn't offer any. He saw them in action. Knows we're lucky to be alive. "They have access to weapons and technology that no one else does." Back to Lilly. "This is not 'capture the flag,' and the BlackGuard are not us. No offense to any of you, but these guys are out of our league."

"And if you get in trouble?" Maigo asks. "If you get killed? What then?"

"Won't happen," I say, but I know she'll see straight through the bravado. "Just...stay safe. If we need your help, we'll call."

"Better keep us on speed dial," Lilly quips with a half smile that reveals a sharp canine tooth. Her tail whips back and forth, revealing the agitation she's keeping out of her expression.

"Collins, Woodstock." The rest goes unsaid and they both nod. Not only is Collins my most trusted partner, but these two have been by my side since first contact with Nemesis. Collins is willing to walk into the belly of the beast, so to speak, and Woodstock is always there to pull us out. I turn to Alessi. "We'll need a plane to get us there, and a chopper when we land. Can you swing that?"

Her grin says she can. I'm not sure what her position at Zoomb really is, but she's got pull, and for now, with GOD and maybe even a goddess to deal with, I'll take what help I can get.

B.F.S.

12

"Dammit," Alicio Brice muttered. While Building-K was sealed and the exits all covered by highly armed men, the BlackGuard would not be arriving to take care of this problem. They had been diverted by the one person at GOD whose authority superseded Brice's, Zach Cole, the program's director. He wasn't a scientist. Lacked the mind for that kind of work. But he was ruthlessly efficient and a cunning man, not to be trifled with. And he was the man Brice would have to answer to if this problem wasn't taken care of in a quiet manner.

While the GOD research facility was located on the Pacific Coast, outside Lompoc—the flower seed capital of the world—their main offices were located beyond the countless fields of flowers, in town, rising high above the city's valley-sandwiched grid of two-story homes and businesses. If things got loud, Cole would know about it.

So the guards at the exits were armed with silent, non-lethal weapons—stun guns and sticky foam guns—as well as more conventional sound-suppressed weapons. They would try to take it alive, but at the first sign of trouble, they had been authorized to use lethal force on the Tsuchi, or on anyone implanted by it. Harsh measures, but the men understood. They'd seen Wood's body, and they knew the creature had emerged from his skull. Mortal risk came with guarding the incubators. They lost men every year. Brice saw it as evolution in action. The men who had been with GOD the longest were the best. The fittest. And it was them he was sending into Building-K.

He stood outside the massive warehouse, smelling the ocean breeze. He rarely went outside; the salty, cool air felt unfamiliar and invigorating. Despite the potentially hazardous security breach, a smile spread across his face. *It's going to be a good night,* he thought, looking up at the darkening sky. He decided to go out. Have some Mexican by the ocean. Maybe invite that woman from Level 3. What was her name? Dee Hardy? Dee Haddrill, that was it. He'd ask her.

"Sir?" a man said, standing a foot taller than Brice, looking down at him through the reflective night-vision goggles that would colorize and illuminate the dim confines of the giant warehouse.

Brice blinked out of his dinner plans and looked up at the man. He didn't know the man's name. Could barely see his face. But he was the senior guard on duty. *What do we call his rank?* "Yes? Uh, Captain?"

"Chief."

"Right. Sorry."

"I asked about containment protocols," the large man said.

"Oh, right. Just immobilize the Tsuchi—"

"The Dark Matter."

"Yes. These have been designated 'Tsuchi.'"

"Sushi. Good to know."

"Tsuchi," Brice repeated, pronouncing it correctly with the Japanese TS sound emphasized.

The Chief offered a phony smile. "Heard you the first time."

Brice took a deep breath and let it out slowly. The Chief of GOD's guard was rubbing him the wrong way. "Immobilize it with the spray foam. I will come to collect it. If that isn't possible, destroy the target, and I will come to collect it. Should any of your men be...stung...by the creature, they must be eliminated immediately. Any delay could be—"

"I get it."

"I hope you do," Brice grumbled.

The Chief's faux grin faded. Without another word, the man turned around and headed for the five men waiting by the door, which would be opened just long enough for the six-man team to enter and split in two.

Brice checked his watch. 5:12 pm. If they wrapped this up in the next thirty minutes, his dinner plans might still work out. The Chief, now standing at the ready, beside the entry door, glanced back at Brice. He waved them in like he was shooing them away.

It took all of Chief Reynolds's restraint to not punch Brice in the nose. The man was insolent, cocky and disrespectful to anyone not as smart, which, admittedly, was most people. He also had direct authority over Reynolds and his men. He would still mention the man's lack of respect to Director Cole, who was reasonable, fair *and* respectful to the security force. But that would come later. For now, Reynolds was on the job, and life-or-death circumstances waited for him and his men, on the other side of the metal door.

"Comm check," he said.

One by one, the five men with him spoke their last names: Talbot, Ellis, Gilmour, McAfee and Cross. When they were done, he said, "Non-lethals are preferable, but I honestly don't give a rip. If you feel you're in danger, use lethal force at your discretion. Teams of three. Ellis, Gilmour, you're with me. We'll take the east end. Talbot, McAfee, Cross, head west. Sweep the perimeter, and converge on the far side. We'll tackle the 'Valley' after that."

All five men spoke their agreement.

Reynolds tapped the armor covering his chest, stomach and back. "We're well protected, but should any of us be...stung, for lack of a better word, the resulting effect will be lethal inside a minute, and... Well, do yourself a favor and put a bullet in your head. If you can't, I will."

The crackle of a stun gun snapped to life in Reynolds's hand. "Weapons hot." The little data he had on the Tsuchi made it clear that a stun gun would have limited effectiveness, mostly because the thing had a shelled back. To really hit it, he'd have to tag it in the face or the belly. If it was as fast as Brice said, he doubted he'd get a chance to use it. That's why they were leaning heavily on the foam guns, which could slather a target, expand and solidify in seconds, immobilizing anything it touched.

"On three," Reynolds said, raising three fingers and counting down. When he lowered his last finger, Ellis flung the door open and went in, followed by Gilmour. The pair swept the space on the other side and then headed east. Reynolds closed and locked the door behind him, and then he fell in line behind Ellis and Gilmour, while the others headed west.

Building-K was a massive space. Its arched ceiling was covered with lights that really did little to illuminate the wide open space, partly because of the distance and partly because of the giant hangar's contents. He'd heard the building described as a morgue, and it was, in every sense—chilled air, dead bodies, haunting atmosphere—but it was the deceased that made this morgue stand apart from all others. Here, the dead were Kaiju.

The first, of which he was currently walking along the perimeter, was called Nemesis Prime. The ancient monster had been recovered from the frozen wilds of Alaska. The tech company Zoomb, with whom DARPA had contracts, had dismantled the beast and shipped it to a warehouse. They had since lost custody of the creature's corpse, though he doubted they knew where it went. In the wake of the disaster in Washington D.C., Director Cole determined that they couldn't be trusted with the corpse, or its DNA. Moving quickly in the days after the battle that nearly destroyed the country's heart, GOD had used every element at its disposal, including its private security force, to transport Prime, and her spawn, the now deceased Nemesis, to the Lompoc facility. The remaining five Kaiju, also deceased, were taken off-shore to an undisclosed island far above Reynolds's pay grade. But everyone knew that the Kaiju that really mattered, the monster that killed five rivals, was here, lying beside her ancestor at the west end of Building-K.

Moving quickly and silently, the three men reached the far end of the warehouse and rounded the dried-out husk of Prime's head. The ancient, gray skin stretched back to empty eye sockets the size of swimming pools. Despite its mummified, dehydrated state, the disassembled Kaiju had been laid out on its stomach, the way it would have been in life. Had the thing been living, it would have stood eye-to-eye with Nemesis, but with even more bulk. The ancient plates of armor and long spikes rose up toward the ceiling like an alien city.

As they circled around the far corner, a whispered voice tickled his ear. "West end clear." It was Cross. "Coming your way. Over."

"Copy that," Reynolds said. "East end is clear, too. En route. Over and out."

Despite the dark confines of Building-K, the goggles let him see everything clearly, including his men, five hundred feet away. What he couldn't see was any sign of the Dark Matter, Brice's precious 'Tsuchi.' And he didn't really expect to. They were clearing the perimeter as a matter of course, but with all of the Kaiju nooks and crannies, a creature the size of a small dog would have no trouble hiding.

If it wanted to.

But Brice was confident the Tsuchi wouldn't hide. Once they were out in the open, it would attack. And its brazenness would be its downfall.

The two groups merged halfway down the backside of the warehouse.

"All clear," Cross reported, though he didn't really need to. Had they seen something, Reynolds would know about it.

The Chief looked across Building-K's interior. The space was divided by the two massive corpses, one on each side. Between the bodies was a large staging area and a laboratory. Flood lights, currently unlit, surrounded tables of equipment and sample trays. Most of the recent work was being done on Nemesis. While Prime was still a curiosity, Nemesis's fresher body gave up her secrets more readily...at first. Now they had to drill through several feet of hardened, rubber-like skin that had slowly grown back, like a fungus, over the past year. While the body beneath lay still, the outer layer of skin, which some believed was a separate, non-sentient organism, grew a little each day.

Reynolds looked back and forth between Nemesis and Prime. They were equally huge, but only one of them still frightened him. It was why he hadn't covered the west end. He'd never admit it, but being close to the goddess of vengeance unnerved him, primarily because he knew for a fact that he wasn't a good man. None of them were. They were mercenaries with questionable pasts, given asylum and big paychecks, courtesy of GOD, its influence and its black budget. "Form a perimeter around the staging area. Facing in."

"Facing in?" McAfee asked. "You want us to turn our backs on a Dark Matter target?"

"I want you to watch each others' backs. And mine. We need to lure this thing out, and that means making it think we're easy targets."

"Copy that," McAfee said with great reluctance.

Moving single file, the team flowed toward the staging area, but never made it. Gilmour stopped short. "What the hell..."

"Where?" Reynolds asked, switching to his KRISS rifle.

Gilmour pointed toward Nemesis's body.

Reynolds saw it and lowered his weapon, eyes widening. "Dammit."

He knew what the three exercise ball-sized holes in Nemesis's side meant—it meant they were fucked.

13

Reynolds was about to give the order to switch to lethal weapons when Talbot shouted "Contact!" and unleashed a torrent of foam that struck the floor, mushroomed out and solidified. But the man had missed the mark, and instead of locking the Tsuchi in place, he provided it with a springboard to launch its attack.

The creature sprang from Nemesis's tail, where it had been hiding, perfectly camouflaged on the rough, black flesh. Talbot unleashed another stream of foam, this time striking the Tsuchi's underside, but as the viscous goo expanded, the Tsuchi landed atop Talbot's face, wrapping its eight legs around his head and squeezing.

Talbot's muffled screams were punctuated by a loud crack from his jaw. The foam slid into his mouth. Down his throat. And it was expanding. His body twitched and fell back with the Tsuchi frozen in place, unable to escape the foam, but striking him over and over with its stinger-tipped tail. Fortunately, the armor did its job, preventing the stinger from reaching his flesh.

Reynolds dropped his stun gun and drew his KRISS rifle, putting a single round in Talbot's head, and putting the man out of his misery. Then Reynolds sent a stream of bullets into the Tsuchi's tail, severing it. The long, whip-like tail fell to the ground, writhing and spinning on for several seconds, before it fell still, like the Tsuchi itself. The creature was locked in place, unable to move its limbs, trapped in the foam. It was still alive—for the moment—which would please Brice, but it was the least of their problems.

"Stay sharp," Reynolds said. "There are three—"

"Argh!"

The high-pitched shout spun Reynolds around. It was Gilmour, suspended in the air upon what looked like a spear tip emerging from his chest. It had punched a hole through both layers of armor, but that wasn't the most shocking thing about the scene. The tip of the spear looked like a giant-sized hypodermic needle. The hole at the end was clogged with Gilmour's guts, but they shot out with a slurp and were followed by a spurt of white fluid. The gore landed at Reynolds's feet, red flesh mixed with white fluid, all surrounding a writhing, white larva. Then the spear-needle withdrew and stabbed Gilmour twice more while he was held aloft by two, long, spidery arms, tipped with scimitar-sized talons. Each thrust shot a new larva into the air, none remaining inside the body, which Reynolds knew was a good thing. Gilmour's body was then cast aside, revealing the horror behind him.

At the most basic level, the creature resembled a Tsuchi—eight limbs, a spider's face and mandibles, and a long, twitching tail. But the comparisons ended there, because this thing was much, much worse. The first, most obvious discrepancy was the size. The armored shell on its back, stretching from head to tail in a series of overlapping armored plates, was the size of a Volkswagen Bug. The creature's eight eyes glowed bright orange, as did several basketball-sized spots on its underside. Given the evidence of the Tsuchi's birth,

Reynolds understood what the glowing membranes meant. The eight legs, still thin and spindly, were now covered in thick armor, like Nemesis, but with a bluish, almost iridescent hue. In fact, all of the armor had an almost oily quality, as though energy were flowing through it. It was the tail that held Reynolds's attention the most, now arched up behind the monster's back, poised to strike.

But the monster didn't move. It regarded the four remaining men, one after the other.

"Ellis, Cross," Reynolds said, "hose this thing down when I give the word. McAfee, switch to lethal. Aim for the head. Do *not* hit the orange membranes, or we're all toast." He didn't wait to hear confirmation from the men. They hadn't run away, which meant they were listening. "Fire!"

Twin streams of foam shot out, striking a few of the Tsuchi's scythe-like limbs, but not all of them. Spinning sideways, the monster shot one forelimb at Ellis and snapped its tail at Cross. The latter's shout of surprise was cut short by a loud crack—the giant needle punching through his armor, body, a second layer of armor and finally, the foam's containment unit. When the tail withdrew, foam sprayed out from the back of the tank, and from the hole in Cross's chest. As it hardened and expanded, Cross was lifted off the ground like he'd been nailed to some kind of ancient sacrificial altar.

Ellis fared no better. The sharp talon at the end of the limb hadn't pierced him, but it slid up and under the man's armor, yanking him off his feet and into the creature's talons, even as the tail stabbed through Cross. When both talons dug into Ellis's shoulders, his body convulsed. Blue sparks leapt out and streaks of electricity sparked between the two points. When he hung limp, the Tsuchi began to chew, dragging Ellis's body further inside its widening maw with each bite.

It wasn't until Cross was frozen in hard foam, and Ellis was fully consumed, that McAfee and Reynolds recovered from their shock and opened fire.

The Tsuchi bucked and twisted under the barrage of high caliber rounds, clearly confused about what was happening. But Reynolds could tell they weren't doing any real damage.

"I'm in my office on the fifth floor, and I hear gunfire," a voice said in Reynolds's ear. It was Brice. "Have you killed it?"

While Cross continued to fire, Reynolds reloaded his rifle without looking. "The target Tsuchi is dead."

"Then why do I hear gunfire?" The scientist sounded irritated, unaware that his research facility was about to go to hell.

"Because the thing reproduced!" Reynolds shouted, backing away and firing as Cross reloaded. The Tsuchi was still twitching from each round, some of them actually punching through its thick, black skin, but most of it ricocheting off its armor plating.

"I told you to shoot your men if—"

"Most of my men are dead," Reynolds said, his magazine empty again. "The Tsuchi reproduced with Nemesis's corpse!"

The line fell silent.

"This thing is the size of a truck!" Reynolds opened fire again, stopping when his back struck the far wall. He wasn't far from the exit.

"But there is just one?" Brice asked. "The Tsuchi reproduce in sets of three."

Reynolds glanced toward the holes in Nemesis's dead skin. Three of them. "I've seen only one, but there is evidence of three."

"My god..." Brice said. "I'm coming down."

"I feel better alread—"

A long, armored tail snaked down from above. Reynolds looked up and saw a second Tsuchi clinging to the wall. He shouted a warning, but it was too late. The spear tip stabbed into McAfee's back, three times in rapid succession, each time spurting a white blob and writhing larva onto the floor. But the Tsuchi must have seen this and understood the man wasn't a host for its young, because it lifted McAfee up and shoved him head fist into its open maw, every mandible chomp crackling with electricity. A torrent of blood fell between Reynolds and the exit.

As he considered running through it, a roar, like a high-pitched squeal mixed with a gurgle, echoed through the massive hangar. Reynolds gasped as a third over-sized Tsuchi flew through the air, spinning out of control. It landed inside the jumbled remains of Nemesis Prime.

What the fu—

A shift of movement, so large he nearly missed it, slid across the western side of the building.

It was an arm.

The size of three buses, end to end.

Dropping his useless weapon, Reynolds ran through the curtain of McAfee's blood. There was nothing he could do to stop what was coming. Nothing any of them could do.

Nemesis was alive.

Even worse, she was awake.

14

I snap awake at the sound of a text message chime. In a daze, I dig my phone out of my pocket, then fail to punch in the unlock code three times, before finally getting it right, looking at the screen and realizing the text wasn't mine. With a yawn, I look around the interior of the big rental SUV. I'm alone in the back, sprawled out over the seat. Collins and Alessi are in the front. We left Woodstock at the Santa Maria Airport, where a shiny, dark blue, Bell 525 Relentless, one of the world's most expensive corporate helicopters—sporting a Zoomb logo—awaited him. It didn't have a mounted gun, like helicopter Betty, but it would get us around in style...if necessary. The helicopter would be used for a quick getaway, but we were hoping to get in and out without being noticed, using fake GOD IDs, also courtesy of Zoomb.

I'm not sure Alessi's allocation of Zoomb resources could possibly go unnoticed, especially while she is 'on leave,' so I'm sure there are unsaid strings attached, or an alternate agenda, but right now I don't care. The FC-P—my family—is under threat because of these guys, and I'm going to do what I can to turn that around. For the moment, I'll play the role of Faust.

I blink my eyes open wider and sit up. We pass a sign for Vandenberg Air Force Base. I could have very easily requisitioned a flight directly to Lompoc, landing minutes away from our destination, but there is no doubt our arrival would have been noticed. Alessi's thumbs tap out a message on her phone. Collins sits behind the wheel.

"Welcome back," Collins says.

I slept on the flight across the country, my third in far too few hours, and I never really woke up as we transferred to the vehicle. "What are the odds that these phony keycards will get us into GOD's cafe? They must have great coffee, right?"

"Look to your right," Collins says.

I turn my head and find a cup of coffee, steam slipping through the hole in its plastic cap, sitting in a cup holder. "We stopped?"

"You slept through it." Collins glances back at me. "Pushing yourself too hard."

"Don't really have a choice," I say, raising the coffee cup as though making a toast and taking a sip. The warm liquid seems to spread out through my body, waking my mind, and reminding me how much I already ache. Ignoring the pain, I lean forward and peek over the seat.

"That Endo?" I ask Alessi.

She hits 'send' on her message and angles the screen so I can't see it.

"No? Maybe your BFF?" I get no response. "But that can't be right. I don't have a text."

The slightest hint of a smile shows I'm getting through. "Seriously, what's going on?"

Her phone chimes again, and like a trained monkey, I put my hand on my pants pocket, about to remove my phone. Ignoring the fact that I'm already halfway to being mind controlled by electronics, I lean forward, trying to read what's on Alessi's screen. But she hides it from me again. What she fails to hide is the surprise on her face.

"What is it?" I ask.

"We need to go in," she says.

Collins shakes her head. "We're not ready."

And she's right. The plan was to hit a hotel, take showers, dress like science-nerds and try to blend in with the research personnel.

Easy for me, the balding white male, and Alessi, the serious Japanese woman—we fall within the stereotype. Collins on the other hand...she'd stand out and be noticed, no matter how nerdy she dressed. Her disguise was an expensive power suit, the kind someone with authority might wear—the kind that science-nerds avoid eye contact with and security guards ogle. But if we go in now, dressed in T-shirts, jeans and a lone, red beanie cap, we'll stand out for our casualness.

"There isn't time," Alessi says. "And they'll be distracted."

"With what?" I ask, sensing an answer that's going to make my ass pucker.

"A Tsuchi is loose," she says. "But it's not in the main building. It's in Building-K."

"Annnd what is Building-K?" I ask.

"I haven't been told," she says so quickly it sounds like the truth. "All I know is that it's big."

"How big?" I ask, puckering in progress.

Alessi looks back at me, understanding my fears, and the true nature of the question. "Big enough."

"Great."

"Turn here," Alessi says to Collins, and I sit back. I don't like this, running into the unknown, led by someone I don't trust, who is, in turn, led by someone I want to kick in the nuts most of the time, a man whose...obsession has mirrored my own on occasion.

While Alessi gives Collins directions to the GOD facility, I put on a pair of fake glasses and remove my beanie cap. At the very least, I'll look like a scientist rushing back to work late in the day, perhaps called in because of the emergency situation.

We pull up to the gate five minutes later. The gate house is two stories tall, with windows surrounding each of the two floors. Beyond the gate is a tall building, not quite a skyscraper, but dwarfed by what looks like a hangar for the world's largest plane. Technically, this land is still part of the Air Force Base, which stretches along the coast to the Space Launch Complex, built in the 1950s for ballistic missile testing and later converted to a space launching facility. So something like a giant hangar would go overlooked in this area. It's just one of many strange looking Air Force buildings. But this one contains a loose Tsuchi, and hopefully nothing else.

I turn my attention back to the guard house. Currently, there is no one standing by the security window. We stop in front of the gate. No one home.

"Should we drive through?" Collins asks.

"They're in there," Alessi says. "They're distracted, but blasting through the gate will definitely get their attention, in the wrong way. Honk like you're agitated. Like you've been waiting for a while."

Collins lays on the horn, letting out one long blast, followed by a barrage of irritating shorter honks.

The man who comes to the window is wearing black fatigues, like he's ready for action. A handgun is holstered on his hip. He's already shaking his head as he approaches and opens the sliding window. "We're locked down. No one gets in."

"But—"

"You can either wait, or come back tomorrow," the man says, indifferent to Collins's feminine wiles.

As the guard starts closing his window, I roll mine down and fix him with a squinty-eyed stare. "Why do you think we're here? Hmm?"

The man pauses, glancing at me. I'm not sure if it's the words I'm saying or the annoying nasal voice I'm using, but he looks irritated already. Irritated, but listening.

"Do you think we'd come back this late in the day just for fun? For kicks? I was sitting down for dinner! What's your name?" It's the kind of question only people who believe they can get you in trouble will ask. It does the job.

The window slides back open. "Why, exactly, are you here...sir?"

"You and I both know that Dark Matter has gotten loose." My knowledge of what's going on inside along with my use of GOD slang quickly piques the man's attention. "I was summoned to help eliminate the problem."

"I'm sorry, sir. But I'm not sure how you could help eliminate the threat." He's not being sarcastic. The question is honest, which means he's still on the hook.

"Euthanasia," I say. "Killing things is my specialty. The sooner you allow us access, the sooner I will be able to put your infected compatriots out of their misery."

This last line appeals to the man's fears, both for himself and any friends he might have actively dealing with the escaped Tsuchi. Also, I got to use the word 'compatriots' in a sentence, which is a first.

The guard looks back over his shoulder, then toward the facility and finally back to the SUV. He reaches out his hand. "IDs."

He takes the photo IDs, checks the pictures while bending down to look at us each in turn. Then he scans them one at a time. With each digital beep from the computer, I expect an alarm to go off, but nothing happens. The man hands the IDs back to Collins and asks me, "How serious is it?"

"Deadly serious, I'm afraid," I say, and then I dig for information. "As you'd expect any breach inside Building-K to be."

The man shakes his head. "I wouldn't know."

The gate lifts away and we pull through, speeding down the straight drive and arriving in a wide, half-full parking lot. I can see action by the massive Building-K—a lot of security, but they're not really moving. More like waiting. But definitely distracted.

We park close to the fifteen-story main building's front door. It's a bleak government building, square with tinted windows. There are three sets of double doors leading in. Alessi takes point, entering through the center doors like she owns the place. Inside are three card terminals and a windowed security booth. The guard inside looks surprised to see us, but he says nothing. When I see the metal detectors ahead, I glance at Alessi, trying to hide my worry while at the same time conveying it to her. She gives a subtle shake of her head that says, "Don't worry about it." We head toward the card scanners, swipe through them one at a time, and push through the turnstiles and metal detectors with no problem.

But how? I wonder. *Our weapons should have set off the alarms.*

Then I notice what looks like a car alarm remote in Alessi's hand. She takes her finger off a button, gives me a slight grin and pushes the elevator call button on the far wall. We stand silently before the polished marble wall, waiting for the elevator. When it dings and opens, a lone man is standing on the other side, skinny, white, blond and balding, except that unlike me, he's trying to hide it with a poor comb-over rather than a hat.

The man looks confused by our presence, looking first at Alessi, then to Collins with widening eyes and finally to me, with a gasp. This man knows exactly who I am, Clark Kent disguise or not, and he opens his mouth to shout for help.

15

The three of us act in unison, but uncoordinated. I take a swing at the man's head. Collins punches low, going for his gut. And Alessi brings the tech, a crackle of electricity revealing a stun gun thrust at the man's chest. Each response is justified, I think. If the man sounded the alarm, we'd have to fight our way out of here, and there's a good chance we'd lose that fight. But all three of us connect at the same time, and the man crumples to the elevator floor like Peter Griffin after falling down the stairs, arms askew, legs twisted. It's a pitiful sight.

We quickly step inside the elevator, and I jam down the 'close doors' button several times, hoping no one will notice the man lying at our feet. The doors slide shut, and I relax, looking down at the sprawled man. "Okay, can we all agree that this guy got a raw deal, even if he works for GOD?"

"Is he alive?" Collins asks.

I check for a pulse, watching a wash of purple spread over his swelling cheek. "He's going to wish he wasn't when he wakes up."

The man suddenly groans, giving me a start. Driven by self-preservation instincts, I nearly punch him again.

The man cradles his face, then his gut. "W—what did you do to me?"

"I believe the scientific term would be, put the smack down." I take the man's white lab coat in one hand and let him see my other, clenched in a fist. "Who are you?"

He raises his hand in defeat. "What do you want?"

"Pretty sure I asked for your name," I say.

"Brice."

Alessi glowers at the man. "Alicio Brice?"

He looks up at her, surprised. Confirmation enough.

"This is who we want," she says.

Collins hoists the man up so I can get in his face properly. "Take us to..." I look at Alessi. "Where do we want to go?"

"His office."

I look back at Brice. "...your office. Now."

"Fifth floor," he says, and I punch in the number. "But...you don't want to do this. Not now."

"Because you're dangerous?" I ask, my tone mocking. "Because you'll hunt us down? I wouldn't make threats if I were you."

"You don't understand. A Tsuchi is loose. I have to—"

"We know," I say.

He squints one eye at me. The other is starting to swell shut. "You didn't..."

"Let it out?" I say. "We're not crazy. That's your department."

"You know nothing about what we do," he says.

The elevator stops and the doors open, but I don't step out. There are, no doubt, security cameras in the hallway. I was concerned the elevator would have them, too, but since no alarm has been sounded, I don't think that's true. I put my foot in front of the door to keep it from closing or returning to another floor. Alessi draws her sidearm and peeks into the hallway. Since she doesn't start shooting, I assume we're in the clear.

I probably shouldn't, but I decide to blow Brice's mind. "You work for GOD, but I doubt the Good Lord looks highly upon what the Genetic Offense Directive actually does, which is basically playing god, coming up with new and horrible chimeras. Weaponized biology. Like Kaiju, capital K, who died on Island 731. Or the Tsuchi, which killed so many of your men on the island that you had to fire bomb it, a tactic you repeated in Oregon because your men, the BlackGuard, did a shitty job. You should really have a talk with that

Silhouette guy. He tends to let targets slip through the cracks. And yeah, I'm supposed to be dead, too, which is the real reason you're so surprised to see me, not because you admire my awesomeness and envy my kaiju, *lowercase K*, mojo, but that's probably also true. And to top all that off, you've got Nemesis's body stashed inside your hangar outside, and if that's true, you're really screwed."

Brice looks equal parts confused and surprised. I've hit the nail on the head and didn't even know the hammer existed. Or something. To his credit, he doesn't try to deny anything. "Why...would we be screwed if Nemesis's corpse were in the warehouse?"

"And here I thought you were a smarty pants." I can't help but grin. "Because she's not dead, and she *really* doesn't like bad men who do bad things. Maybe you noticed that when she destroyed half the East Coast to take vengeance on a single man."

"I can assure you, she is quite dead."

I was just guessing that Nemesis was in the hangar, but he's just confirmed it, and despite his insistence that she is deceased, I know what Maigo and I felt. I turn to Alessi. "We need to do this fast." Then to Brice. "Lead the way, mon capitan. I don't think I need to tell you what will happen if you give us a hard time. You've already had a taste of the triple threat."

Brice sneers. "I have always loathed your sense of humor."

I'm not sure if he's talking about my few appearances on national news, or footage they have from spying on us, but I don't ask. The more it seems like I'm in control of the situation, the better. I wipe the smile from my face. "I think you'd prefer me funny, than not. Now lead the way."

We enter the hallway doing our best to look casual. Alessi has the taser positioned behind her back, and I'm standing behind her to block the view of it, but any keen-eyed observer will see the fresh shiner around Brice's eye. But even if they do, security has their hands full with the loose Tsuchi.

There's three doors on the left side of the hallway. Brice heads for the one in the middle. When he reaches it, he swipes his keycard and the door pops open. We step inside and stop, shocked by what's on the other side. The first thing that surprises me is the scope of the place. The bright white room stretches from one side of the building to the other. But I quickly forget the size when I see the line of clear domes, each containing a horrible creature, the likes of which I've never seen, or at least, never seen in this combination. But I do recognize the creature closest to us, not from personal experience, but from Hawkins's description. The crocodile spins toward us, moving fluidly in two feet of water. As we walk past, its mouth opens, unfurling two long tentacles that slap against the curved glass. Had there been no partition between us, it could have snatched me and yanked me into its gaping mouth.

"This place is a freak show," Collins says, mirroring my thoughts.

Brice leads us to a lone desk at the center of the room, holding a single, thin laptop. All of it white, like the room.

"A little too space-age hipster in here for my taste," I say, but I'm ignored.

Brice stops beside the desk, probes his swelling eye with his fingers and asks, "What now?"

"Log in," Alessi says.

Brice starts tapping keys. "Even if I log in, the system is text based. You're not going to find what you're looking for."

I glance at the screen and see something like a DOS prompt appear, but nothing really familiar. They've got their own operating system. Of course they have their own operating system.

"Are you saying you're not going to comply?" I ask, the threat in my tone says the rest.

"I'm saying you don't have time."

I'm not entirely sure what he's talking about. Security, in theory, could already be on their way, but how would he know that? I draw my handgun from behind my back and aim it at his head. "The remaining Tsuchi. Where are they?"

He points to the left, and I see them, lying on their backs inside a dome, legs curled up. "They look dead."

"They're pretending," he says.

"Destroy them."

His eyes widen a touch. "They're priceless specimens."

"Do it."

"Do you have any idea how many people lost their lives to—"

I chamber a round. "It's you or them."

"You're no killer," Brice says.

"Not of men," I say. "But I make exceptions for monsters, and I think you qualify."

I mean what I'm saying, and I'm pretty sure he can see that, because he starts tapping keys, bringing up a diagram of the room. He taps the screen, highlighting the dome containing the Tsuchi and then taps a red icon. When a warning message pops up, he taps Continue. A moment later, the glass dome is awash in flames. The Tsuchi bound into the air, slamming against the glass and writhing until they fall back into their faux death poses, no longer acting.

A sound like distant gunshots tickles my ears, barely audible, but a constant stream. Somewhere, a battle is being fought. Sounds like a lot for one Tsuchi.

Brice glances toward the sound, but hides any concern it might give him. "What now?"

"Now," Alessi says, "You can step back."

She pulls a USB flashdrive from her pocket and plugs it into the laptop. The screen immediately fills with preprogrammed commands. Software opens and closes faster than I can see. Databases scroll past. Diagrams. Case files.

Brice looks horrified. "You're with *them*, aren't you?"

"Them, who?" I ask.

He looks at me, a wild look in his eyes. "Zoomb. They have been trying to infiltrate our operation for months. You should be careful who you get into bed with, Hudson."

"What are you doing?" I ask Alessi.

"Erasing their database," she says. "Everything they have ever researched, created or stolen is being erased. Including everything they have about the FC-P, and your friends."

"No!" Brice says, and tries to grab the laptop. Collins holds him back. He struggles for a moment, but realizes Collins is more than a match for him and gives up. "Can't you see? She's not simply erasing the data, she is copying it! You are helping a corporation perform espionage on a government agency. This is treason!"

Despite the despicable nature of what they do here, he's technically right, especially if Alessi is indeed copying their data with the intention of handing it over to her employers. The good news is that GOD could never publicly tell anyone what they really do here, and if I need him to, the President would have my back. The bad news is that data or no data, the FC-P will be dead center in GOD's crosshairs. Not that we weren't already, but they're not going to simply come looking for Lilly. They're going to come for vengeance.

That is, if they know we did this. Which brings me to the dilemma at hand.

Brice.

If I let the man walk, I'll be starting a war. But the alternative... Could I really kill the man? *No*, I decide, but I suspect Alessi might, and I'm not sure if I'll try to stop her.

A vibration shakes the floor beneath us.

"What was that?" Collins asks.

"Time's up," Brice says.

The laptop screen goes black, leaving only a blinking red cursor. I snap my hand out and pluck the flashdrive out before Alessi can. She glowers at me for a moment, but says nothing.

A second vibration rattles the building.

"What's happening?" I ask Brice.

"The Tsuchi. It multiplied." A grin spreads across his lips. "With Nemesis's corpse."

Well, fuck.

That's horrible news. But Brice has missed the obvious. "The Tsuchi only implant *living* hosts."

Brice is about to argue, but is cut off by irrefutable evidence in support of my claim. The building shakes, as a roar, so loud and familiar, tears through the air.

Nemesis *is* alive, and she's pissed.

I turn toward the door and start to run—when Nemesis is waking up a few hundred feet away, it's the only sensible action—but I spot Brice back at the keyboard. I raise my weapon, but he hits a final key, steps back and raises his hands. The asshole knows I won't shoot him.

But he's forgotten about Alessi. She fires twice, both shots striking the man's chest and exiting through his back, spraying the white wall behind him with twin splotches of bright red. But the damage has already been done. From one side of the room to the other, the glass domes lift off the floor, unleashing their living weapons.

16

"Do we really have to do this now?" Lilly asked, hands on her hips, tail snapping back and forth, watching the scale's digital display blink.

"You're overdue," Joliet replied, clipboard in hand. While she was giving Lilly her bi-annual physical, something she insisted on because Lilly had grown so quickly, she was dressed in cotton pajamas. Night was upon them, and after the day's excitement and long drive, she felt like turning in early. But not until she finished Lilly's exam. It was a miracle the girl agreed to it at all. The display showed Lilly's weight: 242.

"Son-of-a-bitch," Lilly grumbled.

"Hey," Joliet said. "Language."

"How would you feel if you weighed more than Dad? Look at you. You're a waif. What do you weigh? One twenty? One thirty?"

Joliet sighed. This kind of conversation never went well with Lilly, because there was no standard for comparison. "You weigh more than us because your muscles are denser. It's why you're so strong. And why you can jump seventy five feet down from a tree without getting hurt."

"I get it," Lilly says. "I'm awesome. But I'm also...you know..."

"A cat woman," Joliet says.

"Yeah, except that I'm more than that. You know that better than anyone. You're the one that puts the—"

Joliet raised both hands. "I know what I do."

"And you know that there are parts of me that aren't human or cat. We don't even know what else is in the mix. For all we know, I might end up like my mother. Not you. I mean—"

"I know what you mean, Lilly," Joliet could practically read the girl's mind at this point. Next would come the reminder that she had laid a clutch of eggs.

Lilly threw her arms out to her sides. "I laid eggs. *Eggs!* So you know what that means? I'm *asexual.*"

Joliet blinked. *Okay*, this *is new territory.*

"And even if I got to meet a guy—which I won't, because, you know—" Lilly looked around the interior of the cabin's large bathroom and motioned all around, signifying that she was speaking about the cabin, and probably the reserve where she spent most of her time. "—who might actually be interested in me, he's going to be a total freak. Probably one of those Furry pervs."

Joliet wanted to comfort the girl. To tell her she'd find someone. That she'd find love. But she wasn't so sure herself, and she thought any attempt to encourage Lilly would just sound hollow. So she just said, "You'll always have us." After an awkward silence, she took out her pen light and aimed it at Lilly's yellow eyes. The pupils constricted into thin slits. "You know the drill. Follow the light."

Lilly's eyes remained locked in place while Joliet moved the light back and forth. "Lilly, this only works if—"

"Where's Dad?" Lilly asked.

"Downstairs," Joliet said, feeling frustrated. She had dissected countless sea creatures, including a sea turtle mutilated by a rubber band; she had survived the horrors of Island 731; but she had never raised a daughter, let alone a cat-daughter who was part *whoknowswhatelse.* As far as she knew, she was the first mother in the history of the world to have an adopted daughter like this. She managed by reminding herself that this girl, while strange and having the capacity to be frightening, was sweet and fiercely loyal. "But I thought you didn't want him to—"

Lilly's eyes snapped toward Joliet, the sudden intensity of them was startling. "How much *do* you weigh?"

"One ten, but that's—whoa!" Joliet suddenly found herself lifted off the bathroom floor. Before she could complain about the rough treatment, she was shoved upwards through a hatch in the ceiling and deposited on a floor of pink insulation. "Lilly, what the hell do you think you're doing?"

Lilly looked confused for a moment, but then she blinked and said, "Right. You can't hear them. So, here's the deal. We're surrounded. Maybe twenty men, give or take."

"What?" Joliet shifted back toward the open hatch. "If that's true, I need to—"

"You need to stay here. And stay safe." Lilly slid back out of the hole, clinging to the side with one hand and about to pull the hatch closed with the other. She was hanging in midair, making it look effortless.

Joliet was indignant. She didn't let anyone boss her around, let alone the girl who called her 'Mom.'

"Lilly, I survived the island, I think I can handle this, too."

Lilly hung there for a moment, looking up at Joliet. "The problem is, you weren't my mother then. Before you, my mother was a monster. You...you're too important now."

With that, Lilly dropped to the floor, pulling the hatch closed as she fell. Joliet, lit in the bright white light of her penlight, sighed and then remembered her phone. She pulled it from her back pocket, switched it on and tried to make a call to Cooper. They might be able to get help, or at the very least, let the others know what was happening. But the phone beeped at her. She looked at the screen.

No signal.

But that wasn't possible, unless... The men outside had blocked the signal, which meant they had access to impressive technology, and that told her all she needed to know about who was outside.

Mark Hawkins hated TV. He rarely ever watched cable. But right now all he really wanted to do was watch a mind-numbing SyFy movie, have a beer or two and chill out. Not because he was tired, but because he was agitated. Inaction didn't suit him, especially when it came to DARPA. He'd rather take the fight to their doorstep than hide in the woods.

But right now, the TV wasn't working. The satellite dish sometimes acted up during a storm or thick cloud cover, but the skies outside were clear, save for the stars and the moon. He knew nothing about fixing TVs or the satellite box connections, but like any true man, he pretended to and crouched down in front of the TV to check things out.

After pushing a series of buttons and seeing that everything was working right, he decided that something must have been wrong on the other end. The signal just wasn't getting through.

A loud thud beside him sent him sprawling for cover, but when he rolled back to his feet, it was just Lilly standing in the living room. *Did she jump down from the second floor?* The central living area at the front of the large cabin was open concept, the ceiling peaking two stories up at a line of skylights. When Hawkins saw what Lilly held, he forgot all about how she'd entered the room.

"What are you doing with my shotgun?" he asked.

Without a word, Lilly tossed the weapon to him. He caught it, and then quickly caught the box of shells that followed.

"I already loaded it," she said, looking around the room. "Shades are pulled, so let's leave the lights on. Turning them off now will just let them know that we know they're here."

Hawkins quickly understood. They were under attack, or soon would be. "How many?"

"Twenty-ish."

"Where is Maigo?"

Lilly shrugged. "Probably up in her room. I can't hear her. But she's safer there, so let's leave her be. She'll hide when the shooting starts."

"Joliet?"

Lilly grinned. "I threw her in the attic."

"You *what?*"

"Be glad I didn't put you up there, too," she says.

"Lilly," Hawkins said, his voice stern. "You can lose."

Her smile faded. "I know, I know, this isn't capture the flag."

As though to prove the point, every window on the first floor, and the skylights above, burst inward at once. A number of small devices rattled to the floor.

Hawkins caught sight of Lilly launching toward the roof and slipping out a skylight, while he dove to the floor, clutching his eyes shut, blocking his ears and opening his mouth.

The flash-bang grenades went off one by one, punching Hawkins's body with stunning force, but not permanently injuring him. *They're not here to kill us—not yet—they're here to collect Lilly.* When the last flash-bang detonated, Hawkins opened his eyes to a spinning room. Despite his best efforts to shield himself from the stun weapons' effect, he was still disoriented.

He raised the shotgun, knowing what would come next. Hordes of men would flow through the windows, aiming weapons, maybe firing, maybe shouting orders. The first one who entered would lose his head. The second, well, that would be a toss up. By the third, Hawkins would be screwed.

But that's not what happened. Instead, Lilly fell back through the skylight, her body clutched in some sort of spasm. Hawkins stumbled to her and knelt down beside her, quickly seeing two large darts from an oversized stun gun in her chest. They guessed she'd exit. They were waiting for her.

"Here's the deal," a man said from behind Hawkins. "We can either leave with the girl, or we can kill you and then leave with the girl. The choice is yours, but I don't give a damn, either way."

17

"Back the way we came," I shout, pointing to the far end as a pair of small goats, adorable as hell, hop toward a pig...with wings. I don't think the large swine could possible fly. The wings look too small, and the pigs lack the chest muscles, but then I remember that genetically, pigs are very similar to humans. It makes a sick kind of sense that they'd try this kind of modification on a hog before moving to human trials.

But the goats... They look normal—until they reach the pig. The nearest goat bounds up and dives, its body going rigid. For a moment, I think the thing has passed out, that it's one of those fainting goats, but then its mouth opens and *peels back* over its face. Two wide, hooked mandibles snap open and clamp shut on the pig's pink skin, digging in deep.

The pig bucks and squeals, but the goat, now bleating savagely, remains locked in place while its counterpart trots around. The goat starts wrapping the pig in copious amounts of webbing that's being excreted from *its udders!* What kind of freak show did Brice unleash?

The kind Hawkins warned me about, I realize. This is what GOD is all about: developing genetic monsters used on the battlefield. It's a few insane steps beyond strapping laser beams to the backs of dolphins. On the plus side, this whole facility is on the verge of being flattened by the third coming of the goddess of vengeance. On the downside, we're stuck inside the building with a circus act of scientific horrors between us and the door.

Trying to erase the squealing, winged pig from my mind, I chase Collins and Alessi across the room. I move down the right side of the long room, running along the wall, weapon aimed to the left, but not firing. I nearly trip as I pass yet another freakish battle.

A komodo dragon covered in spines that makes it look absolutely undefeatable swats its tail at some kind of mutated skunk, which turns its ass around and farts out some kind of viscous brown gas. As I run past, skirting the cloud of mutated skunk stank, I see the dragon's tail stab into the shrieking skunk, but then passing through the gas, the tail melts and falls away. The fight takes just three seconds and ends with both creatures dead.

Luckily, most of the creatures inside the domed containment units have attacked their neighbors.

Most.

At the end of the room, the tentacled crocodile twitches its head back, swallowing its neighbor—some kind of monkey I think. When it's done, it lowers its head toward Alessi, the closest of us, and drops its jaws open. The two tentacles unravel as though in slow motion, but I think it's just building pressure, because the two things suddenly spring out and wrap around Alessi's feet. She shouts and falls back, striking her head and dropping her weapon.

Collins dives without missing a beat, catching hold of Alessi's outstretched hands. But if the extra weight adds any strain to the tentacles, the croc doesn't show it. The monster reels in both women, the pulsing tendrils bulging and pulling, bulging and pulling.

"Stay down!" I shout, taking aim. I slide to a stop, knowing that I'll miss if I shoot while running. The room echoes with the sound of each shot. The croc gives a throaty growl and thrashes its head to the side with each hit, but it doesn't release the women. If anything, it doubles its efforts. I unload the clip, walking slowly forward, closing the distance between me and Collins to twenty feet. The fleshy mouth is oozing blood, but the croc's mind is intact, and whatever primal instincts it has tells it to not abandon its prey, no matter how much pain it endures.

I eject the magazine and slap in my only spare, taking aim again. As I pull the trigger, my arms are struck. The round hits the floor just beyond Collins's head. But that's all I see, because the world becomes a blur of movement and pain a moment later. I'm being assaulted.

But by what?

With my arms raised over my face in a classic boxer's stance, I try to peek around my forearms and get a look at what I'm sure will be a hideous attacker. Instead, I see a small army of emperor tamarins with small black monkey bodies, large, white, old-timey mustaches and...talons. Large ones, like five oversized claws had been merged into one, ice-pick sized, curved claw, one in place of each hand and foot. Right now, they're hurling themselves at me, curling into solid little balls. I can take the punishment, but if one hits my head, it could be sleepy time for Jon Hudson.

I try for my gun, hoping to shoot the croc while deflecting the monkey assault with my free hand. But the little jerks change tactics, opening up out of their balled forms and swinging those claws at me.

The first connects with my shoulder, putting an inch-deep puncture wound in meat.

Instincts take over, and I forget all about the gun. I grab the monkey from my shoulder. It bites my hand, but it can't stop me from flinging it across the room. I meant to throw it across the room and bash it against the wall, but an aggressive seagull swoops through the air and plucks it away. There are several more of them circling the battle, which will soon leave only the most badass genetic monsters. It's like accelerated evolution. Survival of the fittest. The human race came out on top of the real deal, but in this mutated competition, I'm not so sure we're going to pull through.

I reach down toward a stabbing pain in my thigh without looking, tear the monkey away and hurl it upwards. A seagull cries out and snatches its prize. A few of the others give chase, but then they seem to notice there are many more of the small meals on the floor, encircling me. They circle and dive. The monkeys, having met their match, forget about me and turn their attention to the dive-bombing seagulls, which I now see have mouths like piranhas.

"Jon!" Collins shouts.

I turn and see Alessi just feet from the croc's mouth. Collins has gotten to her feet and is leaning back, playing tug-o-war with the monster.

A monkey and seagull thrash around atop my handgun on the floor, locked in mortal combat, where I'm happy to leave them. I jump over the pair, run to Collins's side and draw her .50 caliber sidearm.

"I can't...hold her...much longer," Collins grunts. Alessi says nothing. Her eyes convey her message clearly enough: *please.*

The croc's eyes track me as I run to the side, aiming the weapon at its head. I'm about to fire when one of the tentacles releases Alessi and snaps to the side, slapping against the small of my back and sticking.

Mother bitches, that hurts!

The tentacles aren't simply suction cups, they're covered in barbs!

Knowing I'm about to be yanked back and into the croc's mouth, I dive forward, pulling the monster's head into view. My dive is arrested for just a moment, as the tendrils pull taut. I squint, aim and pull the trigger.

The tentacle yanks me back, and I never see if my aim was true, but I find out a second later when I'm slapped down on the floor. I lean up and see the croc, a hole where its eye used to be, lying dead on the floor. Collins quickly peels the tentacle off Alessi, which elicits a shout of pain. I stand with a grunt, the weight of the tendril still pulling on my back. When Collins steps up next to me, I say, "Do it quick."

"It's like a wax," she says. "Women do it all the time."

She yanks, and I feel hundreds of tiny pops as the barbs tear out of my skin. I grind my teeth, thinking for a moment that I'll manage to stifle my scream, but I fail when the air hits my back, bringing on a sharp stinging unlike anything I've ever felt. I'm going to bathe in antibiotics if we make it out of here.

Speaking of which, our path to the door is now clear. I hobble toward the door as quickly as I can, and I all but fall into the hallway. A lone African American scientist in some kind of clean-suit stands at the far end. His suit is covered in blood. Brice must have opened all the containment units in every lab. I limp down the hallway toward the man, keeping my gun low, trying not to spook him. He's hammering the elevator's call button like a manic woodpecker.

The elevator, still fifty feet away, dings. The doors slide open.

"Hold up," I say to the man, like it's just another casual day at the office.

The man steps inside, and when it's clear he's not going to hold the doors, I fire a few shots into it, just to vent my frustration. One of the rounds strikes the call button, which bursts with sparks.

The doors remain open. Well, that's a stroke of good luck in an otherwise craptastic day.

"What did you do?" the man shouts from inside the elevator.

Or not...

I peek inside. The panicked man is jamming the 'close door' button, but the elevator isn't responding. He looks up at me, incredulous. "You broke it!"

"Listen, buddy," I say, aiming Collins's big gun at his head, but I never get to finish. At the far end of the hallway, a door bursts open with enough force to send the door across the hall and through the window on the other side. The scientist all but squeals in fright.

And then I see why.

The wall around the doorframe cracks and then shatters, leaving a gaping hole. The biggest damn gorilla I've ever seen struts into the hallway, its skull cleaved cleanly off, brain exposed, snapped wires dangling freely from it. Blood drips from its arms, and I'm pretty sure it's not the ape's.

"Oh, god," the scientist cries, going back to work on the button with no result. "Oh, god!"

"Here!" Alessi says from the far side of the hallway. She's standing in an open doorway, a stairwell behind her. Collins and I quickly join her.

"Up or down?" Collins asks, but a roar from below answers for her.

Up it is.

I tap my throat mic for the first time. "Woodstock, where are you?"

"En route," he says, his voice clear through the perfectly disguised earbud in my ear. "Run into trouble?"

"You could say that. ETA?"

"Five minutes."

"Doooctooor!" The shout shakes the air with reverberating bass so loud I'm sure it wasn't human.

"Go!" I urge Alessi and Collins higher. I turn back to the hallway. The scientist across the corridor peeks out of the elevator, looking down the length of the hallway.

"The hell was that?" Woodstock asks.

I ignore him and look around the corner, to the gorilla. It points at the scientist again and hollers, "Doctor will die now!"

Holy planet of the fucking Kongs, I think, and I wave the doctor across the hall, shouting, "Let's go!"

The man wastes no time debating it. His choices are: stay and die horribly, or run with the man who might shoot him, and maybe live a few minutes longer. We take the stairs side by side, rounding the single flight toward the open roof doorway, where Collins waits.

Out of breath, I finally reply to Woodstock. "I don't care what laws you break, or how dangerous you fly. I need you here in two minutes, tops."

"Music to my ears, boss," Woodstock says, followed by a "Whoop!" that is cut short, first by a second, angry roar from Nemesis, which seems much louder now that we're outside (though it's still muffled) and the resounding thunder of an over-sized, intelligent silverback making short work of the stairwell behind us.

18

Hawkins placed his shotgun on the floor and slowly raised his hands, putting all his willpower into not spinning around and diving at the man behind him. Not only was the man armed, but he might not be alone. Attacking was most likely a death sentence, and that wouldn't do Lilly any good. If they took her now, he needed to survive so he could get her back. Dying in her defense, however noble, would only make her situation worse.

"Turn around," the man said. "Real slow."

Hawkins did as instructed, taking in the scene with calm determination. He'd take in every detail, commit them to memory and use the information to hunt these men down. But he didn't really need to take in details. He recognized the four BlackGuard men, but they weren't alone. Behind them stood four more men, who looked like regular soldiers, their uniforms dark camouflage, their faces masked, but eyes revealed. The four BlackGuard were hidden behind black masks and those reflective goggles. The man talking was known as Silhouette.

"I'm sorry," Hawkins said, "you brought a small army to take care of us, but only the four of you to handle an army of Tsuchis?"

If the man was surprised, it was impossible to tell. He just tilted his head and said, "I thought you looked familiar. A little different without the mud on your face."

Hawkins felt an odd sort of tension fill the room. Men were shifting, like a fight was coming, but it had nothing to do with him.

The man snapped his gloved fingers, the sound muffled, "Dustin Dreyling, right? The new FC-P hire."

Hawkins just stared at the man, trying to find his eyes through the reflective glass.

"No," Silhouette said. "That's not right. Well, not the truth, anyway. Hawkins. Mark Hawkins. That sounds right. You know, for a while we thought you might actually be dead. You and your girlfriend—" He glanced at Lilly. "—and your pet. But here you are, alive and living right under our noses in a vacation home funded by the same assholes who pay our bills. Ironic, don't you think?"

Hawkins didn't take the bait. He knew the man was just looking for an excuse to get violent.

"But the real problem lies within a single word of what I just said." Silhouette leaned in close, whispering. "Do you know what that word is?"

Hawkins said nothing, but pondered the question, replaying the man's last words in his mind. Then it came to him, along with an understanding of why the men were tensing for a fight, despite the situation being under control.

Alive.

The BlackGuard operative, Specter, had been ordered to kill him and Hudson. Not only had he spared them, but he'd also left the goggles behind. The goggles that had allowed them to uncover the Lompoc location. But it was the same goggles that had revealed Lilly and the FC-P to GOD.

Specter, recognizable as the smaller of the four men, slowly stepped to the side, away from the others, his stance non-threatening. "I didn't think you'd approve, but I—"

"You're God-damned right I wouldn't approve," Silhouette said to Specter. "Give me one good reason why I shouldn't put you next to this asshat and put bullets in both of your heads."

Hawkins paid attention to the conversation and noted the revelation that despite the man's claims to the contrary, Silhouette was planning on killing him, which meant he *had* to act. The question was, when?

And how?

There were nine men in the room, four of them highly trained killers, the other five potentially as deadly. With Lilly out of commission, Hawkins would have to rely on his shotgun, but there weren't enough shells in the weapon to take out all eight men, and he wasn't even sure if the pellets would get past their armor. His only real hope was that things would go south with Specter and that distraction would give him time to act.

And then, probably, die. But he had to try. He watched the conversation, tensing to move.

"I thought I recognized him," Specter said. "You had already left, so I made the call."

"And didn't tell me about it."

"The results speak for themselves, I think."

Specter's confidence was surprising. Silhouette was clearly in charge, but Specter had no problem questioning the man's authority. But was this cocksure attitude considered acceptable? Or was Specter just digging his own grave?

Hawkins saw his chances of success dwindle to nothing when Silhouette shook his head and laughed. "You're a ballsy sonofabitch. Now do me a favor, and put a bullet in his head this time."

Silhouette stepped aside, allowing Specter a clean shot.

Hawkins glanced down. The shotgun was at his feet. If he was lucky, he'd have enough time to duck, grab the weapon and pull the trigger. If he was really lucky, the shot would strike the man's legs. But after that, no amount of luck would change his fate.

Specter took aim.

Outside, a shrill scream grew louder. Everyone looked toward the front of the house, from where the sound had come. The scream wasn't getting louder, though. It was getting closer. A thunk above marked the man's impact with the ceiling. He rolled down the slanted roof and fell past one of the shattered windows, hitting the ground outside with a thud.

Silhouette toggled his throat mic. "All teams report."

The man was quiet for a moment, then turned his attention back to Hawkins. "Who's out there?"

Before Hawkins could reply, several more screams filled the air. One by one, men slammed into the house. The first struck the outside wall, his shout cut short by a loud crack. The second man struck the roof and rolled off. The third man also struck the roof, but then toppled through one of the broken skylights and fell to the floor.

"Looks like there's something worse than the BlackGuard out tonight," Hawkins said and immediately regretted it.

Silhouette lifted his own weapon at Hawkins's head, finger on the trigger. But he never got a chance to pull it. A shotgun blast struck the man, throwing him across the room.

"Now, Mark!" Joliet shouted from the second floor balcony. She pumped the shotgun and fired a second time, striking one of the less armored regular soldiers, killing him instantly. Hawkins crouched, looped his finger around the shotgun trigger and yanked it back. The weapon fired, shredding furniture and striking the largest of the BlackGuard in the legs. The shot was intended for Specter, but the lithe man had already dived away. The shot still had the desired effect, though. While the big man fell, Hawkins dove away, hiding behind the large, stone, fireplace chimney.

Joliet got off one more shot before the counter attack began. The BlackGuard didn't just fire at her, they shot up through the floor, their KRISS rifles making short work of the wood. Joliet was forced back, diving into a bedroom.

The chimney burst into a cloud of chipped stone, as bullets tore around Hawkins. He ducked back, waiting for a break in the fire. The break came a moment later when two more men fell through the skylights.

What the hell is happening out there?

He got his answer a moment later when the front door was kicked off its hinges, and Maigo entered. Not only had he never seen the girl look angry before, he'd never seen *anyone* this angry in his life. She looked possessed. She looked...like Nemesis in human form.

"Stop!" Maigo shouted. Her voice was so loud and commanding that everyone obeyed. But that didn't stop everyone in the room—including the recovered Silhouette, whose armor had protected him—from aiming their weapons at the girl.

"Maigo," Hawkins yelled. "Get out of here!"

"Maigo?" someone asked, sounding surprised, but Hawkins couldn't see who had said it. Instead he heard the staccato roar of a KRISS rifle, followed by Silhouette bellowing, "What *the fuck*!" and the chaos of returning fire, none of which was directed at Hawkins.

Hawkins stepped out from hiding, shotgun brought to bear, and took in the scene. One of the BlackGuard laid on the floor, blood oozing from his head. The rest of them were firing across the living room at Specter, who had just dived into the kitchen, sliding behind the island.

Maigo took hold of the nearest man, one of the regular soldiers, with surprising speed. She lifted him by his arms and threw him into the ceiling two stories above. He fell back down, limp.

More men poured into the cabin through the back, ready to join the fight, but several were cut down by Specter, hiding in the kitchen.

Joliet opened fire from the second floor, striking one of the newcomers, but drawing heavy fire. She fell back with a shout of pain, clutching her side.

Lilly stirred on the floor, her eyes snapping open, taking in the scene. She let out a screeching cry, but she was still too weak to move. Maigo crouched beside her, eyes wary for danger. But the BlackGuard and their support were focused on people with guns, which Hawkins remembered, included him. He fired the shotgun at the men, striking two of the regular soldiers.

Silhouette returned fire, but missed as Hawkins ducked back behind the chimney.

Over the roar of gunfire from both sides of the battle, high pitched screams tore through the air from the back of the house. Men retreated from the back door, pursued by three large black cats. Lilly had called in reinforcements. The tide of this encounter had shifted dramatically, and everyone knew it, including Silhouette.

The BlackGuard leader slapped something against the kitchen's outer wall, ducked and covered his ears.

"Fire in the hole!" Hawkins said, covering himself, too.

The explosion rocked the inside of the home, the sound reverberating off the walls and striking everyone with the same numbing force. Hawkins forced himself past the pain and leaned out from hiding, raising his shotgun. He fired once, but missed his target. Silhouette and the big man had already fled through a hole in the wall.

Several of the soldiers still moved, but Lilly's girls set upon them, quickly snapping necks, which was unfortunate. A living captive would have provided them with a lot of information.

"Back!" a man shouted. "Hawkins! Call them off!"

It was the short man, Specter, who for some reason had helped save their lives twice now. He was still alive.

"Lilly!" Hawkins said, and she understood. She let out a cat-like cry, and all three big cats bounded over to her, nuzzling calmly, like nothing had happened.

Hawkins headed for the kitchen, shotgun raised. He glanced at the girls, still on the living room floor. Maigo gave him a too-old-for-her-age nod that said, "I've got her."

Joliet tromped down the stairs, clutching her blood-soaked side with one hand, still wielding the shotgun with the other, pausing for a moment to address Lilly. "Don't you dare ever put me in an attic again."

Hawkins looked at Joliet, the pained expression on her face, and then at her side, where blood was slipping out from beneath her hand. Before he could ask, Joliet said, "It went through. Pretty sure it missed anything important. I think I'll live. But a hospital would probably be a good idea...after we get some answers from this guy." She motioned to the kitchen, where Specter was hidden.

Hawkins smiled. *Shot and still feisty.* His kind of lady.

Side by side, the pair entered the kitchen.

"Show yourself," Hawkins said.

Specter stood slowly from behind the counter. He was unarmed, hands raised. "My weapons are on the floor."

"Who are you?" Joliet said.

"A friend," the man replied, reaching up to his mask. He peeled off the goggles and mask as one, revealing a face Hawkins recognized.

Katsu Endo.

19

"Head for the far side!" I shout as I run, pointing to the other side of the roof. There's nothing strategic about the far side of the roof, where several air conditioning units, antennas and satellite dishes are located; it's just far away from the stairwell.

As we near the edge, the warehouse comes into view below. The curved metal roof is just thirty feet below us. If we had a rope... But we don't, and pondering what we could do isn't nearly as helpful as figuring out what we *can* do.

"Is there another stairwell?" I ask the scientist, who's bent over, hands on his knees, heaving each breath. This is the first time he's been chased by a giant killer monster. I've kept in pretty good shape since I realized my job would involve creatures who could cover a hundred feet in a single step.

Through heavy breathing, the man points across the building. "Other...side..."

I slap the back of his head. "Could have mentioned that when I pointed this way and shouted 'head for the far side.'" I turn to Collins. "Any bright ideas?"

She holds her hand out. "Yeah, give me my gun back."

I hand her the weapon, not because it's hers, but because she's a better shot, and we both know it. Alessi has her weapon drawn, too, but I'm not sure the 9mm will do any good. Collins's .50 caliber is our best hope.

A low growl that shakes the fifteen-story building rises from below.

While we wait, I take the scientist by the collar and give him a shake, "Is that Nemesis?"

"Nemesis is dead," he says, shielding his head like I'm going to punch him. And I might, if he doesn't spill the beans.

"Is her body in Building-K?"

He nods vigorously.

"Well, she doesn't *sound* dead."

His nod becomes a shake. "I—I don't know. Her dermis regenerated over the past year, but she wasn't breathing. There was no pulse. No brain activity."

"But her skin was growing," I point out. "That's got to be a sign of life, right?"

"The dark colored skin is like a separate organism. Like a fungus."

"A bullet and bomb-proof fungus." My words are drenched in sarcasm, but the man nods.

"Yes."

"So you kept a three-hundred-fifty-foot-tall, alien goddess of vengeance in a hangar within stomping distance of a U.S. city? Did it ever occur to you that the body, which I'm assuming didn't decay, was in some kind of stasis while the fungus grew?"

"Alien?" he asks, eyes widening.

"Really? That's what you took away from—"

The stairwell at the center of the roof explodes up. The door launches away. The roof bulges out. The walls crumble apart. And then all at once, the silverback pushes its way through the now gaping exit.

The roof shakes as the silverback plants one foot on the rough, stony surface. It turns left, looking for us, and then right, finding us. It roars at us, strands of drool flapping like flags caught in a stiff wind, visible even from here.

"Woodstock," I say. "ETA?"

"You should hear me coming," he says. "One minute tops."

I pause and listen, but some kind of tumult within the warehouse behind me, and the sound of the now running silverback's charge, block out any other sounds.

"We're on the east side of the building," I tell him, "but I'm not sure if we'll be here when you arrive."

"Just keep me posted, bossman."

I was implying that we'd be dead, but I decide to let him keep his glass half full.

Collins takes a step toward the charging ape, weapon raised. "Stop!"

The beast continues its frothy charge.

Collins fires a shot, clipping the ape's arm. "I said stop!"

The silverback digs its feet in and grinds to a stop.

"I can't believe that worked," I whisper.

To our collective surprise, the gorilla thrusts his finger out at the cowering scientist. "I want doctor!"

Collins shakes her head. "Not going to happen."

The ape turns his finger to his exposed brain. "He do this! To family!"

Collins's aim waivers. I don't blame her. Unlike much of the world, who have been conditioned, through movies and novels, to view monstrous things as simple-minded killing machines, we know better. They're complex creatures with genuine emotions that are sometimes deeper than we can comprehend. It sounds like this great ape saw his fate befall his family before it was done to him. I don't know what family means to a gorilla, but I suspect it's similar to a human family: children, a mate, maybe even brothers, sisters and parents. It wouldn't surprise me if GOD took an entire troop of gorillas from the Congo.

"I gave Tilly to Nemesis for less," I say.

The scientist flinches like I've just punched him. "You can't be serious!"

"Did you do this to him?" I ask the man.

His silence is answer enough, and I step away from the man.

"Jon..." Collins glances at me, the look in her eyes is stern, but unconvincing.

"Would you stand in my way if they did this to our children?"

"You people are crazy!" The scientist says, and he breaks away, running along the edge of the roof. He doesn't know it yet, but he's just triggered his own doom and taken away some of the burden I might have felt if I had simply stood aside.

The roof shakes beneath our feet. At first, I think it's from the charging gorilla, but the sound of wrenching metal spins me around, and I see the hangar roof bending upward.

"Coming in low," Woodstock says. "From the n—what the hell is that thing on the roof!"

The hangar roof is struck from below, two long, blade-like spines punching through.

"Holy sheeit!" Woodstock shouts. "Is that—"

"Meet us on the west side of the roof," I shout, running toward the still charging gorilla. "West side!"

As we pass the silverback, it makes eye contact with me, and it's the strangest thing, not because it's a giant talking ape, but because I see intelligence in there. It grunts and dips its head in thanks, before continuing past us toward the scientist, who has realized he has nowhere to run and has turned to meet his end face on—and screaming.

Several things happen at once.

First, the silverback reaches the scientist. It doesn't stop, doesn't speak, doesn't grant mercy. It simply tackles the man, crushing bones and internal organs, as it lifts him off the rooftop and launches into the air, intending to end both of their miserable lives.

Second, the warehouse explodes, sending massive sheets of curved metal sailing through the air. One of these giant hangar pieces spins around, and slams into the GOD building. I don't see it happen, but the whole building shudders from the impact. *The first of many*, I think, running as fast as I can.

Third, the Zoomb helicopter rockets into view, spins and angles too fast to the side, and then, somehow, miraculously—what Woodstock would call just another day at the office—sets down hard on its wheels, just thirty feet ahead. The door springs open automatically.

And finally, last, but most graphic, Nemesis rises, her mouth agape. Just as the gorilla and scientist reach the apex of their leap, the Kaiju snaps its jaws over the pair like a trained dog. The crack of her teeth coming together is like pealing thunder, and if not for the chopper's rotor wash pushing me in the other direction, it would have knocked me off my feet.

Standing beneath the spinning helicopter blades, I can't help but turn around and watch Nemesis stand. She's as massive as I remember, shedding building debris as she pushes her massive girth up, until she's standing nearly twice the size of the building I'm standing atop.

I've been in a similar position more than once before. But this feels different.

Nemesis feels different.

And that's when I realize I am feeling her. Not like before, when I touched Maigo, but just a hint...like an instinct. I feel her anger. Her hatred. Her loathing.

And then, she feels me.

Nemesis's giant head turns down, looking at me. *Her eyes*, I think, *they've changed.* Where Nemesis used to have almost human brown eyes, they're now lifeless and glowing orange, like the membranes covering her neck, chest and torso. There's nothing of Maigo left in the monster, which means there is no affection left for me. No protection.

"Oh, shit," I say, just a moment before Collins wraps her arms around me and wrenches me back into the chopper.

"Go, go, go!" Collins shouts, and the chopper pitches to the side even as it lifts off, pulling us west, across the roof and away from Nemesis.

The goddess of vengeance roars. I'm pretty sure everyone in the helicopter shouts in pain from the sound, but I can't hear anyone, not even myself. Looking out the side window, I see a giant arm swooping down. The massive hand, tipped with five long, hooked claws, will pass through us like we're nothing more than air. We will simply cease to exist.

The roof fades away below us, and the swinging arm strikes the building, disintegrating it and all those horrible experiments. A shock-wave rattles the chopper, but we've made it out of range, thanks to the building's sacrifice. But that doesn't mean we're out of danger. Nemesis doesn't give up easily.

But then the giant flinches, her arm snapping up to something on her chest.

A Tsuchi.

An elephant-sized Tsuchi, with its tail poised to strike the orange membrane on Nemesis's chest, unknowingly dooming us all.

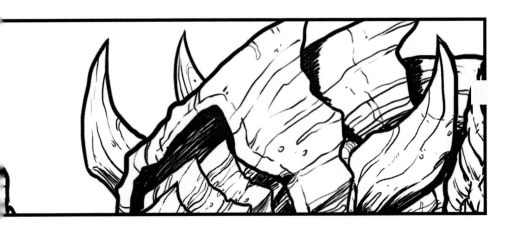

TSUCHI

20

Raw anger boiled through Nemesis. Her blood felt like acid. Her skin, fresh and thick, squeezed her body, making every movement a fight. But she was alive, and the world around her assaulted her senses.

The pain that had awakened her had numbed some, but she still felt as though something had been stolen from her. Part of her body. Her essence. But that wasn't the worst of it. The entire world and all its misery washed over her. Crimes committed around the globe filtered through her mind, lighting fire to her synapses and bringing back memories of tortures at the hands of those who...attuned her to injustice. She could feel them all. The murdered. The raped. The enslaved. The atrocities of mankind fueled an ancient furnace that flickered to life and then burned white hot. She would smite them with glorious vengeance until the injustice and misery broadcast by every wronged person fell silent, or until there were no more people left.

But there was something else, something missing. She felt...alone. And cold. And unrestrained!

Nemesis twisted her body and stood. She met a momentary resistance, but then she shoved against it, and like everything she encountered, it yielded to her might. The metal roof sheared away, and Nemesis saw the sun. She also felt a sudden and ripe burst of injustice, just above her, dangled out like a treat. She opened her jaws and snapped them closed, uncaring that she'd consumed both wrongdoer and victim. She felt the tiny bodies in her mouth, and she crushed them with her tongue, silencing their blaring moral foghorn. Millions more remained, but the nearest of them was—

As she stood to her full height, more nearby voices reached her. Hundreds of them. All coming from the building below her. She turned her head down toward the offending structure. So many voices in one location, all crying out for vengeance, could not be denied.

Then she saw him. A man standing on an adjacent roof, eyes turned up. He was afraid, but he did not cower from her judgment. Memories of this man returned in flashes, but she didn't understand them. The places and words and emotions associated with that face lacked meaning. All she felt for him was indifference, and while he did not deserve her wrath, many of those cowering in the building beneath him did.

Nemesis raised her massive, armored arm, the dark gray skin between the thick plates bending and flexing. She watched the tiny man run toward an awaiting helicopter. She didn't direct her blow toward him, but she didn't try to avoid him, either. He was simply a curiosity. Something from a past she no longer felt anything about.

The building provided no resistance for her strike. It crumbled beneath her massive claws, as though it were little more than air, but it did provide her some relief from the anguish oozing out of its walls. The voices within were silent now.

After unleashing a victorious roar, Nemesis noted the small man still lived, carried away through the air. She watched him for a moment, able to pinpoint his tiny face, framed by a window in the moving vehicle. And, for a moment, she felt something. It was fear, but not just for himself. He was afraid for them both. But why—

Then she felt it.

On her chest.

At first, the poking of its talons into her skin was a mere itch, but now she felt the thing. *Really* felt it, the way she felt most life, by detecting the lightness or darkness of its soul. In this case, the creature scurrying up her chest, both familiar and unknown, exploded with darkness. Not only that, it bore a resemblance to Nemesis herself. She recognized the traits that came from her, and for a moment, she felt a kinship, the way a mother might feel for her spawn. But then she remembered. This is what she'd seen upon waking. What she had struck away. This is the creature that had stolen from her. Had *violated* her.

And it was poised to strike.

Nemesis knew what would happen if the creature pierced the membrane on her chest. The creature would cease to exist in a fiery explosion. Had the creature been a bigger threat, she might have been inclined to let the thing have its way. But such an attack was reserved for far graver threats.

Moving with surprising speed, Nemesis brought a single claw up to scrape the creature away. The small thing didn't strike, but Nemesis didn't hit it, either. The creature leapt away, wrapped its long tail around Nemesis's wrist and then swung onto her forearm, where it did strike.

Three times.

21

My relief at Nemesis taking action against the Tsuchi is short lived. The creature, while much smaller than Nemesis, is agile and lightning fast. I flinch when it leaps away, wraps its tail around the Kaiju's arm and swings onto her wrist. "Oh, crap," I say, when I see the thing's tail jab Nemesis's wrist three times.

Nemesis backhands her arm into what remains of the GOD building, and it comes away free of the Tsuchi, but the damage has already been done. The skin on Nemesis's wrist bulges and then splits.

The massive Kaiju roars in pain, sending shockwaves through the air. The chopper shakes, but we're far enough away now to not be in any real danger.

"Woodstock, hold us here," I say, and the helicopter levels out to a smooth hover, the rotor blades almost silent in the regal interior. "Collins, get on Devine." The Digital Vanguard Intelligence Network, designed to help us coordinate a response to Kaiju threats across all emergency channels, including the military, has been unused for the past year. "I want airstrikes on the—"

Two F-22s roar past. I'm about to ask how they got here so fast, and then I remember that we're technically still on an Air Force base. The two jets, America's most advanced 5th generation fighters, unload their full payloads. Between the two fighters, twenty-four missiles streak through the air.

My body tenses for a moment, as the white smoke trails seem to point toward Nemesis's chest, but the missiles angle upwards, locked onto Nemesis's head. While there is no threat of detonating one of Nemesis's membranes, they've just guaranteed she's going to be really pissed off, and with a city of 43,000 people within stomping distance, that seems like a really bad idea.

The missiles strike Nemesis in the side of her face, pitching her sideways as the cracking bulge on her wrist ruptures with bright red gore. She roars, sounding more angry than hurt.

Part of me wonders if the combination of modern military mixed with the Tsuchi assault might be enough to take Nemesis down for good, but I know that's the wrong call. Small Tsuchi are a threat to the whole planet. I hate to think about what an army of giant Tsuchi could do.

I turn to Collins. "Tell them to target the Tsuchi! Not Nemesis!"

Collins has her smartphone to her ear. "They're not going to know what Tsuchi are."

"The spiders!" I shout, remembering their more descriptive name. "The big fucking spiders!" I see Alessi, sitting beside Collins, but looking past me, out the window, widen her eyes.

I turn back to the action in time to see Nemesis twist and arch her back in pain. But it's not from the missiles. The smoke from those twelve strikes rolls away from her face, revealing no damage at all. The old girl is as tough as ever...if you ignore her wrist. As she bends back, Nemesis lifts the offending wrist up, letting out a sharp wail as her flesh bursts from the inside out.

Three new Tsuchi, smaller than the one that implanted them, tear out of the arm, twitching and shaking gore away from their bodies. Like the first, they're much bigger than a normal Tsuchi, and even from this distance, I can see they share some attributes with Nemesis. These aren't the spindly, turtle-shelled monsters I fought in Oregon. These are Nemesis-Tsuchi, having borrowed some of their DNA from the Kaiju.

How big will they get?

Nemesis reacts to the new creatures with her normal unhinged vengeance, slapping her massive hand down on the opposite wrist. All three Kaiju Tsuchi, still young and unfocussed, are crushed. A flash of light bursts from beneath the giant hand, and then, all at once, an explosion is released. Nemesis's hands separate, unleashing the bright orange fluid contained in each new Tsuchi. The creatures are torn apart, along with what remains of the GOD building.

I avert my eyes from the brightness and hold on, as the shockwave shakes the chopper. When I look back, Nemesis stands alone, surrounded by a black, charred circle and a giant pile of rubble that used to be GOD. Beyond, I see what little remains of the mammoth hangar, inside of which are the mummified remains of a second Kaiju, similar to Nemesis, but thicker, even in death.

Nemesis Prime. I've never seen the body before. She's uglier than I imagined.

"More F-22s are en route," Collins says. "Targeting the Tsuchi. ETA thirty seconds."

Then I see movement on the ground. A Tsuchi, larger than the first, scurries away, heading south. A second one, still larger, bolts east.

"Let them know there are three targets," I tell her. "One engaging Nemesis, one headed south and one headed east. We need to intercept all three before they reach civilization." A map of the region pops into my head. Downtown Lompoc is seventeen miles away by car, but that's via a long winding route. To a giant Tsuchi, able to run right over the tall hills separating us from the town, that distance would be cut in half. "Priority should be given to the Tsuchi headed east!"

Nemesis, turns south, clearly intending to give chase, despite the obvious speed advantage the Tsuchi have, but she doesn't make it more than a step.

The charred corpse of the GOD building bursts open, and the first Tsuchi, the smallest and boldest of the three giant spiders, leaps onto Nemesis's back and scurries up, working its way through the double sets of towering spikes. Nemesis reacts quickly, spinning in circles, leveling the area with her long, trident tipped tail, trying to reach the Tsuchi.

The giant spider stops at Nemesis's shoulder, clinging with all eight legs. Nemesis tries to bite the thing, but can't reach it. As she lifts her hand to crush it, like she did the others, the Tsuchi strikes with its tail, three times. But the syringe-like stinger can't pierce the armor on the Kaiju's shoulder.

Nemesis's big hand hits hard, but there's no explosion. The agile Tsuchi suddenly appears on the far shoulder, striking with its tail again, to no effect. Then it's gone, and faster than seems possible, it's atop Nemesis's head.

In a flash, I see how this could all end. Three new Tsuchi, bursting from Nemesis's head, destroying her brain and forever killing the Kaiju.

Before Nemesis's raised hand can crash down on her own head, the Tsuchi does something new. It bites down. Blue arcs of electricity spark between the two mandibles. The charge can't be enough to incapacitate the much larger Nemesis, but it does make her flinch long enough for the Tsuchi to raise its tail, ready to strike.

It never gets the chance. A lone missile streaks in from the south, striking the Tsuchi. The armored spider spins away through the air, its legs like the spokes of a bike wheel, spinning madly.

Before the Tsuchi hits the ground, a line of white web streaks from its backside and strikes Nemesis's wrist, just below the fresh wound, which appears to have been cauterized by the explosive end of the three newborn Tsuchis. The spinning Tsuchi's fall is turned into a swing, bringing it around toward Nemesis's back. The BFS's legs splay wide, ready to land. Its tail arches and twitches, ready to strike.

But the Tsuchi fails to hit its mark. Nemesis's large but fast tail swings around and strikes the Tsuchi like a baseball bat hitting a golf ball. The impact's force snaps the web line and sends the now limp Tsuchi sailing—toward us.

Woodstock angles the chopper to the right, pulling us out over the ocean. The Tsuchi falls short of striking us, landing on the ground and rolling several hundred feet, stopping just before toppling over a cliff, into the ocean.

"Pulling back," Woodstock announces. Since Nemesis is charging in our direction, I offer no complaint. She roars at us, perhaps seeing the chopper as a threat now, or maybe as competition for her prize, but when we're far enough away, she ignores us and turns her full attention back to the now twitching Tsuchi.

Nemesis leans over the creature, and with surprising gentleness and accuracy, places one of her colossal claws on the Tsuchi's underside. The pinned spider flails, its tail stabbing at the claw but ricocheting away. While the Tsuchi goes ballistic, Nemesis reaches down with her free hand and with a quick flick of her finger, she severs the tail, effectively castrating the thing.

The Tsuchi's legs go rigid with shock for a moment, but then it starts twitching again. Nemesis reaches down, and one by one, she flicks off the spider's eight legs, which continue to twitch, despite being separated from the body.

My stomach sours. As much as the Tsuchi hurt Nemesis, and needs to be destroyed, this kind of torture is new for Nemesis. She generally dispatches her foes with brutal efficiency, preferring to silence the cries for vengeance as quickly as possible. This behavior is...sadistic.

Whatever fondness I have for the monster fades away. Everything good about her is now living on the other side of the country, as a teenage girl named Maigo. This Nemesis is, I think, closer to her pure, goddess of vengeance self. We're getting a taste of old-school Nemesis now, seeing her the way our ancestors might have, the way some alien race designed her to be.

Lacking any appendages, the Tsuchi is now motionless. Its mandibles open and close slowly, but the creature isn't going anywhere...unless it regenerates like Nemesis. But the giant Kaiju has no intention of allowing the Tsuchi to live.

"Further away!" I shout, as Nemesis brings both hands up and links them together.

The helicopter's engine whines as we're lifted up and further away.

The first explosion to rock the area is created by Nemesis's fists slamming down atop the Tsuchi. The legless spider is instantly pulverized, along with a hundred feet of cliff face. The second explosion happens when Nemesis lifts her fists, exposing the Tsuchi's ruptured membranes to the air.

While a normal explosion of this kind is a horrible thing, from the force and from the nearly nuclear temperatures generated by the blast—the most powerful non-nuclear explosion known to man—this one is compounded by the fact that it originates from within a crumbled cliff. Much of the stone is pulverized to dust by the blast, but just as much is tossed into the air, some of it baseball sized, some of it the size of a car.

Lucky for us, gravity tugs those large boulders down fast. Unlucky for us, those baseball-sized stones beat the tar out of our helicopter. Woodstock pulls some impressive maneuvers in an attempt to avoid the wave of debris, but before my stomach stops flip-flopping from whatever it is he did, I hear emergency alarms.

"Buckle up!" Woodstock shouts. "We're going down!"

While Collins calls in a mayday over Devine, I look out the window. Below is the bold blue ocean. Straight ahead are Nemesis's eyes, watching us drop past her. A year ago, still influenced by Maigo's connection to me, the Kaiju might have reached out and caught us. Now the brute just watches us fall. And then, as we pass by, she turns and steps into the ocean, leaving us to our fate and leaving the two remaining Tsuchi to do whatever it is they're going to do.

For a moment, I think Woodstock is going to pull us out of the fall. I hear the rotor spin faster for a moment, and my ass is squeezed into the seat. But then a jarring impact shakes us from below, and the setting sun is blotted out by the Pacific Ocean, which in this part of the world is thousands of feet deep.

22

Nemesis stands before me, blazing orange eyes staring down, dwarfing me. Judging me. And finding me wanting. I turn to run, but it's useless. Not only can she outpace me, the way I might outpace an ant, but I'm on a rooftop, and this time without a wing suit or a parachute to carry me away. So I turn to face her.

Die with a little dignity, Jon.

The wet sluicing of shredding flesh fills the air, accompanied by a pungent smell—fish and blood. Nemesis arches her back, flexing her chest outward. The back skin stretches and splits. The process repeats all over her body. The greatest molting on Earth.

She tears at the stuff, leveling apartment buildings with each discarded, airplane-sized hunk of thick skin. Beneath it, a glorious white form emerges, in some ways more hideous, more defined, almost skeletal in appearance. The transformation completes as two massive wings, incapable of flight, unfurl and put the city behind her in shadow.

Where am I? I wonder. The city is both familiar, but not.

The rising sun warms my back, casting a long shadow on the metal rooftop. The light is caught by millions of glittering diamonds—what we call Nemesis's feathers—which are highly reflective sheets capable of focusing the sun's light into an intensely powerful energy beam. But just once, so it's reserved for the worst of the worst.

In this case, for me.

But what did I do?

What crime have I committed?

As the wings curl, flecks of light dance around the rooftop, racing toward the center and merging with a growing spotlight centered on me. I can already feel the heat. When it happens, the intensity will be so fast and focused that I'll be vaporized, along with everything behind me.

Nemesis roars in victory, the focus nearly attained.

And then it's blocked.

Someone is standing in front of me. Taking my place. I recognize the silhouette.

"Maigo, no!"

I launch to my feet, oblivious to the tug on my arm until it stings. I glance down, breathing hard, coming out of the nightmare. An IV needle twists in my arm. I yank it away, stumbling back onto the bed. Dazed and confused in a non-Matthew McConaughey fun way, I search the room for clues about my location.

There's no window. No mirror. No cabinets or counters. Definitely not a hospital. The medical equipment beside the flat, normal looking bed is nominal: an IV bag and a heart monitor, which is still beeping away, rather fast. I glance down at my hand and pull the heart monitor clip from my finger. The beep becomes a droning squeal, announcing my death. And yet, no one comes running.

It's an illusion, I think. Someone is trying to make me think I'm being cared for. *But is it totally?* I reach up and touch my aching head. Instead of my beanie cap, I find a bandage. The last thing I remember is hitting the water...and my head? And then water rushing up over the helicopter. Everything after that is...nothing. I passed out.

Or I died.

Which would make this what? Hell? Purgatory? I'm not arrogant enough to assume I'd be quickly spirited away to the pearly gates. "Hello?" I say to the ceiling. "Anybody there? God? Steve Jobs? Mother Teresa? Uh...Bazuzal?"

Nothing. I figured that if a human being was listening in, that might get a response. Of course, if I *am* dead and it *is* God listening, does the guy even talk to people anymore? And if so, how? There isn't even a bush to burn in the room.

My next observation is an embarrassing one. I'm buck naked. And there aren't any clothes or even a johnny in the room. "Looks like it's time to go Roman," I say to myself. "Senator style, not Olympian."

I pull the top sheet off the bed and wrap it around my body like a toga. I feel ridiculous, but this is as good as it's going to get. I head for the door and open it, jumping back with a start, because of the proximity of the person on the other side. "Holy geez, Ash."

"Like your outfit," Collins says, lowering the hand she was about to use to knock on my door.

I look her up and down, noticing her own sheet turned toga. "Et tu Brute?"

"That makes no sense."

I shrug. "We're a regular Grumio and Metella."

"A what?"

"Look it up."

"I think you should lie back down," she says, looking honestly concerned. "You hit your head pretty hard."

I half take her advice and sit down on the bed. "What happened? After we crashed."

Collins scours the room, no doubt looking for clues about where we are. "You were knocked unconscious. Woodstock, too."

"Is he okay?"

"I haven't seen him. This was the first room I tried. I was next door. But he was alive last time I saw him. In bad shape, though. Bleeding a lot. Broken bones. Alessi got him to the surface, while I dragged your sorry ass up. A chopper pulled us out a few minutes later. Unmarked. Black." The kind government agents know to avoid because they're the kind we use. "Last thing I remember was a needle going into my neck." She moves her curly red hair aside, revealing a small needle puncture with bruising around it. Whoever jabbed her hadn't been gentle.

I feel my neck for a needle wound, but there's nothing. I was out cold already.

"What about Nemesis?" I ask.

"Out to sea."

"And the Tsuchi?"

"I didn't see them again."

I push myself back up, head spinning a little, but I steady myself, set my resolve on ludicrous and head for the door. "Let's get some answers."

The hallway beyond is white, like the room. Bland and featureless. Linoleum floors. *The hell is this place?* I stop at the door next to mine and glance in.

"That was my room," Collins says.

It's identical to mine. I move to the next door and try the handle. It's locked. The next three doors I try have the same result. We turn a corner and we're faced with an open door. Beyond it, darkness.

"Feeling a little like a mouse in a maze," I say. "And I don't think we'll get cheese at the end."

Collins steps around me and into the dark. "If they wanted us dead, we would be already."

"You don't always have to be braver than me, you know." I follow her in. Lights in the ceiling click and blink to life, illuminating a rectangular room. Three of the walls are mirrored, reflecting endless duplicates of each other. The effect is nauseating.

With a hydraulic hiss, the door behind us closes and locks. Aside from the door, the room is featureless. No furniture. No outlets. Just a ceiling full of long light bulbs and the same white linoleum floor.

I turn my attention to Collins, focusing on her instead of the mirrors.

"So," she says. "Planning to propose, are you?"

"*What?* Really? Now?"

She shrugs. "I'm not going anywhere."

"You know at least one of these walls is one-way glass, right? We're being watched."

She looks at our refection. "Everything about this place is designed to make us uncomfortable. To keep us off balance. I'm saying, let's find some balance."

Her eyes lock mine in place. The intensity of her gaze would be enough to make most men look away. I just get lost in them. "Fine. Yes. I'm working on it."

"Nothing big, I hope," she says. "No song and dance, or in front of a crowd or a ring in a muffin."

I hold my breath. While I haven't decided anything yet, I was feeling some pressure, like a lot of guys do, I suppose, to come up with something grand as a demonstration of my love. I might not put a video of it on Facebook, making a spectacle of our relationship, but I did think something...grand...was expected these days.

"Just...ask. Okay? When you're ready."

I feel a weight I didn't know was there fall away. First because she's removed all the social pressure, which is liberating, and second because she's basically indicated what her answer will be. She *wants* me to ask. She's going to say *yes*. My eyes widen just a touch.

Collins puts her hand on my chest and quickly says, "But not now."

"Right," I say, waving my hand in the air, overdoing my denial. "Pssh, I wasn't... Totally. I—"

"Okay," a man's voice booms from some unseen speaker. "I get it. You're unfazed by your surroundings. Congratulations."

The man sounds annoyed and maybe a little revolted by our romantic talk.

"Now," the man says, "turn around and look at the mess you've made."

Collins and I both turn around. The mirrored wall has gone clear, revealing a city in ruins. It's night, but the crumbling city is lit by a number of fires. I step toward the wall of glass, looking down. The destruction ends a block away, but stretches from one end of the city to another. Amid all the chaos, I see people.

Bodies.

They litter the street. But not one of them is whole. I've seen this before. When Nemesis first escaped Maine. She went on a rampage, but not for the joy of destruction. She was feasting, on people, to fuel her rapid growth. But this wasn't Nemesis, and we're not in Maine. This was a Tsuchi. We're looking at what remains of Lompoc, California.

"It ate them," I say. "It's growing."

"Yes," the man says. "*They* are."

23

"Where are they?" I ask, watching the emergency vehicles' futile attempts to put out fires and rescue the dying. We should be down there, coordinating a response. This is our job, and this ass... I take a deep breath and steady myself. Losing my cool will do no one any good.

"We don't know," the man behind the mirror replies.

"How could you *not* know?" Collins asks, sounding just as close to losing her patience as me.

"In case you have failed to notice, the sun has fallen."

I turn to the mirrored wall behind me and stab out a finger. "In case you failed to notice the past thirty years, there is now such a thing as infrared."

The man's response is calm, lacking any trace of defensiveness. "The Tsuchi's body heat is concealed within its armor. A normal Tsuchi can hide from thermal imaging when it is retracted within its shell. But these new...Kaiju-Tsuchi are armored, top to bottom, making them all but invisible to FLIR or any other thermal imaging. And before you ask, yes, that includes our digitally-enhanced vision system."

"That's a lazy name," I say. "Don't you think?"

Collins backhands my shoulder.

"What? It doesn't even spell anything. Devs? 'Hand me my Devs.' 'Looking through these Devs is like—'"

"Enough!" the man shouts, showing that he can, at least, be irritated. "How you people are still alive is a mystery to me. You respond to chaos with more chaos. You operate out of an old brick building and a cabin in the woods."

Collins and I both tense, but if the man behind the glass notices, he doesn't say anything. He knows about the cabin.

"Tell me, what is your plan now, Jon Hudson? If I were to set you free, what would you do?"

If I'm honest, I have no idea. He's right. We play this stuff by ear, adapting as we go, because there is no precedent for what we deal with, and there still isn't a weapon in the U.S. military's arsenal capable of killing a Kaiju. I know from experience that the Mother of All Bombs (MOAB), the most powerful non-nuclear weapon we have, doesn't work. And I'm not about to authorize or request that a nuclear device be used on U.S. soil, putting people at risk and maybe, at least in the case of Nemesis, who is a walking bomb, just making her angry. In her white form, it might work, but now? It's not worth the risk. So I have no idea what to do, not without more intel. But I'm not about to let the man behind the curtain know...though I'm sure he already suspects.

"Remain silent if you choose," he says. "Maintain some pride. But the truth is, you're broken. Your team is broken, separated by thousands of miles, in hiding or injured."

"Where is Woodstock?" I ask.

"Recovering," the man says. "In a hospital. He was lucky to have survived."

"And..." I'm about to ask about Alessi, but then I realize her identity might be worth concealing. "What about Lucy?"

"Lucy?"

Dammit. It was the first name that came to mind. I have always associated Alessi with Lucy Liu. They look a lot alike. But I can't use that name. What's a good Japanese last name?

"Are you referring to Maggie Alessi?" the man asks. "Half-sister of Katsu Endo, Zoomb employee and participant in corporate espionage, which in this case amounts to treason?"

I nod. "That's the one."

"She is alive."

"Can we see her?" Collins asks.

"She will remain with us until her purpose is fulfilled."

"And what purpose is that?" I ask.

"To ensure the cooperation of Mr. Endo, of course, who I have just come to understand has been operating under our noses. He's quite a cunning character."

"Yeah," I grumble, "He's a peach."

"You should be grateful to the man," the mystery voice says. "He played a part in your...team's survival tonight."

I want to make threats. To pound on the glass. But I know the effort will be wasted, and it'll make me look like an idiot, in part because I'm trained to deal with stressful situations like, oh, I don't know, three-hundred-fifty-foot-tall monsters, but also because I'm wearing a God damned toga!

Realization sneaks past my anger. Endo was undercover at GOD, and in a position to rescue the others, which means they raided the cabin, but took Endo along for the ride. "Specter."

"He was quite good," the man says. "Played by the rules and was happy to break them when asked. But he does have weaknesses, doesn't he? Had we known he cared so much for his family and friends, we would have never hired him. But then, we didn't know he had family or friends. The man must care about you, Jon. He risked exposure, and his life, to save you."

The idea that Endo...*cares* about me is frustrating. Yes, we worked together—reluctantly—and yes, we had a kind of weird, adversarial bromance going on when dealing with the last Kaiju crisis in Boston and D.C., but the man is a criminal. A murderer. The only thing we really have in common is our...what—Love? Obsession? Relationship?—with Nemesis. Or in my case, with Maigo.

"And again tonight, to save Maigo," the man finishes.

"Excuse me?" I say, tensing in a way that's impossible to hide.

"She is unharmed," the man says, "But she is no longer hidden."

I stalk toward the window, but only manage to stare myself down. "She will *not* become one of your Dark Matter—"

"There is no need to worry about that. Dr. Brice and his Dark Matter research is no more. As of last night, the collection and research branch of GOD has been cleaved away."

"Like the island," Collins says.

"Less intentionally, but yes."

"But isn't that what GOD did?" I ask. "Without the lab, what's left?"

"The lab was an invaluable part of GOD's mandate, and it will be missed until it can be replaced, but the research already conducted is still enough to carry us into the future." The mirror in front of me fades, becoming partly transparent to reveal a squat man in a suit coat.

He looks more like a mafia don than a government agent. At least he has the mustache. He'd fit right in at the DHS. "My name is Zachary Cole. I'm the Director of GOD. What remains of my organization is focused on practical application. We take the raw material provided by Brice and turn it into something useful."

"By useful, you mean weapons," Collins says.

"Sometimes yes. Sometimes...yes." The man smiles, his teeth perfect, as though chiseled from marble. "The point is, while you talk to the media and make a spectacle every time you face a Kaiju threat, we have been hard at work creating solutions."

I say nothing, not because I don't have a handful of Hudsonisms to fling at him, but because I'm listening.

"I'm pleased to see you're interested," he says.

Collins snaps her gaze toward me. "Jon, you can't make a deal with this guy."

"Sometimes you have to make a deal with a demon to kill the Devil," I say, and I turn back to Cole. "That's pretty much what you're proposing?"

"And when we are done, you can go back to your work and we will go back to ours, and your pretty little family of freaks can live without looking over your shoulders...as long as they behave. While you might have deemed those two girls harmless, we are already developing ways to...negate their potential."

"So, let's break this down," I say. "You have Woodstock and Alessi as collateral. You're willing to look the other way when it comes to Lilly and Maigo. And you're going to let us go."

"Yes."

"In exchange for what?" Collins asks.

"Do your jobs. Destroy the Tsuchi. *Kill* Nemesis."

"And leave the bodies," I say.

"Yes. You may not like what we do," Cole says. "You may not approve of our methods. But you are going to appreciate the results."

Again, I keep my quips to myself, because I fear he's right.

"Now, let's go back to your original question. Where are the Tsuchi? While we have been unable to track them, scattered reports of sightings and attacks have been filtering in all night. The smaller of the two is heading south. It will reach Los Angeles valley, and the millions who live there, at daybreak. The second, larger specimen is headed our way, and can wait."

"*Our* way?" I ask, turning back toward the window. "I thought it already left?"

"Looks can be deceiving, my friend."

I'm about to tell him he's not my friend and to screw off, among other surly things, but then the lights overhead blink off, plunging us into momentary darkness. Then the roof—the whole friggin' roof flickers and disappears. *What the...* The walls go next, transporting us outside. I spin around, watching the hallway and empty rooms pixelate and blink out of reality. The floor beneath my feet transforms from linoleum to bare concrete. The whole thing, including Cole. "A hologram?" I ask myself.

"But we touched it."

"Holodeck tech..." I say, in awe. "No offense, but if I ever get a chance to play with this, I'm going to have to program myself some Deanna Troi."

"As long as I get Jean Luc," she says, and we fist bump to seal the deal.

I turn in a circle. We're not in Lompoc. Never were. The air is hot and dry. The hard-packed sand around us stretches for miles in every direction, ending at distant mountains, revealed by the sliver of a rising sun. Other than that, the only thing I can see is an airplane, the likes of which I have never seen.

"I know where we are," I say, looking at Collins. "This is Groom Lake."

"Where?"

"Area 51."

A phone rings. It's coming from the plane.

Collins and I walk cautiously toward the blaring ring, which is the only sound for miles. The phone's glowing screen lights the way. I recognize the model. It's a Devine phone, putting us back in touch with the emergency services we coordinate. I answer it.

"Like the plane?" Cole asks. "Get in. You're racing the sun."

"Hate to break it to you, but neither of us can pilot this thing."

"No one can," he says. "It's a prototype VTOL X-35. Now, get in."

VTOL stands for Vertical Take Off and Landing. Looking at the thing's weird, almost diamond shape, I'm surprised the thing can even fly.

"In case the impending destruction of a major U.S. city isn't impetus enough, I failed to mention that Hawkins, Endo, Lilly *and* Maigo are en route...to LAX. Their flight lands in an hour. In fact, they're not far from you now, albeit thirty thousand feet up. Would be a shame if the Tsuchi was there to greet them instead of you."

"You didn't mention Joliet," I say.

"Injured, I'm afraid. But alive and well. Her hospital stay will be short."

Good to know, I think, and then I shift back to the topic at hand. "So, how do we stop it?"

"Everything you need is on board."

I look at the strange vehicle's lowered ramp, and then to Collins. She gives an almost imperceptible nod. We ascend the ramp together and stop when we see who's waiting for us. "Aww, c'mon."

24

I recognize the uniforms of the two men, but not their unmasked faces. But the size difference gives away their identities, or rather, their codenames. They stand in the large plane's cargo area, side by side, arms crossed, faces set on intimidate.

The smaller man, and by smaller, I mean he's my size—the other man is a giant—has the high and tight hair of a military man, but the skin and confident eyes of Denzel Washington. I reach my hand out to him. "Silhouette, right?"

"Agent Hudson. Nice to see you again." The man's smile and voice match Denzel's, too. I really don't like this guy. He takes my hand, a firm shake—not the crushing squeeze that alpha males deliver to prove their prowess, but which actually reveals their insecurity.

I turn to the bigger man, and point at him. He's a good foot taller and wider than me. All of that extra bulk is muscle. He's bald, but bearded. "Bruticus." He frowns. "No, that's not it. Grape Ape?"

The giant gives me all his attention, unfolding his arms and clenching his fists. "You think you can take me, little man?"

"Me? Hell no." I hitch my thumb at Collins. "But she'd kick your ass."

Collins just grins at the man with the same confident air as Silhouette.

"You about done?" Silhouette asks, climbing into the open cockpit and taking a seat.

I take the seat next to him without being invited. "Just trying to gauge how quickly Grape Ape over here switches to the dark side. If we have to work together, I need to know he's not going to go 'roid rage on us." I look back at the man. "You going to 'roid rage us, Obsidian?"

"My men are the best in the business," Silhouette answers quickly, preventing Obsidian from answering.

"From where I'm sitting, you're down two BlackGuard since the last time I saw you, and if I'm right, you got your ass kicked by a former park ranger, a biologist and two teenage girls."

The man's confidence falters as he looks at me. "Is that what you tell yourself? They're not even human. You might be the United States' golden Kaiju boy, but we've been dealing with Dark Matter threats since long before the FC-P existed. Those girls are going to grow up. And when they do, they're going to turn on you, like any wild animal does."

I'm about to say something pithy when he adds, "Your *girl* killed eleven men tonight."

While I have no doubt that any action Maigo took was in self-defense and in the defense of the others, taking a life is never an easy thing. The psychological ramifications are intense. And if he's telling the truth, Maigo killed eleven men. But...this is Maigo. She has memories of killing thousands, of *eating* hundreds. Another eleven might not have any effect on her at all, and if that's the case... I shake my head, trying to ignore what someone like that would grow up to be like. For the past year, Maigo and I have become family. I trust her with my life, and she trusts me like a father. But she hadn't been pushed until tonight, and the result was eleven dead men.

"That's what I thought," Silhouette says, and he starts the X-35, which is really just a gentle hum. He turns back to the cargo area, where eight seats line either side of the space. "Buckle up. This thing accelerates like you wouldn't believe."

Collins buckles herself in across from Obsidian.

The only indication that we've lifted off is the slight lurch in my gut. The engine just hums a little louder.

"Geez," I say. "What's under the hood?"

"Prototype," Silhouette says. "I don't know the technical details, but they call it a 'repulse engine.' Was designed by some robotics guy. I think his name is Mohr. Let's us take off and land, just about anywhere, and without making any noise. Now, best put on the mask. Unless you want to be unconscious."

Silhouette takes a mask down from a hook on the ceiling and straps it over his nose and mouth. Two tubes rise into the ceiling. I find my mask and put it on, while Obsidian and Collins do likewise in the back.

Without waiting to hear if everyone is all set, Silhouette guns the engines, and we go from a complete, airborne standstill to *Godknowshowfast* in sixty seconds. Even with the mask on, breathing is hard. I feel myself getting light-headed. And then, at speed, the G-forces wear off. There's no engine roar. No turbulence. The only indication that we're moving is the scenery below, just a thousand feet down, blurring past. When Silhouette takes his mask off, I do likewise.

"Shouldn't we be—" I point up, "—like thirty thousand feet higher?"

"The X-35 makes no noise. It's undetectable to radar. And we're moving so fast that no one on the ground will really get a good look at us before we're out of sight, and that's if they happen to be looking up. And if something happens to get in our way, we'll know about it in time to—" He flicks the controls to the left, spinning us in a rapid roll. I'm not sure how many times we spin, but my head keeps going even after he's stopped. "It's the fastest, quietest, most maneuverable plane on the planet. Even if someone managed to lock a missile on us, we're only moving at half speed. There isn't a missile in the world that can catch us."

What he's telling me isn't exactly comforting. I've never really had a desire to ride inside a missile. Still, it means we'll be in Los Angeles in—I do the mental math, estimating the distance at three hundred miles—eight minutes.

Holy shit.

Good news is, we're going to beat the sun. I watch out the window as the landscape grows darker beneath us.

"So," I say. "I have two questions."

Silhouette just glances at me.

"First. We're headed to Los Angeles to stop the Tsuchi. And I mean really stop it."

"Stop it dead," he says.

"How?"

He looks at me, more than a glance this time, then taps a few buttons on the very futuristic-looking console and lets go of the controls. He slides off the seat and steps into the back, where Collins and Obsidian sit in silence. He sets himself down beside Obsidian and waits for me to join Collins. Then he reaches up and pushes a button on the slanted wall above him. A panel in the floor opens, revealing three black devices that look like futuristic land mines.

"And these are?" I ask.

"Bacteria bombs."

"Bacteria...bombs?" Collins says. "Are we going to make them sick?"

"Bacteria do much more than make people sick," Silhouette says. "It also eats just about everything, including metal, arsenic, nuclear waste and any and every kind of flesh. Even Kaiju flesh. Once this stuff works its way into the target, it will eat its way from one side to the other, and then it'll spread out through the whole system. It replicates fast. If placed near the brain, death could take just minutes. Maybe less."

"Sounds like something that could kill a lot of people," Collins says. "How do you contain it?"

"Salt water," he says. "Or incineration."

"Sounds too simple," she says.

"Brice designed it that way. Simple solutions are the best. There are a fleet of C-130 airplanes fitted with Modular Airborne Firefighting Systems, loaded up with salt water, waiting for a green light. We just need to keep the Tsuchi out of the ocean after the device has been planted, and that shouldn't be a problem for them, since they can't swim."

"You *think*," I say. "They're not just Tsuchi now. They're Nemesis-Tsuchi, and in case you didn't notice, Nemesis is as at home in the water as she is on land. Also, just a quick nitpick. You used the words 'placed' and 'planted' when talking about the bombs. Since these things don't look like they can be launched, I'm assuming someone needs to get close enough to physically attach them."

"Close enough to toss it," he says. "Yeah. The launched system was less reliable, missing the target or dispersing the bacteria over too wide an area to be quickly effective. Once contact is made, the system will take over, drilling the device into place and exposing the surface to the bacteria."

I already suspect the answer, but I need to ask, just to be sure. "And who is going to do that?"

He offers that winning smile of his. "The only two people on Earth with that kind of hands-on Kaiju experience."

"Me..." I say, trying to think of who the second person would be, and already preparing to argue with Collins about it. But she doesn't make sense. None of my people do. While she's had some close calls, she's never been that close to—*oh no.* "Seriously? Endo?"

"It's why we recruited him. We were aware of his involvement with your efforts to combat Nemesis and her five siblings. What we didn't know is that he worked for, and has continued to work for, Zoomb."

"So you're sending us both off to die, is that it? Take care of the threat and your competition at the same time."

"Whether you die or not will be in your hands, Hudson. Always has been. But as much as we might like to see Endo suffer, Cole has ordered us to support your efforts. And we will."

Until we're done, I think. Then the gloves will come off. Cole promised to return Woodstock and Alessi, and to leave the FC-P alone. But even if Cole was being sincere, which I don't believe, I'm pretty sure the BlackGuard are going to hold a grudge for the men they've lost.

But for now, the enemy of my city-destroying Kaiju is my frenemy. Or something.

Silhouette looks into the cockpit. "Three minutes until we decelerate, which is going to be as fun as the acceleration. So let's wrap this up. What was your second question?"

I look down at myself and then at Collins, thinking it must be obvious. "Are we expected to fight the Tsuchi and Nemesis dressed like Grumio and Metella?"

Silhouette shows no reaction, but Obsidian chuckles.

"Grumio est coquus," the big baritone says, correctly identifying Grumio's profession.

"Really?" I say. "Someone finally gets the reference, and it's the oaf?"

"The oaf took Latin for four years," Obsidian says. "At Harvard."

Silhouette pushes another button behind him, and a second panel opens. This contains two BlackGuard uniforms, folded in neat stacks. He then heads for the cockpit, joined by Obsidian. "You have two minutes. I hope you can change fast."

Collins and I lose the togas, and start getting dressed. While I rarely miss the opportunity to steal a look at Collins dressing, I barely notice now. The three bacteria bombs sitting beside our clothes hold my attention, not because I fear one of them might go off and eat us all, but because they have the potential to kill Nemesis. While I can logically understand why that needs to happen, I'm not sure how Maigo is going to feel about it, and if she has a problem, what she'll do about it.

Eleven men...

25

When people back home asked Pixie Brearley where she lived in Los Angeles, she always replied, "On Sunset," and watched as people were either impressed or afraid. The reaction depended on what they knew about Hollywood's infamous Sunset Strip. It was a haven for actors looking for cheap rent at the heart of tinsel town. It was also populated by a large number of seedy elements, from drug dealers to porn actors to general freaks of nature that would make her conservative parents pass out. But it was where a number of stars got their start.

It also was a good eighteen miles away; a thirty minute drive without traffic, and there was *always* traffic. Brearley silenced her alarm clock and stared at the ceiling. She had two auditions today, one for a grocery store commercial she would probably get, and one for a sitcom that she wouldn't. She had a face that got her into auditions, but there was something—her voice, delivery, mannerisms, who knew?—that kept her from landing the big roles. This ever-present dichotomy depressed her. She was always on the cusp of having a career. A real career.

She knew she shouldn't complain. She got enough work to pay the bills. But it really just felt like a tease. Like if the Church had asked Michelangelo to do a comic strip instead of the Sistine Chapel. Sure, she might not be on the same level as a Michelangelo, but she had the potential. Or, at least, she believed she did. "Just like every other asshole in this town," she said to herself, sitting up in bed.

It was 6:00 am. The sun was rising, but her apartment building was still cast in the shadows of the San Gabriel Mountains rising up behind Montrose. The small town, technically a part of the much larger Glendale, was on the fringe of Los Angeles, but it had a small-town feel. It let her be close enough to work, without having to deal with the stifling inner-city life other wannabe actors seemed to enjoy.

Maybe that's my problem, she thought, *I need more angst.*

She stood and stretched, thinking she needed to get back to taking Yoga, but it was such a cliché LA thing to do, it drove her nuts. She wanted all the glory Los Angeles had to offer, without losing her Maine sensibilities.

That's probably the real issue. I'm not ditsy enough.

She turned to the chest-high bedroom window that stretched from one end of the room to the other and looked at the view. Or rather, the lack of view. Despite living quite close to the base of the San Gabriel Mountains, the grayish-brown smog stuck in the valley completely erased the surrounding landscape. Out the windows at the front of her apartment, she had an equally non-existent, stunning view of downtown Los Angeles. But she really only saw the mountains and the city from her apartment on the few days a year it actually rained.

While the rest of Los Angeles went ballistic over a quarter inch of rain, she just enjoyed the views and the ability to see more than a hundred feet. Right now, the towering mountains were vague silhouettes, backlit by the rising sun.

Something about the light held her interest. While she rubbed the crust from her eyes, she watched the sunlight shift about through the haze, like when someone walks in front of a light, breaking it up with a mobile shadow. But on a grand scale. That shadow loomed larger. Menacing. Her thoughts immediately shifted to the Kaiju known as Nemesis. She had been safe in Los Angeles during both of the creature's prior appearances, and the West Coast had been totally unaffected by the monster, or by the five others that had smashed a path of destruction around the world. Los Angeles had earthquakes, violent wind storms, brush fires and lung-burning smog, but *not* Kaiju. Despite that, she paid special attention to the monster, because its origins in Maine were only an hour away from her childhood home in Mechanic Falls.

The shadowy shape warbled through the view, almost vibrating, and then, it quickly shrank away to nothing. She rubbed her eyes, fixed on the shadowy mountain, but she could see nothing other than the blank slate of gray light.

Her phone chimed, prodding her onward toward her day. Every part of her morning was programmed into the phone as a series of reminders. Otherwise, she languished in the shower, or ate too slowly, or forgot to iron her clothes...and without fail, she'd show up late to an audition, which was the quickest way to lose the part, unless your last name was Lawrence or Johansen. *Do they even have to audition?*

She picked up the phone and headed for the bathroom. Normally, she'd hit the exercise bike first, then eat, then shower, but today's early audition meant skipping all that and eating an energy bar on the way. In the bathroom, she shed her clothing, turned the shower to scalding hot and waited for the steam to start rising. While LA, to her, was hot all year long, especially now in the summer, she still hadn't broken the habit of taking a hot shower.

Steam curled up over the shower curtain, and she pulled it open. She put one foot in the shower and stopped.

Was the ground shaking?

Another earthquake? She stood still, attuning her body to the floor beneath her feet. She could take a few steps back and be in the doorway, a not bad place to take cover during a bad earthquake, but she was on the second floor. If a bad quake hit, she'd feel better being outside. But here she was, buck naked and living next door to a guy she called 'Dirty Phil,' partly because he was a grubby kind of guy, but also because he was a leering perv. If she had to run outside because of an earthquake, she was going to do it fully clothed.

The shaking returned, rumbling steadily under her feet. She'd felt several quakes since moving to LA ten years prior, but none felt like this. They normally came in waves, lifting up and then sliding away. This was constant.

Increasing.

Maybe the wave is still coming? she thought. If so, it was going to be huge.

She yanked her foot out of the shower, bolted into the bedroom and reached for her clothes. The shorts went on first, commando style. She started to pull the tank top over her head, but she turned to leave. She could dress while running. But as she neared the door, a loud crash pulled her eyes toward the window.

I'm too late, she thought, turning, muscles coiling in preparation to run through the living room, out the front door and down the steps to the palm tree-filled courtyard.

But what she saw outside the window locked her in place, not because standing still was a better idea, but because some primal part of her brain knew that running or not would have no bearing on how things played out. She finally understood the deer-in-headlights phenomenon that everyone in Maine talked about. She could see into the future. Her fate was set. She was going to die.

The creature outside her window, charging down the hill, through Montrose and on a trajectory that would take it to the more densely populated cities of Burbank, Glendale and Los Angeles beyond, was *not*

Nemesis. But as it emerged through the haze, she could see some of Nemesis in it—the bright orange patches that could set cities on fire, and the overlapping plates of armor—but the comparison ended there. This...was a giant spider, with a wicked looking tail that whipped back and forth, shattering homes and lives. The creature itself was a hundred feet long, and nearly as wide thanks to its eight legs, but the tail added another hundred to its reach.

The worst thing about the monster wasn't its appearance, massive size or shocking speed. It was that as it ran down the hillside, flattening everything in its path, it was also plucking people up—from where they stood outside, through building windows and out of cars—and cramming them into its mouth, gobbling them down. It was like its many eyes, limbs and tail were working in tandem to guide it forward and simultaneously feast on the smorgasbord of humanity. There were ten million people in Los Angeles county. If this thing was just here to eat...as Nemesis had done on its way to Boston, it could act like a lawn mower, carving a path of destruction up and down the valley, tearing people from every nook and cranny of the over-populated cities beyond Montrose.

All of this flitted through her senses and mind in the two seconds it took the Kaiju to close the distance. As the monstrous form reached her building, and plowed right through it, Brearley clutched her arms over her head and ducked. She wasn't in a doorway. Wasn't protected by anything other than her own hands.

But she survived.

A breeze tickled her arms, and she lifted them away from her head. The back wall of her bedroom still stood, though the window was cracked. But the side walls and the entire front of her apartment, along with most of the building, was crushed to the ground. She looked up at the spider Kaiju as it continued down the hill, lifted Dirty Phil in one of its long arms and shoved his screaming form into its gnawing mouth.

I'm alive! she thought, and then she started forming a plan. She glanced left, looking to the car park, where her Toyota sat, unmolested. *I'll head east*, she thought, *through the Angeles National Forest and keep going until I reach the East Coast. What are the odds that this would happen in Maine again?*

She took one step to the dresser where she kept her keys and stopped. The world around her shifted. The apartment fell away. As nausea spread out through her body, she thought the second floor had collapsed beneath her. But when the whole world fell away, she knew that couldn't be. She looked down at the fading landscape and saw a long pole, like the end of an elephant tusk, protruding out from her gut.

Realization came in time with her ear-shattering scream that would have landed her a starring role in a Hollywood slasher film. The tail had swung back as the Kaiju continued forward, punching a hole through her back and lifting her up and over the monster, pulling her down, into the creature's gaping maw, which twitched and ground its previous victims like metal in a junkyard auto shredder. She was deposited in the jaws feet first, her mind exploding with pain, and then she was sent to merciful oblivion as the two mandibles shoved her in, jolting her body with a lethal dose of electricity once both made contact with her shoulders.

26

The butterflies in my stomach go Kaiju on me, tearing at my insides with ruthless ferocity, their razor blade wings slicing me into little *Yan Can Cook* chefs. *A little there. A little there. Done!* It's not because I'm expected to place a bacteria bomb on the back of an extremely lethal Nemesis-spawned Tsuchi, it's because we're about to disembark a DARPA aircraft to meet our team, along with two of the men who raided the cabin, shot Joliet and would have killed them all—if not for the interference of Maigo, whose abilities are now out of the bag, for the team, and for the enemy. As is Lilly's location. To heap even more insult after injury, Collins and I are now dressed in GOD uniforms.

"They'll understand," Collins says. She's seated across from me, looking as good in a black, armored uniform as she does in everything else.

"We'll see," I say.

Maigo, despite her constant state of near-silent glum, is a calm person. I'm not expecting much of a reaction from her, but then, I've never seen her face-to-face with men who tried to kill her and the people she cares about. She killed eleven men. So, I suppose she's really a wild card, which puts her in the same category as Lilly and Hawkins. While Joliet is the most rash of us, the normally cool-headed Hawkins has been holding this grudge for years. And while I can't say I blame him, knowing that GOD's experiments resulted in the deaths of his colleagues and friends, he might be quick on the draw. And then there is Lilly, who not only survived Island 731, but was born there, to a monster created by GOD. It wouldn't surprise me if her very DNA was patented by the secret organization. Of all of them, she has the most reasons to see GOD taken down, not to mention the ability to make it happen. I'd love to see it happen, but right now we need GOD, their fancy flying machine and their weapons.

The X-35 sets down on the tarmac with nary a bump, the VTOL repulse engines blowing my mind. Where will we be in thirty years?

Probably dead.

Or fighting zombie robots.

One of the two.

"Let us go out first," I say to Silhouette and Obsidian. "Smooth things over."

"No argument here," Silhouette says, and I give Collins a knowing smile. As badass as these guys are—and I've seen them in action—they're in no rush to deal with...with who? Not Lilly. From what I understand, Lilly never really took part in the fight, a fact that must be eating her up. It's Maigo they're afraid of.

Collins and I stand at the back hatch. I dial Hawkins on our new Devine phone. He picks up on the second ring. "Who's this?"

For a fraction of a second, I'm surprised by the tone, but then realize they haven't heard from us since our last known location was pancaked by Nemesis, and this phone no doubt shows up as an unknown caller. "It's me."

"Hudson." He sounds relieved. "Where are you?"

"Did you see the weird plane set down about three hundred feet from your Zoomb jet?" I ask.

"You mean the DARPA plane that Lilly is already on top of and we all have our weapons pointed at?"

I smile. "You guys are on the ball."

"We try."

"Well, when the hatch opens, it would be great if Lilly didn't gut me."

"That's you?" he says. "Did you steal it? I know Woodstock is good, but a UFO?"

"It's a little more complicated than that," I say. "And before I open this door, I need your word that no one is going to get violent."

"I don't like the sound of this..."

"How's Joliet?" I ask.

The question throws him, softening his tone. "She'll live. But she's going to be in the hospital for a few days."

"Then all of our people made it out of Maine, okay?"

"Who's in there with you, Jon?" Hawkins tone has shifted again.

"If I can work with Endo, you can work with these guys." My patience starts to wear thin, but I remind myself that he doesn't know about the Tsuchi threat to this area. "Just call Lilly back, and let's talk this out face-to-face. We have bigger problems."

The phone muffles for a moment, and I hear Hawkins whistle through his fingers and then shout something. There's a gentle thump on the roof. "Okay," he says. "She's pulled back."

"Coming out." I look back to the cockpit. "You guys are horrible at making friends. You know that, right?"

Obsidian gives me a sort of half smile and presses a button. The back hatch slides open without a sound and settles on the tarmac. We're on the southern end of the airport, where private jets are kept. Most of the small planes around us are gleaming white luxury planes, but the bright yellow Zoomb jet, sporting a logo on its tail and wings, shines like a beacon, despite the still rising sun just starting to peek over the distant mountains.

At the bottom of the ramp, the FC-P awaits, and they're not happy. They are, I note, dressed for war—even Maigo, who is wearing our standard, night-op garb and armor, which isn't as sophisticated as the gear Collins and I are wearing. Lilly is crouched, ready to pounce, but she doesn't move. Hawkins is trying to look around me, into the X-35. But Maigo...

She steps around the others and hugs me, breaking the tension. I squeeze her back as best I can with all the armor between us. "You okay?" I say into her ear.

"I'm not hurt," she says.

"That's not what I mean."

She leans back. Looks me in the eyes. "Been better...but I've been worse, too."

Good perspective, I think, and I smile. "That you have."

"Hudson," Hawkins says, but I hold up my hand before he can finish.

"First thing we all need to agree on is that sometimes, to do our job and protect the world from the kinds of threats the FC-P is charged with facing, we have to work with people we don't like. Take Lilly for example—"

"Hey," the cat-woman says, but smiles.

"And sometimes we have to work with people we loathe." I acknowledge Endo for the first time and offer my hand. He shakes it, and I add, "Been a while, douche-breath. How's the corporate espionage thing going?"

"Where's my sister?" he asks.

"And there is the problem," I say. "Your former employers, or faux employers, whatever you call them, currently have possession of Alessi and Woodstock. I'm going to assume you're all bright enough to understand the position that puts us in." When no one responds with anything more dramatic than Endo's twitching lip, I continue. "What do you know about Lompoc?"

"Nemesis is alive," Maigo says quickly, and with a trace of excitement.

"And you're lucky to be," Hawkins adds. "Nemesis did a number on Lompoc and the GOD facility."

They don't know.

"Well, you're right and you're wrong," I say. "Nemesis destroyed the GOD laboratory, but not Lompoc."

Endo puts his hand on my arm, and I have to fight the urge to sock him in the nose. I manage to resist, mostly because he'd probably dodge the punch and then level me with a spinning kick of some kind. "What happened?"

"Short version—" I start to say, but I'm cut short by what sounds like an air-raid siren. I'm about to ask what it means when I remember that I'm the one who picked it out. The sirens, installed in all major coastal cities, warns of an impending Kaiju attack. "—that."

"What is it?" Hawkins asks.

Collins lifts the Devine phone to her ear, saying, "A Tsuchi," before turning away, listening to the voice on the other end.

"I thought the Tsuchi were little," Lilly says, and then she reveals why hers and Buddy's relationship is the most strained at the FC-P. "Like a stupid dog."

"They are. Until they find a living Kaiju and do their thing to it."

"The Tsuchi implanted young into Nemesis?" Hawkins asks, jaw slack.

"And now we have Nemi-Tsuchi running amok. Yeah. Two of them. One here in LA and one headed east, whereabouts currently unknown. When I first saw them, they were the size of elephants, but I think we should assume they're growing."

"And fast," Hawkins adds. "As fast as Nemesis grew, the Tsuchi are faster. As long as they have the raw material to fuel it, they could be as big as Nemesis in a day."

"What raw material?" Lilly asks, her suspicious tone suggesting she's already figured it out.

"People." Maigo looks haunted as she speaks the words, no doubt recalling her own feeding frenzy.

"Lots of them," Collins says, turning back to the group. "The Tsuchi is making a beeline through Burbank toward downtown, eating everyone it comes across on the way, and here, that's a lot of people, even this early."

Unlike Nemesis, the Tsuchi won't have to go far to find more people to eat. There are enough to keep it busy for a long time. And if it can grow as fast as Hawkins thinks, it's not going to have any trouble finding enough food to fuel its Kaiju growth.

"Police put it at two-hundred-feet long, with a hundred of that being tail." Collins waits, the phone still at her ear.

"Have emergency responders, local, the National Guard and FEMA—everyone—filling the gaps behind it, but never, and I mean never, crossing its path. Any emergency vehicles already in its path should clear the area and move to the communities already affected. Triage protocols." Collins is about to relay the orders, but I stop her with, "And get me every military aircraft available. I want rings around this city thicker than Saturn's. But under no circumstances are they to engage until the order is given."

"Why not?" Hawkins asks, as Collins relays my orders.

"Because," I say, "We might have a way to kill it." I glance at Maigo. "And Nemesis."

She tries to hide her frown, but fails. Endo does even worse, but says nothing. I reach out for Maigo's hand, lock her fingers in mine and squeeze, leading her into the X-35, and toward our salvation, or our doom.

Possibly both.

27

"Where are we?" Lilly asks, straining her neck to see through the cockpit windshield. She's not the only one. Of the six of us, seated on either side of the plane's small cargo hold, only Maigo seems uninterested in the view. As usual, she's got her head down, face hidden by her long, straight hair. Normally, she's hiding from the world. This time, I think she's trying to hide her emotions from us. Nemesis, as horrible as the monster can be, was—and still is—part of her.

Endo reaches for the control panel Silhouette had used to open the floor panels. He pushes a series of buttons, looking comfortable, like he knows what he's doing. Of course he does. He was part of this outfit for six months. This isn't his first ride on the X-35.

The walls and floor around us flicker and then disappear. Lilly yanks her feet up in surprise. Endless city buildings zip past below. Nothing recognizable, just thousands of homes and businesses. And people. Lots of people. The air raid siren has warned them of the danger, but in a city of ten million, an evacuation quickly becomes gridlock.

"What the—" I say, but catch myself before I sound too stupid.

"There aren't any windows," Endo says. "Even the front windshield is an illusion. The images are captured in real time by thousands of high def cameras embedded in the aircraft's skin and displayed on the interior, which is really just a series of large, flexible screens."

"Just another piece of tech for you to take to Zoomb?" Silhouette says from the cockpit.

"I was never here for your technology," Endo says.

Obsidian backhands Silhouette's shoulder playfully. "He's got a Kaiju crush, man. That's why he spent so much time at Building-K."

Endo ignores them and stands, leaning toward the wall at my back. "They're touch sensitive, too." He places both hands on the wall and slides them away from each other. Like a giant iPhone touch screen, the image zooms in, bringing downtown Los Angeles into focus. He swipes the view up a touch and then zooms again, honing in on an aberration. His next zoom brings it into focus.

The Tsuchi.

It's bigger than was reported, and as it yanks an endless number of people from the city it's crashing through, stuffing them in its mouth, I understand why—it's growing. Fast. Just like Hawkins warned.

"Contact with Dark Matter in thirty seconds," Silhouette says. "Sort your shit out."

The first thing we all did after entering the X-35 was argue about who was going to plant the bacteria bomb on the Tsuchi's back. In some ways, it would be easier if none of us wanted to do it, and we were forced to draw straws. In the end, cold hard logic won the day. As much as I would love to not do this, I have the most experience with this kind of thing—aside from Endo, who did not volunteer. I'm not about to risk the others' lives on something that is my responsibility, and I outrank them. But...I'm not going in alone.

Much to Hawkins's chagrin, Lilly is coming with me, for obvious reasons: she's faster, stronger and can cling to a Kaiju-Tsuchi back like Spiderman on a wall. While Maigo's strength might surpass Lilly's, she's in a bad place and hasn't been training with the team the way Lilly has.

The view shows the city, and the Tsuchi, growing closer as the X-35 descends toward the U.S. Bank Tower, LA's tallest and most iconic skyscraper.

"You ready?" I say to Lilly. "No screwing around. No showing off. As good as you are, you've never dealt with anything like that." I point at the floor as we fly a thousand feet above the Tsuchi, now on the very outskirts of downtown.

She nods silently. She's either trying to be on her best behavior, or she's earnestly intimidated, which would be my preference.

I turn to Endo. "Arms out, I glide, arms back, I drop?"

"Like the wingsuit in Boston," he says. "But you can accelerate, once, for five seconds. The trigger is beneath your chin. Tap it twice. Or you can try flapping."

"I'd rather eat a bird than be a bird." Lilly is wearing an identical, all black wingsuit designed by DARPA and used by GOD. Except for the all-black design, it functions very similarly to the wingsuit designed by my ex, Jenn. While I don't think Jenn works for DARPA—she was way too anti-establishment to work for any kind of Man, government or corporate—I suspect this suit design might have been inspired by my wingsuit leap a few years back...with a few improvements. Unlike the bulky wingsuits worn by thrill-seeking enthusiasts, the ultra thin, super-strong fabric—made from goat-spider silk of all things—isn't bunched up between my arms and legs, restricting movement. It's all tucked away in the arms and legs, waiting for me to slap the button on my chest before springing out.

"Deployment in ten...nine..." Silhouette continues his countdown as the back hatch descends.

I turn to Hawkins and motion toward the cockpit. "Keep an eye on them, but take no action unless there's no other choice." I then turn to Collins and point at Endo. "Watch this asshole like a hawk." And then to Maigo. I take her hands. She looks up at me through her hair.

"We'll figure it out," I tell her. "We'll get through this, no matter what."

"Be careful," she says, and then to Lilly. "Don't let him get hurt."

Lilly gives a salute and leaps out of the still descending aircraft, landing on the rooftop thirty feet below.

Silhouette reaches "Three."

"Love you," I tell her, which gets a smile. I glance up at Collins, who is seated next to the girl. "Both of you."

There's a slight bump as the VTOL aircraft sets down on the roof. I pick up my bag and head down the ramp. Lilly waits for me at the bottom.

"That was mushy," Lilly says.

"Yeah, well, I'm sure your Dad would have appreciated a goodbye, seeing how it's likely we're both going to die."

Lilly looks up at the now rising X-35, its hatch sliding shut. She manages to exchange a wave with Hawkins. Then they're off, cruising over the rooftop and diving down the far side. Lilly looks a touch despondent. I must have hit a nerve.

I give her shoulder a whack. "Don't sweat it kid. I was just joking."

"Nice try," she says, and heads across the large, round helicopter landing pad on which we've been deposited. The landing pad is a massive white circle, with two red rings, one on the outer fringe, the second around a huge number 12. There's a one-story drop to the deck below and then a short, jagged wall that surrounds the roof like a child's drawing of the sun.

"All aboard," Lilly says, reaching her arms out to me. I throw an arm around her neck and hop up. She holds me in her arms with ease.

"My hero," I say, and then Lilly jumps. My stomach lurches and catches up with me a moment later when we land on the next level. Lilly deposits me on the floor, and we both head for the wall. In the distance, I can see Dodger's Stadium, or at least, what's left of it. I then lean over the wall for a view of Los Angeles's financial district below...and the monster destroying it.

The Tsuchi is two blocks away, making short work of a bunch of short buildings, all with tennis courts on the roofs. I don't think it's trying to cause destruction. It's more like a kid with a savage hankering for peanuts, destroying the shells to get at the morsels inside. In this case, people. I'm not sure how it's able to find all the people it's plucking from the buildings and vehicles nearby. It's like it can detect them without needing to see them. While the eight legs stomp through the short buildings, the tail whips back and forth, stabbing into the windows of the 55-story Bank of America building, pulling impaled victims out like an anteater does ants.

The creature is definitely larger than was reported. Its body and tail are both a good fifty feet longer, making it three hundred feet from one end to the other, but most of that is tail and limbs. The bulk of its body is still 1/3 the size of Nemesis. Big enough to land on if it's standing still, but its uncanny ability to pluck people from buildings has me concerned. Luckily, I've got a buzzing fly to distract it with.

The X-35 swoops around the square Bank of America building, its lines of windows looking like oversized pinstripes...at least, the ones that haven't been punched through yet. The Tsuchi pays the plane no heed, that is, until a chain gun emerges from its underbelly and opens fire.

As the line of bright orange tracer rounds stretch toward the monster, I cringe, hoping Obsidian, who I'm sure is behind the gun controls, knows to avoid hitting the bright orange membranes. Luckily, most of the Tsuchi's membranes are on its underside, but there is one on either side of its neck. Its eight eyes look like they could be made of the same explosive stuff, or they're at least covered by a protective layer of it.

My worry, it turns out, is misplaced. The thousands of rounds being spewed by the X-35 don't come close to any of the membranes. But they do hit the layers of impenetrable armor, ricocheting away into the city. I duck down as a window one floor down explodes from a burst of deflected chain gun fire.

The buzzing gun falls silent a moment later. In the brief pause that follows, the sound of falling glass rings out around the city.

Hundreds of shattered windows. I peek up over the wall. The chain gun decimated the facades of several skyscrapers, but it also did its job. The Tsuchi is now focused solely on the X-35, which is hovering at five hundred feet, back out over the path of destruction where the Tsuchi can't do much more damage than it's already done. It also puts the monster's back to us, which is what we've been waiting for.

"Let's go," I say, putting my hands on the wall, prepping to jump up and over.

A vibration rattling up through the building, and then through my body, stops me. I grab hold of Lilly's leg. She's already perched on the edge, about to leap. "Hold on!"

"What?" Her talons dig into the wall, rooting her in place.

The vibration rattles through us again. Through the whole city. And it doesn't coincide with anything the Tsuchi is doing.

No, I think, turning west. *Not now.* I run around the building's rooftop, stopping when I reach the western side.

In the far distance, through a curtain of light brown haze, visible only because I'm atop a thousand-foot-tall building, is a line of blue ocean. But the view is marred by the rising, black figure of Nemesis. She's huge, but moving fast, built for power and speed. It will only be a few minutes before she arrives, and there's no doubting why she's here. The Tsuchi. The fiery injustice Nemesis feels when mankind commits crimes against itself must pale in comparison to what the Tsuchi did to Nemesis. She's not interested in the city or the people in it. She's making a beeline toward downtown, flattening block after congested block, and she won't stop until she gets here.

"What should we do?" Lilly asks. "Let them fight?"

My face twists like I've bitten into a lemon grown in hell. "That's a horrible idea. This is a U.S. city with millions of people in it, not a Kaiju battleground. We're going to do what we came here to do, hopefully in time to turn Nemesis around, before any real damage is done." I climb up onto the wall and leap off. Lilly bounds over the wall after me.

28

As my fall rapidly approaches both terminal velocity and a terminal meeting with the ground, I slap my chest, and the wingsuit fabric snaps out. While my fall isn't exactly arrested, it is redirected and slowed, allowing me to pull away from the U.S. Bank building. A snap of fabric pulls my eyes to the right. Lilly glides beside me, a smile on her face.

Her confidence, while potentially misplaced, bolsters my own. After all, even if we die, what cooler way could there be to die than to wingsuit jump onto the back of a Kaiju-spider in defense of mankind. *History books, here we come.*

The wind rushing all around me blocks out all other sound, until the Tsuchi roars. The high pitched wail strikes me like a shockwave. Had I been standing on the ground, it might have stumbled me, but here, moving through the air, I punch right through it and continue on my downward trajectory, a human missile with a bomb strapped to his waist.

We streak past the ruined Bank of America building, twinkling panes of glass still fluttering from its gutted side, and then over what little remains of those weird tennis-court-topped buildings. Ahead is a flattened hotel, office park and the 110 freeway, where the X-35 hovers, just out of reach. They've lured the creature onto the freeway to avoid more structural damage, but the many lanes are already clogged with vehicles. Traffic is stopped to the horizon in either direction, with most people abandoning their vehicles and making a run for it. Despite the X-35's distraction, the Tsuchi continues its feast, plucking up fleeing people and devouring them whole. I can almost see the thing getting bigger. But the real problem is that it's picking off people without looking.

It's going to sense us coming. Our only hope is that people moving at 100 mph are harder to catch than those scurrying along the ground. I try to glance back over my shoulder in search of Nemesis, but I'm quickly pulled off course. I correct my aim back to the Tsuchi and fold my arms back, dropping down and speeding up.

Lilly follows suit, her ability to watch and mimic other people making her look like a seasoned thrill seeker, which I suppose in some ways, she is. After living on an island fraught with danger, she's been cooped up with the same group of people for a year. This must feel like a vacation. When she gives a loud, "whoop," I'm sure of it.

When we're within a few hundred feet of the Tsuchi, I splay my arms and legs wide, slowing down to make sure I hit the target, rather than flying right past. As Lilly and I slow, movement to my left catches my eyes. The long tail, pulling back from the Tsuchi's mouth, is swinging around, the giant jousting lance pointed straight at my side. It looks like it's moving slowly, but that's just because it's so damn big.

"Lilly!" I shout. My voice is lost in the wind, but Lilly's keen hearing picks it up anyway. She turns in my direction, eyes widening as she sees the impending attack.

I'm about to fold my arms back and hope the increase in speed will help us dodge the attack, but Lilly has other plans. She angles her body to the side and then rolls up and over me. Before I can understand what she's up to, I feel her land on top of me, her claws digging into my armor, locking us tight together. I don't see or feel her tap the button beneath her chin, but the two small rockets at the back of her wingsuit kick on and launch us forward, and down.

As we rocket toward the Tsuchi, accelerating past 150 mph, I catch sight of the giant stinger, sailing past, uncomfortably close. Simply diving wouldn't have done it. Lilly saved my life. Temporarily. We're still about to become smears on the Tsuchi's armored back.

Lilly's claws retract and we separate with just five seconds left until impact. It takes me two to reach up and slap the button on my chest again, and another two for the rapid deployment chute to explode out and unfurl, catching the wind and snapping my descent to a 20 mph impact. The remaining second is stretched into five, thanks to the chute, but the impact with the Tsuchi is still jarring. I hit the solid plate hard on my side, slamming my head against it. The Tsuchi rises up for a moment, and I slide toward the ground, the chute catching air once more and then snagging on one of the monster's many spines. I'm slammed back down again, a cowboy on a bucking Kaiju.

Hanging in place by my parachute, I toggle my throat mic. "We're down! Back off, so this thing stops thrashing like there's a bear trap on its nuts."

"Copy that," Silhouette replies, and the X-35 accelerates up into the sky, far enough away that the Tsuchi loses interest and settles back down onto all eight limbs. Silhouette's voice returns a moment later, trying to conceal his surprise, but failing. "Uh, are you aware that Dark Matter Three is en route to your position from the coast?"

"Her name is Nemesis," I say, trying to roll over onto my stomach. "And yes."

With my hands and knees under me, I get my bearings. I'm on the Tsuchi's back, but toward the tail end, which is the opposite end of where I want to be. But still, I wingsuited onto the back of a Kaiju. That's pretty impressive on its own. Now if only I could keep up that level of awesomeness... I unclip myself from the parachute and am immediately thrown to the side as the Tsuchi turns its attention back to downtown Los Angeles, and eating people. I roll hard, reaching out, but I'm slammed against a spine and spun around.

Then, all at once, I'm locked in place. For a moment, I think the Tsuchi has reached up and caught me, but when I look up, it's Lilly I see. With her talons locked into the armor's porous texture, she stands easily, bending her knees to absorb the vibrations rippling through the thing's back as it moves. Luckily, its eight legs mean the trip is fairly smooth.

Lilly grips the armor on my back and lifts me up. "Why are you here again?"

I squeeze my fists into balls, twice in rapid succession, the way Endo showed me. Hooked metal claws not too dissimilar to Lilly's pop out of the finger tips. "Now we both have claws." The DARPA climbing gloves are yet another high tech toy found in the X-35's many compartments, which, according to Silhouette, "contain the most advanced equipment and weaponry that the world's most elite covert-ops team could need. We have every potential situation covered."

"Claws, but not muscles," she says, tossing me ahead of her and then climbing past me with ease.

Using the claws to find good handholds, I climb over the Tsuchi's back. Lilly helps me up and over the overlapping armor plates, which grind and shift with each rapid step of the creature's eight legs. Once we're past the downward slope leading to the tail, we crest the top. I look down at the monstrous head, where the screams of people are crushed to oblivion, and a slew of eyes will see us coming. "It's all downhill from here."

I unbuckle the bacteria bomb strapped to my stomach. The round, black disc is fairly simple, and it already has a one-minute timer programmed in, just enough time for us to make our getaway...maybe. Odds are, we'll have to ride this out until the Tsuchi's mind is consumed by bacteria and it's dead on the ground. "I'll attach the bomb," I say to Lilly. "You make sure I don't fall off. But if I do, or something else happens to me..."

Lilly pats the other bacteria bomb buckled to her stomach. "Then I'll finish the job. Got it."

"Let's go—ooh!" The Tsuchi stops suddenly, and forward momentum pitches me forward. I tumble onto the creature's armored back and roll toward its head, coughing out air as I topple over the overlapping plates. I stop at the bottom, on my back. I open my eyes to Lilly, descending through the air. She lands next to me in an effortless crouch. "Smooth."

When she pulls me to my feet again, I freeze. We're standing, dead center, on the Kaiju's head. It's stopped moving now, and all eight of its eyes, though lacking pupils, are locked on us. But will it attack its own head? Not wanting to find out, I crouch down slowly, placing the bacteria bomb onto the armored shell. The device whirs loudly as the bolts automatically spin, digging into armor, locking the device in place. I push a single button, and stand, mission accomplished.

But before I can declare victory, jump ship or be skewered by the Tsuchi, my happy ending is ruined by the sound of a skyscraper plummeting toward Earth. The Bank of America building topples like a felled tree, pitching over sideways, and landing atop the clover leaf-shaped Westin Bonaventure Hotel. A shockwave rolls through the city, bursting windows. A cloud of tan dust and debris explodes out into the city, rolling between buildings and covering the freeway to the northwest, while leaving our position in the clear. All around, I can hear car alarms mingled with horrified screams.

The Tsuchi, Lilly and I all remain rooted in place, attention fixed on the fallen building and the towering column of smoke left in its wake. The rising soot is moving unnaturally.

Orange light flickers from within the cloud. It swirls away, pushed by something large from the other side. And then, she's here. Nemesis. The Queen of the Monsters steps through the smog and debris, orange eyes fixed on the Tsuchi.

She bellows a roar that makes my insides quake, but it's not nearly as loud as the shriek returned by the Tsuchi. I'm not sure if it's actually louder, but since we're at ground zero for a Kaiju roar, the sound sends Lilly and me down to our knees, hands over our ears.

When the roar fades and I open my eyes, my heart skips a beat. We're in motion, headed straight for Nemesis...and she's headed straight for us, arm raised to swat the Tsuchi like an oversized...well, like an oversized spider. Without shouting a warning, I leap onto Lilly's back, wrap my arms around her and stand straight.

As Nemesis's massive claws descend, I tap my chin down twice, triggering the jumpsuit's rockets. They're designed to gain altitude, or speed, when already moving, not for lift off, but they're powerful enough to do the job. My arms strain as Lilly and I are lifted off the Tsuchi's back. The first two seconds of propulsion only lifts us a hundred feet, but then, as Nemesis's arm swishes beneath us and slams into the Tsuchi's side, we cut through the sky, lifting up past Nemesis's snarling face.

With just a second of propulsion left, the X-35 swoops into view, its back hatch open. I angle us toward it just as the rocket cuts out. Momentum carries us forward. I reach out with one hand. The clawed finger tips catch on the ramp's outer edge. The jolting stop pries Lilly from my grasp and she falls, but not before we lock arms. Dangling by the ramp, I feel like I'm being drawn and quartered. My shoulders are about to pop out.

"How...much...do you...weigh?" I say to Lilly.

She gasps up at me, suddenly a teenager again. I'd laugh if it wasn't for the pain and the fact that I'm about to drop us on top of Nemesis's head.

29

I'm caught from above and look up into Collins's eyes. She's got me, both strong hands gripping my arm, Hawkins behind her, holding her belt with both hands. But Collins can't lift us both. Like me, her shoulders will give before she can haul us up. Maigo steps calmly into view, lays on her stomach and reaches out over the edge. She locks up for a moment, looking at Nemesis far below, but then she reaches out further, to Lilly. "Take my hand."

Lilly lunges up, tugging me down, and catches Maigo's hand. The weight falls away, granting relief. But then Maigo surprises me by taking hold of my arm and lifting both Lilly and me up onto the ramp. We all crawl back up into the X-35, its ramp already closing.

Endo, standing above the group as we huff and puff on the floor, greets me with, "Did you do it?"

"Yeah, we're fine," I say. "Thanks for asking."

Endo crouches in front of me. "I know that humor is how you communicate, but right now, my sister—"

"Is alive," I say.

He lowers his voice to something like a growl. "You have no idea what kind of people these are."

"I imagine they're a lot like you," I say, and that shuts him up, not because it was the world's most witty comeback, but perhaps one of the more accurate. "They have Woodstock, too. I don't intend on letting them keep either of them. As bad as you think they are, we're equally good, and I don't mean that in a happy-go-lucky kind of way, I mean that in a kick-ass kind of way."

"Damn straight," Lilly says.

"Now if you can back off, there are a pair of Kaiju destroying Los Angeles."

Endo stays locked in place, staring at me.

"Right. Yes. We put the bacteria bomb on the Tsuchi." I pull myself off the floor and into one of the cargo seats. I look down through the floor at the action below. "It should have gone off by now." I turn toward the cockpit. "Did the bacteria bomb explode?"

"They don't explode," Silhouette says. "They open, exposing the organic material to the bacteria. Then they eat their way through."

"How long does that take?" I ask.

"For the armor? A few minutes. After that, it should be like acid on a head of lettuce."

"A few minutes?" Sonofa... "That's too long. What else can we do?"

"Let them fight?" Obsidian suggests.

I throw my hands in the air. "What the hell? Are you all quoting a movie or something?"

"Actually," Lilly says, but I cut her off.

"Never mind," I say, watching the Tsuchi topple through the city, landing at the base of Wells Fargo Tower, a fifty-four-floor building shaped like a blade, perfectly matching its sister building, the KPMG Tower. The thousands of windows normally reflecting the sky, burst, sending twinkling shards of glass down onto the Tsuchi, which is struggling to right itself atop a McDonalds. As Nemesis heads for the creature, her back to us, I look at Lilly and she nods. I hate to say it, but today, that cat-lady and I are simpatico.

I look at Maigo, her scowl deep and concerning. As much as I'd like to talk this out with her, there are people dying down there, and it's my job to put a stop to it. The Nemesis below us is not Maigo anymore. She's—*it's*—a monster, no different from the Tsuchi. I stand, and grunt from the effort, my battered body resisting every motion.

Collins puts her hand on my arm. "You're in no condition."

"I'll go," Endo says, pulling out a wingsuit. But before he can start dressing, Obsidian steps into the cargo hold, already dressed to jump and with the third bacteria bomb strapped to him. The whole point of two people going was so that if one died, the other could finish the job. The bomb—a generous word for a device that simply opens—on his stomach ends the conversation. The back hatch opens again.

Obsidian smiles at Lilly and gives her a wink. "Just you and me, pretty kitty."

She hisses at him, while Hawkins sneaks up behind the big man and puts a knife to his throat. "If you come back without her..."

Lilly smiles up at Hawkins, puts her hands over her heart and silently says, "Aww."

"Yeah, yeah," the big man says, not at all intimidated. He puts his fingers on the blade and pushes it away from his throat. Then he steps to the edge of the ramp. He looks back with a slick grin, "Watch yourself, Ranger. We know all about your bear-killing days, your girlfriend back East, your old Indian step-dad, and—"

The man's threat is cut short when Lilly takes hold of the man and throws him out the back. She gives a wave and jumps out after him.

Pure, unadulterated rage flowed through Nemesis's body with the speed and energy of lightning. The raw power of it felt good, but not nearly as good as the rush she would feel when she took vengeance for the crimes committed against her. She learned that, when she had awakened. She had been struck first by the knowledge that she had been violated, her very flesh stolen from her. And then she had sensed the cries of hundreds of living things inside the building. While she had managed to exact vengeance on one of the creatures that had sprung from her body, she had also destroyed the building and those in it who had been guilty—of what, she did not know. Still, she had felt empowered when they were dead.

While the world around her cried out for vengeance, nothing called to her as loudly as the two remaining creatures. She recognized part of herself in her opponent, but she felt no kinship with it. The creature was a corruption. An abomination. And it needed to be destroyed. Not only because she had been wronged, but because its eradication would feel so right.

She craved it.

Hungered for it.

And yet, there was something else tugging at her thoughts, quietly whispering for her attention. Something familiar was nearby. Something... missing. And welcome.

The gentle tug pulled her attention upward, to a strange diamond-shaped object hovering above her. She had no memory of it. No knowledge about why such a thing would feel familiar. So she ignored it...too late.

Her opponent recovered from the blow that had sent it tumbling through the city. With impressive agility, it rolled back to its many feet, leaped up and clung to the side of the building. Its eight eyes glared at Nemesis with hunger of their own, but a different kind of hunger. If Nemesis fell today, she'd be eaten. But she felt no fear, only surprise as the creature sprang forward, limbs outstretched and open, tail pulled back and poised to strike.

The creature landed on Nemesis's chest, its eight arms wrapped around her, its bladed talons slipping past armor and into her thick, black skin. Nemesis roared, but her voice was cut short when the creature's mandibles bit into her neck. Bright blue bolts of electricity sparked in the air, coursing through her body, paralyzing her as the long tail stabbed toward her side.

But then, like Nemesis, the creature went rigid for a moment, as though struck by the same paralyzing energy. The blue arcs stopped, and Nemesis quickly regained her senses. She took hold of the long tail, stopped just feet from her side, and yanked. The eight blade-tipped limbs slurped from her back, and the creature came free, suddenly back to life and thrashing. Nemesis spun, swinging her enemy out, into and through a building.

As the building toppled, Nemesis released the creature, sending it sprawling into yet another building. The creature's back impacted the tall structure, holding it in place for a moment, before gravity pulled it out. The creature fell, landed on its feet, and charged.

But its aim was off. It ran sideways, stumbling about.

Injured, Nemesis realized, and her body flowed with energy once more, vengeance and the rush it brought within her grasp. She tilted her head back and roared into the sky.

30

Holy shit, Lilly thought as she watched Nemesis throw the Tsuchi through one building and into another. Joliet didn't like it when she swore, but she let the curse words fly in her thoughts. How could she not? Uncle Jon used them so often, and so creatively. He'd exposed her to the wonders of colorful language.

Obsidian, on the other hand, had no filter. The man was a few feet below and ahead of her. His voice was caught by the wind and dragged out as he soared on his open wingsuit, shouting a single word for a hundred feet, "Fuuuuuck!"

Despite his evident fear, Obsidian angled himself toward the back of Nemesis's head. It was a much smaller landing zone than the Tsuchi's back, but the dark skin up there wasn't armored. It would be a softer landing, and the bacteria bomb would work faster, too. Of course, if Nemesis made any sudden movements, they could be cleaved in two by one of the massive blade-like plates protruding from either side of her back, or they might roll off the side of her head, into one of the spikes, or they might follow countless other paths to doom.

Of all the potential for error, there was one problem Lilly had to overcome in the next few seconds—she had already used her chute. She had a secondary, but it was just your run of the mill parachute, not a rapid-deploy chute. In the time it took her parachute to expand, she'd hit the ground, or Nemesis. And even her physical abilities couldn't overcome terminal velocity.

She tucked her arms back, dropping and picking up speed, as Obsidian opened his arms and legs wide, slowing down in preparation to deploy his chute. She ducked her head, zipping right under the big man, and then, with a quick spin, turned and faced him, reaching up and grabbing hold, adding her weight to his own.

"The *fuck!*" the man yelled. She couldn't see his eyes behind the mask, but she imagined they were twisted up with fear. And that made her happy.

She looked ahead, her view upside down. They were rapidly approaching Nemesis's head as the creature kicked its way through heaps of debris, closing in on the Tsuchi, which now seemed confused. As Obsidian tried to shake her off, Lilly extended her claws into his armor and reached between them with one hand, triggering the man's rapid deploy chute. It burst up, filled with air and then snapped them to a stop—just twenty feet above Nemesis. But the Kaiju was moving fast. She'd be beyond them by the time the chute lowered them the rest of the way. Lilly reached up and swung her claws out, cutting through the cables. She and Obsidian fell the remaining distance. Lilly landed first, catching Obsidian and putting him down on his feet...on top of Nemesis's head.

If the monster felt their arrival, it showed no indication.

And if Obsidian felt any thanks for her catching him, he didn't voice it. Of course, he hadn't really reacted much to her hitching a ride, either. In place at the landing zone, he was already going to work, extending his suit's claws and removing the bacteria bomb from his waist. She was happy he was the one doing it. Nemesis might be a killing machine, but she could see Maigo still felt a connection to the monster. For the sake of their relationship, she didn't want to be the one ultimately responsible for the Kaiju's death, but she also couldn't ignore what she felt was her duty.

After leaving Island 731 with Hawkins, Joliet and Uncle Bray, Lilly had felt lost and alone, hiding from the world on a Ute reservation. Then came the FC-P, with Kaiju and action, and she helped save Washington D.C.! She might still have to hide from the world, but she was also living. Really living. And being part of this team meant everything to her. It was their job to protect the world from the weird, and that's what she intended to do. But in this case, she was happy Obsidian was the one pulling the trigger. And while he set the bacteria bomb, Lilly watched the Tsuchi stumble through the city.

It's working, she thought. *The bacteria is eating its brain.*

Lilly's heightened senses suddenly warned of danger. She ducked and spun around, claws extended, muscles ready to spring. Black tendrils reached out for her, snaking out of a weird-looking opening where Nemesis's neck met the head, just above the massive carapace that hid her deadly wings. It looked like a slimy, orange cocoon of some kind.

It wants to pull me in there. But why?

She backed away, bumping into Obsidian. "Hey, watch your—" He stood suddenly, eyes on the tendrils reaching for them. That also happened to be the same moment the Tsuchi twitched its legs out and caught Nemesis in the gut. The Kaiju pitched forward, flinging Obsidian from her head. Lilly reached for him, but the man fell down, straight into the waiting jaws of the Tsuchi, which, despite its melting mind, was still eating everything, and everyone, that it could.

Lilly lowered herself down, clinging to Nemesis's warm flesh. She checked the bomb. It was counting down. Fifty seconds left.

As Nemesis righted herself, the three-hundred-fifty-foot-tall behemoth came level with the now windowless thirty-fifth floor of the KPMG building. Lilly sprang out, leaping the fifty foot distance, but she fell several floors before reaching the building's exterior. She caught hold of an empty window frame on the thirty-third floor, the impact knocking the air from her lungs. She dug in her claws but felt the ruined wall giving way. Before she could fall, a pair of hands reached over and took her arm. "I have you," said a man with a thick Mexican accent.

While most of Lilly's cat-like features were concealed by the tactical suit she wore, her hands and face were exposed. The man showed a moment of surprise, but then started pulling. Lilly reached up and put her claws into the floor, pulling herself up. The man helped, but he couldn't have pulled her all the way inside by himself. Inside, they both fell back onto the floor.

"Are you like a super hero or something?" the man asked.

Lilly smiled at the man, who was dressed in a blue uniform sporting the logo of a cleaning company. "Let's go with: 'yes.'"

Nemesis's massive form moved past the building, her arms grazing the facade and peeling it away. The whole structure shook, but instead of running away, Lilly moved to the open window and watched. Nemesis dove forward, landing atop the now twitching Tsuchi, its brain and insides being turned to putty. The impact rattled the building top to bottom. Lilly watched as the sister Wells Fargo building, already weakened at the base, swayed back and forth.

The janitor stood next to her, looking down at the carnage. "Ay Dios mio."

"No shit," Lilly said. The Tsuchi was crushed beneath Nemesis's girth, but the larger Kaiju was still moving, slipping its massive claws between her and the Tsuchi. *What is it—?* Lilly realized what Nemesis was up to just a second before the claws pierced two of the membranes on the Tsuchi's belly. Exposed to the air, the fluid within detonated. The force of the blast struck the earth first, and then the Tsuchi, decimating the creature. Then, as the force met Nemesis's body, it exploded outward in a razor-sharp ring of destruction, slicing the bases of four skyscrapers—including the KPMG building. All four buildings toppled inwards at once. As the ground below came into view, Lilly grabbed the janitor, whose calm demeanor was replaced by a high pitched scream, and they ran for the far side of the crumbling building.

Desks, chairs and other office detritus rolled toward them, tumbling out of cubicles and offices. As the building's angle increased, the bombardment became airborne. Fighting gravity, Lilly dug her claws into the carpeted floor, using her legs and one arm to run, and the free arm to hold the man. As the floor's angle passed forty-five degrees, an office on the far side of the building exploded, releasing a desk, a chair, two filing cabinets, reams of loose paper and a photocopier. It also opened a clear path to the windows on the far side.

Leaping over the desk and shoving off it, Lilly toggled her comm and was immediately greeted by Hawkins's worried voice. "Lilly! Where are you!"

"KPMG building," she replied, shouting over the cacophonous rumble of a crumbling skyscraper."

"Oh God," Hawkins said.

"I'm not dead yet!" Lilly spun around a water cooler, getting splashed in the face as it passed. She looked at the janitor. "What floor is this?"

"Treinta-tercer!"

"In English!"

"Thirty-third!"

"Thirty-third floor," she shouted to Hawkins. "Near the middle of the building. We'll be out in five seconds."

She heard Hawkins yelling to someone and then to her. "We'll be there!"

Lilly focused on running the distance, ducking, dodging and scaling up the sides of the floor-bolted cubicle walls when she needed to. A ream of paper struck a cubicle wall and burst open, obscuring her view. With no other choice, she pushed through it and was greeted on the other side by the falling photocopier. It struck her left side hard, knocking her back, clipping the side of her head, breaking ribs and her arm in two places.

Lilly roared in pain and frustration, but she didn't fall. Her feet remained rooted in the floor. She turned to her passenger. "You need to hold onto me!" She put him in place beneath her, and the small man clung to her underside the way she had held onto Obsidian. With screamed exertion, she pulled herself back up and dug her right hand into the floor, which was now nearly vertical.

She glanced back. The ground raced toward them. Scaling the angled floor, Lilly charged upward. The way forward was empty of debris now, which had all fallen past them. Blue sky beckoned her upward. She roared again, pursued by the explosive sound of the building reaching the ground.

She leapt, slipping up and out of a window on the far side.

Smoke exploded up behind them.

Lilly looked for rescue, but didn't see it.

Then, at the apex of her leap, the X-35 swung around, its hatch open, Maigo in the opening. Their eyes met, and for a moment, she saw anger in her adopted sister's eyes, and then worry. They reached out in unison, catching each other's wrists, and through mutual, superhuman strength, they swung Lilly and the man inside the cargo hold. The rescued duo sprawled onto the floor, and passed out.

31

"Pull up!" I shout to Silhouette, but it's not really necessary. I've taken Obsidian's place in the cockpit, so my view of the building toppling toward the X-35's front end is the same as his. The towering building is mirrored glass from top to bottom, topped with a giant Deloitte & Touche logo, that's now peeling away, one letter at a time. When all but the first and last five letters fall away, I nearly laugh, but then I catch our reflection in the windows. "Faster!"

"Everyone hold on!" Silhouette says.

The shifting reflection of the falling building is dizzying. For a moment, there is sky, then the distant city and then the destruction below. And then, in a sudden tunneling of my vision and crushing force against my chest, it all slides away.

I'm nearly unconscious by the time the X-35 comes to a halt. In seconds, we've traveled miles. Adrenaline fuels my pounding heart, returning blood to my brain. "Take us higher. I want to see."

We rise up steadily, and the view of a mostly flattened and smoldering downtown Los Angeles comes into view. The fleet of C-130s can be seen far below, disgorging their contents, not on the fires, but on the dead Tsuchi to prevent the bacteria bomb from spreading.

I look back at the group. Collins is tending to the stranger dressed like a janitor. Hawkins is leaning over Lilly, and he notices my attention. "She's hurt pretty bad. Going to need a hospital."

"We'll get her taken care of," Silhouette says.

Hawkins looks ready to dive into the cockpit and start throwing punches. "The hell you will."

"Look," the now teamless BlackGuard leader says, "I saw what she did down there. Despite our actions against your people, she tried to save my man. That counts for a lot with me. I won't let them take her, even if Cole orders me to. You have my word."

"Aww, look at that, Hawkins," I say, "you have your very own frenemy." I glance toward Endo, who is still seated, paying me no attention, eyes out the front window...or projection. Whatever they're called. "Isn't it fun?"

"She's rising," Endo says, his voice a reverent whisper. He stands up and moves behind Silhouette, watching.

Maigo steps around the group, standing beside Endo, her face grim.

"She's too strong for them," Endo says to her. "She will not be defeated."

I'm not sure if he's just being hopeful or honestly confident that the bacteria bomb, which clearly worked against the Tsuchi, won't be effective against Nemesis. But we're going to find out soon enough, and I'm undecided about which outcome I'm hoping for. The same cannot be said for Endo and Maigo, who watch the unfolding scene like Red Sox fans do the last pitch of the final game in a tied World Series.

"There!" Endo says, pointing to the heap of destroyed skyscrapers lying over each other. The mound of crushed buildings rises, splits and then gives birth to Nemesis.

She stands slowly, shedding building remnants as she rises, getting to her feet and then shaking off Los Angeles like a wet dog. Beneath her is a charred swath of city and the crispy remains of the Tsuchi, recognizable only because its layers of armor are somewhat intact.

On her feet, Nemesis turns her head skyward and lets out a bellowing roar, looking more powerful than ever, as if the battle, instead of wearing her down, has only stoked the fires within her. She kicks her way free of the wreckage and surveys the area. Apparently satisfied, she turns first to the coast, and then inland, to the northeast.

Toward the second Tsuchi.

She takes one step to the north, which will take her through countless, densely populated cities, many of which have already been ravaged by the Tsuchi.

But then she stops, looking stunned. She turns her head back and forth, like someone who's just been tapped on the shoulder, but doesn't know by whom. And then the big Kaiju flinches, snapping her head back and roaring in pain.

At that same moment, Maigo winces and grabs her head, falling to her knees. The connection then projects to me as a dull headache.

"It's burning her," Maigo says.

Nemesis stumbles out of downtown, headed east now, toward the coast. She rakes at her head with the big claws, tears at her thick skin, no doubt removing the bacteria bomb in the process, but not the bacteria. It's too late. It's eating through her several feet of skin and will soon reach her brain.

Maigo closes her eyes and lowers her head. For a moment, I think she's simply calming herself, but then I hear her gently whisper, "Run...run!"

And Nemesis does. I'm not sure whether Maigo actually managed to issue a command, or a suggestion, or if she still knows how Nemesis thinks, but the monsters runs.

Straight for the ocean.

For salt water.

Entire blocks of Inglewood neighborhoods are flattened.

How many people is she killing this time?

"She can save people, too," Maigo says to me, once again knowing my thoughts. "From things that no one else can."

"Killing thousands to save millions?" I say. "You think that's okay?"

"What if it's billions?"

I have no argument for that. The old Star Trek 'Needs of the many outweighs the needs of the few,' is a logical statement. But what good is logic, and saving lives, if you have to sacrifice your soul to do it? There are people dying below us. Children. Where is the justice in that? Who will take revenge on Nemesis for the death and pain she causes?

Just two miles from the ocean, skirting the edge of LAX, she flinches, roars and catches her foot on the swirling overpasses where the 405 and 110 freeways intersect. Nemesis stumbles, falls and rolls, leveling the Airport Courthouse building and the surrounding neighborhoods.

Is that it? Is she down?

"Get up," Maigo whispers, tears in her eyes. "You're almost there."

Once again, the monster seems to hear her words. Nemesis stands, stumbling to the side, her mind feeling the first effects of a bacterial assault. Then she's up and moving again, headed toward the now nearby coastline.

From our position high above, I can see what lies ahead. The neighborhoods come to an end, which is a good thing, but in their place is a treeless path of earth absolutely covered in massive, white oil tanks. "What is *that*?"

"Chevron refinery," Endo says.

I'm torn by indecision. If we let her go through the refinery, we're going to have an ecological disaster on our hands, at best. At worst, the place will go up in flames and take half of the city with it, maybe more. But if we can somehow force Nemesis around the refinery, she'll be once again storming through neighborhoods.

"There's nothing we can do," Silhouette says, ending my silent debate. He's right. There are no weapons on board that she'll even feel. We just need to hope the bacteria does its job in time.

But it's clearly not. While Nemesis's gait is awkward and stumbling, she never slows her pace or trajectory. She reaches the refinery, crashing through a field of oil tanks. One by one, they rupture and disgorge their contents like thick, huge, milk cartons full of black milk.

But nothing explodes.

That is, until the squadron of Air Force jets I called in when this began decides to take matters into their own hands. I see a group of five swoop around, heading for Nemesis. I call back to Collins, "Call the Air Force off! There's no—"

"Too late," Silhouette says, and the seatbelt digs into my chest as we rapidly decelerate.

Missiles streak out from the array of jets. The pilots are no doubt locals, or have lived in the area long enough to feel an affinity for it. Whatever the case may be, their bleeding hearts have led them astray.

As we decelerate to a stop, the missiles close the distance to Nemesis as she nears the far end of the refinery, and the coast just a beach beyond that. I take Maigo's arm. She snaps out of a trance-like state and looks up at me. "Buckle up! Everyone buckle up!"

She leaps back into her seat, and I'm relieved to see that Lilly, still unconscious, is buckled in next to Hawkins, and the stranger next to Collins, all ready for what's about to happen. I turn to Silhouette. "Mach 6, huh?"

He nods, punching buttons. "I'm setting the autopilot to disengage in sixty seconds. Any more than that and we'll be paste."

"Sounds fantastic. DARPA should open an amusement park." The missiles are seconds away from Nemesis, who is coated in oil and standing in the world's largest oil spill, surrounded by how many gallons of oil? Millions? More? Whatever the case may be, in a few seconds it will all be gone. "Better hurry."

The missiles make contact, the first few striking Nemesis's back, doing her no damage, but setting the oil coating her on fire. The flames streak down her back, but will they reach the refinery before she reaches the ocean?

I root for her, hoping she'll make it three more long steps to the water before the fire streaking down her back reaches the ground. And then, in a flash, it doesn't matter. A missile strikes and breaches one of the bright orange membranes, unleashing a force equivalent to a small nuclear strike. I catch a glimpse of light, Nemesis sprawling sideways, the oil refinery going up at once, and then, as quick as I can snap my fingers, it all shrinks away, growing smaller, and then dimmer, until there's nothing left but darkness and the sweet relief of unconsciousness.

32

My senses return slowly, starting as a prickling in my toes and working upward as the blood flow in my body normalizes. The pins and needles stabbing my limbs wakes my mind. I open my eyes to a view of what used to be El Segundo and Manhattan Beach. The area is a smoldering ruin. A two-mile-wide black circle of earth surrounds the decimated refinery, of which there is now no trace. At the fringe of the circle is an ever-widening ring of fire, eating through neighborhoods, fueled by the ocean breeze.

I turn my attention to the now-glass beach just beyond the refinery. The burned black circle ends at the water, which is slick with burning oil, but nothing else.

"She's gone," Endo says.

I turn to find him sitting beside me in the cockpit. A glance back reveals Silhouette in the back, buckled in, gagged and bound at the wrists and ankles. Despite being stripped of his uniform, dressed only in black boxer briefs and a black T-shirt, he's sitting calmly. Biding his time.

Endo glances back. "We can't trust him."

"I don't trust *you*." I look at the others. Hawkins and Collins are starting to stir. Lilly and the janitor are out cold. Maigo is wide awake, looking past us, out the front window. "Maigo."

Her eyes snap toward me.

"You okay?"

"She almost died," the girl says. "You almost killed her."

I've got nothing to say to that. It's true. And I understand how she feels. There was a time when I wanted to save the monster, despite the destruction she wrought, but that was when Maigo was still a part of the monster. Now, Nemesis is just...Nemesis, an ancient and alien goddess of vengeance who cares nothing for the people she crushes underfoot.

I turn to Endo. "What now? I'm assuming you have a plan, since you've hijacked our ride."

Endo works the controls, and the X-35 pulls up and away from the carnage. "Emergency services are doing what they can here. DARPA's C-130s dumped their payloads on the city, but are being reloaded to help stop the fire." That he knows and addresses my concerns before giving an answer irks me. I don't like being known by this man. He sets his eyes on me. "*We* are going to get our people back."

He spins us around and accelerates, but not so fast that I need to put on the mask.

"And how do you intend to do that? Fly into Area 51, waltz inside like we own the place, maybe with Hawkins as a prisoner, and stroll back out with Alessi and Woodstock?"

He smiles and points at Silhouette's uniform resting on the floor behind us. That's exactly what he plans to do. "Seriously? We're borrowing rescue plans from Star Wars now?"

"We even have a furry prisoner to take with us," Endo says. "We can have her wounds tended to before leaving."

I stare at him, confounded. Area 51, while no longer a big secret, is still a heavily guarded military base in the middle of nowhere, and apparently one of many installations where DARPA, or perhaps just GOD, operates. Even dressed as Silhouette, I don't think we'll make it past the tarmac.

He must sense my impending line of questioning, because he says, "We are going to be the least of their worries." I wait for the punch line, and he delivers it. "The second Tsuchi spent the night charging northeast, through California and into Nevada. It was last reported in Pahrump, just fifty miles from Vegas."

"Geez," I say. Vegas's population is just over six hundred thousand, but tops out at two million if you count the surrounding suburbs. It's potentially double that if you count the tourists. "Area 51 scrambled its forces to defend the city, didn't they? The base is vulnerable."

"Uh-huh," Endo says.

"Then we need to go to Vegas, too. It's our job to—"

"The Tsuchi isn't going to Vegas," Endo says.

"What makes you think that?"

"I understand them."

I try hard not to roll my eyes. Endo is obsessed with Kaiju, Nemesis in particular, but he fancies himself a regular monster whisperer. "And what do you understand?"

"That a creature begotten by Nemesis might have a thirst for more than flesh and blood."

There are two things I really hate in this world: *The Golden Girls* and Endo being right. While the first Tsuchi showed a clear preference for densely populated areas and the people within them, the second charged northeast. I'm sure it's had plenty to eat along the way, but a good portion of its path was empty desert. If all it wanted was food, it could have headed up the coast, while its now dead sibling went south. So it was being drawn by something else: vengeance. Like Maigo, it might retain the knowledge of what had been done to the Tsuchi who spawned it. The creature held a grudge, against GOD. "It's going to Area 51. But why? It left the GOD building in Lompoc alone."

"It's after Brice," Endo says.

"Brice is dead."

"One of them is."

"One of them?"

"Alicio Brice was one of the first U.S. scientists to work with Unit 731 after the war. He formed GOD and established Island 731 as an official black operation long before there was a DARPA organization to hide behind. The first Brice has been dead for thirty years. The man you met was one of many clones, all created by the first, all instilled with his knowledge and ruthless search for knowledge."

I'm about to point out Endo's similar personality flaws, but hold my tongue. If I'm stuck working with the man again, I need him on our side, at least until I'm in a position to bring him down. I also know now that Cole was lying about ending GOD's biological weapons program. With a cache of Brices, the research could continue indefinitely. It's then that I realize I haven't even questioned the notion of clones. Has my life become so insane that human cloning is barely a blip on my weirdar?

"The remaining Brices, ranging in age from twenty to forty, operate out of Area 51. If the Tsuchi senses them the way Nemesis would a single offender, it will be drawn to them, its thirst for vengeance overpowering."

"And what about Cole? Is he a clone, too?"

Endo shakes his head. "He's a genius, like Brice, but not in the scientific way. He's not a fan of Brice, or much of what he does, but he appreciates and utilizes the weapons being developed."

"Ends justify the means," I say. "I get it. So when does the shit show begin?"

Endo glances at the X-35's digital displays. There are screens full of numbers and instruments I can't make sense of, but the map, with a dot quickly moving atop it, is clearly our position in the world. "We'll be there in ten minutes. Better get dressed. And wake the others."

Nine minutes later, after dropping off the shell-shocked janitor outside the Little A'Le'Inn—a small restaurant and inn welcoming

UFO fanatics to the outskirts of Area 51, where he was excitedly received as an abductee—I've exchanged my GOD uniform for Silhouette's, which is just different enough to be recognizable. Thankfully, we're close enough to the same size that it fits well. The ensemble is completed by the head piece and mask, which Endo claims the man rarely removed. Apparently, the BlackGuard leader preferred to keep people guessing, even his superiors.

Hawkins has also dressed in a uniform and concealed his face behind a mask. He's bigger than me, and he'll be playing the part of Obsidian. He's not quite as big as the BlackGuard behemoth, but if no one scrutinizes him, it could work. Endo wanted to leave everyone but Lilly behind. Her injuries would grant us access to the infirmary, where he was sure we would find Alessi and Woodstock. But Hawkins wasn't about to let Lilly out of his sight, and if Endo is right and a Tsuchi is going to attack the base, I'm not about to leave Collins and Maigo on the surface. Silhouette on the other hand, bound and seat-belted...he's on his own.

"Two miles out," Endo says. "We'll be on the ground in forty seconds. When the hatch opens, follow me." He looks at me. "If anyone questions us, keep your answers short and terse. Lower your voice an octave, if you can. Everyone, even Cole, should feel like you're on the verge of getting violent. No one wants to be on your bad side."

I glance at Silhouette. He's staring right at me. We are most definitely on his bad side. That could be a problem someday.

Endo taps my arm with the back of his hand and points out the windshield. "Look."

Looking out the front, it takes no effort to find what he's pointing at. The Tsuchi, a good four hundred feet from mandible to tail tip, races across the barren terrain below, leaving a towering trail of dust behind it. "Why haven't they spotted it yet?"

"They're watching Vegas," Endo says, "but they'll know it's coming when it passes the motion sensors a mile out from the base."

We cruise over the Tsuchi and a line of mountains. Area 51 comes into view ahead and below. We swoop down toward it, the Tsuchi closing in, and our friends, according to Endo, are fifteen stories underground. This...is going to suck.

33

By the time the X-35 ramp lowers, the base is coming to life. Soldiers run about, armed and ready for war, most of them lugging heavy weapons instead of standard rifles. Several large auto turrets, like those used by the BlackGuard in Oregon, but much larger, rise out of the concrete. They're joined by several missile systems rising from the ground. They look like surface-to-air missiles, but I suspect they'll work just fine against something that's two-hundred-feet tall. It's clear that all the action has nothing to do with us, and everything to do with the Tsuchi cresting the 6000-foot-tall Papoose Mountain, just south of the base. From above, the Tsuchi didn't look too dissimilar from the first, but I can now see that its four rear legs are stocky and powerful, with wide, split claws at the base, rather than the scimitar blades.

I wave the others down the ramp, saying, "Let's move. Go, go, go."

When everyone, except the bound Silhouette, is out, Endo steps up next to me. "Try to slow down. Stay calm." He motions to Silhouette. "You're supposed to be him now." I look at our captive, tied up and gagged in the back of a vehicle that might get tromped by a Kaiju Tsuchi. Despite what I would call a worst case scenario, he's calm as can be, like he's got the situation under control.

"Right," I say. "Lead the way."

Endo strikes out at a relaxed pace, not even glancing up when two AH-64 Apache attack helicopters loaded for bear fly overhead. Our small group, all dressed in BlackGuard uniforms, faces covered by masks, head across the tarmac. Lilly is similarly dressed, her face hidden, but she lies on a field stretcher carried by Hawkins and Maigo.

The buildings ahead aren't very impressive, and I think that's the point. The base remained a secret for a long time, thanks to its uninspiring facade. Long hangars, single-story buildings, bland structures all the way around. Looks more like a low budget construction company than a top secret base developing and testing the most advanced tech in the world.

According to Endo, and conspiracy theorists, it's all a sham. The real action is underground, and even if the entire world knows it, who cares? They still can't see what's going on here. But we're about to.

It takes all of my restraint to not look back when I hear missiles take to the sky, multiple explosions and the Tsuchi's high pitched roar. But I manage to stride on like it's no big deal.

Endo leads us to a small building that looks like a double-wide mobile home. The steps look like old wood, but they're solid metal. At the top, the door, also faux worn and solid steel, slides open smoothly. The short hallway on the other side of the door ends at an elevator, one of many hidden in the buildings around the base—or rather, bases, plural—with each elevator leading to a different black operation, all protected by the U.S. Air Force, who likely has no idea what really goes on below ground. Two guards, dressed in black, flinch at the sight of us. They're either spooked by the knowledge that a Kaiju is approaching, or by the sudden appearance of the BlackGuard.

We head straight toward them and stop. I wait in silence, glaring at the men, letting them think it's Silhouette behind the mask. Finally, I say, "Dark Matter for the infirmary."

One of the men, let's call him Chuck, looks past me, at Lilly. "Looks like one of ours."

He's right, so I lift off her mask, revealing her feline face. She twitches, but doesn't wake, still out for the count, which is definitely concerning. Endo better be right about getting her some fast help here.

Perhaps bolstered by Chuck's questioning, the second man, we'll call him Bob, inspects the rest. "I heard you lost men."

"New recruits," I say, slowly turning my reflective face on Bob so he can be reminded about how worried he looks.

Bob forces a laugh and hitches his thumb toward Collins. "Since when does the BlackGuard recruit wom—"

Collins cold cocks Bob in the side of the head, dropping him in a crumpled heap.

Chuck reaches for his gun, but Endo, Collins and I are all faster on the draw. Before he gets the weapon from its holster, he's got three muzzles leveled at his face.

"Are you aware of what we lost today?" I ask, making sure my voice is low and threatening.

"Ye-yes, sir."

"Then you must also realize that I am in a really, *really* bad mood." I push my weapon into his forehead. "You know they won't care if I shoot you, right? You are dispensable. I am not."

Chuck is shaking a little bit right now. I've never instilled this kind of fear in someone before. Silhouette must have a seriously nasty reputation.

"Now call the God. Damned. Elevator."

The man places his hand on the palm print scanner. Blue light flashes back and forth, and the elevator doors slide open. Once we're inside, the doors closed, Collins says, "Too much?"

"Just right," Endo replies. "And not the first time one of them has been punched." He pushes one of three elevator buttons.

"Only three levels?" I ask.

"Three main levels, each with more elevators going down. But we are primarily interested with what is on levels one and three. Any lower could be...dangerous. Even for the BlackGuard."

"What's below level three?" Hawkins asks.

Endo looks back at Obsidian's doppelganger. "Answers."

"To what?" Collin says.

"To everything."

"Okay, thank you Captain Cryptic," I say. "But why level three? I thought the infirmary was on the first level."

"It is, and you'll see. It's not something I can easily explain, but...you need to know what you're really up against."

"Make sure you add mysterious and foreboding to your eHarmony account." I straighten my relaxed posture as the doors open, but the act is for nothing. The hallway on the other side is empty...and gloomy. The hall is round, like a large sewer pipe. A grated metal walkway is mounted to the curved floor. The lights along the ceiling are yellow and caged. This place is built like a Cold-War bomb shelter.

A vibration moves through the tunnel. The Tsuchi is waging a war on the surface, but can it reach us, GOD and the Brice clones down here? Feeling a sense of Endo's foreboding, I head down the hallway, each footfall echoing loudly on the metal floor.

"Second door on the right," Endo says.

As we pass the first door, I glance through the window into a sophisticated control room with large, interactive displays, tech I don't recognize, Zach Cole and more than one Alicio Brice. My plan is to continue past without stopping, but I fail to stop myself from doing a double take. Not because of who I saw, but because of what was on the large screen—Nemesis. On land. Not in LA or pre-recorded anywhere on the East Coast during the last two years. The barren desert she's stomping over is definitely West Coast, meaning this picture is live.

It takes all my will to move forward, but I need to get Woodstock and get out of here before the Tsuchi puts the smack down on this place. As we approach the second door on the right, I note that it is guarded. Not wanting to dick around with the guy, I walk up to him, look him in the eyes—and he steps aside, unlocking the door with his handprint. I was going to knock him out and use his hand, but this worked out well enough. Our group files inside. It looks like a small hospital, with rooms on either side of three hallways, left, right and straight ahead.

Endo points to the right and looks at Hawkins and Lilly. "You'll find a large, clear, pill-shaped device at the end of the hall. Put her inside, seal the hatch and step back. Do not interfere until it is finished." He points to Collins and me. "You two with me."

"You sure about this?" Hawkins asks me.

"If you're not comfortable, we can wait, but we don't know how she's doing."

"I have no reason to lie," Endo says, "And I harbor the girl no ill will."

Hawkins stands motionless for just a moment and then makes up his mind, leading Maigo and the unconscious Lilly down the right hallway.

A nurse steps out of a nearby office and looks surprised to see us. "Oh. You guys again." She's also not very intimidated.

"Looking for the old man and the young woman brought in with him."

"You mean Old Timer Magnum P.I. and Lucy Liu?"

On the inside, I'm shouting "Yes!" and hugging the woman for seeing the world through the same sarcastic lens as me, but I maintain my cold exterior and say, "Sounds like them."

She points straight ahead. "End of the hall."

Without a thank you or nod of appreciation, I head down the hall with Collins and Endo. The door at the end is locked, a hand print reader beside it. The nurse clearly believes that Silhouette or the BlackGuard could unlock the door. We've been lucky to have quasi-willing guards at the other doors.

"Maybe you're still in the system?" I say to Endo. "It's still a government facility."

He's already removing his glove. "They could have flagged me, too."

"Just do it," Collins says, and Endo obeys, placing his hand on the scanner. A moment later, the door unlocks. Inside are a surprised Woodstock and Alessi, sitting in comfortable chairs, drinking soda and playing what looks like poker.

Woodstock, whose head is bandaged and right arm is in a futuristic-looking blue cast, and who is dressed in what looks like a bright blue flight suit, throws down his cards and says, "Really? I'm about to drop a royal flush down, and you bunch of yahoos are gonna—"

"Don't," Endo says to Alessi. "It's me."

Alessi's eyes widen. "Endo?"

"Don't what?" I ask.

"Hudson?" Woodstock says, his surprise matching Alessi's.

Endo, Collins and I lift our reflective goggles so they can see it's us.

"Well, damn," Woodstock says. "Alessi here was about to shank you!"

Alessi holds up her right hand. She's holding a long, sharpened piece of metal. "Took it off my bed," she says.

"They would have killed you," Endo chides.

"They were going to anyway," she argues.

"We decided we'd rather die fighting than wait it out." Woodstock grunts and stands. "And to be honest, we weren't sure we'd see you all again. Now, let's get this pony show on the road."

The nurse looks alarmed when we exit with Woodstock and Alessi in tow. "I wasn't told about any transfers."

"Hey," Maigo says, suddenly appearing beside the nurse. She slugs her and the woman sprawls over a desk, spilling dramatically to the floor. Before I can get upset, Maigo points to Collins. "If she can do it, I can do it."

Why is everyone in my life always right?

"Where is Hawkins?" I ask.

"Still with Lilly. And a doctor. He's helping, but not happily."

"We have time," Endo says to me. "You need to see."

"I need to come with you," Maigo says. She's not being demanding or young, so I believe her. Whatever is down there has something to do with Nemesis, and that means it has something to do with Maigo.

Surprisingly, Endo looks to me, waiting for my answer.

I nod. "Collins, you're coming with us, too." I hand Woodstock my sidearm. The KRISS rifle over my back, taken from the X-35's small but well stocked armory closet, would be too much for him to handle with one arm.

Endo gives Alessi his KRISS, and says, "Ten minutes. Then we'll all leave together."

"Stay here by the door," I tell them. "If anyone not us comes in—"

"We'll use our best discretion," Woodstock says and gives a lopsided grin. "Of which I have none."

Endo heads for the door, opens it and leans out. The hallway is empty. The guard now missing. When he catches my odd expression, he says, "Must be the Tsuchi." Then he points to my mask and pulls his down. Collins, Maigo and I do likewise, and we follow him into the hallway. We backtrack toward the elevator, and I steal a second glance inside the control room. The large viewscreen is now split, one side showing Nemesis, still charging over empty desert, the other side showing the Tsuchi above us. Helicopters swoop around it, firing missiles and chain guns, all with no effect. It's no longer walking. It's stopped in the middle of the base and appears to be...digging.

The people inside the room are moving about quickly, gathering equipment and laptops, driven by Zach Cole, who is clearly shouting, but unheard thanks to the thick door.

"Looks like they're bugging out," Collins says.

A vibration rocks the tunnel.

Endo, against his own advice, breaks into a jog, and we follow. We quickly reach the elevator. Endo punches the 3, and the doors shut.

"Why the rush?" I ask.

"The base will be liquidated before risking the release of what's below."

"And what is below?"

The elevator stops and opens. No guards.

Endo jogs down the metal-floored hallway, identical to the one above. When he reaches the first door, he stops at the palm reader and places his hand on it. The door clicks open, and he enters.

Maigo tenses, gripping my arm.

"What is it?" I ask her.

"I can feel them."

"Feel who?"

She looks at the open door. Collins is inside with Endo, standing still. She glances back. "Jon... You need to see this..."

I hold my hand out to Maigo. "Whatever it is, we'll face it together. No matter what."

She takes my hand, and we step inside together, both of our grips tightening as we see what's inside. As my heartbeat ratchets up, I ask, "Endo, what... Who are they?"

He turns to me, and then Maigo. "You don't recognize them?"

And then, at once, I do.

And so does Maigo. Her hands go to her head as she screams in pain, the very sight of these...things...returning her to a memory of ancient tortures that are fresh for her and faded for me.

We're looking at Nemesis's creators.

MEGATSUCHI

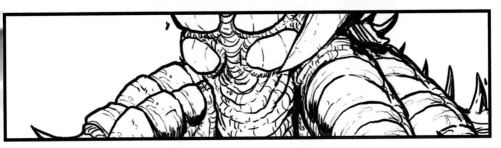

34

Alan Baxter stood on the tarmac of Area 51, surrounded by his fellow Marines—a special detachment assigned to the defense of Area 51. They waited amidst rising waves of hundred degree summer heat and abject chaos. The monster was approaching. He had no other name for it than *Kaiju*, the generic designation now used for the gargantuan creatures that seemed to be a part of the world. He'd never seen one in person before. Never had a desire to. And now that he was up close and personal with one, he wanted nothing more than to run the other direction. Not because he was a coward, but because he knew a losing fight when he saw one.

Like most of the men streaming out of hangars, he carried a fifty pound FGM-148 Javelin missile on his shoulder. The missile was powerful, and the fire-and-forget capability meant he could take a shot and run, but he didn't see how it would help. While the missile could punch through the thickest modern armor, giving a lone Marine the ability to take out a tank or a helicopter, the Kaiju approaching the base had already shirked off an array of surface-to-air, surface-to-surface and air-to-surface missiles, all of which outclassed the Javelin.

He'd seen the other Kaiju spider on TV, just an hour ago, as it rampaged through Los Angeles, wreaking destruction on a massive scale. If not for the arrival of Nemesis, the monster might have continued up and down the coast. Looking at the Kaiju spider on the outskirts of the base, he could clearly see it shared some of Nemesis's physical traits, just like the monsters that had attacked D.C. the year before. And if that was true, this thing would likely be just as resistant to modern weaponry as Nemesis, who took a MOAB in Boston and shrugged it off. While no one had tried to nuke the monsters yet, he really hoped they didn't try it now. Although there wouldn't be civilians to worry about, he was pretty sure that the higher-ups and eggheads who worked below ground were important enough to not obliterate.

"Baxter!" It was his friend, Scott Smith, who was smiling like an asshole. He was an action junkie to the core. Complained daily about being assigned to the most boring security detail in the world. The only action they ever saw was when, once or twice a year, a UFO enthusiast would cross the fence, set off alarms and be stopped before making it fifty feet. But this...this must have been like a wet dream come true for Smith. He looked almost giddy as he ran toward the Kaiju, which had reached the first in a series of hangars.

"Let's do this, man!" Smith said.

The man's excitement was infectious. Baxter picked up his pace, running toward the Kaiju. His instincts screamed to head the other way, but the danger was minimized by two things. First, all he had to do was fire the missile and run. By then, once everyone figured out they were just wasting ammo, the situation and the tactical response to it would probably change to more of a 'lock down and wait it out' strategy. Second, there were now hundreds of men, Humvees, helicopters and jets all vying for the monster's attention. The odds of being attacked were as small as the Kaiju was large.

But then, the Kaiju got larger.

Even Smith stopped running.

The spider pushed off the ground with its four front limbs, rising a good two-hundred-fifty feet in the air. Its long tail doubled its length. It wasn't quite as tall as Nemesis, he knew, but it was big enough. The monster rose up quickly, its body cracking and snapping into a new position, held aloft by its four, rear, wider legs. Its eight-eyed, snapping mandible face craned downward, making it look much less like a spider, and more like Nemesis, with four thin arms ending at wicked looking blades.

An F-18 Hornet swooped in from behind the creature, and unprepared for its sudden rising, tried to pull up, but was clearly not going to make it. The pilot must have seen it, too, because he ejected just a second before the plane collided with the Kaiju's armored back. While the jet went up in flames, the pilot, still strapped into his ejection seat, rocketed away, his chute quickly deploying.

"Oh my god," Smith shouted, laughing. "Did you see that?"

As Smith continued laughing, Baxter made a mental note to reconsider their friendship. This was not the kind of man with whom you wanted to share the battlefield. He was what many of the younger, video-game playing, troops referred to as a 'Leeroy Jenkins,' the first to charge, the first to die and the demise of the men with whom he served.

Smith's laughter was cut short when the Kaiju turned, reached out and skewered the pilot on the tip of its taloned limb. It then shoved the man into its mouth. If the man screamed, no one heard it over the continuing thunder of exploding missiles. But then all noise was drowned out by the Kaiju's high pitched roar. The battalion of Marines, three hundred strong, all stopped as one, placing hands over their ears and falling to their knees.

When the wailing cry finished, the Kaiju dropped back down to all eight legs, decimating the hangar beneath it, which must have contained a fuel truck or a fueled jet, because the whole thing went up in a ball of flame.

The Kaiju slid out of the rising black smoke, its frenetic energy gone. Its smooth movement and lowered head reminded Baxter of a lion slowly emerging from tall grass, stalking prey.

About to charge.

We're its prey!

Someone else must have realized the same thing, shouting, "No, no, no!" and firing off his Javelin before sprinting in the opposite direction: duty done, commence ass saving.

A high-pitched warbling growl slid through the air, rippling from the Kaiju as its eight orange eyes locked on the battalion of men. The lone Javelin missile struck its face and exploded harmlessly between two eyes. But the detonation triggered the monster's charge.

It roared again, paralyzing the men with its volume. Baxter wanted nothing more than to fire his single missile and run, but the sound kept him on his knees, hands over his ears. When it ended, the Kaiju was through the hangar and charging toward them, closing the distance.

A barrage of Javelin missiles ripped through the air at once, meeting the Kaiju head on. But it just plowed straight through the bright orange balls of light, lowering its head and snatching up men. Stunned, Baxter stood still for a moment, watching the monster's long tail swing across the base, leveling three more hangars, the last of which exploded.

Apache helicopters rained down Hydra rockets, Hellfire missiles and chain-gun fire.

F-22 fighter jets roared past, adding Sidewinder missiles to the mix.

The cacophony of explosions, sent shockwaves in every direction, knocking the wind from Baxter's lungs every time he tried to take a breath. The wave of impacts kept him on the ground, which was now shaking from the monster's approach.

Men screamed all around as they ran. Those who ran the fastest seemed to attract the most attention, and they were impaled or simply sucked up into the grinding mouth. The mammoth creature darted back and forth with surprising speed, plucking men from the ground with ease.

Baxter looked at Smith, who was just getting back to his feet. He looked shell-shocked for a moment, but when the two men made eye contact again, Smith cracked a big smile and shouted, "Aww, yeah, mother bitches! Time to fuck some shit up!"

He might as well have added a shout of "Leeroy Jenkins!" but instead, he fired off his lone and completely useless Javelin missile. Instead of running, Smith watched the missile streak toward the monster and connect with its side, the explosion just a small orange circle, causing no visible harm. What it did though, was get the Kaiju's attention.

When it turned toward them, Smith bolted, all of his fervor sucked away, a scream tearing from his mouth.

Baxter wanted to run, too. God, he wanted to run. But he stayed on his knees, as though in supplication, bowing to this god on earth, begging for mercy. But he wasn't really doing any of that. He was simply trying to not be noticed.

The spider-thing skittered across the tarmac, tearing it to shreds, until the creature stood directly over Baxter. Smith screamed again as he was skewered, lifted up and silenced inside the monster's mouth. It then spun in a circle, plucking up other nearby men. From beneath the colossal creature, Baxter looked all around him. The tail swept out, flattening buildings and smearing men. Explosions rocked the monster on all sides. Eight legs, moving with surprising speed, spun the thing one way and then the other, faster than he imagined possible.

He was in the eye of the storm. Safe, for a moment. Protected by the swirling mass around and above him. But it wouldn't stay here for long. More distant men were getting away. He thought about running, but discounted it. The first to be captured were the runners. But it gathered the motionless with equal efficiency. And, he noted, without even looking at them.

It already knows I'm here, he thought. *It will take me along with the rest as soon as it steps away.*

So what can I do about it?

Nothing.

I'm going to die.

The only real question left is: how am I going to die?

The answer came from the voice of a Drill Sergeant, "If you die in combat, I expect the bullet to hit you head on. Anything else means you were running away, and I don't train cowards, do I?"

"Sir, no sir," Baxter said to himself. But what could one man with a single Javelin missile do to a Kaiju spider built like Nemesis?

Baxter found the answer when he realized the ground around him was still brightly lit, despite the Kaiju above him blocking out the sun. He turned his eyes upward. Like Nemesis, the Kaiju had large, bright orange membranes on its underside. He could see the luminous liquid above him, swirling with catastrophic potential. Then he recalled the footage from this morning. The Kaiju in Los Angeles had been destroyed when Nemesis ruptured the membranes on the creature's underside. The explosion destroyed buildings, and would likely now do the same, killing men on the tarmac, and maybe those below ground, too, but the Kaiju *could* be destroyed. By one man, with the power of Nemesis.

It was a hell of a way to die. He smiled, feeling oddly like Smith for a moment, then he aimed his Javelin straight up toward the orange membrane, just fifty feet above his head. Once he pulled the trigger, the missile would cover the distance in a second. The resulting explosion would be faster.

It's not going to hurt, he told himself. He'd be there one moment and gone the next. But if it worked...if it worked, he would be remembered forever.

Good enough, he decided, and pulled the trigger.

35

Mark Hawkins stood by the machine in which Lilly lay. The base was like an operating table, but with eight robotic arms emerging from the flat surface. Lilly laid on the table, beneath a clear plastic shell. A series of sensors swept over her body. At first, he felt apprehensive, but then medical reports, x-rays and other information were displayed on a wall-sized screen behind the strange machine.

It showed multiple fractures in one arm, three broken ribs and a fractured skull. Lilly had taken a beating saving that man from the falling building. It was a foolish and risky thing to have done, but he'd never felt more proud of her. She might have inherited some of Joliet's brashness, but she'd also inherited her strident sense of right and wrong. A willingness to risk her life to save others was a quality that parents feared, but also hoped their children would develop. Part of him said that if Lilly had better training, she might have made it out unscathed, but he knew that no one else on the planet could have escaped that falling building alive, let alone with a startled janitor in tow.

The machine then went to work, administering general anesthesia and quickly cutting away her clothing. Next, it set bones and cleaned wounds, the robot arms, all bearing a logo reading *Mohr*, moved in a perfectly choreographed dance. Wounds were glued shut and bandaged. Her set arm was sprayed with a foam that expanded and hardened from her wrist to her shoulder.

Hawkins wondered if the machine would have made the same call if it knew Lilly was covered in hair. That foam was going to be hard to remove.

Lilly was then lifted up, and her torso was wrapped in a wide, white, rib belt that would protect her from jolts and keep everything in place. Her head was wrapped next. Lilly was placed back on the table, and then the robotic arms slid silently back into holes that sealed behind them. A message blinked on the screen.

Bed rest – 2 weeks.
Rib belt – 3 weeks.
Cast disintegration – 6 weeks.

At least the cast will take care of itself, Hawkins thought.

A small tray extended from the side of the machine. It contained a single orange pill bottle labeled:

Percocet - 5mg/325.
Take orally as needed.
Max 12 tablets in 24 hrs.

The clear cover lifted away with a hiss, and the machine fell quiet. While Endo was right, that Lilly's injuries would be tended to quickly, he still had an unconscious girl, who outweighed him, to get back outside.

The facility shook from some kind of impact, the lights flickering. Hawkins turned his eyes to the ceiling. He didn't know how far below the surface they were, but that they could feel the impacts of the Kaiju above told him they weren't quite deep enough to not worry. To make matters worse, they were behind enemy lines with three of their party injured.

Hawkins searched the large medical room for a gurney or wheelchair to roll her out in, but found nothing. *Looks like we'll have to use the field stretcher*, Hawkins thought, heading toward the door to get Alessi. He was stopped by a weak voice behind him. "Why do the cheeseburgers taste like pancakes?"

Hawkins did an about-face and dashed to Lilly's side. "Hey kiddo. You feeling okay?"

"I wanted a cheeseburger, but all they have are pancakes...and tweetie birds." Her face fell flat for a moment, and then she laughed. "Tweetie birds aren't real food, are they? But, they are for Sylvester." The laughter just as quickly transformed to pouty crying. "But I wanted a cheeseburger."

Hawkins wasn't sure which was worse, an unconscious and still Lilly, or a mobile tripping Lilly. He put his hand on her good shoulder. "Hey Lilly, look at me."

Her head lolled, but she made eye contact. Her pupils were dilated, causing her to squint when she saw the lights on the ceiling. "So bright in here." Then she gasped. "Are we on a spaceship? Oh. My. God. We were abducted!"

The smile that came to Hawkins's face was unbidden, but he couldn't hold it back. Their situation was precarious, but he still wished he had a video recorder of some kind to capture this.

A sudden commotion from the hallway caught his attention. Shouting voices. But no gunfire.

"Lilly," Hawkins said, making eye contact again. "Do you know who I am?"

"Daddy," she said with a smile, and she leaned her head on his chest.

You're breaking my heart, kid, he thought, wanting to just hug her until her head cleared. Instead, he pushed her back. "Lilly, I need you to wait right here. No matter what you hear, just wait for me to come back."

She seemed to sober a little. "And if you don't come back?"

"I will."

Her eyes glazed over again. "Get me a cheeseburger."

"Tomorrow," he said, heading for the door. "Tomorrow, you can have all the cheeseburgers you want."

Lilly tried to clap her hands, but was befuddled by the cast that kept her arm bent at an unmoving forty-five degree angle. "Awww."

Hawkins pushed his way through the doors into the hallway, and then he stopped. Woodstock and Alessi had taken cover behind medical equipment and were aiming their weapons down the hallway, where Silhouette, once again dressed, but without his telltale reflective mask, stood with four non-BlackGuard soldiers. While the soldiers had M4 rifles, Silhouette appeared unarmed.

"Ahh, Ranger," Silhouette said. "Was wondering where you were. Is your kitty all patched up now?"

"Go to hell," Hawkins said. He had a sidearm, but hadn't thought to bring anything bigger, as he had been preoccupied with carrying Lilly.

Silhouette smiled. "How about this? You and your pals can walk. We'll hang on to Lilly."

"What happened to your word?" Hawkins said. "You said you wouldn't take her."

"It's called psy ops," Silhouette said. "Hearts and minds, Hawkins. Hearts and minds."

Hawkins was in motion before he gave it any thought. Even if they managed to escape, Silhouette would hunt them down, would eventually find Lilly. Silhouette—and GOD—had to be stopped here and now, or Lilly would spend the rest of her life looking over her shoulder. And that wasn't going to happen with a gun fight. That would just get them all dead. But if he was right, Silhouette, like most tough guys, wouldn't back down from a fight.

When Silhouette stepped forward, rolling his neck, Hawkins knew he had pegged the man's personality right. But now came the hard part. Hawkins had been in a few fights, had survived an island of monsters and gone toe-to-toe with a grizzly bear and walked away from it, but he wasn't the world's most skilled fighter, like Endo, or Collins. Still, he was tough. And he swung first.

His fist struck the side of Silhouette's face with all the force he could muster. The blow sent the BlackGuard leader sprawling into the wall. But when the man rebounded and spun around, it was with a smile on his face and a blur of motion.

Hawkins was struck three times, and he only caught a glimpse of the first strike, an open palm to his forehead that snapped his head back. The second punch struck his gut, bringing him forward and into the third strike, a solid blow to his sternum that slammed him into the wall behind him and stole his breath.

The pain just fueled Hawkins. Before he was ready, he flung himself off the wall, big hands reaching out for Silhouette's throat. But he never made it. Silhouette was as fast as he was strong. He dove to the floor, wrapped his legs around Hawkins's feet and twisted, flinging him to the floor.

Hawkins landed hard, but rolled over and got back to his feet where he was immediately greeted by a trio of punches to his face. He stumbled back, toward the wall. He could feel his face swelling and the wet warmth of blood flowing over his face.

"How did a man like you ever survive the island?" Silhouette said, sounding disappointed. "How did you ever kill a bear?"

Hawkins pushed off the wall. "Because I don't stop getting back up." He rushed forward, diving for Silhouette with his arms spread wide. The tackle couldn't be avoided, and both men dropped. Hawkins gave Silhouette a strong headbutt, stunning him momentarily. "And because I don't fight fair." Hawkins then reached behind his back. He drew his eight inch knife from its sheath just as smoothly as he slipped it into Silhouette's side, between the man's ribs and into his heart.

Silhouette's body seized, and an expression of surprise froze on his face, his legs twitching and kicking. Hawkins glanced up at the four soldiers, their guard lowered, shock on their faces. But it wouldn't last long.

"Fire!" Hawkins shouted.

Alessi and Woodstock opened fire, Woodstock taking one man with three clean shots and Alessi spraying the other three in the same amount of time, thanks to the KRISS's rapid rate of fire and lack of recoil.

Hawkins withdrew his blade, wiped it off on Silhouette's sleeve and slipped it back into its sheath. He stood with a groan.

"Sthuffering thucatash," Lilly said from the end of the hallway. Her eyes were wide, a half smile on her face. She giggled, but she was cut off by a massive rumbling shockwave pulsing down from above. The whole facility shook and then went black.

36

"You're okay," I tell Maigo, crouching in front of her, my arms around her back, my forehead leaning against her hair. Despite my encouraging words, I'm feeling the same abject horror about the creatures in this room, but to a lesser degree. I don't think anyone could walk into this space, memories of past tortures or not, and not be disturbed. A glance up at Collins confirms it. Of all of us, she's got the toughest emotional skin, built up to deal with her previous abusive husband, and even she looks mortified, a hand over her mouth.

"They're dead," I whisper, glancing toward the three, square, liquid-filled tanks. They look like oversized fish tanks, each a perfect cube, each with a different occupant. "They're all dead."

I don't try to push her. This girl who was one part of a city-destroying Kaiju, and has the strength of who knows how many men, is shaking under my arms. So I just rub her back and turn my attention to understanding what I'm seeing.

The tank nearest us contains what looks like a very pale, very blond human man. But I'm pretty sure he's not human. The first tell is that he's a good ten feet tall, but not in the lanky way abnormally tall humans look. He's built like a professional wrestler—the Hulk Hogan variety, not Andre the Giant, who'd look small next to this guy. And then there is the symbol on the man's chest. It's not a tattoo, it's like an indentation, like it was carved out of him, but with perfect edges. There are three circles, one inside the other, centered on the man's broad chest. A single line protruding down from the center circle extends downward through the next two. I have no idea what it means, but I commit it to memory.

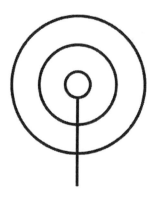

The next tank contains something that is very much not human, and completely unrecognizable to me. In some regards, it's humanoid, with a head, two arms and two legs...but that's where the comparison ends. Its face is fugly, covered with boney horns that look like they punched out of the skin. Its mouth, frozen open in death, is full of large white teeth. It has three red eyes on either side of its long domed head, which ends at a mane of hair, flowing out behind it in the water. Its body is powerful, like a cross between the blond giant and a hairless, gray lion. Its hands and feet are tipped with long, deadly looking claws. Its long, powerful tail is tipped with a tuft of hair, like a painter's brush. While its body isn't as big as the alien Viking fellow, it looks like it could make short work of him.

And that brings us to the third tank, where the creature Maigo and I both recognize from Nemesis Prime's memories is contained. It's not the whole creature. Just its head. At its full height, the creature would probably be a good fifty feet tall. It's not Kaiju big, but these are the things that captured Nemesis Prime, tortured her and turned her into something she might not have been without them. It reminds me of the way people train elephants for the circus; the smaller, but smarter life form, plucking the larger, more malleable-minded giant from its habitat and training it, often through violence, to perform a duty. I look at its two, basketball-sized, black eyes, and even in death, I see a ruthless intelligence. The bald head was covered in gleaming white skin, stretched down to where its mouth was hidden by a mass of tentacles that remind me of spiky star fish limbs.

"What...are they?" Collins asks.

Endo steps up to the center glass tank containing the gray creature. "I don't know the details, but they're not of this Earth. Like Nemesis Prime. Our Nemesis is different. Thanks to Maigo, she is, at least partly, of this Earth. But I think these creature have something to do with Nemesis."

He doesn't know, I think, and for some reason, I decide to tell him. "The big one on the right...trained Nemesis Prime and brought her to Earth. Or, at least, his species did."

Endo looks uncommonly surprised. "You've seen them before?"

"In Nemesis's memories." I rub Maigo's back. "We both did. Saw them and *felt* what they did to her, how they made her the goddess of vengeance."

"Why didn't you tell me before?" Endo asks.

"You're not exactly a team player," Collins says on my behalf.

Endo frowns, perhaps reconsidering his life choices, but probably just pouting about not being the all-knowing Nemesis fanboy.

"I'm okay," Maigo says as her shivers stop. She holds onto my arms, and we stand together. She turns toward the contained monsters. "Why are they here?"

Maigo steps out of my arms, her strength and resolve that of a Kaiju, returned in full. She heads for the big, tentacle-faced floating head. She stares the thing down, and I wonder for a moment, if she faced this thing, at its full height, would she be strong enough to take it down? She might be, but I hope to never find out.

With a sudden roar, Maigo draws her fist back, ready to punch the glass. A voice stops her.

"I wouldn't do that," Zach Cole says, standing behind us, having entered the room without making a sound.

Maigo glares back at him. "Why not?"

He shrugs. "It'd make a mess. And you could destroy a one of a kind specimen."

"Just another one of your sick collections?" I ask, slowly lowering my hand to my sidearm.

Cole boldly steps up beside Maigo, his hands clasped behind his back. I'm not sure what's more surprising, that he seems unafraid of Maigo or that the ample bellied man in a suit can reach his hands that far back. "This *collection* might help the human race survive long enough to have a future."

"Explain," Endo demands.

Cole smiles at his former subordinate. "The BlackGuard command is yours if you want it, Specter. You've proven yourself more than a match for our best, and Silhouette..." The man looks up toward the ceiling, which shakes as if on cue. "His fate is uncertain."

Endo considers the offer, but then shakes his head. "My fate lies elsewhere."

Cole shrugs and turns his attention to me. His arrogant body language sets me off, and I take a swing, desiring to put him in his place before letting him continue his diatribe. My fist is on target, but it strikes nothing. My follow-through pulls me forward, and I stumble to the floor. No way the fat man could have moved so fast. I turn around in time to see the amused Cole flicker.

A hologram.

"You're not even here anymore, are you?" I ask.

He shakes his head. "Long gone." He motions to the specimens. "Now, if you're ready to hear me out..." I pick myself up without a word and wait for him to continue.

"What you see before you is the reason GOD exists." He motions to the gray creature and the floating head. "While we've only known about these creatures for ten years, these brutes—" He points to the blond man. "—have been on our radar since World War II. The Nazis fancied themselves the descendants of these giants, and to a degree they were right. These men joined the human population thousands of years ago, their blood commingling with ours over millennia the same way ours did with Neanderthals, but their bloodline has been severely diluted by time."

"Who are they?" Collins asks.

"That's where it gets complicated," Cole says. "While they are not human, or even from this planet, we all know about the fabled Atlanteans. But they weren't an advanced civilization of humans. They simply lived among us, and we think, were sent here to strengthen us."

I step up to the tank containing the blond man, my guard still up, but curiosity officially piqued. "Sent here?"

He points at the gray creature, "By them."

"The Atlantean looks like the smarter of the two," Collins points out.

"Looks can be deceiving," Cole says and nods at me, like he knows me, like he's earned the right to rib me. I really don't like this guy. "But this is where our knowledge takes a sharp uptick."

"There was an encounter," Endo concludes. "Contact made."

Cole nods. "Like I said, ten years ago. In the Arctic. A team of scientists, funded by Brian Norwood's Global Exploration Corporation, in the northernmost part of the Queen Elizabeth Islands, in Northern Canada, raised a complete mammoth from the tundra. From the mammoth came a woman. And in her arms, a beacon. It led them to an ancient citadel buried in the ice. They were pursued by these—" He motions to the gray corpse. "—creatures. The Ferox. The research team lost most of their crew, but a few of them survived and relayed their story to me, after we tracked them down and recovered what remained of their conflict, including this specimen. In a way, the Ferox made us who we are today: warring people capable of great violence and the ability to create weapons of unbelievable destructive capability."

Collins glares at Cole. "That's your defense for monsters like the Tsuchi? For experimenting on human beings? For warping nature?"

As much as I abhor the idea, I can see where Cole's logic is leading. Fight monsters with monsters. But that doesn't make it right.

"It is the nature instilled in us by the Ferox, who have taken human form, and over thousands of years, molded us—trained us—into a true fighting force. They strengthened us by interbreeding humanity with the Atlanteans. They also rebelled strongly against the idea of being enslaved. Freedom is everything to humanity today, because it is everything to the Ferox and the Atlanteans."

"And why would these Ferox do this to us?" I ask and turn my attention to the floating head. "It doesn't seem that dissimilar to what these guys did to Nemesis."

"In the long run, it's not," Cole admits. "And that's probably because they're cut from the same cloth, so to speak. There was a time when the Ferox and this race of giants, the Aeros, were one species."

"They look a little like Cthulhu," I point out.

Cole chuckled. "Brice theorized that Lovecraft was influenced by a Ferox, in an attempt to train the human race to fear creatures of Cthulhuean appearance. And you'll note they have almost nothing in common with the Ferox, despite their shared genetic history. As they spread through the cosmos, two distinct races emerged, and a race war began with the more intelligent and cunning Aeros driving the Ferox back. In a bid to turn the tide, the Ferox found developing worlds and molded their higher life forms into warriors willing to aid their cause. It's a war that's been waged since before homo sapiens were the dominant species on Earth."

"How does this all involve Nemesis?" Maigo asks, her voice quiet, her glaring attention still locked on the large floating head.

The ceiling shakes from an impact high above. When we all look up, listening to the rumble, Cole says, "We're safe down here. Not even a nuclear blast can reach us. As for Nemesis, we believe Prime was sent to Earth by the Aeros as a kind of watchdog. So when the Atlanteans, brought to Earth by the Ferox, set up shop, Nemesis Prime exacted her vengeance on them. In the end, Prime was defeated—how, we don't know, though the corpse shows signs of a battle with something equally large—but not before the battle destroyed Atlantis and scattered the few survivors."

"Okay, thanks for the history lesson, chubs," I say. "But you still haven't given me a good reason to not hunt you down and shoot you, put you in the Viking's tank, and arrange you in an embarrassing pose."

Cole's face gets serious, but I don't think it has anything to do with my blatant disrespect. "Ten years ago, when the citadel in the Arctic was raised, we detected a powerful signal sent from near-Earth orbit and into deep space. We later learned that the Ferox attacking the scientific crew were simply trying to *prevent* that signal from being sent."

"We've been compromised," Endo says. "Their influence on us revealed."

"Yes." Cole takes a deep breath and sighs. "And the Aeros are coming back." He looks me in the eyes. "We don't know when, but they'll eventually come, and we're doing everything we can—" He turns to Collins. "—including breaking every rule in the book, in an effort to save the entire God damned planet. Imagine what a single Tsuchi could do if it was set loose in an enemy ship. We'd stand a real chance of surviving—"

"But at what cost?" Collins asks. "If we have to become something worse than human to survive, do we deserve to survive?"

"Anyone they didn't kill would be enslaved."

"There has to be a better way," Collins says.

"When you figure it out, you let me know. In the meantime, I would appreciate it if you would all leave without further conflict." He puts his hand to his ear, where I see a small earbud. "It seems your friends have survived an encounter with Silhouette—"

As much as his words tense my muscles, the impact is dwarfed by a sudden impact that jolts the floor beneath us and fills the base with an echoing rumble. The lights flicker and go out.

The darkness lasts just a few seconds, and then power is restored. Cole is headed toward the wall, which in his location, must be a door. "Leave now, while you can. If you stay, I will consider you all property of GOD, to be used however I deem necessary." He stops in the doorway. "Hudson, if these guys come back..."

"Call me," I say.

Collins looks ready to clock me, but if everything Cole has just said is true, then we can't be kept out of the loop. If I can make deals with demons, I can make deals with devils, too, especially if it means saving the human race, which at the moment contains a good number of people I care about.

"No one will stop you on the way out," Cole says. "But you're on your own now. The Tsuchi and Nemesis are your problems."

"But the Tsuchi..." Endo starts.

"Is retreating northeast, I'm told." He taps his earbud. "As is Nemesis."

"Cole," I say, stopping his exit. "You'll leave us alone?"

He ponders this for a moment, and then says, "You don't step on my toes, I won't step on yours."

Collins takes hold of my wrist. She doesn't like bowing to evil men. She'd rather knock them senseless. "This is for the girls," I say, and she loosens her grip. I turn back to Cole. "Done."

He nods and steps toward the wall, pixelating and fading away, leaving us with the manipulators, invaders and potential destroyers of the human race. I stand there for a moment, looking at the bodies, feeling a powerful sense of impending doom...but that could have more to do with the Tsuchi above us and Nemesis closing in. Sometimes, this job sucks.

37

Back in the elevator, Collins, Maigo, Endo and I are all silent, digesting the unbelievable information Cole has just laid on us. How much of it is true and how much is speculation, or exaggeration, I don't know, but one thing's for certain, the FC-P is going to need a bigger budget. I turn to Endo. "How much of what he said do you believe?"

Endo answers without thought. "All of it."

"Multiple races of aliens. The manipulation of the human race for thousands of years. At-*freaking*-lantis."

"You say that like Atlantis is the strangest of all those revelations," Collins says. "And I'm not sure why, but I believe him, too. Not that it excuses the way they have been preparing for the Aeros. And you—" She burrows into my skull with her eyes. "—you will not be collaborating with these people."

As tempting as it is, I know she's right. Becoming monsters to fight monsters has never been our style...if you ignore the fact that Lilly is a cat woman, Maigo has Kaiju strength and I once controlled a Kaiju by taking over its mind. Ignoring all that, our humanity is still intact. "Can we agree that milking them for information is acceptable? We still have no real idea what we'd be up against, should said invasion ever take place. For all we know, it might not happen for another hundred years. If the Aeros and Ferox have been duking it out for thousands of years, I doubt they operate on the same time scale as us. That they're not here yet, ten years later, means it's probably not a hop, skip and a jump through a wormhole or something."

"Milk away, but don't drink the Kool-Aid," Collins says.

"That was one of the worst mixed metaphors I've ever heard," Endo says.

Collins, Maigo and I all crane our heads toward him at once.

I shake my head. "Seriously, why does every asshole in the world think they can pal around with us?"

Endo stands grinning. "You're easy targets."

Collins and I are both surprised when Maigo lunges forward, picks Endo up by his chest armor and slams him against the elevator wall. "Not as easy as you." The tone of her voice is dark and brooding. The creatures we saw, and the memories they conjured, must have deeply affected her.

I put my hand on her shoulder. "Easy now. Maigo..."

"I won't let them hurt you," she says to me. "I won't let anyone hurt you."

The sentiment seems overly simple, but is familiar. It's basically how Nemesis acted a year ago, when Maigo was still part of the monster. In response to my helping the creature exact revenge on Maigo's murderous father, Maigo bonded to me. While our relationship has become a more complex father-daughter affair, today's events have returned her protective nature to the surface.

Endo bows his head. "Apologies, Maigo. I meant no harm. It wounds me to know that I have upset you. I will respect your...parents from now on."

While his apology sounds sincere, he definitely had to force the word 'parents,' and I can't blame him. As much as he would like to have a relationship with the girl who was once Nemesis, she sees us, even though we're not married—yet—as adoptive parents.

The elevator pings, and the doors slide open. Guns are thrust in our faces. We nearly spring into action, but Lilly stumbles into the elevator, throwing up her hands, a sharp-toothed smile on her face. "My peeps!"

Guns are lowered. Hawkins, looking like he went a few rounds with a Ferox, steps into the elevator. He's followed by Alessi and Woodstock.

"Going the hell up," Woodstock says.

"I heard Silhouette caught up with you?" I ask Hawkins.

"A few minutes before he caught up with the Devil," he replies, dead serious.

The mood in the elevator is heavy and serious, but then Lilly does an exaggerated Hawkins impression, "'A few minutes before he caught up with the Devil.'" She starts laughing, breaking the tension, and we all join in. Even Maigo, who finally lets go of Endo.

The elevator pings.

The doors open.

Our laughter stops.

The elevator has risen up into an empty space that used to be hidden by a small building, which is now just rubble around us. And beyond the rubble...is an unimaginable field of black death. The charring covering everything, from the steaming tarmac, to the smoldering buildings, to the hundreds of small, smoking heaps that I think are bodies, tells me that the Tsuchi's explosive membrane was ruptured. But without Nemesis lying on top of it, forcing the Tsuchi to absorb the brunt of the explosion, the Kaiju here was probably launched into the sky like a tossed coin.

I step out of the elevator and look to the northeast, where Cole said the Tsuchi was headed. My flipped coin theory appears validated by the crumbling side of Bald Mountain, where the flipped Tsuchi, weighing fifty thousand tons, give or take ten thousand, must have landed on its back. A cloud of dust streaking into the distance reveals its course, just like Cole said, to the northeast.

So what's to the northeast?

I run my thoughts over a mental map of the country. There is literally almost nothing between here and the Nevada border. A few roads here and there. Minimal people to worry about. It's mostly arid, flat desert cut through by rugged mountainous terrain. My imaginary map continues northeast, crossing the border of Utah, following an imaginary path right to Salt Lake City, its surrounding suburbs and its millions of residents. If I'm right, the Tsuchi is still after food, but also moving away from Nemesis, who is also headed northeast in pursuit of it.

I turn around as the others step out of the elevator. The doors close behind them and the whole unit slides down into what used to be the floor. *That's how it wasn't destroyed.*

"What now, bossman?" Woodstock asks, but he's in no condition to do much of anything. The same goes for Lilly and Hawkins, though he's not going to be happy to hear that. But I can tell by the way he's standing, with the slap-happy Lilly actually helping to support his weight, that he took a serious beating. Vince Neil and crew were never this motley.

"We need transportation." I turn my attention from my people to the surrounding area. It's a wasteland.

"We have transportation," Endo says, stepping out of what little remains of the blackened building. Alessi heads out with him, locking her arm in his and putting her head on his shoulder, just for a moment. The affection is brief, but it seems even someone like Endo can be loved, and that might be weirder than aliens... A smile slips onto my face. There *are* aliens at Area 51! The nerds would be so happy to find out, though they might not sleep again if they knew the details.

I follow Endo with the rest, and for a moment, I think he's lost his mind. Stretching out before us is a mile long circle of black. Beyond it is desert, and then mountains, and then nothing. But something emerges from the black as my perspective changes. There's something there. Something resting on it. When we're standing beneath the blackened form of the X-35, I ask, "How?"

"The X-35 isn't just designed to replace helicopters and fighter jets," Endo says. He looks up at the blue sky above.

"No," I say. "Are you kidding me? This thing can fly in space?"

"It survived the blast because it's designed to exit and re-enter Earth's atmosphere. Given what we just learned, is it really that surprising that we'd be developing a fighter capable of space travel?"

I reach up and rub the blackened hull. The char rubs away, revealing the unharmed, shiny surface beneath.

"Slap my ass and call me Sally," Woodstock says. "Can we keep it?"

I lock eyes with Endo, suspecting he might have his own plans for the X-35. Oddly, he acquiesces with a nod. I turn to Woodstock. "Woodstock, meet Future Betty."

Woodstock gives a whoop as Endo lowers the cargo bay ramp.

We quickly board the vehicle, and I let Woodstock take the cockpit seat so he can watch and learn how Endo pilots the craft. Once everyone buckles up, Endo pulls the X-35 up to a height of just fifty feet, and hovers. "Where to?"

"Cheeseburgers!" Lilly says.

As hungry as I am, a burger joint is still third on my list of potential destinations. The first, most obvious target is the Tsuchi. I look Lilly over. She's clad in black like the rest of us, but the black covering her is natural fur. The uniform and the bacteria bomb are missing. I nearly ask, but the answer is obvious; when Lilly was patched up, the bomb was removed along with her clothing, and while getting beat up by Silhouette, Hawkins hadn't thought to bring it. So there goes that strategy.

"Any ideas?" I ask.

"The Tsuchi's destination is most likely Salt Lake City," Alessi says, accessing the X-35's wall screen system with such fluency that it's clear she's had inside information from Endo.

"It will take time to get there," Collins says. "Time enough to evacuate at least some of the population."

People will die in the ensuing panic-filled evacuation, too, but Collins's plan reveals she holds no hope of actually stopping the Tsuchi's progress. And that's discouraging, because what good are we? Without weapons developed by people like Cole, we're basically lucking our way through these messes.

Alessi scrolls through several streams of information displayed on the screen. "If the Tsuchi moves in a straight line between here and Salt Lake, it's just over three hundred miles. With a top speed over a hundred miles per hour, it won't be that long before the Tsuchi arrives."

Lilly giggles, but says nothing. Whatever drugs she was given seem to be wearing off some.

"What about Nemesis?" I ask.

Alessi taps and swipes her way to the information. Live aerial footage of Nemesis charging across a group of large green circles in the middle of a desert appears. The label at the bottom of the news feed identifies the location as Oasis, California. "Oasis is four hundred miles from Salt Lake in a straight shot. With a similar top speed, Nemesis is just an hour behind the Tsuchi. If it stops in Salt Lake, there's a good chance she'll catch it there."

"So, best case scenario, Nemesis takes care of our pest problem."

Lilly giggles again.

Maigo loses her patience. "What's so funny!"

"Nemmy has tentacles."

I'm about to write her off and keep working on our futile plan, but then she adds, "On her head. She tried to hug me. Wanted to pull me into her hole." She cracks up a little, laughing, but I'm not. I unbuckle and kneel in front of Lilly. She's still drugged, but trying to tell us something. I lift her face so her yellow eyes are looking at me.

"What did the hole look like?"

She blinks hard twice. "Like...a peapod...on the back of her neck. They just wanted a hug. Just a little hug. I think she's lonely." Lilly puts her hand on Maigo's knee. "She misses you, Maig. Think she wants you back...or whoever is convenient, I guess...whoever gets too close. Almost got me, but I don't swing that way." She laughs again. "Sorry, Nems, I don't like you that way."

I look at Maigo, whose face shows an inner conflict. "Not a chance."

"But if it could save people, we have to—"

"*Not* going to happen."

"Isn't that what we're supposed to do?" Maigo argues. "Save people?"

"I'm not going to sacrifice you," I say. "I'm not going to give you back. You don't deserve—"

"It's not up to you," she says. "Nemesis is part of me. She's in my head. And I'm still part of her. I hate it. It sucks. But I might be able to steer her. Guide her. Without me, she's just a monster. I can give her a conscience again."

We stare at each other for a moment. Then I stand and sit back down, calmly buckling myself in. I turn to Collins. "Get in touch with Watson and Cooper. I want them coordinating a staggered evacuation, starting with everyone southwest of Salt Lake. Send them east. Then work their way up, moving people in every direction except for southwest."

"Endo," I say. "How long to get to Maine without killing us?"

"An hour," he says.

"Then we'll be back in time to see Salt Lake City laid to waste."

I ignore the grumbling voices all around me. I understand what Maigo is suggesting. I can see how it would work. And aside from our close bond, I'm not sure how I can really argue against it, or take it away from her. But I'll be damned if I let her go without reminding her of what she's signing up for.

"Take us home."

38

"Why are we here?" Maigo stands with her arms crossed, but she's no longer shrunken in on herself, hiding behind her bangs. She's got the long black hair tied back in a tight ponytail. This might be the first time I've really seen her whole face at once. Not that I can see her very well. It's dark and my flashlight sucks. There are GOD goggles in the X-35, but I don't want them knowing where we are, or recording this conversation.

"For perspective," I say, stepping through the doorway into the morgue beneath the ruined laboratory in Maine. "This is where it started. Where you started."

"And you wanted me to remember what it's like to kill people?" She's on the defense, putting up walls like a typical teenager, which is really what I want for her. "I haven't forgotten. How could I?"

"No, I—"

"It would be different. I'm stronger. My will is stronger. I could control her."

The last sentence is spoken with a trace of doubt. While both of us are certain that Maigo's rejoining Nemesis would restore the beast's conscience, would she really be able to reign the instinctual monster in? Or would she be locked inside, while it rampaged again? Would she relieve the horrors that plague her? Would she be reminded what human flesh tastes like?

I step up to the wall where the word Nemesis is scrawled in ancient Greek, in blood. The boney remains of the woman who was slain to write this message lay to my right. *When this mess is over, I really need to have her taken care of.* Some part of Maigo was more human than Kaiju back then. She could think, could write in a language she never knew in life.

"I want you to remember what you're giving up," I say. "And to understand what you're asking me to give up."

She's silent. Maybe waiting for a classic Hudson punch line. But I'm out of jokes. I point to the wall. "You remember doing this?"

She nods.

"Do you remember waking up?"

"It's...it's fuzzy. Like a dream. Not really." She looks up at the blood that dripped from the word before drying. "This is my first real memory...after my... After my murder. *Her* murder."

Maigo knows that she's not the same Maigo who was killed, but only the carrier of her memories and DNA. That girl is still dead and buried, her soul gone to wherever the souls of innocent children go. Probably someplace better. Someplace without monsters.

"What about the second time?" I ask.

"What do you mean?"

"When you were—in a non-religious way—born again, from Nemesis."

"I...I remember waking up in Beverly. You were there. And Ash. And Buddy." She smiles at the memory.

"Do you remember how I looked?"

"Relieved," she says. "And...injured? You had bruising around your neck. And the side of your face. That was from the Washington fight, right?"

I shake my head. "That was from you."

She stares at me. "You woke up once in the three days between when Collins and I found you and your first memory. For ten minutes."

I can see she's afraid to ask, but she manages to get the words out. "What happened?"

"Can you still get in my head?"

"I've been trying not to," she says. "Since I blew the whole engagement thing."

"Good call," I say. "But I want you to try to do it now. Just like when it's Christmas morning and we're both kids, but I want you to let go. Let me direct the path."

She doesn't say "okay," or put her hands on my head, or anything else. One second we're standing in an abandoned morgue, the next we're standing beside a Christmas tree in my childhood living room. But neither of us are kids. We came here because I was thinking about this scene.

I shift my attention forward in time, to the day following Maigo's recovery from Washington. We managed to sneak her back without anyone knowing. She was cleaned up and attended to by a doctor we had sign a DHS non-disclosure agreement. The diagnosis was something close to a coma, but with a lot of brain activity. She called it 'a deep sleep brought on by extreme exhaustion,' and felt confident Maigo would wake soon.

And she did, later that day.

The memory returns.

I'm sitting beside Maigo's bed, bleary eyed and twisting my red beanie cap in my hands. Maigo's eyes are closed, but shifting back and forth rapidly, like she's in some kind of frenetic REM sleep cycle. Just as my eyes start to slide shut, Maigo lunges up in bed, eyes open wide, gasping.

The sound and sudden motion pull me to my feet. But it's a mistake.

Maigo reels toward me, acting on defensive instinct, throwing out a punch that catches the side of my head and knocks me into the wall. Then she's out of bed, slamming her body into mine and wrapping her fingers around my throat.

Tears streak down her cheeks.

Her breathing is fast and deep.

She looks back and forth, eyes darting, confusion enveloping her.

Despite having the life choked out of me, all I feel is pity. I can't bring myself to fight back, and when Maigo finally looks at me, her grip loosens. Then her eyes widen with recognition. "Jon?"

"If...you...don't...kill me."

She releases me and steps back, bumping into the bed and sprawling around, looking for an attack. *She's used to being Nemesis*, I think. Used to being attacked every time she steps out of the ocean. Her last memory would have been of dying.

Of saving me.

"You remember me?"

Her head snaps back toward me. "Christmas."

When I nod, the strength goes out of her, and she falls into my arms.

"Are we alive?" she asks.

"Yeah."

"Am I safe?"

"You are."

"We protect each other, right?"

It's then that I know I'm talking to the will within Nemesis, who had been protecting me, in Beverly and again in Washington. This is the girl who gave her life for mine, and I would do everything I could to return the favor. "Always."

She reaches up for my swelling face, grasping it with both hands. A flash of...something, like memories, but simpler. Something like love, like what fathers—the good ones—feel for their children, drives its way into my soul, taking root, depending on me for growth. For life.

And then she's gone. Unconscious again.

The memory stops, but we haven't left the dream room. Maigo is still in my arms. But she opens her eyes. Stands. "I understand now."

Thank God.

"I knew that you loved me. That you accepted me like a daughter. I never doubted that. But I didn't know about this. I didn't know what you promised me. I didn't know you *really* felt like my father."

"Kinda weird, right?"

She smiles. "I'm sorry."

"For what?"

"For doing this to you."

"I've never regretted taking you in. I never will."

"That's not what I meant."

"What did you—oh..." I walk to the window, which isn't real, and look out at the view of Beverly, which isn't charred like it is in the real world. "You're still going through with it."

"I have to."

"Why?"

"Because you're my father."

"That's...stupid," I say.

"Because you taught me what's right and wrong. From the first time I saw you, and tried to eat you, you have been risking everything to help other people. And now I have a chance to do the same, and maybe make up for some of the horrible things I did with Nemesis."

"That wasn't you."

"Part of it was. Nemesis might have blinded me to the death and destruction, but the thirst for revenge? The need to kill Tilley? That came from me. I need to do this..."

When I say nothing, she steps up next to me, our faces warmed by the sun. "Dad?"

"Yeah?"

"This is what Hudsons do, right?"

I turn toward her. "What?"

"When Watson created my new identity, we made my last name Hudson. It was going to be a surprise..." She smiles up at me. "Surprise."

Adopting Maigo was never a possibility, because she was, technically, dead. I knew Watson had created a new identity for her—which we can easily do as a division of the DHS—retaining her first name, but I'd never asked what they used for a last name, and it never came up. And now that I'm thinking about it...

"Take us back," I say.

The dream ends, and we're back in the bleak underground morgue. We head back outside, and I pull my phone from my pocket, dialing Watson. He answers on the second ring. "Are you back in the Crow's Nest?"

"Yep, we're just settling in now. Coop is coordinating with—"

"Never mind that," I say. "Can you access Maigo's credentials? Her Social Security card? Birth certificate? All that?"

"Yeah," he says. "We did make them, after all. Why?"

"Make her my daughter." While I can't go through the normal adoption channels, I *can* change the records.

I hear Maigo gasp next to me.

Watson is silent.

"Watson?"

I hear typing keys, but nothing else. I check the phone. Full signal. "Watson?"

"Done," he says, and I hang up without saying goodbye. I turn to Maigo. "*Now* you're a Hudson."

I'm expecting a hug or something more stereotypically girly, but Maigo gets serious. "Then now we can do what Hudsons do." She takes my hand. "Together."

The last thing I want is to help this girl, my daughter, now on paper and in my heart, rejoin Nemesis. She will lead a life of violence and chaos, of pain and battle. But...she could save people. Millions of people. Knowing the weight she feels from her past as Nemesis, I can't take that from her. And she's right, Hudsons save people. "We might not share the same blood, but sometimes nurture wins over nature. Let's go kick some ass." My toe strikes a rock on the ground, and I sprawl into the dirt.

Maigo helps me up. "Definitely don't share the same blood."

Ten minutes later, we're back in the X-35, minus Hawkins and Lilly, who are now being cared for by a few stunned and NDA-silenced doctors in Portland. Neither were happy about it, but Hawkins's internal injuries needed tending, and Lilly, while returning to her senses, was still craving cheeseburgers and hardly in fighting shape. But they were happy to be reunited with Joliet, who was recovering nicely. They were being visited by their loud friend, and fellow Island 731 survivor, Bob Bray.

Woodstock is still with us, watching and learning as Endo lifts us off the ground and plots our course across the country. Alessi, Collins, Maigo and I sit in the back. Everyone knows the plan. No one likes it. But no one fights it, either, which is a good thing, because I'm still struggling with the idea of giving Maigo back to Nemesis. The trouble is, I can't think of any other solution, and we're going to be face-to-face with the giant in an hour.

39

With every massive step, the earth quaking beneath her, Nemesis felt herself gaining on the last remaining beacon calling for her to smite it. She understood that this creature had wronged her, and that she had to destroy it or forever be pricked by its continued existence. She also knew it would feel good, that in wronging her, the enemy had also given her a gift. It had awakened her mind to the knowledge that silencing the voices through vengeance not only gave her peace, it made her feel good.

But at the same time, the energy each kill gave her, also felt empty. From her first memories in this new body, Nemesis had been a plural. A warring duality.

That second part of her, the voice that tamped down the thirst and drove her to consider the lives of the tiny people who trembled in fear, was missing. Her primal nature raged at the very concept of...missing that part of her. The longing remained constant, though a distant second to the siren call drawing her toward the violator.

And then to the rest of them. The humans. She could feel the missing part of her. Distant but alive. But without that second voice, she couldn't deny her thirst for vengeance.

So she charged on, the memory of her dual nature a slight voice in the background, washed out by bloodlust.

Her target had stopped. Or slowed. Either way, she would reach it soon. Each step increased her thirst. Her towering legs moved faster, kicking through homes and vehicles and endless stretches of dry land, the heat itching her black skin. Driven by ravenous desire, Nemesis leaned forward, shaking the ground as her hands impacted the ground and her claws dug caves. Then she lunged, propelling herself with her powerful back legs.

The ground beneath her blurred.

Her speed doubled.

The desert gave way to neighborhoods.

With each lunge and landing, the landscape around her crumbled. Alarms sounded. Explosions filled the air. People screamed, their voices lost in the quaking rumble of each step forward. A mile high cloud of dust and ash trailed in her wake, cast up by her tail, which thrashed a zigzag of destruction, whipping back and forth.

But as she closed in on her enemy, she also felt the presence of her former self growing stronger. She was coming. But still an afterthought.

Nemesis looked to the horizon.

Beyond the manicured neighborhoods and emptied downtowns, she saw smoke. She smelled it, too, mixed with blood. Her stomach churned. She hadn't eaten since waking. The little people scattered about wouldn't sate her hunger, but her enemy would.

Nemesis roared, her voice booming, the sound waves streaking out ahead of her, leveling everything in her path before she crushed what remained underfoot and swept it all away with her swishing tail.

A high-pitched wail replied from the distance, but it didn't sound afraid.

It sounded defiant and angry.

The enemy hadn't stopped running because it was distracted by food, it had stopped to fight.

Nemesis bellowed again, and still three miles away, she began lurching, her chest heaving, her throat constricting and flexing. As she lunged up and came down on her massive arms, she expelled a bright orange glob, which slurped free and shot out with a pop. The projectile soared toward the horizon, pursued by Nemesis, and announced her approach by unleashing the fires of hell and harsh judgment on the violator and everything else around it.

The shockwave from the explosion washed back over Nemesis, stumbling her. Her hands fell back as her torso ground through the city, but her legs never stopped pumping, and she quickly got her arms under her again, charging into the wave of heat generated by the explosion.

A wall of smoke blocked her view of what lay ahead, but she charged onward, parting the black cloud with her mass, the swell of air around her kicking the ash skyward.

Then she saw the enemy, blackened, but unharmed. It stood boldly on four thick legs, its four talon-tipped arms open wide to embrace her, a city at its back. The creature was easily her size now, perhaps larger, but Nemesis never slowed. Instead, she roared once more, shoved off the ground and dove into the waiting arms of her enemy, sending them both catapulting into the city beyond.

40

Katsu Endo sat at the X-35's controls, but he was only pretending to fly. Once he'd input the flight path into the system, including preferred altitudes, speeds and airspace, he could sit back and let the vehicle's onboard radar system automatically avoid any obstacles it came across. Endo couldn't fly a plane, or a helicopter, but to operate the X-35, you didn't really need to know how to pilot. While you could pilot manually, all you needed was basic competency with a touch-screen operating system. And when you did need to manually pilot, the designers had made the controls as simple as a video game, no doubt understanding that future pilots would be most comfortable with a flight stick and simple foot controls. And with the repulse engines, it was possible.

So instead of piloting, he was listening.

And planning.

Hudson didn't trust him entirely; that was no secret. But he didn't loathe Endo as much as he pretended to, and despite his frequent threats of legal action, Hudson had yet to attempt subduing Endo, despite ample opportunity.

It's because, Endo knew, *the solution to the Kaiju problem is far more complicated than black and white.* Both men occupied gray territory and had done questionable things to protect entire cities, and the ones they loved. And, by the sounds of it, Hudson wasn't done.

If Endo understood correctly, Nemesis was looking for a partner. The monster had been born half-human after all. It made sense that, now lacking Maigo, Nemesis would want her back, to share life. Nemesis Prime had been a lone beast, destined to smite in solitude, but Nemesis was different. She required a partner to be whole. At least, that was the way Endo understood it.

Lilly had spoken of a spot on the back of Nemesis's neck, an opening, where black tendrils had reached for her. Endo could only assume, as Hudson and Maigo clearly were, that entering that space would then link Maigo and Nemesis once more.

It was a bold plan. Even for Hudson. While the man could be... thorny, Endo had come to respect the man's creative solutions to problems, and his willingness to enter the gray areas of morality. But could he handle what Cole had revealed to them? Could the man sacrifice Maigo, and then, lacking her strength, work against an invasion?

Endo didn't think so. What Hudson was about to do would break him.

There were few people on Earth, save for Endo himself and Cole's people at GOD, who had the qualifications to handle, without losing their minds, an event on the magnitude of an alien assault. Losing Hudson would not be good. But...Hudson would do everything he could to save the people of Salt Lake, including sacrificing Maigo, who Endo had overheard, was now legally Hudson's daughter.

Endo marveled at the girl's willingness to sacrifice herself. She was as brave as he imagined a girl born from Nemesis would be. But like Hudson, Endo suspected her loss would be detrimental in the long run.

Sacrifices have to be made sometimes, he told himself. And what greater love was there than to lay down one's life for one's friends?

Friends... The word had become a stranger to Endo. While Alessi was his half-sister and bound to him by blood and common exploits at Zoomb, his only real friends considered him an enemy. He glanced back at Hudson, Collins, Alessi and Maigo. He would never tell Hudson, but he considered the man a friend, and a trusted ally.

A twitch of motion pulled his attention to Woodstock's mustache. The man was smiling.

"You ain't even flying, are you?" Woodstock said.

Endo smiled and took his hands off the flight stick. The X-35 continued forward, rocketing across the country at Mach 3.

"God damn, I love Future Betty something fierce!"

I turn to the cockpit, wondering what has Woodstock all worked up. He's talking animatedly to Endo, who is actually smiling. What the hell? Given Woodstock's gesticulations, I can tell they're discussing the X-35. So I tune them out and turn back to the three ladies sitting across from me.

Collins has her hand interlocked with Maigo's. For some reason, seeing them together like this, daughter and future mother—I hope— makes what we're about to do so much harder.

"Then we're all agreed," I say. "You're not going in until it's safe. Until the battle is over."

Maigo nods, doing her best to keep up a brave front, but the tightness of her jaw and the uncommon bounce in her leg give her away.

"Then..." I take a deep breath, trying to stay calm. "You'll jump— are you sure about that? You've never done it before."

"I think I can figure it out," she says, channeling Lilly's false confidence. "And if I'm honest, I'm pretty sure I could just jump without a parachute."

Collins raises a finger in the air, looking uncomfortable. "I'm sorry to even mention this, but what's to stop Nemesis from eating you on the way down?"

"She can feel me, and I can feel her. She'll know who I am."

"And she's just going to let you land on her back and...climb inside," Alessi asks, showing her first signs of doubt about our plan.

"Something like that," Maigo says. "If Lilly is right."

"And if she's not?" Collins asks.

"Then she's going to bug out," I say. "And call us for a pick-up."

Maigo nods, but I can see she's not counting on that happening. The hope of it even being a possibility might be enough to derail her nerves.

"Coming up on Salt Lake," Woodstock says, "and it's a hot mess."

The walls and floor of the X-35 display the feed from the cameras on the exterior. Salt Lake City lays ahead, the majority of its buildings still standing. But that's about to change, because as I watch, Nemesis dives headlong into the Tsuchi, which now matches Nemesis's three-hundred-fifty-foot height. The pair rise into the air like a tidal wave, crashing down on a rocky shoreline. But instead of breaking on the rocks, they break straight through them, flattening a long building that looks something like a giant, covered, silver casserole dish. But as the pair arc back toward the ground, I recognize the building behind the Tsuchi and cringe.

The Tsuchi's eight limbs twist back, catching the ground on either side of the ornate Salt Lake City Temple, the largest Mormon temple in the world and the headquarters for Salt Lake City's bike enthusiasts. The Tsuchi's fall comes to a grinding halt, its strength matching Nemesis's. The giant spider's back seems to tap against the golden angel, Nephi, that tops the temple's tallest spire, and then stop, as though supported by divine power.

But then Nemesis roars in anger, stands tall, lifts a foot and drives it into the Tsuchi's chest. The eight-limbed Kaiju crashes back, flattening the temple beneath its girth.

Well, the Mormons are officially going to hate Nemesis, now.

Nemesis doesn't let up, lunging forward and jabbing one of her long claws into the Tsuchi's side. The Tsuchi lets out a high-pitched shriek, but it's far from finished. While Nemesis, looking absolutely frenzied, eyes radiating energy, teeth bared in a snarl, raises her free arm for a second strike, the Tsuchi's lightning fast tail swoops around and tags Nemesis in the side, one, two, three times.

Oh no...

Never in all our planning had we considered the possibility that Nemesis might lose this fight, and we'd be stuck with an ever-growing Tsuchi fueled by a hunger for *all* men.

Nemesis cries out in pain and staggers back, placing her colossal hand on her side in a very human gesture of pain. Her cry becomes sharp. She flinches as though struck, being consumed from the inside.

While Nemesis is distracted, the Tsuchi rights itself, standing upright on its rear four legs, and in that position, standing as tall as Nemesis, its four, armored, spidery limbs twitching in front of it, arcs of electricity crackling between its bus-sized mandibles, I think it's even more frightening than Nemesis or even her five siblings—Typhon, Karkinos, Scylla, Scrion and Drakon.

Next to Nemesis, the Tsuchi is nearly the tallest thing in Salt Lake City, with only three buildings being taller, by only fifty feet, give or take. Okay, so... Now it's a MegaTsuchi. Knowing it's inflicted a mortal wound, the Tsuchi hangs back and waits, its tail thrashing back and forth, decimating the facades of the buildings behind it.

I glance at Alessi. "Don't tell me those are all..."

"Mormon church buildings," she says, tapping a touch screen, reading information. "But most of downtown has been evacuated."

Maigo kneels on the floor, hands pressed against the digital display showing us the action taking place two thousand feet below us. She cringes suddenly, seizing in pain. It hits me a moment later. I kneel beside her, wincing as my head blazes with pain transmitted from Nemesis and filtered through Maigo.

Maigo screams in time with Nemesis's shrill roar, and I watch as three elephant-sized Tsuchi tear out of Nemesis's side.

41

Nemesis spins in a circle, reaching for her side as the Tsuchi emerge. Her trident-tipped tail sweeps around behind her, hewing down the

Church History Museum, the Plaza Hotel and the Family History Library—which contains the genealogy of just about everyone on the planet. The buildings crumble in unison, and I hope the church made digital backups of their genealogy information.

The emergence of three more Tsuchis is far more shocking than the destruction being wrought. They have the potential to destroy the world. The last Tsuchi leaps down from Nemesis's side, revealing a bloody wound through her black skin, and the softer white flesh hidden beneath.

With a roar unlike anything I've heard from Nemesis before, the Queen of the Monsters enters a kind of berserker rage. The nearest newborn Tsuchi, still finding its legs, is stomped under foot, three times. On the third crushing blow, the small amount of explosive fluid in its body hits the air and detonates with a *whump* that's muffled by Nemesis's foot. But she doesn't stop. She lunges at the second small Tsuchi that's scaling a thirty-story apartment building. Before the small arachnid reaches the top, Nemesis's long index finger punches through the creature, and the building. On the far side of the building, the claw exits with the Tsuchi dangling limp. When she extracts the claw, the Tsuchi is scraped away.

The third newborn is a brazen little bastard. It leaps off the top of a nearby building, legs splayed out, tail cocked back and ready to strike Nemesis's head. I hold my breath. If the Tsuchi manages to tag Nemesis in the head, would that be it?

"Turn!" Maigo says, and once again, Nemesis seems to hear her, craning her massive head to the left and snapping her jaws open. Instead of landing atop Nemesis, the Tsuchi finds itself inside the massive jaws, which snap shut with the relative speed and power of a bear trap. The intense pressure bursts the Tsuchi's insides out, the small amount of explosive fluid incinerating it all. Nemesis gives the limp, charred body a good thrash and then spits it out.

Rising smoke and dust swirls into the sky, obscuring much of the flattened church buildings, the surrounding city—and the big Tsuchi. It's dropped back down onto eight legs.

Nemesis, coming down from her berserker rage, moves in a slow circle, her orange eyes squinting and suspicious.

"I should go now," Maigo says.

I shake my head. "Not a chance."

"I could help her. She'd be smarter with me."

Collins crouches on the other side of Maigo's kneeling form. "Jon's right, honey. The way things are down there right now, you might not even make it down. You've seen how the Tsuchi detects people without even seeing them."

"Nemesis would protect me," Maigo says.

"And leave herself open to attack." Collins rubs the girl's back. "We need to protect you. Both of you. This only works if you both survive."

"Here it comes," Alessi says, turning our attention back to the battle raging below.

A swirl of motion in the debris cloud behind Nemesis reveals the Tsuchi's presence. It moves with such speed that Maigo can't even project a warning to Nemesis.

The Tsuchi rises up out of the smoke, flinging its massive form onto Nemesis's back. While its back four legs grip Nemesis's broad thighs, its four arms wrap around her, stabbing the scythe-like tips into her chest and shoulders, locking itself in place.

Nemesis reaches back with her hands, but two of the blade-tipped spider limbs snap up with shocking speed, impaling both colossal hands. As Nemesis roars in pain, the Tsuchi pries her arms out to either side, exposing her chest. Locked in place, hands and limbs impaled, bleeding from her side, Nemesis turns her head skyward and lets out a cry that sounds something like defeat.

As monstrous as Nemesis is, the sound breaks my heart. Nemesis has met her match.

"No!" Maigo shouts and punches the floor hard enough to put a dent in it and shake the X-35.

Below us, the Tsuchi's long tail slips up over Nemesis's head, the tip aimed toward her chest. The giant mutated spider lunges down, piercing Nemesis's shoulder with her mandibles. Blue bolts of electricity tear through Nemesis, shaking her body, and silencing her booming voice.

"No!" Maigo screams. "Do something, you brainless bitch!"

Nemesis snarls. I'm not sure if she's felt Maigo's insult or is just moving beyond her pain and back into her berserker state, but the defeated look in her eyes is replaced by something else.

If I were Nemesis, what would I do?

The answer comes as the Tsuchi strikes.

"Get us higher!" I shout, and I'm crushed to the floor as Endo quickly complies, launching us upward at surprising speed.

As the view of the world below shrinks away, the Tsuchi's tail stabs into Nemesis. But it misses the intended target, striking the membrane on the left side of Nemesis's chest, one of the two largest on the creature's body. The power in the cell is enough to level cities, and the Tsuchi seems to understand this, refusing to withdraw the stinger, perhaps trying to think of a way to avoid what will happen next.

But Nemesis, that ruthless and cunning monster, has no desire to wait. She flexes her chest exposing a small amount of the orange fluid to the air, igniting it, shooting the stinger free and unleashing the bright orange death within.

The light reaches us first, whiting out the cameras on the outside of the X-35, and sparing us from its blinding brightness. The shockwave hits us next, shaking the aircraft, but not endangering us, as we're at least 10,000 feet above the action now. The cacophonous sound reaches us next, rattling the ship and my internal organs.

As the light fades, the view of the city snaps back on in time for us to see the explosion's results. A wave of flame spreads southwest through the city, leaving a blackened half circle that I've seen before, in Beverly, in Boston, in Washington, D.C.

The explosion has also launched Nemesis and the Tsuchi back. The massive spikes on Nemesis's back have impaled the Tsuchi's chest, including two of its orange membranes. The pair are stuck together. They crash out of the Mormon district and into the more secular part of the city, demolishing buildings and ensuring the city won't recover for years or decades.

When the giants roll and separate, the Tsuchi's impaled membranes erupt with a second, blinding explosion that hammers Nemesis into the ground and launches the Tsuchi across the city. We're once again blinded, holding on as the shockwave and rumbling din rolls past.

When the light clears, the two Kaiju are revealed. They're separated by a half mile of ruined city. Nemesis lies face down, surrounded by burning city. The Tsuchi is on its back, its eight limbs clenched up over its body. I have no illusions that either Kaiju is dead, but they're both knocked silly.

"I'm sorry," Maigo whispers toward the floor, toward Nemesis. I realize too late that the apology is meant for me.

With speed I haven't seen yet, Maigo grasps my wrist, slaps a handcuff around it and locks the other side to the leg of the seat in the cargo hold. Collins starts to react, but what can she do against someone as fast and strong as Maigo without hurting her? Nothing. Before I can complain, Collins is similarly locked in place. Maigo gets to her feet and thrusts a finger at Alessi. "Don't try anything."

Alessi just raises her hands. While Maigo might have only had two pairs of handcuffs—*Where the hell did she get them?*—Alessi doesn't stand a chance against the girl with Kaiju blood. Maigo hits the button for the cargo ramp and it slowly, noiselessly opens.

Smoke-tinged air floods into the X-35. The sounds of crumbling buildings, sirens and alarms reach up from below.

"Maigo," Endo says from the cockpit. "There's another way."

I'm not sure what Endo is getting at, but the fatherly side of me hopes he's telling the truth. "Hear him out."

"Love you," Maigo says. She crouches down and kisses my head. Then does the same to Collins. "You'll make great parents."

You'll make... Future tense.

"Maigo," I say, "If it doesn't work—"

"I'll call for a pickup," she says, and jumps.

My despair is quickly replaced by shock as Endo leaps from his seat in the cockpit and charges into the cargo hold. He stops by Alessi for a moment, whispering in her ear. When he steps away, she reaches out for him, but he jumps out after Maigo.

My Devine phone rings, the tone telling me it's Cooper, who is coordinating the evacuation and the military response, which, thus far, has been none. At my request. Missiles and bullets only cause more damage and put my people in danger. But if Nemesis falls...we're going to throw absolutely everything at the Tsuchi while it's injured. Since Salt Lake City is pretty much a wasteland already, we won't have to hold back.

I answer the phone, and Cooper doesn't wait for me to speak.

"Things aren't going well," she says, her voice calm and measured.

"Considering Salt Lake City is in ruins and my daughter and pilot just jumped ship, no, things are definitely not going well."

"The military is...eager to get involved," she says.

"What good have they ever done against a Kaiju?" I ask.

"Do you want me to relay that message?" Her calm demeanor irks me.

"Why are you so calm?" I grumble. "People are dying!"

She clears her throat, and equally calm, says, "Spunky is feeding."

I can't stop the laugh that comes. Cooper is breast feeding her son—whose actual name is Ted Watson-Cooper, but who was nicknamed 'Spunky' because of how much he kicked in utero—while she's coordinating the U.S. military in response to a Kaiju attack. We are, without a doubt, the strangest government organization on the planet.

"Just keep them back," I say. "But...if Nemesis falls, I want them to hit the Tsuchi with everything we have."

"*Everything?*"

"Let's hit it with multiple MOABs first. If that doesn't work, then yes, everything." Everything meaning nukes, and the idea makes me want to puke, because I'll be responsible for dropping nukes on a U.S. city. Granted, the city is screwed already, but nukes will make the region off limits for hundreds of years and will likely increase the civilian casualty numbers by thousands. "Just get as many people out of the area as possible."

"Will do," she says. "What's your plan, now?"

"Now?" I say, looking at the open cargo door my daughter leapt from. "I was thinking about praying, but not to Mormon Jesus. I'm pretty sure that guy hates us now."

"Good luck," she says.

"Thanks, Coop, and...if things go sideways for us—"

"You'll be fine," she says, and hangs up. It's abrupt, but Cooper doesn't do well with the mushy stuff from anyone other than Watson. Strong emotions make her uncomfortable, so I take her sudden departure as a compliment. Means she cares.

Alessi hits the button to retract the cargo bay hatch and then crouches beside me, unlocking my cuffs, and then Collins's. "What now?"

I turn to the cockpit. "Woodstock?"

"I got this!" he says, hands on the controls. Future Betty rocks to the side, forcing us to hang on, but then levels out. "I got this," he says again, less sure, but more focused.

"Jon," Alessi says, her use of my first name grabbing my attention. "What are we going to do?" She's worried about Endo, just as much as I'm worried about Maigo.

I look her in the eyes and deliver the news she doesn't want to hear. "We're going to wait."

42

A shifting breeze lifted more dust and smoke into the air, obscuring the ruined city below Maigo, and hiding her target. The plan was basic, but not simple: land on Nemesis the way Jon and Lilly had done on the Tsuchi in Los Angeles, and then...she wasn't exactly sure. If Lilly's report, and her intuition, were right, Nemesis would take care of the rest, pulling her in, rejoining her to the monster.

Making her a monster.

Again.

Where are you? she thought, her arms and legs splayed wide, stretching the wingsuit fabric taut. She glided in circles, looking for some hint of the Kaiju before she was forced to land on the ground.

But maybe the ground was where she should be. Nemesis had fallen, and was clearly still down. But not dead. Maigo could still feel her connection to the creature, though it felt hazy now. Had the blast knocked Nemesis unconscious? Was that even possible?

Maigo yelped in surprise when something struck her hand. She was a thousand feet above Salt Lake City, so what could have touched her? She looked left and found Endo gliding expertly beside her, matching her speed and altitude with the ease of a bird. She thought she'd been doing okay. Her strength made operating the suit easy, but she now saw how a graceful and experienced user looked.

"What are you doing?" she shouted over the rushing wind that smelled of a dead city, an odor she'd become familiar with over the years. Once upon a time, she had relished the scent.

"Helping," Endo replied.

"Helping who?" She didn't want to have to subdue Endo, too, if Jon had sent the man after her. The city below was the last place someone should be unconscious. Even conscious and running, the odds of escaping the Kaiju battlefield were slim...that was, if the two giants ever got back up. She stole a glance at the Tsuchi, still on its back, still clutched in some kind of rigor. But then, a limb twitched. The Tsuchi was waking up.

"Maigo!" Endo says. "Follow me!"

Endo banked to the left and dove, swooping down into the tan cloud of pulverized city. Not seeing any other clear path, Maigo did her best to mimic Endo's maneuver and half glided, half fell after him. She nearly plowed into his back, but snapped her wingsuit open wide, caught the air and glided beside him again, just four hundred feet from the ground, which was steadily approaching.

"Look for...her light," he said, coughing from the air.

The air didn't bother Maigo, either because she was accustomed to worse—a Kaiju's breath was repulsive in a way she couldn't explain—or because her stronger body and lungs resisted the irritation better.

Maigo looked ahead, using her powerful vision to cut through the darkened ruins below them. Then she saw it. A faint orange glow. Then another, and another. Maigo finally recognized the glowing pattern as the side of Nemesis's neck. On the ground. Unmoving. But still glowing. Still burning with unspent primal energy.

She motioned toward the light with her head. Endo looked, but didn't see it until they had cut the distance in half.

They glided straight toward the massive neck. It wasn't a small target to land on, but this was Maigo's first attempt. Endo seemed to know that, too. "I'm going to deploy my chute first. I'll need more time to land. But you can take a hit. Deploy at the last second, and you'll hit your mark. Ready?"

Maigo glanced forward. They were just three hundred feet from Nemesis, moving at a 100 mph. She didn't have a choice. "Ready!"

A hundred feet from Nemesis, Endo's chute exploded out, catching the air and yanking him back. Maigo slapped her chest a half second, and half the distance later, when impact seemed unavoidable. The chute burst out, filled with air and yanked hard on her body for just a moment, before she collided with the armor-plated carapace that was Nemesis's back. A strong, hot wind took hold of the chute and dragged her across Nemesis's back, slamming her into the towering, bone-like blade extending from the creature's shoulder blade. Maigo used the momentary pause in motion to detach the parachute.

Endo, smaller and weaker—lacking Maigo's Kaiju blood—landed beside her, on his feet. He detached his parachute in time for the wind to carry it away from him. He did it with the same ease someone else might open a door and step through, but looking much cooler.

He smiled down at her obvious admiration. "Let's move."

A rumble of movement spurred both into action. Nemesis was waking up.

"Move it," Endo said, running over Nemesis's massive back, toward her head. He looked like an ant running over a person. As Maigo ran, she realized she was seeing the world through Nemesis's eyes, her mind mentally preparing for the coming perspective shift. Right now, she was still just another ant.

She caught up to Endo as they ran over the rough folds of thick black skin and armored plates. Then she saw it, thirty feet ahead, at the base of Nemesis's skull. It was an opening big enough for a person. Black tendrils were already stretching out toward them.

Before they made it another two steps, Nemesis took a deep breath. Her back flexed up into the air, pushing up on their legs. It felt like gravity had suddenly tripled. Endo and Maigo both dropped to their hands and knees.

"Hold on!" Endo shouted, extending the claws on the fingertips of his gloves and digging into the thick skin.

Maigo realized she was wearing the same kind of suit and extended her claws with a grin. This was what it was like to be Lilly. But then the ground fell out from beneath her. She shoved her arms down and caught hold before Nemesis's exhale pulled the creature's back out of reach. Maigo snapped down and slammed into the back, watching smoke and dust spiral away from Nemesis's breath. With a constant vibrating rumble, Nemesis lifted off the ground. A moment later, the level floor beneath Maigo began angling up.

Nemesis was standing.

"Hurry!" Endo shouted, starting up the rising incline.

Maigo started up after him, but the shaking was so intense that each step was a battle. They were within fifteen feet now, the black tendrils frantically snaking. Endo paused, watching them slither back and forth. She couldn't tell if he was horrified or mesmerized.

The angle suddenly sprang up to vertical. The sudden motion pulled Endo free with a shout. Maigo reached out, caught him by the arm and pulled him back. He dug in his claws, clinging in place.

"Thank you," he said.

"Why are you here again?"

He just grinned, but then his eyes went wide. "Hold on!"

Maigo turned to see the Tsuchi slide out of the smoke, moving on its four back limbs, standing tall.

Nemesis still hadn't turned around. The Tsuchi, despite its size, moved silently. Its mandibles twitched hungrily, eight eyes focused on Nemesis, and then...on them.

"It sees us," Maigo said, remembering how quickly a Tsuchi could pluck a person up and eat them. *It could eat us both and still have time to catch Nemesis off guard.*

She glanced up. She could lunge up once, maybe twice, and reach the tendrils, maybe in time to avoid the Tsuchi's sneak attack, or at least to turn the tide of this battle. But she'd have to leave Endo to do that. She didn't know him well, but she knew Hudson had a complicated relationship with the man. She didn't know if they were really friends, but there was a mutual respect between them. And while Endo had his own goals, he'd been helpful in the past. He'd saved people. He didn't deserve to die here.

During Maigo's deliberation, the Tsuchi took one more step, two of its forelimbs clearly poised to strike out.

"Maigo," Endo said. "Sacrifices have to be made."

Is he telling me to leave him?

"But not always the way we expect. Or want."

"What are you saying?"

"I'm saying." Endo digs his claws deeper into Nemesis's skin. "You need to let her go."

Before Maigo could react to the words, Endo struck out, his speed like that of a Tsuchi, striking the small button beneath her chin, twice, in rapid succession.

"Why—" Maigo started to say, but she was ripped away as the two rockets on her back fired for a full five seconds. She didn't watch her rapid ascent. Instead, she kept her eyes on Nemesis, and the Tsuchi closing in. "No!" she screamed. "Turn around!" But it was too late. The Tsuchi launched its attack, burying its talons in Nemesis's back.

But if Nemesis felt the giant blades slipping into her flesh, she didn't show it. She stood there silently, and then, as though a dog irritated by a puppy, she began to growl, the throaty warble shaking the ground, which now raced up to meet Maigo.

Maigo deployed her secondary chute, which didn't fully deploy, but added enough drag to slow her to a survivable speed. Her tough body, covered in high-tech armor, absorbed the impact from the landing and the sprawling roll that came next. And then, without missing a beat, she got back to her feet, running toward Nemesis. Endo hadn't saved her, he'd doomed them all...unless she reached the monster, scaled her body and finished what she had come here to do.

43

"I can't see anything," I shout. "Take us lower!"

"Any lower and we might land on one of their heads," Woodstock complains. "We're liable to get slapped as it is."

He's right, I know. After Maigo and Endo jumped, he took us down to an altitude of five hundred feet. We're dealing with three-hundred-fifty-foot-tall Kaiju, with hundred foot reaches and who knows how high of a vertical leap—not to mention the possibility of another explosive immolation. We are definitely in the danger zone.

The view outside is like a swirling desert with a blue sky above. The tan dust and smoke cover the city to an altitude of four hundred feet, hiding both Kaiju and any remaining buildings.

"There!" Alessi says, the desperation in her voice matching my own. As much as I care about Maigo, Alessi cares for her half brother. She points to our port side, where the dust cloud swirls, rises and disperses, revealing the Tsuchi. It stands tall, flexes its four upper limbs back and turns in a slow circle. Then it stops like it's detected something we can't see.

Like how it can find people without seeing them. Part of my mind considers that it might be able to detect electromagnetic fields like a shark, or a platypus, but the rest of me just doesn't give a rip. Right now, all that matters is that it's found something and is already closing the distance.

And then I do see it. A half mile away, smoke and dust billow up and away. A moment later, Nemesis stands, her head cutting through the smoke, facing away from us. Away from the Tsuchi.

She's too far away for us to see Maigo, if she even made it. "Get us closer to Nemesis."

"I'll try," Woodstock says. So far, all he's done is lower our altitude. Flying a UFO-like aircraft that moves fluidly in three dimensions isn't exactly the same as flying a helicopter. But he's an experienced pilot and—

"Whoa!" The X-35 tilts sharply to the side, but goes nowhere.

"Figured out how to roll us," Woodstock said. "Sorry 'bout that. This'll be easier when both arms are working."

We start moving sideways a moment later, without any detectable tilt.

"There we go," he says, petting the console. "Good, Future Betty."

The Tsuchi closes the distance in time with us, but thus far is ignoring our presence. Nemesis stands still, her back to the approaching Kaiju spider.

She doesn't know it's there. Is she still stunned?

"Turn around," I say, but I lack the connection to the beast that Maigo has. I look for the girl, but between the smoke and filtered sunlight, I can't see the back of Nemesis's head clearly.

"I see someone," Collins says. "On the back of her head."

I squint, trying to see. Someone is definitely there, but it's just a small, black-clad shadow moving over Nemesis's skin, quickly scaling the neck. I place my hands against the large touch screen, pulling them apart to zoom in. The cameras mounted around the ship's hull obey the command, focusing in on the action. I catch sight of the figure's legs, but I moved too fast past it. When I sweep back, I stop at the sight of a thousand thin, black tendrils wrapping around the figure and pulling it back into Nemesis's head.

She made it. God dammit, she made it.

The Tsuchi crashes into view, slamming into Nemesis's back, driving them both to the ground and kicking up a fresh bloom of dust. Woodstock pulls up, keeping us above the cloud. The dust swirls beneath us, kicked up by furious movement I can't see.

Is the Tsuchi still attacking?

Is it killing Nemesis?

Is it killing Maigo?

Maybe she'll be expelled again?

Too many questions, and no answers imminent.

A flash of light filters out through the dust.

"Hold on!" Woodstock shouts, accelerating straight up.

The explosion isn't as big as the previous immolations, but it kicks the dust cloud away, giving us a clear view of Nemesis, and giving Nemesis a clear view of her adversary.

That was smart, I think. *Too smart for Nemesis.*

Maigo...

Kick its ass, kid.

The Tsuchi, being of small mind and infinite aggression, isn't impressed by the explosion, or the way Nemesis is flexing her body, opening and closing her fingers, like she's just getting warmed up—or simply getting used to her body.

Dropping down and scurrying over the blackened battlefield, the Tsuchi darts forward, standing suddenly and spinning around. Its massive tail swoops around, moving at incredible speed, directed at Nemesis's side.

The ancient goddess of vengeance just stands there, calm as can be. And then with a burst of speed of her own, she snaps her hand up and catches the stinger, which looks small in her gargantuan hand's grasp. The Tsuchi, perhaps thinking it has struck flesh, spurts a rhinoceros-sized larva into the air. The glistening white super-slug arcs toward the ground, where Nemesis grinds it under foot.

The Tsuchi attempts to pull its tail back for a second strike, but Nemesis holds it fast—and squeezes. There's a moment of resistance, but then the stinger snaps and crumbles, spraying blood and viscous white fluid.

The Tsuchi writhes and shrieks, yanking its tail, but failing to free it. And then Nemesis pulls, dragging the Tsuchi back. But the Tsuchi falls forward, digging all eight legs into the ground. The two Kaiju have reached a stalemate, but Nemesis is already shifting tactics.

Thinking.

Adapting.

The berserker rage is gone, replaced by a cold, calculating logic.

Nemesis twists her body without letting go of the Tsuchi, pulling the tail tight and swinging her own tail, heavy and tipped with three large blades. She brings her tail down like an executioner's axe, striking the Tsuchi's long tail at the half-way mark.

The blow doesn't sever the tail, but cuts half way through. The Tsuchi reacts by running forward. Nemesis leans back, her powerful fingers locked onto the tail as the sliced open wound stretches, and then tears. The Tsuchi, suddenly free, spills forward, while Nemesis falls back, the tug-o-war coming to an abrupt end.

The Tsuchi, still on its feet, spins around and scurries back at Nemesis, who is rolling over and climbing to her feet...too slow. The spider lunges, catching Nemesis in the side. Its four rear limbs cling to Nemesis's leg while its mandibles bite into her shoulder, shuddering her body with a stunningly bright lightning display. All the while, the four forelimbs become a blur of frenzied strikes, shredding Nemesis's thick skin and drawing blood from the softer flesh hidden beneath. Not even our most powerful bomb was capable of inflicting that kind of damage.

C'mon, Maigo. You can do this!

And then, she does.

Nemesis flexes her arms out, dislodging the Tsuchi and flinging it away. But before the Tsuchi can fall all the way back, Nemesis reaches out and catches the spider Kaiju with both massive hands. *What is she doing?* I wonder, and then all four occupants of the X-35 lets out a loud "Ooh!" like we've just seen a spectacular football hit. Nemesis pulls the Tsuchi in closer while thrusting her head downward, slamming her head into the Tsuchi's face, delivering the world's most brutal headbutt.

"Where did she learn to fight like this?" Collins says to me. I have no answer. I thought Maigo rejoining Nemesis might give the Kaiju a boost of intelligence, but this is more than I expected. Even if they're sharing their brain power 50/50, Maigo is adding some serious fighting skills that none of us knew she had.

A burst of electricity flings Nemesis's head back from the headbutt, but she doesn't slow. She snaps forward, quickly biting one of the two mandibles and yanking. The small limb snaps and peels away, robbing the Tsuchi of its electrified abilities.

That was purposeful, I think. *A calculated move.*

The Tsuchi turns its half crushed face skyward and lets out a pained shriek. The tide has officially turned. And Nemesis proves it by raising both of her massive arms above her head and bringing them down hard, locking her fingers together as massive blades. The downward swipe catches the Tsuchi's arms on both sides, severing all four and sending thousands of gallons of blood spraying over the landscape.

And then, strangely, Nemesis backs off. The Tsuchi makes a feeble attempt to strike Nemesis with its tail, but the phantom limb hits nothing. Nemesis circles her opponent, keeping a watchful eye on it. The Tsuchi attempts to retreat, dragging its limbless front through the ashes.

Nemesis lunges to the Tsuchi's side, lifts her gargantuan foot and slams it down on the Tsuchi's back.

The giant spider kicks and struggles, but can't break free.

What's she doing? I think, and then I voice the question. "What's she doing? Why isn't she killing it?"

Collins shakes her head. "Maybe Maigo's conscience is kicking in? Feelings of mercy?"

"No..." Alessi says. "That's not it."

Nemesis moves, cutting off Alessi's comment. We watch as Nemesis slowly, torturously impales the Tsuchi's back, and peels off a layer of armor. The Tsuchi quakes and squeals as the armor plate is torn from its back.

Maigo, no... Just kill it!

And then she does. Slowly. Nemesis slips her claws into the Tsuchi's soft flesh, moving painfully slow, exacting her vengeance in a very personal way. Maigo is giving in to the rage now, giving in to the thirst for vengeance. She's going to lose control, and then where will our plan be? I'll have to order an attack on Nemesis and my daughter? I'm not sure I can handle that.

The Tsuchi spasms once, twice, and then falls still.

"How could she do that?" Collins asks, no doubt sharing my concerns for the girl who might have become her daughter.

"It wasn't her," Alessi says.

Collins looks exasperated. "Nemesis doesn't—"

"Wasn't Nemesis, either."

We both stare at her.

"I've seen that before," she says. "Once."

The earbud in my ear crackles to life. "Dad?"

My heart skips a beat, and I jump to my feet. "Maigo?"

"I'm okay," she says. "I'm two blocks east of the Tsuchi. Falling back now. Wouldn't mind a ride."

"But..." I'm stymied, my brain slowed by the revelation that Maigo is alive, well and *not* inside Nemesis.

"It's Endo," Alessi says, looking down at Nemesis. "He gave himself to her."

Endo?

Endo!

My jaw drops. *That sonofabitch!* This is what he's always wanted—proximity to Nemesis. A relationship even. He'd been jealous of my connection to her when Maigo was part of the Kaiju. And now...he's got all of that in spades. I should have seen it coming. The question is, can he control it, and if he can, will he play nice?

"Take us down!" I shout to Woodstock. "Right in front of her face."

I'm a little surprised when Woodstock complies without complaining. The X-35 drops down as I open the cargo hatch. Nemesis's massive head slides into view, standing above the Tsuchi. Her giant eyes, no longer glowing orange, but reverted back to their brown, almost human gaze, stare back at me. I've stood here before, but I'm still unnerved by her size. That does nothing to stop my outburst.

"You asshole!" I shout. Nemesis just stares back at me. "You were a pain in the ass when you were a person, and now I have to deal with you as..." I motion up and down at Nemesis. "...as this? Fuck you, Endo." We stand there, eye-to-giant-eye for a moment. My shoulders sag. "And...thank you. For everything."

Nemesis stands still for a moment, and then huffs, the rank air nearly knocking me over. With an almost indifferent air, she turns west and strikes out, following the plan. *Just go*, I think. *All the way to the coast and stay there. Eat whales and enjoy being a monster.*

I step back and raise the cargo hatch. "Woodstock, do me a favor and pick up my daughter."

The thick mustached man looks back with a grin. "You got it, boss."

I turn to Collins, who has remained unscathed during the last few days. She's looking fine in her armor, red curls hanging on her shoulders. I feel like crap, and probably look worse, but I find myself smiling, perhaps fueled by relief, or adrenaline. "Hey."

She turns to me, smiling.

"Wanna get hitched?" I ask. "Like right now?"

She nods, and laughs. "Let's do it."

I turn to Woodstock, but the man reads my mind. "First stop, Maigo. Second stop, Vegas."

44

We didn't quite make it to Vegas immediately after finding Maigo in the blackened city. We escorted Nemesis west as she followed her direct path back to the coast. She moved at a steady 70 mph clip, not quite a run, but she wasn't taking her time, and I suspect she wasn't moving faster because of the injuries to her side, her hands and all the internal injuries we couldn't see. But she never slowed.

Military jets swarmed around us the whole way, eager to take a crack at the city destroyer, but it was easy to see that Nemesis wasn't attacking, and no one wanted to be responsible for setting her on a rampage.

Like Boston, Washington D.C. and Los Angeles, several suburbs of Salt Lake City, and the central part of the city itself were a total loss. But the early evacuation efforts saved several hundred thousand people, including the suburbs to the north and southeast. The loss of life, combined with the destruction of Los Angeles, Lompoc and everything in between has been estimated to be upwards of five hundred thousand, most of them lost during the battles with the Tsuchi or consumed by the Tsuchis, fueling their rapid growth.

That number makes this the most deadly Kaiju attack since Nemesis first appeared. The FC-P, once again with Endo's help—and sacrifice—managed to aid Nemesis and stop the Kaiju threat. Strangely, despite the loss of life, and previous actions in Boston, Nemesis is getting a reputation for being mankind's protector, even if she's also our judge, jury and executioner. She's now, very publicly, stopped seven other Kaiju whose threat to the planet was even more severe. The question I have is this: will Nemesis, bonded with Endo, be content to remain in the ocean?

Not a chance, I think. When you come right down to it, Endo was a very serious, very deadly fanboy. He's not going to want to swim around the oceans munching whales. He's going to want the full experience. Maigo says that he'll feel Nemesis's thirst for vengeance just as strongly as the goddess. He'll just process it differently...and I hope, differently enough to show a little restraint and maybe avoid casually strolling through cities while en route to his targets. Of course, the hardest part is that it's going to be my job to stop Nemesis.

It was night when the Queen of the Monsters reached the ocean and slipped into the waves without a look back. We parted as allies, but if she returns for anything other than putting the hurt on another Kaiju...and puts people in danger, I'm going to have to hit her with everything we have. And yeah, despite Endo being a part of the Kaiju now, Nemesis will always be a 'she' to me.

It's been two days since then, and we're back in Beverly, most of us walking around the joint like it's a geriatric home. But we're not complaining. While Woodstock, Lilly, Hawkins, Joliet and I are bruised, broken and perforated, Maigo, Collins, Cooper and Watson are doting on us, and Buddy makes the rounds licking people's feet, and arms, and hands, and pants—his stubby tail wagging madly the whole time. I think he's losing his mind, or just really happy to see us alive. Even Lilly is letting the dog lick her.

I've talked to the President and briefed representatives of every agency involved in investigating and responding to the aftermath, which, thankfully, isn't our job. The last few days have been a blur of phone calls and meetings. And right now, sitting on the deck of the Crow's Nest, hard cider in hand, sun on my face, it all feels a million miles away. With my eyes closed, head tilted back, I try to forget the horrible things I've seen. But I can't.

Of all the things I've seen—destroyed cities, people eaten whole, genetic monstrosities—my thoughts keep wandering back to Area 51, and what's hidden beneath the sands. What it means for all of us.

The sound of a shifting deck chair pulls me back to the here and now. Collins sits down beside me, beer in hand. We look at each other, sharing words without speaking until we both smile. I hold my bottle up in a mock toast. "Hello, wife."

She clinks her bottle against mine. "Husband."

Yeah, we eventually made it to Vegas. The brief ceremony was conducted by a stunned justice of the peace, who watched us land in what was essentially a bona fide UFO—which we are *definitely* keeping. The service was attended by Maigo and Woodstock. Alessi had been with us when we set down, but she had quickly disappeared into the city. The wedding was a quick and simple affair, followed by a flight back to the East Coast.

"I'm trying to think of a good honeymoon location," I say. It's a white lie, but a good subject to distract me from the truth.

"Someplace not marred by Kaiju attacks," she says.

"Siberia? I hear it's nice in the summer. We could spend a few weeks in the gulag. Just the two of us."

"I'm thinking Rome," she says. "And Greece."

"Pretty sure that part of the world saw its fair share of Nemesis back in the day."

"Good place to start if we're going to find Atlantis," she says.

I freeze, hard cider tilted, almost at my lips. "Are you serious?"

"This is our life now, Jon," she says. "We might as well embrace it."

The bottle lowers as I smile. "It would be a pretty epic honeymoon. But...we're not roughing it. Search by day, fine food and four-star hotel at night."

"Deal."

"So," Maigo says from above us. "We're going to Greece?"

Collins and I look up. Maigo and Lilly are clinging to the brick wall above us. Lilly is healing quickly, but still acting like her bold self, despite the cast and bandages. She's giving Maigo pointers on being super human, and Maigo is officially out of her shell.

She no longer feels the connection to Nemesis. Endo's bonding to the monster seems to have broken it. At first, I thought she might be disturbed by the loss, but it really just set her free. She keeps her hair tied back now. She laughs more. And she's embraced the parts of her that aren't human. Lilly has taken to the task of schooling her 'sister' in how to push the limits of their abilities.

Maigo's connection to me, however, remains. It might even be stronger. She promises she's staying out of my head, but I occasionally see her laugh when I've thought of something funny. As long as she's not in there all the time, especially when I'm alone with my wife, I can deal with it. Maigo is, after all, a Hudson. *Holy crap...in the last week I've become a family man.*

I'm about to tell Maigo that Collins and I will be going alone, but Collins beats me to the punch. "If we're lucky, we'll find Atlantis, too."

I guess we're all going.

Collins takes my hand, "But we need to check out the lay of the land first."

"I know what they'll be laying," Lilly says, nudging Maigo with her elbow.

"Aww, c'mon!" I say, but I can't stop from laughing.

"Lilly!" Maigo says, embarrassed.

Collins just laughs.

Our laughter is cut off by the sudden roar of a helicopter surging over the Crow's Nest roof and swinging around toward the lawn below us. There is a landing pad on the roof, but it's currently occupied by Helicopter Betty and Future Betty, from which we've taken armor, weapons and tech we're still trying to figure out. The dark blue, Bell 525 Relentless is instantly recognizable, not only because of its resplendent appearance, but because the Zoomb logo is hard to miss.

I remain seated while the helicopter lands in the yard. It takes a lot to ruffle my feathers these days. So I sit and sip my hard cider, waiting to see what unfolds. The girls, however, are on guard. They climb through a window back into the building, and disappear.

I have to admit, I'm a little surprised when three figures exit the helicopter dressed in armor and facemasks that resemble the BlackGuard's. The deck door opens. Joliet steps out, shotgun in hand. The ghost of Old Mrs. Rosen, who was known to chase trick-or-treaters off with a shotgun, is probably watching with a grin.

Hawkins emerges next, limping, but carrying a KRISS rifle taken from the X-35.

"What's the situation?" Hawkins asks.

"I'm just having a drink with my lady," I say.

He squints at me. Lowers his weapon. Looks back at the girls in the doorway behind him. They both look a little sheepish and defensive. Who can blame them for being jumpy? Lilly had been hunted by men wearing uniforms a lot like these.

The three armored visitors stop at the bottom of the brick stairway. "Can we talk?"

I recognize the voice as Alessi's. While Endo has always been on and off my shit list, Alessi hasn't done too much to irk me, even if she is his half-sister. "Come on up."

She removes her mask and starts up the stairs. While Joliet ushers the others inside, Alessi pulls a chair around, facing us. She sits, takes the cider from my hand and takes a drink.

And now *she's* on my shit list.

When she doesn't speak, I decide to. "What did he tell you? Before he jumped."

"That's kind of what I'm here to talk to you about." She leans back in her chair, looking exhausted, but also with a trace of fire in her eyes. "Endo was a...resourceful man. In the last year he managed to coerce, bribe, manipulate and threaten his way into being the primary shareholder of Zoomb."

The news straightens me up in my seat. "Endo *owns* Zoomb?"

She shakes her head. She takes a deep breath, holds it and lets it out slowly. "I was a ten percent share holder before. Endo...I'm not sure how he did it, though I suspect certain people might have been beholden to him in the same way the President is to you. The end result is that he managed to take control of fifty-one percent of the stock, meaning that even if everyone else united against him, nothing could be done about it."

"That was a lot to say before jumping," I point out.

"I already knew all that," she says. "But... He... I'll just show you." She digs into her coat and pulls out a sheet of paper. She hands it to me. I unfold it with Collins looking over my shoulder.

Collins, who is a faster reader than me, says, "Holy shit. *Holy. Shit.*"

And when I get to the real meat of the letter, I have to re-read it three times. "Is this for real?"

She nods. "You are now the primary stock holder of Zoomb. The company is yours. You're the seventh richest man in the world."

"But...but why?"

"I think you know why," she says, but then she elaborates. "There are threats in this world, that even with the President's ear, you are unprepared to face. Black organizations within your own government prefer to remain clandestine, performing their unscrupulous research in the shadows, but never really facing threats head on."

I know she's speaking about GOD, but maybe there are more organizations like them.

"When he learned about the Aeros, Ferox and Atlanteans and their connection to Nemesis, he wished for Zoomb's relationship with the FC-P to improve. He decided to..." She's holding back her emotions. "...merge the organizations through you."

I'm stymied. "But...this is crazy. I don't know how to run a company. The FC-P is enough to—"

"I will run the company for you as I have been for Endo," she says. "But you will have full access to all of our research, technology and—"

"The flashdrive," I say, remembering Alessi's espionage back at GOD. "You have all of GOD's files, too?"

She grins. "All of their biological research, including files on the extraterrestrial life forms and a few hundred other projects I think you'll be interested in looking over...or assigning a team to, which you can do. Or have me do."

Here I was, worried that she was going to hand the information over to her cold corporate bosses at Zoomb, and it turns out that *I'm* the cold corporate boss.

Alessi leans forward, locking her eyes on mine. "I can see you're a little overwhelmed. Who wouldn't be? But here is what I want you to take away from all of this. If they..." She looks up at the sky. "...return, you now have a chance to be prepared for it. And I think you're right, let's start by finding Atlantis."

"You..." Collins says. "How did you?"

"The miracles of advanced technology." Alessi leans back, smiling. "When do you want to start being briefed?"

I look to Collins. The stunned look in her eyes must match my own. I look back to the door. Woodstock, Joliet and Hawkins are there. I turn my eyes up, looking in the Crow's Nest windows where Watson, bouncing his son, Cooper, Lilly and Maigo stare down at us.

Back to Alessi. "We're not going anywhere. Let's get started. But first..." I stand up and address the two masked men at the bottom of the stairs. "You two. Take this beast—" I wave my hand at the big chopper. "—and fetch us some Nick's Roast Beef sandwiches." I clap my hands twice. "Chop, chop!"

When I sit back down, Collins and Alessi are staring at me, slightly aghast.

"What? Should I have gotten Maria's Pizza?" I stand back up and shout to the men who are actually heading back to the chopper. "And pick up a monocle while you're out!"

I sit once more, cross my legs and continue hiding my trepidation behind a mask of humor and casual behavior. On the inside, I'm terrified. Not because I'm suddenly mind bogglingly rich, or am now in charge of a colossal, world-wide high-tech corporation with questionable business tactics, while simultaneously running the FC-P, or because I've now got a wife and a teenage daughter, or because the next time Nemesis surfaces, I might have to turn all these newfound resources, including Endo's own sister against her. I can handle all that. But it's now clear that if—if—the Aeros return to Earth, no one will be better equipped to handle the threat than me...the guy, who just three years ago was happily wasting his time and career pretending to search for Bigfoot. Am I really capable of saving the world from an alien invasion?

Let's hope I never have to find out.

EPILOGUE

Far beyond Earth's gravitational influence and the cloud of man-made satellites, a lone, black cube the size of an SUV, hidden by the infinite darkness of space, circled the blue-green planet.

Watching.

Listening.

Transmitting.

While the device lacked a conscience, its artificial intelligence let it detect the presence of a multitude of life forms, though it was only actively searching for a few. The first, humanity, was in great abundance, populating nearly every plot of land on the planet, save for the south pole.

But they were inconsequential.

The emergence of the Gestorumque, what the humans called Kaiju, or specifically, Nemesis, was an unexpected, yet not unpleasant surprise. The creature's survival for so long was unusual for the species, but the creature would be a welcome ally.

While scans for the Atlantide had revealed nothing living, trace amounts of their DNA had been uncovered in the human population. That, along with the observed behavior of the once-simple human race, along with their technological advances, particularly in the realm of warfare, showed a clear Ferox influence.

The signal sent ten years ago had been accurate. Earth belonged to the Ferox.

The black cube transmitted its findings to the fleet, hidden at the fringe of the solar system's heliopause, eleven billion miles from the yellow star. Forced to slow at the solar system's edge, as encountering even the smallest of objects at near light speed could be catastrophic, the remainder of the journey would take time, but for beings such as the Aeros, whose life-spans allowed them to observe the rise and fall of civilizations, the journey would feel brief.

And when they returned to Earth, it would not be to cleanse the Atlantide; it would be to cleanse humanity.

Every last one of them.

In *all* dimensions of reality.

As the cube finished its transmission, sensors detected an approaching anomaly. It scanned the object, determining it to be an errant Earth satellite. Instead of taking action, the cube simply moved aside.

It was a mistake.

The cube detected the black sphere's presence too late.

The laser strike disabled the cube's communications array, silencing it.

The second disabled its defenses.

The third struck its engines.

And the fourth finished it off, punching a hole through the AI's core, putting the Aeros satellite out of commission without destroying it. Any stargazers or government agencies monitoring the sky from the planet below would detect nothing. If the sphere's actions had been more overt, both the Aeros and humanity would know that while the Aeros were still coming, the Ferox had already arrived.

A NOTE FROM THE AUTHOR

Dear Reader,

I wanted to take a moment to thank you for reading *Project 731*. There was a time (a few weeks before I wrote the book) that I thought it would be the final book for the FC-P and Nemesis. If you've just finished the novel, you know that's not true. Not by a long shot. The FC-P and Nemesis *will* return. You might also be wondering who the Aeros and Ferox are. If so, check out my novel, *Raising the Past*.

I hope that you enjoyed this latest installment of what I hope will become a Kaiju series to rival Godzilla and Gamera...in novels, movies, TV shows and comic books. Nemesis is already on her way to being featured in a video game, *Colossal Kaiju Combat: The Fall of Nemesis*. She's off to a good start, but not even her 350-foot-tall girth is going to reach such a lofty goal without help.

So show your support for Nemesis! Post reviews online, at retailers (Amazon, B&N, Kobo, etc) and on Goodreads. Tell your friends about the book. Post fan art. Spread the word however you can, and let's make Nemesis America's first iconic Kaiju (I don't count Kong...he's too short and not very strange).

Thanks again for all your amazing support, and for reading *Project 731*!

—*Jeremy Robinson*

ART GALLERIES

The following art galleries include the original creature concept designs by the amazing Matt Frank, along with cover sketches for *Project Maigo* by Cheung Chung Tat. And if that weren't cool enough, we've got another amazing gallery of fan art.

MATT FRANK CREATURE DESIGNS

This first gallery includes the original creature concept designs for Nemesis and the new Kaiju, deemed: Tsuchi, in its various stages of growth—BFS, Tsuchi and MegaTsuchi. The designs are by the always amazing Matt Frank, who has provided art for all three Nemesis books so far. You might also recognize his work from many Godzilla comic books. While the sketches were based on descriptions straight out of the book, the concepts also influenced the story, as both took shape simultaneously.

Check him out at: www.mattfrankart.com.

NEMESIS

B.F.S.

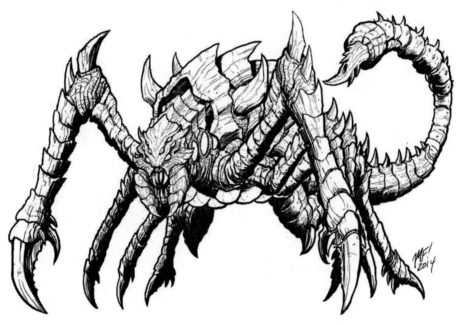

TSUCHI

MEGATSUCHI

CHEUNG CHUNG TAT COVER DESIGNS

I first came across Cheung's work on Facebook, as a Godzilla image he created made the rounds. I was so impressed by his work that I found him on DeviantArt, marveling at the numerous works of Godzilla and dinosaurs. Inspired by his work, I reached out around the world, to Hong Kong, pretending there was no language barrier, and asked if he would like to redesign the covers for *Project Nemesis* and *Project Maigo*, and design the cover for *Project 731*. To my delight, he accepted. And while you might have seen the covers, you haven't seen the sketches that came first, and as a fan of line art, I find them equally amazing. The following sketches are all for *Project Maigo*. And for more of Cheung's art, visit: cheungchungtat.deviantart.com.

Sketch A

Sketch B

FAN ART GALLERY

Soon after the release of *Project Nemesis*, I started receiving fan art inspired by the book. After the release of *Project Maigo*, which included the first fan art gallery in any of my books, I wasn't sure if the trend would continue, but over the past year I've been continually surprised by the amount of Nemesis art being produced, and by the quality. And that's saying a lot, because Nemesis is really hard to draw! I'm an artist in addition to being a writer, and I haven't even attempted drawing Nemesis yet. So kudos to all of you who are brave enough to draw, paint, sculpt and 3D render Nemesis. You guys inspire me every time you send art my way, and I thank you for that.

If you would like your fan art to be featured in any future Nemesis books, send it to info@jeremyrobinsononline.com at a 300dpi image quality. The only real rule is that the images have to feature Nemesis (or any of the characters and new Kaiju from *Project Maigo* and *Project 731*) and cannot feature any trademarked or copyrighted Kaiju, such as Godzilla, Gamera, etc... Thank you very much to all the amazing artists who submitted their work for publication in *Project 731*, and I look forward to seeing more!

—Jeremy Robinson

A GIRL THAT WOULD BECOME NEMESIS
BY RODNEY VAN RODGERS III

BIGBADSHADOWMAN.DEVIANTART.COM

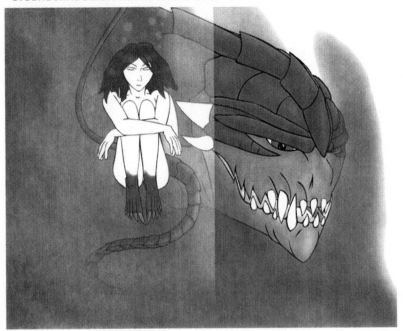

LITTLE KAIJU BY JOHN SCOTT
UCALIPTIC.DEVIANTART.COM

BAKU VS. NEMESIS
BY SHIN ANTHONY
IMNOOBBUTWITHHEART.DEVIANTART.COM

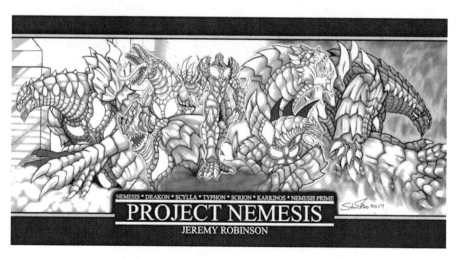

PROJECT NEMESIS BY STEVE THAO
WINTERGAIA.DEVIANTART.COM

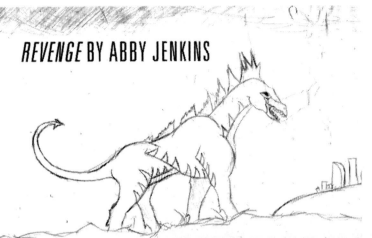

REVENGE BY ABBY JENKINS

"REVENGE"

DESTRUCTION
BY STEVE THAO
WINTERGAIA.DEVIANTART.COM

NEMESIS BROOD
BY ZACHARY RAMSEY
ROSENKRUEX.DEVIANTART.COM

SLUG IT OUT BY ZACHARY RAMSEY
ROSENKRUEX.DEVIANTART.COM

NEMESIS APPROVED
BY ZACH COLE
CRITTERZACH.DEVIANTART.COM

SUPER XERAIMUS VS NEMESIS PRIME BY JENNY MILLER
EXUITIRTEISS.DEVIANTART.COM

NEMESIS SCULPT
BY JORGE ROMERO VÁZQUEZ
MEXICANKAIJU.DEVIANTART.COM

NEMMY LOVE BY ZACH COLE
CRITTERZACH.DEVIANTART.COM

NEMESIS PRIME
BY ZACH COLE
CRITTERZACH.DEVIANTART.COM

PROJECT SPECULATION BY ZACH COLE
CRITTERZACH.DEVIANTART.COM

NEMESIS 3D SCULPT
BY GABRIEL GREGORY
THE-KAIJUENTHUSIAST.DEVIANTART.COM

NEMESIS BUST
BY DAVE JOHNSON
SHNURBINATOR.DEVIANTART.COM

NEMESIS! BY MRTDARK1

PROJECT MAIGO

BY ZACH COLE

CRITTERZACH.DEVIANTART.COM

WITH JAKE WALKER
& SHERRANE SEHOY MCCONNEL

APOCALYPTICGODZILLAX.DEVIANTART.COM

ABOUT THE AUTHOR

JEREMY ROBINSON is the international bestselling author of fifty novels and novellas including *Uprising*, *Island 731*, *SecondWorld*, the Jack Sigler thriller series, and *Project Nemesis*, the highest selling original (non-licensed) kaiju novel of all time. He's known for mixing elements of science, history and mythology, which has earned him the #1 spot in Science Fiction and Action-Adventure, and secured him as the top creature feature author.

Robinson is also known as the bestselling horror writer, Jeremy Bishop, author of *The Sentinel* and the controversial novel, *Torment*. His novels have been translated into twelve languages. He lives in New Hampshire with his wife and three children.

Visit him online at: www.jeremyrobinsononline.com.

ABOUT THE ARTIST

MATT FRANK is a comic book illustrator and cover artist who has worked on well known titles such as *Transformers* and *Ray Harryhausen Presents*, but he is perhaps most well known for his contributions to multiple *Godzilla* comic books. He lives in Texas and enjoys pineapple juice.

Visit him online at: www.mattfrankart.com

WANT TO LEARN MORE ABOUT
THE AEROS AND FEROX?

RAISING THE PAST

SOME SECRETS ARE BETTER LEFT BURIED

"A ROLLICKING ARCTIC ADVENTURE
NOT TO BE MISSED!"
JAMES ROLLINS

JEREMY ROBINSON

BESTSELLING AUTHOR OF RAGNAROK AND ISLAND 731

READ THE BEGINNING
BEFORE THE AEROS COME FOR US ALL

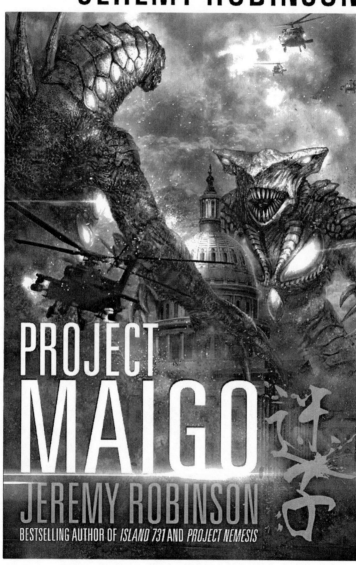

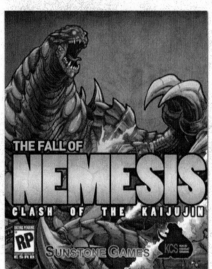

CPSIA information can be obtained at www.ICGtesting.com
Printed in the USA
LVOW11s1918020615

440866LV00006B/922/P